THE LOVE REMAINS

To Ann —
My mentor, my friend
and my dear Christian Sister —
I treasure your friendship.
May your trip to Maui be
all the richer for Kale's story.
me ke aloha pumehana

Katherine
Kapalua
2013

THE LOVE REMAINS

Written by
Katherine Kama'ema'e Smith

Edited by
Robert L. Ball and Kyle Markham

Wehewehe'ana o ka 'Ōlelo Hawai'i e
Henrietta Heneli Mahuna

Hawaiian Cultural Review by
Kumu Aloha Keko'olani, Honolulu Community College

Cover Art, "Kale of Honokahua",
and Design by
John C. Wittenberg, Astrolith Graphics

Honu
Publications
South Bend Maui

The Love Remains

Copyright ©2005, 2006 by Katherine D. Smith

Honu Publications books may be ordered through booksellers or The Islander Group, Booklines Hawaii, Ltd., 269 Pali'i Street, Mililani, HI 96789, 808-676-0116, ext. 206, fax: 808-676-5156 email: customerservice@booklines.com.

ISBN-13: 978-0972-342056

ISBN-10: 0-9723420-5-2

Printed in China

Ua ho'ola'a 'ia kēia puke i nā kūpuna o Honokahua

This book is dedicated to the ancestors of Honokahua

A portion of the proceeds of *The Love Remains* goes to Nā Leo Kia'i
supporting Hawaiian Immersion Education in West Maui

Introduction

Thanksgiving night in Honokōhau Valley, was one of those dark nights when the valley walls seem to close in and hug the riverbed. I was riding in the back of the pick-up and who knows whose dogs were having a jaunt following the wheels down the bumpy dirt road. Silhouettes of kids at play danced in front of a roaring gold bonfire throwing smoke and flickering ashes up into the treetops and "Uncle's" 'ukulele rang lightly behind shouts and laughter. It was the end of a lavish family lū'au. Centuries of ancient Hawaiian feasts suddenly flashed through my mind; knowing that I had been given the blessing to experience this moment made me weep.

When Darryl and Vicky 'Aiwohi gambled on being friends with the Smiths, "those haoles," our lives changed. For Harry, who counts his friends on one hand, Uncle Darryl became a central figure in his life. For me, the niele (nosey) one, Vicky and her gracious Kekona clan, Nā Keiki o Honoapi'ilani, became loving guides in a search that birthed this book.

Darryl and Vicky are among a group of families who grew up on Honolua Ranch at Honokahua, land now known as Kapalua Resort. Some continue to live nearby and work on the property. I was fascinated with their accounts of plantation days and kept wondering what existed at Honokahua before land baron Henry Baldwin created Honolua Ranch in the 1890s. No living persons could tell me.

Five years studying Hawaiian language and researching archival documents led me to the last owner and ruling chiefess of Honokahua, Sarah (Kale) Kani'aulono Davis. In Kale's lifetime, Honokahua's fishing and farming community flourished under a feudal Monarchy and a Constitutional Monarchy; its technology grew from Stone Age to Industrial Age; and its place in the world went from isolation to community with Asia and the West.

The story of Kale Davis, from 1797 to 1867, connects Kapalua Resort to the land of the ancestors and ignites the warm coals of heritage that the remaining Hawaiian families of Honokahua have faithfully kept alive in their hearts. That the kuleana, task of telling Kale's story has fallen to a haole was troubling for me until I realized that preservation of the ʻāina and Hawaiian culture must be carried out by everyone who receives knowledge.

The last three years playing and singing in Henrietta Mahuna's Hawaiian Choir as a part of the Sacred Hearts Mission Catholic Church congregation has been an added blessing. At 85, Henrietta is one of less than a thousand native Hawaiian speakers. She lived with her grandparents and spoke the language of the ancestors until the age of nine. Over many cherished days quilting and singing, Henrietta guided me in the use and nuance of certain Hawaiian words and phrases that have added authenticity to Kale's character. Henrietta's knowledge of the old ways of her grandparents, including living in a pili grass hut and camping in a rock cave, resolved challenging contextual issues.

Although its historical setting is accurate, *The Love Remains* is still a novel. To regard it as a historical work would be a great mistake. Any resemblance of fictionalized historical characters in *The Love Remains* to living persons with the same name is purely coincidental. In order to make the conflicts, challenges, and victories of Kale's life come alive, I have stitched facts together with fictitious dialogue and narrative that includes fictional characters.

No birth, death, or marriage certificates, and no images of Sarah Kale Kaniʻaulono Davis Adams exist at the Hawaii State Archives. Her genealogy at the Bishop Museum Archives cites only names for her husbands and children; in preparing *The Love Remains*, I compiled pedigrees of two subsequent generations from public genealogical resources, and individual names and dates may or may not be supported by two documented sources. My search led me to several direct descendants of Kale Davis, who graciously shared valuable genealogical and family history that authenticated Kale's family history.

The Davis and Young family held Honokahua ahupuaʻa so early that government surveys were never done, and I was unable to find any private surveys. Therefore, the fictional map of Honokahua (see page 263) created to enhance the novel in no way constitutes a historical mapping of Honokahua ahupuaʻa. With the help of Frank Palani Sinenci, Master Kilo Hale, an expert on the selection of home sites for traditional Hawaiian homes, I charted a logical locale for Honokahua fishing village. Kapalua Land Company, Ltd. kindly shared the results of an archeological study done in Honokahua Valley, allowing me to place homesteads in the valley. Because Maui Land & Pineapple Company, Inc. restricts valley access to watershed engineers and company employees, the precious home sites of Honokahua are preserved.

Some West Maui Hawaiians have heard Honokahua pronounced "Honokōhua" by their elders living here since plantation days. In 1963, Mary Kawena Pukui researched the oldest mentions of this place name and concluded that Honokahua was indeed the ancient name. Part of her research is a 1963 tape recording of a conversation with Kupuna Annie Ako, whose family lived in Kāʻanapali for generations before 1900. Mrs. Ako confirmed the name "Honokahua" for this ahupuaʻa, which Pukui translated as "Sites Bay" in *Place Names of Hawaiʻi*. The handwritten Patent of Confirmation signed by Kamehameha IV in 1855 reads "Honokahua" as does John Young's last Will and Testimony enacted in 1835. Based on these findings, I used the Honokahua spelling.

The four documented archeological features of Honokahua are Nā ʻIwi, the sacred burial grounds on the lawn of The Ritz-Carlton, Kapalua, Honokahua Valley habitation sites dating to pre-contact times, the Davis family gravesite, and Paepae fishing koʻa on the grounds of The Ridge at Kapalua. In 1988, Ritz-Carlton Hotels resituated their hotel to preserve the bones of the kūpuna. Alexander and Baldwin Inc. and Maui Land & Pineapple Company, Inc. have faithfully preserved the Davis family gravesite based on a purchase agreement made over 100 years ago, and on their own initiative, have protected the ancient habitation sites of Honokahua Valley. The Association of Apartment Owners of The Ridge at Kapalua lovingly cares for the Paepae.

Descendants of Kale Davis or Honokahua kūpuna may contact me and I will happily identify specific historical facts woven into this novel that I have documented to be true, and share additional information I may have gathered but not used in this novel.

If any inaccuracies, inconsistencies, over-simplifications, or omissions of the true history offend, I apologize for my ignorance; if there are none, it is because God worked a miracle.

Me ka hana, ka ʻike. With the work, comes knowledge. It is my hope that readers will not only enjoy reading Kale's story but also do the "work" of walking Kapalua Resort, experience the places where fishermen and farmers of Honokahua worked, and enjoy the land features that blessed the ancestors and remain today to bless us all.

'O wau me ka 'oia'i'o,
Katherine Kama'ema'e Smith
www.theloveremains.com

CHAPTER 1

Honolulu, November 1817

Kale Davis turned her head into the fresh morning breeze so her long hair would flow back away from her face. It was a long walk to Honolulu Bay, to the brig that would take her to Maui. Her servant boy 'Ulumalu was following behind her, carrying two eke bags that held her kapa cloth and her most prized possessions: Papa's prayer book, Mama's lei palaoa ivory pendant, and the mats and bedding Mrs. Young made for her. *"Ko'iko'i ka halihali'ana? E Kōkua wau?* Is the luggage heavy? May I help?" she asked. He shook his head. Kale often carried her own calabashes and pitched in with farm work, out of pity for maka'āinana commoners who labor so hard and long. But 'Ulumalu had a pride in his work that Kale respected and it was nice to have someone trying to please her. She turned back and continued to walk the sandy beach path that crossed barren Waikīkī plain.

The cool ground under her feet was damp with dew and soon long tentacles of the sun were highlighting the coconut palms and endless beach. The still of early morn slowly gave way to soft sawing sounds of fronds dancing in the cool kona breeze and of chattering birds. The breeze made Kale pull up her white kīhei cape and wrap it around her shoulders for warmth; she was tall and graceful like her Hawaiian mother but slim like her haole father and easily chilled. After another hundred paces, Kale and 'Ulumalu were in front of a small thatched hut nearly in the middle of the plain. Beach pea vines curled up one side and on the ground in front were some white 'ili'ili stones and a few fragments of fishbone. A ball of tattered sun-bleached kapa tied to a stake in the ground indicated the grave of a chief. Here were the bones of her beloved father, Isaac Davis, called Hū'eu-o-kea-lani-pōhai-ali'i, King Kamehameha's trusted gunner and companion.

Kale took one bag from 'Ulumalu, and gathered up a tī leaf-wrapped bundle prepared for her father's grave. As she knelt to put her offering in the hut, a long moan rose from her chest, "U wē–ē! Ku'u Pāpā–ā-ā, U wē–ē-ē!" 'Ulumalu stood quietly; never taking his eyes off her; listening to her mourning chant and watching teardrops make dark spots on her bright yellow pā'ū skirt.

Kale slowly opened the top leaves to expose her offering of baked hog meat and bananas. She slipped the orange 'ilima flower lei from her neck and placed it beside the food. Then she stood up, smoothed out her kīhei, carefully removed the old bunting from the stake, and tied on a fresh white kapa ball. She stood in silent prayer saying goodbye to her father.

She only had to look at 'Ulumalu again and, without a word, he picked up the bags and silently followed her. In a short while, the Honolulu Fort came into full view. Bouncing chop on the bay gently lapped and bubbled against a long coral rock and lava stone pier. Adjacent to the pier were the king's three large thatched storage houses, and the hale noho houses of the king's Kia'i Koa, guards of the harbor. Anchored at the end was the brig *Ka'ahumanu*, a tall ship of Kamehameha's fleet and Kale's means of escape from a drunkard husband and from many lower ranking chiefs of Kamehameha's Court who would pressure her to stay with him.

The last few steps along the jetty seemed to take forever. From the stern boomed a familiar voice, "Well, well, well! And a very good morning to Isaac Davis's lovely daughter!"

"*Hui! Ke Kāpena!* Hello! Captain!" she sang back to Alexander Adams, a family friend and commander of King Kamehameha's sailing fleet.

Alexander, called Alika by Hawaiians, was a tall rugged Scotsman with shining blue eyes that always seemed to be hiding a quip or stealing a glance at something exciting. Kale never remembered seeing him without a smile. His blonde hair was tied back under his braided cap in the style of sailors and the gold buttons of his dark blue uniform jacket glinted in the morning sun. Somewhere in the moment of seeing the strong and confident Captain Adams, Kale's fears gave in to the anticipation of a new life in Maui on the land Kamehameha gave to her father, and her father gave to her.

"Welcome to our humble vessel, my lady." Removing his cap with a gallant sweep of his hand, Adams gestured to the bow, "Tell your boy to bring your luggage down to the bos'un, and I shall show you to your small but tidy cabin."

He offered Kale his arm. "Good news, my lady, you shall have clear weather for your journey to Lāhainā Roads."

Kale felt like she was with her jovial Papa again. She put her hand on the top of Adams' braided cuff and giggled as he paraded her along the deck. "It is good to see you, Captain Adams. I have not had many reasons to smile in the past months and you make me feel happy as my father once did."

"Have I? Very good then." He glanced skyward, "Isaac will be happy with both of us. I shall transport you safely to Lāhainā." He paused to check the lashings on the tender. "I am afraid old Mr. Young talked you into a poor match with that son James of his. There is no living with rum. Do not fret. There are plenty of fish on Maui and you, my dear, are excellent bait!" He enjoyed his own joke so much that Kale could hardly keep from laughing. She could not imagine laughing about those tortuous arguments and fights when James was drunk. Harder yet was the thought of laughing in the face of her shame—leaving James behind in Honolulu and running away to Maui! But here she was, laughing nevertheless, and the irony made her laugh even harder. "Oh, you are such a rascal! It has been even longer since I had a good laugh. Thank you Captain Adams."

"My pleasure, Miss Davis. We shall have more laughing, then." Adams delivered his perfunctory invitation to ali'i passengers, "Will you grace my modest table with your presence at dinner this evening?"

"Of course! For me it will be a pleasure." Kale wondered at her own easy response to his invitation. Alika reminded her of Papa, and how he fussed over her. A tear ran down her cheek and she brushed it away quickly, hoping Alika would just think it a tear of joy.

Adams cleared his throat and turned toward the helm. "Well now, your cabin is just on the left down that first ladder, my lady. Just take your time and hold on to the railing in case a rogue wave decides to play with my ship. I will be on the quarterdeck if you need anything—anything at all."

"*Mahalo nui loa no kou lokomaika'i.* Thank you very much for your graciousness." Kale stayed at the gunwale to look at the sea and savor her parting view of Honolulu as Captain Adams climbed up to the helm. The sky was clear and mist was crawling up the steep, dark green valleys of Mānoa. Diamond Head cut a dark purple form against the bright amber glow of the eastern sky. From the arched coconut palms lining the full length of Waikīkī strand, now and again a canoe would emerge and cut through the long rolls of surf, carrying fishermen to secret deep-sea fishing grounds.

In the harbor, barks, brigs, and a lone whaler swung on their anchors. The old *Ka'ahumanu* tested the strength of the squeaky ropes holding her to the pier and her deck creaked gently under Kale's feet as the wooden rigging clacked against the masts. Deck hands moved quickly about, shouting instructions down the ranks, on-loading cargo, and preparing to cast off.

In a day or two, Kale would be in Maui. Until then, she would enjoy the sea breeze and long-awaited rest. As she gazed at beautiful Honolulu, many sad thoughts rolled through her mind.

Papa was gone seven years but his memory was always with her. Since his death in 1810, Kale, her half-brother George Hū'eu, and half-sister Peke lived with Papa's best friend, John 'Olohana Young on his estate at Kawaihae, Kohala. Mr. Young was a good man, but he lacked the sense of humor Papa had. For most of her four years with the Youngs, Kale preferred to stay with Young's Hawaiian wife, Ka'oana'eha, in her grass hale. Tenderhearted Mrs. Young reminded Kale of her Hawaiian aunties who quietly kept all the old traditions, and Kale was content to work beside her making kapa, weaving, and gathering food from the sea and the land. Kale did not like the stone floors and wooden benches in the "white house" where Mr. Young lived, a whitewashed stone bungalow built in the style of his homeland in England. But she dutifully went up the hill every morning and endured the Bible reading and bookkeeping lessons that Mr. Young held for his own six children and the Davis orphans.

Kale was good at calculations and read perfectly well, but writing always eluded her. Despite the Youngs' kindness, Kale hated the lonely expanses of the Kohala coast and longed for her early days in bustling Honolulu when Papa was alive and she, George Hū'eu, and Peke happily played with all the ali'i children of the court.

When Kale and James, the eldest Young boy, fell in love, she began to dream again instead of counting off each day in a list of routine chores. James loved O'ahu, too, and after marrying they made Honolulu their home. For Kale, the adjustment was not difficult. She was the first-born and had taken care of George Hū'eu and Peke for as long as she could remember. It was easy to turn her nurturing desires to her husband. Away from the discipline of the Young home, James delighted in long nights of socializing at the rum houses near the fort, and before too long, Kale's beautiful childhood memories of Honolulu were scarred by disappointment, pain, and frustration. Leaving James and Honolulu seemed the only remedy but it meant leaving her dreams behind again. This time she was all alone, with no new dreams to chase.

Kōlea, a migratory plover bird swooped over the bow of *Ka'ahumanu* and Kale remembered it was the makahiki winter season when these sojourner birds return to Hawai'i. "I hope your return to Honolulu is better than mine," she said. Tears welled again and she was not sure if they were connected to sadness or joy; but through wet eyes, morning was all the more beautiful. As *Ka'ahumanu* turned south to the channel and light Kona winds etched a fine pattern on the blue-mirrored skin of the ocean, the troubles of her past seemed small.

'Ulumalu padded down the deck to Kale and gave her a small bundle wrapped in kapa. "*E Mrs. Young, pau ka hana āpau. E nui a'e?* Oh, Mrs. Young, done everything. Anything more?"

" *'A'ohe i kēia lā. Mahalo, e 'Ulumalu.* No more work today. Thank you, 'Ulumalu. The sailors gave you a place to sleep. But eat the food I gave you, okay?"

"*Ae, hiki nō.* Okay, Mrs. Young. Maybe sailor food no good."

"And no more say, 'Mrs. Young'; now say 'Miss Davis,' please?"

"Yes, okay, Miss Davis, okay. *E 'olu'olu 'oe e kāhea ia'u.* Please call me if you need me." 'Ulumalu watched for Kale's smile and nod of approval before he returned forward.

Kale filled her chest with the fresh sea air and exhaled a long breath. She was on her way. Kale prayed that Papa would approve.

Above her on the helm, Captain Adams ran through his checklist of departure duties. "What do you make of the voyage today, Ka'aumoana?" he asked his first mate at the helm.

"A good journey, sir. Kona winds will push us through the channel between Moloka'i and Lana'i. Light seas make for smooth sailing but the main swell from the northwest will slow the going until she is under the western tip of Moloka'i." Ka'aumoana 'opioakalani, "young ocean sailor of the sky," was the son of a Hawaiian expert navigator whose ancestors had sailed outrigger canoes to Tahiti and back. Alika never saw Ka'aumoana use a sextant or compass but he was always correct on bearings, courses, and weather predictions. On the way back from Canton, when the *Ka'ahumanu* was lost after a storm, Alika watched in amazement as Ka'aumoana calmly waited for evening and immediately charted the course home based on what he called his "star map." In two days time, they were within sight of land.

Captain Adams didn't have to do anything else but just out of habit, he barked a few commands to the bo'sun and strolled the deck until the sails went taut and she was well underway. Then, with his hands tucked in his vest pockets, he said, "She's all yours, Ka'aumoana," and retired to his cabin to go over the manifest and account for his profit on goods off-loaded at Honolulu. It was a pittance he would clear on this haul, but enough to cover the sailor's wages and keep the old boat afloat. At his desk, he looked at the books and shook his head. "It's a long way off the profits we brought in during the height of the sandalwood trade."

The sandalwood trees that made Captain Adams rich were becoming harder and harder to find. He would have to find other commodities before long. In 1816, the Chinese had seized one of Kamehameha's large shipments to Canton, demanding nearly three thousand dollars in harbor tax. Adams and his crew were lucky to get away with their lives. Kamehameha was a quick learner and declared a tax on all ships anchoring in Honolulu harbor; for the past year, when tall ships sought anchorage at Honolulu, Adams went out by canoe to greet them, collect the harbor tax for the king, and steer them through the narrow coral bound channel into the harbor. He enjoyed conversation with the foreign crews and hearing the latest news from Britain, Russia, and the East.

Until the sandalwood was gone, Adams planned to keep the *Ka'ahumanu* and the rest of the king's fleet busy hauling anything that needed expediting among the islands–including passengers. Kamehameha and his huge entourage of high chiefs, courtesans, and friends whose lives were spent traveling from one playground to another on Maui, O'ahu, and Hawai'i kept him amply busy.

Now he thought about poor Kale, orphaned and leaving her husband. *It is a lot of trouble for such a young lady…the prize of her father's life and now misfortune's slave.* Second Mate Alexander Adams had just arrived in Honolulu when Isaac Davis died, poisoned by jealous chiefs after he thwarted their attempt to kill the king of Kaua'i and take his land. Isaac's best friend, John Young, took to Alexander, and was instrumental in having him assigned as Captain of Kamehameha's small fleet. As a friend of Young, Captain Adams watched Kale grow into a beautiful young woman.

Kale watched Honolulu Harbor shrink away as the *Ka'ahumanu* glided east. The biggest ships looked like tiny toys and low beach huts disappeared into the band of rock points and sandy shoals of the south shore of O'ahu. Above the shore, the Waikīkī plain and green kula lands ran up to carved lush ridges and valleys in the Ko'olau Mountains. Le'ahi, Diamond Head was soon floating in an expansive blue sea and the only visible surf was the waves crashing high on Koko Head.

The hard benches on the aft deck reminded Kale of "white house" lessons. She and James used to sit so close to each other that the tiny hairs on his arm would tickle her. She loved that sensation and for children in a Christian home that was as much pili, closeness, as one ever got. When James was next to her, Kale could hardly hear a word Mr. Young said. But those sweet days were gone. She sighed and tried to focus back to the sea.

"Enjoying the fresh air, are you?" said Adams as he came down the deck from his cabin near the stern.

"Yes, Captain Adams." Kale was happy for the interruption. "The breeze is very lovely and healthy." Kale smiled and pushed back her lauhala hat topped with feather lei. Her long shiny dark hair was tied back to keep it out of her face. "I remember being on your ship when I was a little girl in Honolulu, but never remember making a voyage. Did Papa ever sail with you?"

"Yes, he did; on business for the king, of course. My dear, I must tell you that you have grown into a beautiful woman. Right before me, I see your father smiling. But you must have your mother's eyes. I have never seen such beautiful golden eyes."

Kale blushed and shook her head in shyness but continued, "You knew my mother, too?" Kale was always eager to hear personal accounts of her mother, Nākai, daughter of the chief of Kaʻupulehu on Hawaiʻi. Nākai died in the ʻokuʻu plague of 1803 when Kale was just six years old. Memories of Māmā were few and faint and but Kale remembered being comforted in her warm bosom and carried on her back as she swam in a little rocky cove near Kaʻupulehu.

"No, I am sorry I never knew her. I came to Hawaiʻi just months before your father passed." Kale turned her face to the sea to hide her disappointment and drifted into her memories. The captain didn't say a word, but, when Kale turned back, she saw that he was not looking at the sea but at her. He immediately picked up the conversation, "May I sit down?"

"But of course, Captain." The square proportions of Adam's face didn't look like the other British people Kale had seen. Kale felt drawn to his sea-blue eyes that seemed to be glad with what they saw. "Forgive me, but I was drifting back, remembering how Mama looked. I do not know many people beside my cousins in Kaʻupulehu who remember her."

"I understand. But I have heard a story about your mother. According to Young, Nākai was a wonderful dancer and trained in the old chants. She was tall and beautifully graceful, like you, my dear. Your father taught her to sing Welsh tunes and there was never a party where Nākai was not asked to dance and sing. Of course you have heard how Nākai saved your father's life when the *Fair American* was taken…"

"Yes, but tell me again." She smiled again and nudged a bit closer. Kale was fascinated by Alika's strong chin and broad smile but there was softness in his eyes. *He does not know he is charming. This is a man without guile.* Kale allowed her spirits to rise on his animated conversation.

Adams caught his breath. "Well, then, Simon Metcalf, Captain of the *Eleanor* whipped Nākai's father, Kameʻeiamoku with a rope and the old chief vowed to kill the next white man he saw. Then when Metcalf was trading down at Olowalu on Maui, some other chief stole the *Eleanor*'s longboat for the iron nails and fittings and in the scuffle a sailor on guard was killed. Old Metcalf was incensed and retaliated by opening fire on the next day's trading canoes, killing over a hundred Hawaiians. They called it the Olowalu Massacre.

The local chief put a kapu on further trading, and Metcalf moved on to Kealakekua to meet his son, Thomas, captain of the sloop *Fair American*. Thomas got to Kealakekua before Metcalf, and was the first white man Chief Kameʻeiamoku saw. Kameʻeiamoku sent his warriors and sons out to kill the crew and take the ship, which they did; but Isaac Davis was a strong man and a good swimmer, and they had a hard time doing him in. Finally, they pulled him up on the outrigger and began to beat him with their paddles.

Nākai and your father had found each other, shall we say, attractive, when Isaac was ashore; and now he pled for his life with the only word your mother had taught him, "Aloha! Aloha!" Meanwhile, Nākai was wailing and calling to her brothers from the shore to spare him. They took pity, stopped pounding him, and threw him in a long-boat." Adams stopped "—I have made you sad. Forgive me."

Kale was wiping tears from her eyes. "No please, Captain, go on. I love to hear about my dear parents. Your words warm the love that remains in my heart. It is a good thing."

Adams put his arm around Kale and she smiled at him. "Well, the worst is over, for now Nākai got a haole beachcomber to bring Isaac ashore and Nākai dressed your father's wounds with herbs and stayed with him until he recovered. All the while, she and your father were falling in love. After the battle of Kepaniwai at ʻĪao Valley, King Kamehameha wanted to give Isaac one of his Maui kinswomen as a spoil of war but Isaac would have no other woman but Nākai. Young told me that Kamehameha had a hard time convincing Kameʻeiamoku that Isaac was neither related to Metcalf nor connected in any way to the massacre at Olowalu. And that is the story of Isaac and Nākai as I heard it. It was said that no two people were ever so much in love..." He stopped, and, as he tried to continue, his voice broke, "...except perhaps me and my bride." Adams, obviously surprised by welling emotion, stood up and turned to the gunwale to hide his tears.

"I am sorry. I never knew Mrs. Adams," said Kale

"My dear wife died in childbirth six years ago. She gave me my son Alexander, but I lost her. Talking with you just now, I remembered how much I loved her." He turned back to Kale, attempting a smile. "I am so sorry for bringing my sadness to you, my dear—I can hardly believe I am talking this way. Please excuse me." He looked to the sea again, clinched his jaw, drew a silent breath, and held it.

Kale went to Alika, took his hands in hers, and held them to her heart. "Dear Captain, thank you for telling me about my parents. It helps me hold them in my heart. My father was an important man but he always kept his heart soft and full of the memory of my mother. You are an important man and I see that you too are strong enough to bear a soft heart. It is a good thing to carry the sweet memories of your beloved wife."

"Kale, you are kind and wise beyond your years." Adams looked into Kale's eyes and she could not help kissing his cheeks. He drew in his breath, straightened up, and looked around to see which of the crew may have seen his emotional display. Kale found his straight-laced behavior endearing.

"Thank you, my dear." Recovering his composure, Adams smiled and said, "Well...then, it's time for me to get to work. I and my crew are here to help you if there is anything you require." Kale smiled at the awkward sound of such a formal offer but allowed him to leave.

"Thank you Captain, you have been very gracious to sit with me."

"Very good. We dine at four bells." The broad smile and dancing blue eyes returned. "Mr. Fairbairne will fetch you at your cabin."

"*Ā hui hou.*" Kale bid him "Until we meet again" in Hawaiian, her most comfortable tongue and a signal that she was at ease with Alika. Earlier, the thought of dinner with the captain frightened her but now as the *Ka'ahumanu* plodded over one swell after another she anticipated pleasant companionship at the end of a long important day.

By six o'clock, Captain Adams convinced himself that his emotional response to Kale was a figment of his imagination brought on by compassion for her predicament. He had entertained the lower ranks of aliʻi hundreds, maybe thousands of times in his mess and this was just another dinner companion to while away the dark hours before midnight. The mess was large for a 130-foot brig because Adams had refitted the entire aft deck to make better accommodations for himself, his mates, and passengers. Mahogany wainscots and French Empire style furniture with tapestry upholstered cushions and backs made a mess fit for a king. Thick Chinese carpets covered the planks. Clever Captain Adams even managed to find two windowpanes and a wall mirror to allow ample daylight in his cabin and mess. Tallow was scarce in the Pacific so small kukui nut oil lamps provided effective evening lighting. The second mate, Mr. Fairbairne, was just lighting the last one.

The cook-shipkeeper was preparing baked hen, fresh bread, taro cooked in coconut milk, and bananas for dinner. On shore, coconuts and bananas were forbidden foods for Kale, but on board ship haole customs prevailed so Hawaiian women were quite disposed to visit the *Kaʻahumanu*. After Kale and the Captain dined Kaʻaumoana, Fairbairne, and the bo'sun could eat. The deck and rigging hands got much simpler fare in the dark on the fore deck, but Alika was a good master and all hands made a decent wage and ate their fill of fresh provisions.

"Mr. Fairbairne, please escort Miss Davis to my mess."

"Aye, aye, sir." The second mate left the mess and Adams could hear his measured steps down the hall and his knock on Kale's door. "Good evening, Miss Davis. The captain has sent me to escort you to his quarters." Adams cleared his throat and began to stuff moist tobacco into the barrel of his pipe as Fairbairne returned. The door opened and in stepped Kale. Her loose hair flowed down her back. Her yellow pāʻū was wrapped high to cover her breasts, and, despite the abundant yardage, a hint of her narrow waist accented her hipline. Two maile lei fell almost to the knee and instantly filled the room with a sweet but faint cinnamon smell.

"*Aloha mai!* Sweet welcome!" said Adams, in his best Hawaiian. He meant to sound courteous but feared he was a bit too enthusiastic.

"*Aloha nō, kuʻu Kāpena.* And to you, dear Captain." Their eyes met for a moment too long and Kale silently crossed the room on bare feet, removed one lei, and placed it around Alika's neck.

Alika, who was well accustomed to Hawaiian protocol, bowed his head to receive the lei, as she pulled his head close to hers and gently pressed her nose to his, he breathed out and in deeply with her. Dread flooded his mind as he realized he was becoming aroused. He was not pleased at the prospect of controlling his passion all evening and the idea of having an affair with Isaac's daughter was all but blasphemous. A thought to feign illness and beg recluse shot through his mind. *I am a reprobate, after all.* But Scottish pride outweighed fear. *I have endured battles, famine, pestilence, and I shall conquer this insanity too!*

"Nani, nani ka lei o ka'u hoaloha. Beautiful is the lei of my dear friend," Adams replied. He straightened up to his full height and resumed stuffing his pipe.

"Well, well, well. Have you had a pleasant rest today?" he asked. She didn't seem to notice the beads of sweat on his brow, and surely, she could not perceive his pounding heartbeat. So, for Adams, it was going to be an evening of chess instead of an easy chat. Well enough, thought Alika. *I am fit to the task tonight, but I will not be alone with this girl again.*

"Yes, Captain. I am regenerated by the sailing and our pleasant meeting this afternoon. You make me very welcome on your ship. It is clean and tidy, this ship, and a thing to be proud of." Kale was like a curious child, strolling around the room looking at all the fixtures. "Mr. Young used to have pewter dishes and pitchers just like these," she said, rubbing her fingers over one of the plates on the long polished ebony sideboard.

"Very perceptive. I gave him those plates and pitchers as a wedding present when he married Ka'oana'eha. A fine woman, she is. But I feel sorry for her, having to spend so much time with Young, you know." Kale's eyes widened and Adams reckoned he would have some fun at her stepfather's expense. He cut her a mischievous wink and bellowed with laughter. "I cannot tell a lie! Young and I go a way back and Young above all knows that when God gave out humor, he was busy balancing his books!" He laughed again and Kale could not help but giggle too. Alika knew Young all right, and teasing banter was his strong suit. Yes, he was sailing familiar seas now.

Now that Adams was back in control, he poured some wine into two small pewter cups and offered one to Kale. "Please have a seat, my dear, and a wee dram of port." He offered her a comfortable chair near the writing desk and sat down in his own chair behind the desk. "Boki told me about your problems with James when he made arrangements for you to sail to Maui, but tell me what you are going to do in Lāhainā."

Kale took the cup but did not drink. "Captain Adams, I am not going to Lāhainā, except to pay homage to mother's dear friend Queen Keopuolani. If she gives me her blessing, I will go to live at Honokahua in Kā'anapali and manage my father's land."

"Honokahua? That's a remote place." Adams recalled the small fishing village on the northwest coast of Maui. "After the battle of Kepaniwai at ʻĪao Valley, Kamehameha gave that land to your father, the first haole ever to receive Kingdom land. But he and Nākai never lived there because Kameʻeiamoku insisted they live on Hawaiʻi. Who is the konohiki foreman running Honokahua now?"

"For years it was Piekani, but things were not going well so last year Mr. Young hired a new foreman named Kaholokahiki, an ambitious young sailor who wanted to try his hand at land management. He is preparing for my arrival. When Laura Konia, who owns the adjoining ahupuaʻa at Nāpili, went to Maui last month, she carried my message to him." I asked Kaholokahiki to build me a hale noho pili grass sleeping house, a hale peʻa woman's house, and an open walled work hālau, protected from the wind. Beyond this, I have no plans but to attend to the needs of the people and the land."

"Ah, so you and Laura are friends?" Adams trusted his instincts about people and he had Laura Konia Pauli pegged as a social climber and slacker.

"We are childhood friends. I am a shy plodder. Laura is a schemer, but one is good for the other. Being with her was the only good part of being in Honolulu and I will miss her."

"Kale, I couldn't agree more that you are birds of different flocks. You will not see much of Laura in Nāpili, perhaps once a year. But tell me, how will you get from Lāhainā to Honokahua?"

"By canoe. Mr. Young said there are plenty of canoes for hire at Lāhainā."

"Yes, he is right." Adams could see a host of problems ahead for Kale but it was not his place to point them out. "You are a courageous woman, Kale, and I have no doubt that the Youngs prepared you well to rule Honokahua." Adams smiled and Kale seemed to accept his compliment as approval.

Just then, cook entered the mess with a large tray filled with serving platters and announced that dinner was served. Alika walked to the long polished ebony dinner table and snappily pulled out a chair for Kale. "Please, my lady." He scooted in her chair and moved to the other side of the table where cook assisted him into his chair. As cook presented plates filled with his best fare, water cups, and a pitcher of water, Adams continued his standard compliment. It sounded stilted even to him. "Well, Miss Davis, it is a pleasure to have such a lovely dinner companion. Cook has outdone himself on tonight's feast, I think." The cook smiled as he always did, placed starched linen napkins on each lap and left.

"*Mai, mai e ʻai* Come and eat," said Adams as he picked up his fork.

When Kale was nearly done eating and Adams had finished his best sea stories and ditties, he sensed an opportunity to satisfy his curiosity about how final a judgment Kale had passed on her failed three-year marriage to James Young.

"Now I know where you are going," he said, "but tell me where you have been." It was an obtuse question to warn her of rough seas ahead. Kale blinked and her shoulders moved back just a bit, but she was still smiling. He waited a moment and spoke more clearly, "Could you not find any way to continue living with James?"

Kale's face slowly turned to a painful look of shame. She looked down at her lap and back to Adams, and her eyes pleaded for a way out, but he would not break the tension. He must know the truth because he was falling in love with her.

"I cannot talk about it." Her gaze dropped to her lap again.

Not good enough, thought Adams. He sensed her mental struggle. In the silence the *Ka'ahumanu's* old creaking timbers sounded like firecrackers.

Kale began to weep and words spilled out like water running from a taro patch. "Please Alika, am I to speak to you as I would my father and tell you that I failed to keep my husband?—that I was foolish to marry blindly—that I returned the kindness of your dearest friend Mr. Young by drawing his son away from Kawaihae into a life of depravity in Honolulu?"

Kale never looked up but the words kept spilling out. "I have never said these things to anyone…I tried so many ways to convince James to stop drinking but I failed—I even suffered the indignity of drinking with him but I hated the coarse language and crazy fighting of those people at the rum house. He turned to other women and had no thoughts of stopping. James never drank before I married him; there were no spirits at Kawaihae. And I selfishly convinced James to take up the flamboyant life at the king's court in Honolulu. If we had stayed at Kawaihae, he would have been fine."

Adams had tears in his eyes too but he also was angry that Kale had to endure James' philandering. He wondered what would have become of James if Isaac were still alive.

Kale stopped weeping and there was long silence again. She raised her head but continued looking down. A sudden sob made her gasp. "This is the most painful confession of all, Captain Adams, he forced me to leave his presence and when I returned he beat me until I went away."

Adams wanted to hold her in his arms and console her. With great effort he restrained himself from interrupting. *Patience, lad. Give her time.* He continued to sit and listen.

Finally, after much silence, Kale said calmly, "I tried to stay and Mr. Young intervened to ask James to take me back…James would not listen, so Mr. Young arranged for me to go to Honokahua."

So, that was it. Young rescued Kale from his bereft second son. Not a pleasant task for Young, a man of flawless reputation and great personal integrity. Adams wanted to soothe Kale's pain. No one knew more about the evils of rum than seamen in the Pacific, and no two men were more temperate than Isaac Davis and John Young. Because their lives and fortunes depended on clear thought and quick action, they suffered only sober men around them in war and in business. Young even convinced Kamehameha to give up drink for the good of the Kingdom.

Alika reached across the table and touched Kale's hand and she risked looking at him. Seeing his tear-stained face, she eagerly squeezed his hands and waited for him to speak. He began gently. "Kale, you comforted me this afternoon and I will offer you comfort now." He spoke from his heart. "I will tell you what your father would say if he were here."

Adams spoke slowly, letting each sentence sink in. "You are a courageous woman indeed and I am glad that you are bold enough to tell me what is in your heart." He groped for the right words. "However, I am…afraid that some of your conclusions are…wrong." She was staring at him in disbelief. "Yes, very wrong. First off, no one can foretell which men will be consumed with drink—not even a wife or a father—do you understand?" Kale nodded. "And once a man is consumed, there is no way to rescue him from his drunkenness—even his loved ones cannot do it." Adams watched Kale intently, measuring her reaction. "Do you hear me, lass?"

"Yes…" Kale pulled her hand away to wipe her tears with her hair. "I know all I did was futile but how do you know that nothing will help?"

"Young and I have seen plenty of good men, foreigner and Hawaiian alike, destroyed by rum, spirits, or 'awa. Sometimes by the grace of God, a man will rescue himself, and I have seen it; but my experience tells me you never had a chance to help James." Adams saw that Kale was trying to grasp what he said. *My god, how long has she been suffering under the delusion that she caused James to drink!*

She took his hand again. "I am trying to understand, Alika. Tell me again." He repeated enough to make sure she understood.

Adams stood up, came around the table, pulled out Kale's chair, and offered Kale his arm. "Come, some fresh air will calm you. Let's go out on deck while cook clears and prepares our dessert."

"I am sorry to share my troubles with you…" she started.

He turned and faced her, holding her shoulders squarely. "I must tell you one more thing," said Adams. "I believe your father would agree that you have done the right thing by leaving James." Kale's eyes filled with tears again. Adams took her in his arms and risked kissing her forehead.

She clung to him and finally said, "I don't want to go to Maui. I want to stay on this ship and listen to your kind words forever."

"Come now, lass. A wee bit of fresh air will do good for both of us."

Kale nodded. As Adams opened the mess door, a blast of ocean breeze cooled his face and pushed back Kale's hair. He looked at the curve of her neck and her square shoulders and imagined her arms around his neck. He was glad to be out in the fresh air so he could collect his thoughts and regain his composure. But the prospects were good for Adams. Kale was indeed a free woman and he would risk wooing her.

"*Hū! Ka Mahina Akua!* Oh my! A full moon!" exclaimed Kale as she looked at the eastern horizon. My goodness, thought Adams. I could never have planned a more romantic evening. *God forgive me, this temptation is too great.*

It was Akua, the night of the month when the rising full moon looks twice as large as other nights. The bottoms of a few small clouds shined blue on an indigo sky splashed with the Pleiades on the horizon, and the Hōkūpā constellation overhead. The ocean chop sparkled in the moonlight as the foamy wake of the *Ka'ahumanu* curled off the stern. Kale leaned on the gunwale and looked forward to see the bow wave glowing against the ship's side. Adams put his arm around her and she snuggled her head into his shoulder. Adams resisted the urge to kiss her, especially here on deck where his deck hands could see. It was too inviting, too easy. Even the embrace was not handily explained. Instead, he asked, "Are you cold, my dear?"

"No," she paused. "I just want to be close to you." *Queen's check. Was I so consumed with consolation that I missed her subtle seduction?* His heart was pounding and soon he would be breathing heavily—a terrible mistake to allow this if in fact he had misinterpreted her move. Surely, he just reminded her of her father and any enticement more than that would quickly be rebuffed. *I must be sure. I will not risk being called a lecherous old fool!*

He offered a way out of the embrace: "We should have our dessert so my mates can sit down for their evening meal. Shall we go inside?" Adams thought he might have sounded a bit too paternal but it was done. He offered Kale his arm again and walked her back to the mess. Bowls of baked pudding covered in warm sauce and mugs of steaming coffee were on the table, and the lamps flickered until the door closed. Alika's pulse jumped as Kale walked slowly past the table and into his private quarters. Without turning she asked, "Is this where you sleep?"

Oh God in heaven! He was aroused again. *I am a wretched man!* All he could manage to say was, "Yes."

Kale turned around with her lei in her outstretched arms. "Come in with me, Alika. I want to be close to you." *Checkmate.* He had no choice but surrender.

Alika walked in, locked the door behind, and slipped his arms under hers. She put her lei around him, caressed his face and pressed her nose close to his, breathing with him. "Are you sure, my dear?" he asked gently.

Kale looked up at him and said, "You brought aloha back into my heart today. I am sure if you are sure." His eyes nearly rolled up in ecstasy. He kissed her deeply and the game was over.

As the *Ka'ahumanu* sped toward her target, bowsprit dipping into every swell, Kale and Alika responded to the rhythm of an ancient drum.

Adams lay in his bunk, stroking Kale's face. "Oh Alika," whispered Kale. "I did not ever know this kind of pleasure. You have traded my pain for joy and turned my tears into laughter. I never want to leave this ship."

Adams laughed. "There is a saying, my dear: 'you don't have to go, but you can't stay here.'" Kale frowned but he went on. "Tomorrow morning we anchor in Lāhainā Roads, and soon you will be off to a new life at Honokahua but you will never be rid of me, Kale. A proper Scotsman should have a poetic thing or two to say…all I can tell you is that I have not been in love since my bride passed, but today I fell in love with you. Be kind to an old salt and have me, will you?—I can help you in ways you have not even thought of."

Kale kissed him again. "I will have you. *Aloha nō ho'i wau iā 'oe, e ku'u Alika.* I love you very much, my dear Alex." Adams kissed her again. Kale closed her eyes and soon drifted into a sweet, sweet sleep.

Adams watched her sleep in his arms, wondering at his fortune to win the love of such a beautiful young girl. He knew the stakes. Kale was 20 and he nearly 40. Likely, she would soon rue the day she gave herself to him and he would be heartbroken. How grateful he was that there were no other passengers on this trip. His men would not speak of Kale's indiscretion, and, if she came to her senses in the morning, everyone but Adams could soon forget this tryst.

Kale awoke to the sound of Alika putting on his clothes. He sat on the bunk. "My sweet, I have to receive the usual midnight report. If we have made good headway, perhaps we will see Lāhainā Roads by morning. And whilst I am topside, I will be certain that all hands are below decks so none see you returning to your cabin."

"But I don't want to return to my cabin." Kale rolled up on her elbow.

"Ah, my sweet. Whilst you were asleep, I was scheming how we can have more time together and I have a brilliant plan." In the faint lamplight, Kale could still see the smile in his eyes. Comforted, she leaned back into the pillow. "When we make Lāhainā, your servant boy will stay onboard and I shall escort you to Queen Keopuolani myself. She will no doubt wish to entertain you and perhaps ask you to stay the night at her hale. Just be sure to tell her that you have no need of a canoe because the *Kaʻahumanu* has been commissioned to sail you to Honokahua."

Kale sat up and kissed him. "Oh Alika, it is a wonderful plan. I so desire to be with you." Then she asked, "But Keopuolani's lavish hospitality is renowned. What if I cannot leave for two more days?"

"*E kali nei au iā ʻoe i ke awa.* I will be waiting in the harbor," said Adams and he chuckled. "Remember you are the only one who may redeem your servant ʻUlumalu. He is my assurance that you will return. I shall wait for you, my lady, but I will pine and wither away if you make me wait too long."

" *ʻAʻole loa! ʻAʻole hike iaʻu ke haʻalele iā kuʻu ipo nei.* Never! I cannot leave my cherished lover."

Alika let her vow of love settle in his heart and said, "Well, Kale, I am a practical man and if you should decide in a few days that tonight was not love but a moment of indiscretion, there should be no rumors following you. My men are loyal but it is best that they not see us together, at least until we have left Lāhainā. And if we are truly in love, as I suspect, I would certainly want to tell Young myself and not leave that to court gossips.

"I am so grateful that you know how such things must be handled. You are a wise man and I will do as you teach me."

Kale's submission was a stimulant to Alika. He cleared his throat and mentally squelched a growing desire to make love to her again. He was accustomed to being in charge but Kale seemed beyond his control. And truly, after all his brilliant planning and pleading for reasonability, there was nothing to do except get on his way. "Get dressed, my love. When I return I shall see you safely and secretly to your cabin." As he opened and closed the cabin door behind him, the ship's bell rang eight times. It was just midnight.

CHAPTER 2

Lāhainā Roads

Kale lay cuddled in her bunk, thinking of last night's physical pleasure, wondering at the depth of her womanhood and what delights lay ahead. *What a child I am, not suspecting that a man could pleasure a woman.* Just saying "Alika" to herself made her body ache to welcome him again. As she drifted off, Alika's tender words of love and encouragement echoed in her heart.

A big splash and loud rattle of chain running off the bow startled her awake as the crew dropped anchor at Lāhainā Roads. She was up and dressed in fine white kapa by the time the ship's bell rang four times. There was an instant knock at her door. "Four bells, Miss Davis. Your breakfast is ready in Captain Adams' mess." Kale doubled her hala and maile lei to chest length and put on her maile kupeʻe anklets. "Thank you, I am awake."

Instead of going to the mess, she went on deck just to get her first peek at Lāhainā. Loose tackle on three other sailing ships at anchor and roosters crowing on shore were the only sounds besides small waves breaking on the reef. In the west over Lānaʻi, last night's moon still reflected on the dark water of the ʻAuʻau channel. To the east Puʻu o ʻEke mountains shot nearly straight up, diminishing sunrise to a halo of light above the high ridges; two sparkling waterfalls fell through the backlit cliffs. Kula slopes still in shadow were cultivated right down to the beach with kalo and ʻuala sweet potato patches, maiʻa banana, kō sugar cane fields, and groves of wauke paper mulberry trees. Here and there, light glinted off irrigated kalo loʻi patches and ʻauwai irrigation ditches. Kale had never seen so many kou hardwood and ʻulu breadfruit trees in one place. Their lush foliage was a dark green backdrop for dense groves of gray and olive coconut palms near the canoe-studded shore. Above the ʻulu canopy, wisps of blue smoke curled in the still morning air, signs that many people lived there and were preparing today's food in their underground ovens. One thing seemed unusual—so many fires and so many canoes pulled up on the white sand but only a few small grass huts…*where do the Lāhainā people live—in the mountains?*

By the time Kale went into the mess, the Captain's mates were eating their breakfast and Mr. Fairbairne jumped up to give her a seat next to Captain Adams. As she sat down Adams said, *"Aloha kakahiaka kāua, e kuʻu pua ʻaʻala.* Good morning to the two of us, my beloved fragrant flower."

Kale shyly glanced around the table and grinned when she found Kaʻaumoana was missing. She guessed the others did not speak much Hawaiian. She reprimanded Alika, " *ʻAʻohe e nalo, he haupeʻepeʻe nā kamaliʻi.* Nothing is hidden, for it is hidden by children."

Adams chuckled. "Miss Davis, you are never without a stinging retort to my teasing and I must say that it is a pleasure to have you as a passenger. He winked and she smiled at the wonderful man she had fallen in love with. "I was discussing with my crew your intent to travel on up to Honokahua and I should like to offer the services of *Kaʻahumanu* to take you there tomorrow or the next day. My men are happy to enjoy some time ashore at Lāhainā."

Kale did not miss a beat. "Oh, thank you, Captain. It is a very kind offer and I shall happily continue my travel to Honokahua in your care." She had decided that she would need ʻUlumalu to run errands in Lāhainā and was not willing to leave him here. She tested Adams with a revision to his plan. "My servant ʻUlumalu and I will be going ashore midmorning to visit Queen Keopuolani. We will return to your ship when she bids us depart."

Adams did not flinch but picked right up, "Very good, Miss Davis. I will escort you and your boy as far as the queen's house. Then, as requested by Boki, I will visit Governor Keʻeaumoku and advise him of your intent to take control of Honokahua." Boki, the Governor of Oʻahu, had done no such thing but Kale understood what Alika was doing. The story would create a reason for the *Kaʻahumanu*'s layover at Lāhainā. Moreover, a visit from Captain Adams on Kale's behalf could only cause Keʻeaumoku to treat her with respect.

"Thank you, Captain," Kale smiled gratefully. "It is a great comfort to me that I do not arrive on Maui alone, but under your protection."

"My honor and pleasure, Miss Davis," said Adams at the door. "Mr. Fairbairne will assist you and your boy. I will collect you at two bells. Their eyes met for one last communion; he left and Kale looked down at her bowl of oatmeal porridge, wishing she were in steerage with 'Ulumalu, eating salt fish and cold baked sweet potato. She would never learn to enjoy haole food.

Fairbairne rowed the tender through a small channel and toward the beach. At several points along Lāhainā's three-mile beach people were surfing waves breaking on the coral reef. There was a wooden pier for tenders but at low tide, beaching was more convenient. As they neared the beach, hundreds of people, obviously living outdoors under the 'ulu trees, came into view. 'Ulumalu was the first out to steady the bow on the sand while Kale and Adams stepped out and pushed off Fairbairne for his return trip. Kale and Adams walked up the beach with 'Ulumalu behind, carrying the captain's jacket and a bag containing Kale's gift for Queen Keopuolani.

"It must never rain in Lāhainā," she said.

"Only a few days of rain each year," answered Adams. "How did you figure that out?"

"If they had rain they would have more grass houses for protection."

"Kale, you are a wise woman. Before the civil wars, this place was called 'Lele, the landing place', but Lele could not be defended because the beach was too broad and there were too many ways back into the mountains. Invading warriors cut off the water and starved the people. After the wars, it was called 'Lāhainā,' or 'cruel sun.' You will not see visitors coming to Lāhainā on foot, only by canoe, because of the terrible heat."

They walked under the cool shade of the 'ulu trees along a lovely path that traced the strand. And under the trees, along the entire three-mile beach, gatherings of people were weaving, making kapa cloth, collecting shellfish, fishing, and farming. Not far to the south of the pier, beside a small inland fishpond, was a large kauhale ali'i, royal homestead, consisting of several grass houses. Above the main house towered a tall royal kahili standard topped with three feet of densely woven feathers in a bright yellow, red, and black pattern; the kahili meant that Queen Keopuolani was present. Usually a large hale moe sleeping house like this would have several doors, with one facing the ala path, but Keopuolani's hale had a single door facing the sea. Commoners leave the front wall of the hale hana workhouse open, so workers can see approaching visitors. The queen's hale hana was fully enclosed. Keopuolani is so divinely sacred that anyone who looks at her or intrudes her shadow will be put to death. Even King Kamehameha must remove his clothes and prostrate himself as he approaches her.

From outside the hale, Kale chanted a greeting to the queen:

E aloha iā 'oe, Kalanikauaiwilani Keopuokalani, makuahine o kāu po'e pili aloha. E hā'awi mai iā mākou ke alo o kō kākou mo'i nui ame ka pua kapu a'e o ke akua, ka 'ili o nā mea lani. 'O Kale Davis, ka hua hiapo o Nākai Nālima'alu'alu, kaikamahine o Kame'eiamoku a me 'Aikake, ku'u 'aikane o Kamehameha.

Love to you, oh heart of heaven, mother of your devoted people. Show us the countenance of the highest queen and most sacred child of God, who is the face of all things in heaven. It is Kale Davis, firstborn seed of Nākai Nālima'alu'alu, daughter of Kame'eiamoku and Isaac, beloved companion of Kamehameha.

"Aloha mai, e Kale.'O wai kāu mau hoaloha nei? I feel your love, Kale. Who are your friends here with you?" came a delicate voice from inside the hale.

Kale replied, "*Eia he kanaka lawelawe ka'u a me, kāu alaka'i o Ka 'Aumoku o Ka 'Aupuni o Hawai'i, ke Kāpena Alika Adams.* Right here are my manservant and your leader of the Hawaiian Fleet, Captain Alexander Adams."

"*Hele mai e Ku'u Kāpena! Hau'oli wau e kipa mai 'oe a me ka kaikamahine o 'Aikake i kēia lā 'ano 'ai. E hele mai i ka hale. Ho'opōmaika'i 'ia kākou i ka wā makahiki! E noho pono kākou i ka 'ano haole. Ho'oku'u wau iā 'oukou mai ko'u kapu.* Enter, Captain! I am happy to welcome you and the daughter of Isaac this unexpected day. Come into the house. We are blessed at Makahiki time. Let us behave in the foreign way. I release you all from my kapu."

Kale was stunned. She expected to return after sundown when the sacred queen would give audience without fear of her shadow falling on her visitors. But Keopuplani was so happy to see Alika that she freed them of the taboo to which even King Kamehameha was obligated! Who is this man who does not brag of his friendship with the queen? So, she thought, inside this flamboyant sea captain is a humble man.

Kale motioned to 'Uluwalu to stay outside and she and Alika walked around to the back of the hale where the queen's attendants bid them enter the small door. Out of respect for Keopuolani's highest pi'o rank, Kale and Alika bared themselves to the waist before crawling through the small door.

Keopuolani sat up and smiled when she saw Kale and Alika. Kale loved the smell of a fresh hale woven with fragrant lauwaʻe fern. On the floor were more lauhala mats than Kale had ever seen in one house; she could count twenty or more. The sacred queen was tall and plump, adorned in a simple lavender pāʻū skirt and several light yellow feather lei hulu twined together. In her hair was a poʻo head lei of fresh gardenias and she held a small kahili scepter of red feathers. Her large face and flat nose were not the features of a beautiful woman and her small jet eyes had sadness about them, but her voice was sweet and mellow. "*Aloha mai kuʻu mau kamaliʻi.* Welcome my children," said the queen. When she spoke, the kindness of her expression and calm words put Kale to ease. This is the queen her mother loved.

Kale knelt on the densely soft matting and bowed low as she offered her kapa bundle to the queen. Keopuolani took the bundle and pulled Kale's head to hers for honi, the greeting of shared breath. Alika knelt and bowed too, giving Kepouolani a tin of licorice drops from Canton and sharing honi.

Soon they were chatting in Hawaiian about Kale's move to Honokahua and Alika was recounting all the news from Honolulu and Kailua. Keopuolani was not well, still tired and short of breath a year after suffering influenza. Kale watched her laboriously draw each breath to speak.

Alika begged Keopuolani's forgiveness and asked permission to go see Keʻeaumoku to tell him Kale would be living at Honokahua. Keopuolani agreed he should go, and bid him farewell with a tear in her eye. As they shared a final honi, she said, "*Ā hui hou kāua, e mālama i kou kino ame kō kāu mau ʻaumoana.* Until we meet again take care of your health and your sailors."

Keopuolani inspected Kale a moment and smiled. "You are very like Nākai; she was pretty, full of energy, and quick witted. She was a righteous daughter to me and your presence brings back her sweet memory. I must ask you why you come to Maui instead of staying in Oʻahu with your husband?" After last night's conversation with Alika, it was easy to tell the queen why she left James. However, by telling the queen, Kale risked her whole plan to go to Honokahua. If Keopuolani disapproved there would be nothing to do but heed the counsel of the highest Aliʻi Nui of all Hawaiʻi and return to James. Kale was not prepared for Keopuolani's response.

"My child, life is short and you must do what you can to be happy and find peace." Reading Kale's surprise, she said, "It is not a good thing to run away from the husband of your youth. There was a time I wanted to run away from the king but he married me for the sacredness of our people and so it was a good thing for me to stay with him for their sake. But it is not so with you. At this time, no child depends on you and even your husband has rejected you. You are right to run from the evil rum. Take a new husband and do not cause strife."

Kale wept at the gracious pity of her queen. "I understand now the depth of my Mother's love and respect for you. She told me that those in trouble may throw themselves on the mercy of our beloved Keopuolani."

Keopuolani said, "It is not my mercy but the mercy of heaven. When I was nine years old, Maui was lost to Kamehameha and my mother, Keku'iapoiwa Lilihā, and I, on the back of my kahu, escaped from the slaughter at 'Īao, struggling through the mountain pass to Olowalu with the help of some Honokahua fishermen. From there we sailed to Kalama'ula on Moloka'i, the home of my grandmother, Kalolo."

"Kamehameha wanted the most sacred woman of Hawai'i for his wife and brought his whole fleet of canoes to Moloka'i to capture me. I was a child and had no idea why my uncle would do such a thing, but when my grandmother died he took away my kahu and me, my mother, and my aunt, and we never lived anywhere but in his presence. At twelve, I bore Liholiho, and any dream of falling in love was put aside for the role I was destined to perform for my people as queen. I have been faithful to our gods and my people, and this gives me pleasure. Kale listened intently, unable to stop the tears from rolling down her cheeks.

"Here is the point," continued Keopuolani. "My past makes me merciful. It is because I know heartbreak that I am able to feel compassion for those whose hearts are broken. You have received the same bitter gift. Use it to bring happiness to others." She beckoned Kale to draw close. "Come, child." The queen wrapped her plump arms around Kale and patted her hair. It was as if Kale cuddled in her mother's bosom again, safe and loved. She hugged Keopuolani and kissed her cheek.

"*Aloha 'oe ia'u?* Do you love me?" asked Keopuolani.

"*Ae.* Yes." said Kale.

"If you love me, go to Honokahua; be kind to your farmers and fishermen as I am kind; be merciful to your servants as I am merciful; and do not follow the treachery of the kāhuna and evil chiefs. Evil and treachery has eaten up the men of Hawai'i with war, and the burden of preserving the land falls on the backs of our women; it falls on you.

"Kamehameha conquered the islands with the cannons of your father and Mr. Young. The price he paid for peace was very high. I believe he is right to seek the white man's ways for the good of the Hawaiian people; otherwise, one day they will come and devour us. You are only half white. Your heart is Maoli and the blood of the land flows in it. Rule your land righteously in the old ways of aloha love. Do good for your people at Honokahua and they will do good for the land."

At that moment, Kale understood the enormity of her responsibility at Honokahua. It was not a new home but a role that destiny had carved out for her. Keopuolani could see beyond the circumstances that brought Kale to her today, and, in a few words, she charged Kale with her kuleana life's work as Aliʻi ʻAi Ahupuaʻa, Chiefess of the Land Division. There were no chants or drums, no rites or offerings; but with sweetly spoken words of wisdom, Keopuolani placed the ruling mantle on Kale's shoulders.

Keopuolani released her embrace and Kale prostrated herself before her queen, saying, "ʻO wau malalo o kou leo, Kuʻu Moʻi Nui. ʻO kaʻu keiki paulele, wau. ʻO wau ke koko o ka ʻāina Maoli. E hana maikaʻi ana wau no kaʻu poʻe. I am submitted under your words, my beloved queen. I am your faithful child. I am the blood of the land. I will do good for my people."

Keopuolani took a deep breath and slowly blew on Kale's bowed head. Then she said, "Me ke aloha loaʻa mai iaʻu i kāu hoʻohiki malalo koʻu leo. Aloha wau iā ʻoe e like me kou makuahine. I kēia wā e hiamoe ana wau. E hoʻi mai hou e kipa mai iaʻu. With love I receive your oath under my voice. I love you, as I loved your mother. Now I am going to sleep. Come back to visit me again."

With her face still on the lauhala mat, Kale answered. "Ae, Kuʻu Moʻi Wahine. Aloha ā ola iā ʻoe ā hui hou kāua. Yes, My Beloved Queen. Love and life to you until we meet again." Kale could hear Keopuolani roll over and turn her back so Kale could leave. Kale would not raise her head even to glance at the queen's back. Head down, she respectfully crawled out of the hale backwards as she had seen her mother do so long ago. Outside it was nearly noontime as Kale put on her lei and slowly walked back toward the pier trying to memorize all that had transpired. She thought she spotted Alika on the *Kaʻahumanu*, now surrounded by trading canoes. There were two people on deck but they were impossible to recognize in the distance. ʻUlumalu caught up to her side and awaited instruction.

"Ua ʻai ʻoe? Did you eat?" she asked.

"ʻAole, Miss Davis, pōloli ka naʻau. No, Miss Davis, my gut is rumbling."

"*Aloha ino.* Poor thing. Let's go to the harbor and get some food for you."

From the deck of the *Ka'ahumanu*, Mr. Fairbairne and cook looked down at fifty men and women in canoes filled with vegetables, pigs, fresh fish, and hens. Mr. Fairbairne's red hair was stuck to his sweaty face as he bartered with this farmer and that fisherman, trying to strike a deal. Cook pointed out choice items that would stock his galley for the next two voyages. They were nearly finished and joked about getting ashore for an evening of leisure and female companionship. Ka'aumoana was happily married and volunteered to stay on night watch with the unlucky deck hand who had drawn short straw for shore leave.

Alika, done with his visit to the governor, was back at Lāhainā pier watching Queen Keopuolani's hale through his pocket telescope. "Over here, my darling." he said as he watched Kale come out of the grass hut, look at the ship, and converse with 'Ulumalu. "Now what are you two up to?" Then he saw 'Ulumalu rub his stomach. "Ah...it's food you're after." He watched them all the way back to the pier and delighted in Kale's bright eyes when she saw him waiting for her.

"*Hui! Alika!*" she waved casually according to plan, treating him as a friend, but her big smile and glowing face said she was in love.

Alika watched the woman he loved, relishing her beauty and grace with her every pace, and grateful to be her lover. "Are you ready for lunch after a nice visit, Miss Davis?"

"Yes, we are hungry—for some Hawaiian food!"

"Then you shall have it!" Alika handed 'Ulumalu a coin. "*E hele aku 'oe e kū'ai mai i ka 'aina awakea–na'u, nau ame na ka wahine Davis.* You go and buy some lunch for me and you and Miss Davis." 'Ulumalu happily ran off.

Kale began to tell Alika about the queen's counsel, speaking as quickly as ideas flashed in her mind. "Queen Keopuolani gave me her blessing to rule at Honokahua. She told me to take a new husband and be at peace. Then she told me to be good to my people as she has been to us. Oh, Alika! I learned so much from a short time with her. I know why my mother loved her and I love her too."

"Now, now lass, we have all afternoon and evening to talk about your visit, but you have told it all in one breath."

Kale laughed. "Oh, you are right! Look Alika, over here is a nice place to sit—away from the sun." She took his hand and led him into a shaded coconut grove where a rock outcropping abutted a small patch of tī plants. Alika found a comfortable flat rock to sit on, laid down his jacket and cap, and opened his shirt. Kale sat on the sandy ground at his feet. The cool ocean breeze poured over them. Kale propped herself against his leg and as they looked at the sea; Alika played with her hair.

"You did not tell me that you know the queen," said Kale.

"I wanted to see how you would do on your own; and very well you did, my lady. The queen has helped me unravel some very difficult disputes. She is unmoved by expediency and greed, seeking instead fair and just solutions. King Kamehameha wisely seeks her council and I believe she is the reason for the stability and peace Hawaii has known these last two decades. The king is a powerful deterrent to the treachery of the chiefs and priests, but Keopuolani is the voice of peace and justice. You know, she was never his favorite queen but when he looks back, he will count that she has done more for his monarchy than all the others combined." Kale listened as if she were memorizing every word. "Is this news to you? Didn't Young ever speak of Kingdom politics?"

"Alika, I feel naive and childish that I know so little about my kingdom and so very little about how to manage an ahupuaʻa and village. I have lived in aliʻi families but such knowledge was not shared. I have much to learn."

"Not to worry, my sweet, I am here to help you. You have a konohiki with two years experience and have Young to advise you. Your quick wit and natural wisdom are sufficient to the task." Adams was looking forward to making Kale a skilled and respected chiefess.

"Oh, Alika, I am so happy with you and so happy with my queen. Yesterday I was a lonely, rejected escapee. Today the future is clear to me and I belong to you and to a loving queen. My thoughts are speeding as fast as my heart beats for you."

"And as mine beats for you." Adams gazed at Kale's trusting face and knew that he would spend whatever was required to keep her at his side.

Just then ʻUlumalu returned with three calabashes piled, one upon the other. Alika took them and Kale asked ʻUlumalu, "Did you eat?"

"Yes, Miss Davis. Good fish and ʻulu poi. Plenty more for you and the Captain."

"Good, good. When we have finished eating, you may go and enjoy yourself. I will not need your help until this evening."

"Thank you, Miss Davis."

Alika looked in the calabashes, pulled out a dried ʻōpelu, and began gnawing on it with great gusto. He did not ask Kale to join him. They were ashore now and were required to observe the kapu of separate eating for men and women.

Kale stood up and walked up the beach, looking at clouds sitting atop the southern peaks of Lānaʻi and Molokaʻi.

Kona winds, thought Adams. We will be in Honokahua before noon tomorrow. And tonight—Kale will be mine all night. My God, what have I done to deserve such a wonderful young woman and a ruling chiefess at that? Last night she did not want to get to Maui. Tonight I will not want to reach Honokahua. He pulled poi from the calabash two fingers at a time thinking, *I am as Hawaiian as she is Haole! 'Tis a great match. She is everything I ever wanted.*

Later, when Kale had eaten, ʻUlumalu took away the calabashes and Adams went back to the ship to record the cargo transfers and check the manifest for the voyage from Lāhainā to Honokahua and back to Honolulu. Kale stayed on the beach to swim. From time to time Alika spied on her with his telescope. She was a strong swimmer and never in danger with all the people around her enjoying the surf. But for his work, he could gaze at her glistening brown body all day. Adams took a dip for himself, but it was not for enjoyment. He intended to swim for pleasure, but instead went the circumference of the hull, inspecting her seams and fittings.

At eight bells, Kale and ʻUlumalu pulled up in the long shadows of *Kaʻahumanu* in a small dugout canoe and climbed up the rope ladder. Cook had prepared a cold supper for Adams, Kale, and Kaʻaumoana and regular rations for the deckhand and ʻUlumalu.

Now in light cotton trousers and bare to the waist, Adams sat at his desk, a bit apprehensive about this evening and trying to guess what Kale had in mind. He featured himself entertaining for an evening, but it would be four bells in the morning before there were any distractions at all. He hoped with all his heart that he could keep her happy. Just then, she came into his mess, threw her arms around him, and kissed him deeply. All his fears evaporated as he held her close and felt the softness of her body.

"Alika, are we going to have dinner again here?" Kale was speaking quickly again and he now recognized the cadence. She had a plan, even if he did not.

"Yes…" he said, awaiting a stream of further information.

"Well, if we dine early, we can go out on deck and watch the sunset together."

That sounded very good, relaxing on deck in the cool of the evening. "Of course, my sweet…"

"I have been yearning to be with you all day and I want to pili early so we can go swimming under the Hōkū moon and sleep together the whole night. I don't want to go to my cabin."

"It sounds wonderful, my darling—except for the swimming."

"You don't know how to swim, Alika?"

"No, no, my darling. I swim, and I have dreamed of swimming with you all day but I do not have a way to maintain our privacy because my crew will be on watch tonight. I pay them to watch, but not to watch me and my lady!" He shook his head and laughed. "You are bound to take me to the limits of my comfort."

Kale did not understand his bashfulness. "You do not want the crew to know that we are lovers?"

"They have already seen the love in our eyes—and who could spend so much time with beautiful Kale and not fall in love?" He blushed. "When I even think of swimming with you, my lady, I am aroused and I do not wish to have my crew see me thus."

Kale giggled. "Oh Alika, you want to love me right now. Come, we pili." She took his hand, led him into his sleeping quarters, and shut the door. Plan or no plan, this night would be one he would remember until his dying day.

After a dinner of cold beef, bread, and fruit, Adams and his lady watched the sun set over Lānaʻi and then Kale asked him to take her inside. He bolted the mess door and immediately Kale pulled off her pāʻū and began to hum and dance a kahiko hula step her mother taught her. Adams sat down on the edge of his desk, marveling how the athletic movements showed off the graceful lines of Kale's body. She stopped. "Did you see it, Alika?"

"Yes, go on, yes. All I see is incredibly beautiful, my dear."

"Not everything, Alika, just this." Kale put her hands on her hips and Adams saw them sway back and forward. "When I move my feet and hips like this it is called ʻami. Do you see it is the same way you make me move when we make love?" She came closer and closer to him moving her hips in gentle waves as she whispered, "*E neʻeneʻe mai ʻoe, kuʻu aloha. Ninipo i ke aloha lā, ka wahine haʻalewa i ke kai.* Come and snuggle up, my love. Yearning for love is the woman swaying in the sea." Adams felt light-headed. She was like opium to him and he was happy to return to the depth of her yearning and carry her to heights of his own passion once more.

Cradled in his arms, Kale ran her fingers over his ears and forehead. "Oh Alika, I have never known such sweet pleasure," she whispered. "I was a child yesterday and you have made me a woman. I cannot contain my love for you— it is all I can think of."

Alika petted her hair. "Sweetest heart, it is a good thing for a woman to desire her man, and you are just, so to speak, making up for lost time now because James never sought your pleasure, but as long as we are together I will never stop pleasing you."

Kale wept with joy. "I have never known this kind of love."

"Now, now, my dear, your tears are like pearls, precious to me." He kissed the tears away. "I say we should freshen up with a swim under the Hōkū moon." Adams knew he could hardly embarrass himself after being so spent, and if a swim in the nude would make his lady happy, he would endure the curiosity of two crewmembers.

"Oh, yes!" said Kale. "Oh, Alika! You will love it!" Alika shook his head while Kale, with no apparent thought for her nudity, opened the mess door, walked proudly across the deck to the gangway gate, and dove into the inky ocean.

Adams peeked out the door to see if Kaʻaumoana was on deck. From the helm above, Kaʻaumoana was staring right at him. Adams looked down, avoiding his toothy grin, cleared his throat, and said, "Miss Davis and I are going for a swim."

"Aye, aye, Captain!" shot back Kaʻaumoana, a little bit too loud and definitely too snappily for Adams.

Adams just yelled at the top of his lungs "A-a-ah! me-e-e!" ran buck-naked to the gate, and dove in. Kale squealed with delight as Alika's pale white body flew though moonlight and landed with a great splash next to her. "What a beautiful night for a swim!" he yelled as he came up for air and threw his arms around her.

The brilliant moon illuminated the whole panorama of West Maui. Small misty clouds rested atop the mountains; *Kaʻahumanu* looked like a ghost-ship with only one person on deck. A furlong away, a koholā whale surfaced, blowing a pale white plume into the sky. Adams caressed his lady. "You make me feel like a young sailor again—do you know this is the first time I ever swam at night?"

Kale giggled. "I knew you would love it!" She dove under him, came up behind, and wrapped her legs around him. As the cool salt water pushed against the lovers, the smiling moon invoked the blessing of an infinite scattering of stars and an endless black sea.

Kale could sleep no longer from the anticipation of seeing Honokahua. At two bells she retired to her cabin with one of Alika's oil lamps to pack away her belongings and change into her rust-colored pāʻū. There on her bed was a folded paper. She opened it, held it close behind the lamp, and read:

The Rover's Bride

Oh if you love me, furl your sails
Draw up your boat on shore
Come tell me tales of midnight gales
But tempt their might no more
Oh! stay, Kale whispered, stay with me.
Fear not, the Rover cried
Your bark shall be a prize for me
I'll seize it for my bride.

She recognized Alika's flowing hand and the last word, "bride," was underlined. Kale read it repeatedly, memorizing every word and pondering the meaning. For all her passion and deep respect for Alika, she had never considered what it might mean to marry again, but now she mused about staying with him forever. By six bells, she was out on the deck as Lāhainā came to life, watching the crew return to the *Ka'ahumanu* and wondering what her children with Alika would look like. How much had changed in two days! She watched Alika at the stern and knew she would take this haole man for her husband. *Tonight I will sleep with him in my own hale on Papa's land of Honokahua. He will stay until the sun is high and everyone will know I have taken him for my husband.*

CHAPTER 3

Entry into Honokahua

Sailing up the ʻAuʻAu Channel, the *Kaʻahumanu* passed lush valleys, well-populated near the shore, and vast expanses of uninhabited land separated by seemingly impassible cliffs and peaks. All morning while Alika pointed out various landmarks, Kaʻaumoana regaled his captain and Kale with local lore connected to special places.

Lāhainā's long beach ended at a huge black rock promontory called Kekaha, that Kaʻaumoana called a "jumping off place" for Lāhainā people. "That dry leina plain just inland from the rock is an eerie place to be avoided, especially after dark. Dead people's souls walk across the plain to jump off the rock and return to Kahiki, the home of the ancestors. But some are destined to walk that dry plain forever."

Kale grew very serious. "I know a place like this in Kohala. My stepmother told us kids to stay away lest we interfere with the dead on their trip home. I never set foot in that place and I will not be walking near Kekaha."

Alika laughed. "My fearless lady is afraid of ghosts! Well don't let the ghosties and ghoulies of Honokahua get you…"

"Ghosts?" Kale's gorgeous eyes grew big and Alika laughed again.

"Kale, look there!" Adams pointed and handed her his telescope. "We are now in the Pailolo Channel between Maui and Molokaʻi. Windward Maui, all the way ʻround the north shore to Waiehu, is the moku district called Kāʻanapali, 'divided cliffs'. This is your country, my dear, some of the most verdant valleys in all of Hawaiʻi, and rolling cliffs that chop up the coastline into lovely rugged bays."

Lāhainā's mountains are almost vertical, and flat kula lands at their base run for nearly a mile to the beach. In Kāʻanapali, broad sloping ridges and deep valleys undulate up the coast; distant wrinkles on cloud-topped peaks fan out into broad-backed ridges and deep valleys with wide flood plains, like draping green kapa cloth. Mist and newly formed clouds float over the tallest peaks and black and gray rock points stud the coastline like tentacles of a giant octopus.

Kaʻaumoana pulled to port. "That sandy stretch ahead is Honokōwai," he said. "Where Honokōwai's two streams meet, the flow is so strong it pushes canoes away from the shore. Under the right conditions, those streams will push even our tall ship off course but we won't feel it today because the tide is coming in."

The square sails were pulled taut and vibrated against southerly winds pushing the *Kaʻahumanu* north. Just beyond Honokōwai Kale spotted a fishing village with a large stone koʻa fishing lookout and plenty of canoes; piles of nets were soaking in seawater or drying in the sun. "Is that Honokahua?"

"No, Miss Davis," replied Kaʻaumoana. It is Kahana. See the two streams? Those streams bring plenty mountain shrimp down to the sea and ocean fish come in to eat them. You also have two streams at Honokahua and the fishing is good." He pulled the ship's wheel starboard to follow the coastline. "Do you know of the old King Piʻilani?"

"Yes," said Kale. "He was a righteous king who built the road that encircles Maui."

"He is the one. Six bays of Kāʻanapali were the favorite places of King Piʻilani and are called Nā Hono a Piʻilani, 'The Bays of Piʻilani: Honokōwai, Honokeana, Honokahua, Honolua, Honokōhau, and Hononānā."

"Nā Hono a Piʻilani…" repeated Kale. "And is this why Honokahua is called a sacred place?"

"No…I think it is because of nā ʻiwi—the bones."

"Who is buried there?" asked Kale.

"It is an ancient burial place, but when King Kehaulike's two sons fought over control of Maui in 1738, hundreds of warriors from Maui, Hawaiʻi, and Oʻahu died there; hundreds more died in Honokōwai and Puʻunene.

"On his deathbed, King Kehaulike, Moʻi of Maui named his young son Kamehamehanui, as successor. The older son Kauhiʻaimokuakama and his wife Kahawalu took up arms against the new Moʻi. Great chief and warrior Alapaʻinui offered to mediate between the two brothers, and planned to take Kamehamehanui back to Hawaiʻi, leaving Kauhi to rule Maui. Kauhi thought

Alapaʻi was secretly trying to take Maui for himself and not only turned down the offer, but attacked Kamehamehanui in Lāhainā, causing him and Alapaʻi to flee to Hawaiʻi.

"Alapaʻi and Kamehamehaniui returned to Maui with their forces, took over Lāhainā, destroyed the farms and irrigation system, and drove Kauhi into the mountains. Kauhi sent to Oʻahu for his uncle Peleʻioholani, an enemy of Alapaʻi, to come to his aid. Peleʻioholani and his army sailed past Lāhainā, set up camp in Honokahua and Honolua where water and provisions were plentiful and started to engage Alapaʻi's army, hoping to press them uphill and unite with Kauhi's warriors in the mountains.

"The first battle at Honokōwai ended in heavy losses on both sides and Alapaʻi retreated to Kekaha, but regrouped and struck back at Honokahua, where hundreds of warriors fell. The bodies were buried there, in the dunes."

Kale said, "The bones of warriors are very precious. When one Hawaiian warrior meets misfortune, we all lose the battle. The thought of all those lives lost makes me very thankful that Kamehameha has established peace for us."

"Honokahua was not the end. Peleʻioholani regrouped and pursued Alapaʻi south again all the way to the East Maui plains of Puʻunene. In the pursuit, Kauhi was captured and drowned by order of Alapaʻi and there was no further reason to fight. Before Alapaʻi and Peleʻioholani met face to face and dropped their weapons, eight hundred more valiant warriors died at Puʻunene."

"This was over fifty years before Kamehameha's battles to unify the islands, when even more lives were lost," said Alika.

"Who is kahu of the burial site?" asked Kale

"High Kahuna Hewahewa is kahu. Honokahua is an ancient village, inhabited before Pāʻao and his Tahitian priests came to Hawaiʻi, so our ancient ancestors' bones are buried there too. Hāwea Point is also a sacred place to Hewahewa and he has a camp there."

Kaʻaumoana pointed. "Hāwea is dead ahead." Kale pushed back her hair to look at a massive wide and flat pali where currents caused waves to break in three different directions. "It is named after the sacred drum of Laʻamaikahiki in Kūkaniloko, Oʻahu, where the kings were born. As we pass, you will see Hewahewa's camp."

"I don't like it, Kale," said Alika. "Hewahewa is the most sacred high priest of Kamehameha who wears an eerie grey cape made from pueo hawk feathers. He celebrates the rites to Kamehameha's war god Kūkāʻilimoku at the luakini temples where people are sacrificed. There is no person more powerful than

Hewahewa." Adams looked directly at her and spoke slowly: "I advise you to cater carefully to his needs, my dear, because, as I am sure you are aware, those who break his kapu are surely and swiftly put to death."

Adams waited for a compliant response from Kale but instead she smiled and said, "I am not afraid. I am faithful to the gods and their kapu and such a fate will never befall me." Alika's eyebrows raised and Kale knew she must not let him think her impudent. "If the gods have chosen me to guard and provide for Hewahewa and the sacred ʻiwi, they will protect me as I do it." She felt a twinge of disappointment as he shook his head in disbelief. Kale continued gently. "Alika, I will not succeed as Aliʻi ʻAi Ahupuaʻa without your help; but I will need the help of my gods too." She searched his blue eyes for a glimmer of compromise.

He finally rolled his eyes and smiled. "Even when your gods let you down, you will still be able to rely on me. Just tell me you will steer clear of Hewahewa." Kale nodded and breathed deeply to settle her nerves. Adams smiled and put his arms around her. "Have we weathered our first disagreement? I hope you are not having second thoughts."

She picked up the banter. "Oh, no. I am reconsidering my *third* thoughts."

Alika laughed, squeezed her tight, and kept looking ahead at Hāwea Point. "Forthrightness is the mark of a good leader, and you, my dear, come by that honestly; Kamehameha said he never knew Isaac Davis to tell a lie. It seems his eldest daughter has been blessed with the same honest heart."

With her future just ahead, Kale leaned her head on Alika's shoulder and pondered the idea of her innate abilities; that somehow she might be like her father. To starboard, the rugged green-clad cliffs and valleys of Kāʻanapali looked inviting. To port, the island of Molokaʻi seemed to float in a cobalt sea.

Kale said to Alika, "Papa and Mr. Young left sailing. I wonder why you did not."

"Kamehameha forced them ashore first and then they took to it. As for me, I know nothing but the sea. I had only my mother in Scotland, and, when I signed on in Prestwick at the age of eleven, the sea became my mother and the captain my father. Through the years, I worked my way up to second mate, and, with the help of John Young, became the *Forester's* captain, a position to which most men are born. My dear, what you see is a poor Scottish lad living his life's dream, and with you at my side, there is no other heaven." He squeezed her and she kissed his cheek.

"When will we see Honokahua?" Kale called up to Kaʻaumoana.

"When you see the flat top of Eke Crater we will be at Honokahua," he called back. Inland above them stood a taller peak, Puʻu Kukui "mountain of light," where goddess Pele poured out West Maui.

"Look, Kale dear," said Adams. "Tucked right in front of Hāwea is Nāpili Bay, your friend Laura's place. Isn't it nice you two will be neighbors, so to speak?" Kale ignored his obvious disapproval of Laura. "Thank God she is always gallivanting about the court," he said. " ʻTis less time to take advantage of my lady's generous heart. Don't you worry, my dear, I will be watching after you."

Nāpili's nearly perfect sandy bay lined with coconut palms reminded Kale of a small bay where she learned to surf as a young girl; as she reminisced, the next bay caught her fancy. "Alika, is that my bay, that next one?"

"No it is not, my dear; that is Kapalua Bay where Hewahewa lives. There was no heiau, just a small kauhale group of huts in a coconut grove between the beach and a rock-faced ridge behind the bay. Kale spied for her first view of Honokahua village.

As the *Kaʻahumanu* cut past Kapalua Bay and rounded Hāwea Point, Kale made out the flat outline of the Eke Crater at the very top of the mountains. A thrill of anticipation filled her heart as a filmy white curtain of rain floated across the mountain under a billowed cloud. The hills of Honokahua quickly became a misty backdrop for a brilliant rainbow.

Kaʻaumoana shouted. "It is a very good sign! The omen of the aliʻi precedes you into Honokahua! Your farmers know early rain means prosperity for the coming year."

Kale grinned at Alika. "See how I am blessed by my gods and by you, my beloved?" The small squall moved north, leaving Honokahua's broad hills of light green pili grass and lower kula lands striped with mounded rows of dark green sweet potato vines sparkling in the mid-morning sun. The top of the mountain cleared and Eke crater reappeared, like the top of a huge drum against a bright blue sky.

"This, my darling, is Honokahua!" Adams took Kale's hand and led her up to the helm. "Your people should get a full view of their Aliʻi Nui Wahine as she enters the harbor, like Cleopatra entering Rome!" Kale did not understand the reference but took her place on the quarterdeck anyway.

Kaʻaumoana brought the square-rigger into a calm sandy bay on the north side of Hāwea Point. He pointed to the northeast. "Honokahua Bay is just there beyond Makāluapuna Point, but, Captain, I suggest we put in here in Oneloa

Bay. It is deeper than Honokahua and well protected from southerly winds and northerly swell. To anchor at even three fathoms in Honokahua Bay will leave her out in the swell. If the winds change it is easier to drop back to Kapalua Bay from here."

"Very good, Ka'aumona. Prepare to drop anchor here," said Adams. Turning to Kale he straightened his cap and said with great élan, "Please excuse me, my lady. We must prepare to escort the Ali'i 'Ai Ahupua'a to her fiefdom." Kale shook her head and blushed and Adams laughed as he jumped down to the deck yelling, "Bo'sun! Pull 'er in!"

Just as the bo'sun began shouting orders to deckhands, the deep round sound of a pū shell resonated through the air. Kale scanned the coastline and spotted a lone kahuna standing on a rock platform built into the ridge above Hāwea Point. She recognized his mapele heiau temple of Lono by the tī-leaf-thatched hut and towers on either end. His large Ku'ula Stone boulder was tied with a red sash, and two large white kapa flags announced the Makahiki harvest season. Honokahua's Kahuna was alerting his village of their arrival.

Kale watched the clear turquoise seas of Oneloa Bay licking rocks and lava tubes between the two points. A honu sea turtle popped his head up for a gulp of air and dove back down to feed on seaweed. People were gathering at the beach at Oneloa Bay and Kale could hear paddlers shouting as they shoved off to greet the brig.

The anticipation was over. About 80 of Kale's people were coming to greet their chief, half of them women, a couple of elderly men, and the rest youngsters, most under the age of ten and all skinny. The canoes approaching the ship were not full of trading items as in Lāhainā but loaded with just one or two small baskets of dried fish and sweet potatoes. Kale did not see any young man who might be her foreman, Kaholokahiki.

"Are these all the men you have?" asked Alika, "You may have inherited more problems than you bargained for."

Finally, the canoes gave way to let through the only young man in the welcoming party, their Konohiki. Adams did not call out a greeting. Kale looked at him, but he just smiled at her and said, "Go ahead, Miss Davis, address your people."

She lifted her voice. "*Aloha 'oukou E ku'u po'e o Honokahua!* Dear people of Honokahua, greetings to all!"

"*Aloha Mai!*" the people called back.

" *'O Kale Kani'aulono, ke kaikamahine o 'Aikake a me Nākai Nālima'alu'alu, kē ia. He Ali'i 'Ai Ahupua'a maika'i wau. He mau po'e maika'i kākou. Ke hele mai nei au mai Honolulu no noho i Honokahua me 'oukou. Eia ka ho'ohiki ka'u, iā 'oukou. E hana ana kākou me pū, no ka maika'i o ka 'āina.* I am Kale Kani'aulono, the daughter of Isaac and Nākai Nālima'alu'alu. I am a righteous chief. You are a righteous people. I come from Honolulu to live with you at Honokahua. Here is my promise to you. We will work together for the good of the land."

The Konohiki smiled and called back, "*E aloha iā 'oe, ku'u Ali'i 'Ai Ahupua'a maika'i. E komo mai 'oe i Honokahua, e noho mai ma lalo o ka mālama 'ana o nā akua ame kāu po'e.* And greetings to you, good chief. Join us in Honokahua and live in the care of the gods and your people." The people cheered and then became silent again. The konohiki continued, "Please come ashore that we might honor you." Immediately the rest of the canoes cut a course around Makāluapuna Point, straight to Honokahua village, tucked in the north end of Honokahua Bay.

"Something is amiss here," whispered Adams to Kale as he climbed down the rope ladder first and assisted her into Kaholokahiki's canoe. 'Ulumalu waited until the tender was lowered and then disembarked with Kale's bags, a sea chest, and boxes of extra provisions that Adams had arranged to be off-loaded at Honokahua. Kale's canoe followed the other canoes; the heavy tender lagged behind.

As they neared the stream estuary Kale noticed the sea was reddish-brown with red silt running out of the Honokahua stream. She said to Kaholokahiki, "The run-off looks like blood running into the sea."

Kaholokahiki did not turn around but just said, "It is the blood of the living land and it beats in the hearts of all of us." A tear came to Kale's eyes as she saw the pitiable state of her people and she wondered how she could help them.

Once on shore, she was relieved to see four middle-aged men and another four men in their twenties standing beside a large load of sandalwood they obviously had just hauled down the mountain. Adams said, "I am glad to see that Honokahua has a few resources. I was beginning to think there were no able-bodied men here at all. Maybe you will be able to pay your taxes after all." Then he asked Kaholokahiki in Hawaiian, "*Aia ke koe o nā la'au 'iliahi ihea no ka 'auhau o ka Makahiki?* Where is the rest of the sandalwood for the makahiki tax?"

Kaholo looked at Kale and then dropped his eyes and answered, "This is all we have brought down the mountain." Kale did not understand exactly what they were talking about but she knew by Alika's stern demeanor that it was not a good report.

Alika looked at Kale and then back at Kaholo. "Tell your chief about the problem now."

Kaholo looked ashamed. "We are required to pay the district tax collector ten loads of sandalwood for the Makahiki which begins in six days. We have only a few men and myself who are able to do heavy work. We have cut all the wood but have just now started to haul it down…"

Adams, the sandalwood trader broke in, "With eight men, it's a two-week venture to sort, tie, and haul down the remaining nine loads. The Makahiki begins in six days and if you don't have the sandalwood ready, the tax collector has the power to confiscate this land and give it back to the King for redistribution to another ali'i." Now the two men waited for a decision from the Ali'i Wahine.

Kale's mind was running. She knew that Alika probably had a solution, but he expected her to find an answer on her own. After a long moment of silence, it came to her. She spoke softly and forced herself to speak slowly: "Kaholokahiki, why are there so few men here to do the work?"

Kaholo explained that many men were lost in the civil wars between Maui and Hawai'i but the conscription for Kepaniwai Battle at 'Iao Valley had been the worst, drawing all males fourteen and older, and losses were great. The only men to return were two fishermen who helped Keopuolani escape through the mountains, and they are now elderly. Kale suddenly made the connection: it was her father who gunned down Honokahua's men at 'Iao. Now by a cruel turn of events, she was to rule over their widows and children. She bit her lip to keep back the tears.

"Such a great loss…" She could not think of what else to say. "How have you been able to manage the sandalwood obligation all these years?"

"Until just this month, we have not been asked to cut wood. All Honokahua women work in the fields and even at fishing; Kū'ula, the fishing god, and Lono, god of the harvest, have been good to us," said Kaholo.

"I understand. Are there any other Makahiki tax items in shortage?"

"No, my chief, all are sufficient and some in excess."

"Good, good, good. Please thank your people for coming to greet me and allow them to return to their work while you, Captain Alexander, and I think about what to do concerning this sandalwood obligation. Kale turned around so that all the people could hear her. "I declare all rites of greeting and honor to the Aliʻi Wahine kapu for five days."

Kaholo called two young boys to his side and told them to run and tell everyone in Honokahua about the kapu. Kale saw relief on the faces of her people, who were already dispersing. Now she understood that they intentionally brought little of value to trade lest precious work time be wasted. *My people are industrious.*

Adams was beaming with pride. "And for that wonderful demonstration of leadership under fire, I shall offer my able but reluctant crew to help with the hauling; and, as Kaholo has done, I shall put my own back to the effort."

"Oh, Alika!" Kale threw her arms around him and kissed him. "Thank you for helping me and my people!" Adams first reaction was shyness and he stiffened; then remembering that Honokahua was Kale's domain, he picked her up and swung her around, yelling, "Anything for my bride!" Kale and Alika were laughing and Kaholo looked uncomfortable, but he managed a grateful smile.

The crew of the *Kaʻahumanu* did not laugh when they heard they would be at hard labor in Honokahua for five days. Adams promised them a substantial bonus he would make back with interest on an extra load of sandalwood he negotiated with Kale. It would make this run a worthy business venture after all. By noon, Adams brought all but one deck hand ashore and caught up with Kale who was sharing aloha with everyone she met; at this moment, she was with Manu, the old Kahuna Kilo Iʻa, priest and fishing expert.

"Alika! Manu was on the heiau as we sailed in."

"*Aloha e ke kumu,* Love to you, teacher," said Adams, and shared honi. "*Pono mai kākou i kāu mau pule, no ke ola o ka poʻe.* We all need your prayers for the life of the people." Then he turned to Kale and bowed. "May I have audience with the Aliʻi Wahine? That is, if she has time for an old salt soon dispatched to hard labor in the mountains of Honokahua."

"Yes, of course." Kale and Alika excused themselves from Manu, and Alika led his bride through a gulch toward the beach path leading back to Honokahua village. "Where are we going?"

"Kale dear, forgive me for being practical, but do you have a house to live in here? I should like to know where you are when I return tonight."

"I don't know. I asked Kaholo to build me one, but perhaps he did not have time to do it. We must find ʻUlumalu. He brought all my belongings ashore."

"Well, my dear, if tonight you are longing for your Rover, do sing out in the dark so I may find you and 'Ulumalu." He sang out in a falsetto voice "Oh, Ro-o-o-ve-e-er!" Kale giggled and then squealed with glee as this tall rugged man, still in his captain's trousers, began swinging his hips, imitating her 'ami hula steps. "Ah, me! Ro-o-o-v-ve-e-er!" he yodeled. Kale tickled his belly and ran down the path with Alika in playful pursuit.

Back at the village, two kūpuna elders, Keahi and Umuwena led 'Ulumalu to a freshly constructed pili grass and naio wood hut tall enough to stand in and roomy enough to sleep eight adults. It was above the south bank of the Honokahua stream, far enough inland to be protected from both trade and kona winds, and high enough up the hill to see all the other houses. One door faced east and another south. Kou and banana trees shaded tī planted by the doors to keep away evil and lauwaʻe ferns to perfume the air. Morning glories already started climbing the west wall.

The kūpuna told 'Ulumalu to put all Kale's belongings outside the house and tell them any other furnishings or provisions she would need. When everything was collected, they told 'Ulumalu they were ready to cut the umbilical cord of the house whenever the aliʻi wished.

'Ulumalu spotted Kale and Alika entering the village and he called: "*E Miss Davis, e hele mai kākou, i kou hale. Hoʻomākaukau kākou no ka pule kuwā.* Oh Miss Davis, let us go to your house. We are all ready for the house-opening prayer."

Kale cut a glance at Alika. "I told you! My people have built me a house!" Then she answered, "*E 'Ulumalu! Ke hele mai nei māua. E hahai mai ana māua iā 'oe i ka hale.* 'Ulumalu! We are coming. We'll follow you to the house."

When Kale saw the large sturdy hale, she wept and thanked the two men for their careful work and loving care to every detail, the grand size, fine workmanship, and thickness of the pili grass roof. It was better than Mrs. Young's house in Kawaihae and a much finer house than some aliʻi at court could afford. "*Nani nui loa koʻu hale noho!* My sleeping house is most beautiful!" Keahi and Umuwena just kept looking down at their feet, murmuring about the graciousness of their Aliʻi Wahine. It was the humble way of the people of Honokahua.

Keahi gave Kale a flat stone to hold under the long trailing pili grass purposely left untrimmed at the top of the main door opening. As old Umuwena cut through the grass with a small ax, he chanted in rhythm with chopping sounds ringing off the rock:

"Severed is the piko, umbilical cord of the house; the thatch that sheds the rain, that wards off the evil influences of the heavens…that the house dweller may prosper, that the guest who enters may have health, that the lord of the land may have health, that the chiefs may have long life…'Ā *mama* it is free."

Keahi uncovered a small offering of 'ōpae, red fish, and bananas, dug a hole under the threshold, and buried the pili grass cuttings with the offering. Then they both stood back for Kale to enter. She went in and deeply breathed the comforting sweet fragrance of new grass…*Beloved home.* 'Ulumalu and the old men followed her inside, carrying her favorite belongings and so many new ones. They carefully padded the sleeping area against the back wall with dried sweet potato vines and spread out Kale's finely woven lauhala mats. Coarse mats covered the ground for sitting or walking. They placed Alika's chest in the middle for a table, with Papa's prayer book on top. While Keahi and Umuwena hung fans and nets on the walls and kukui nut torches from the ridgepole, Kale picked up her precious book and opened the chest she knew was from Alika. Inside was an oil lamp and four shiny pewter plates and cups—the wedding gift. Tears welled up again and she turned to see the expression on Alika's face, but he was gone.

The kūpuna men kept bringing in utensils: coconut shell cups and various sizes of platters and calabashes made from koa and gourds. In one corner, they set a basket full of tools: fly swatters, brooms, digging sticks, an adz, and various cutting tools. They even gave Kale a calabash full of fishhooks, lines, and sinkers. It was a fine house.

The 'auinalā afternoon work time began so Kale decided to take her new net bag up to the kula and find a farmer to help. Walking up the hill she saw Honokahua Valley below, a flood plain between Honokahua and Mokupe'a Streams, wide enough for two dozen taro patches. Kale guessed that fishermen lived in the four homesteads built on the south kualapa ridge above the estuary. Against a rock cliff, that was the northern boundary of Honokahua Bay, three more hale were supported on pilings, so they sat above the estuary's flood stage. Thick pilings were anchored in the mud by stone kahua foundations, and wa'a canoes were moored underneath the house next to a small makaha fishpond.

There were many farmers' kauhale up the valley, but Kale headed for one of four homesteads on the broad hill above Makāluapuna Point. As she neared the even rows of robust 'uala 'ie'ie, sweet potato vines she heard voices—little girls chatting and laughing—but the vines were raked into mounds so high Kale could not see them squatting on the ground, harvesting potatoes.

"Auwē Oh, dear!" Kale said in a loud voice. "*Wela ka lā!* It's hot today!" The chatter stopped and three heads popped up to see who spoke. Seeing the Ali'i Wahine they immediately hid again. Kale laughed. "*Mai maka'u 'oukou. Ke hele nei au e kōkua iā 'oukou me kō 'oukou kā'ai 'ana* Do not be afraid. I have come to help you with your digging."

There were frantic whispers and then a tall girl with a stupefied look on her face stood up, wringing her hands. Kale laughed all the more. "Stop staring at me. What is your name?"

The girl looked down and whispered, " *'O Mapuana wau.* I am Mapuana."

"Come here, Mapuana." Kale shared honi with the skinny Mapuana and hugged her. "Do not be afraid. Show your respect as you have been taught, from the love of your heart, not from fear." Mapuana smiled and looked at the other two girls who were standing up now and giggling. "Yes, I mean that for all of you." Kale walked over to their basket and saw big, well-shaped sweet potatoes like ones she grew for Mrs. Young in Kawaihae. "Very good, your harvest."

The girls grinned and the tiny one said, "My name is Pi'ikani!" And the shyest girl with reddish hair just whispered, "Kaehu."

"*Hau'oli wau e 'ike i nā pua u'i o Honokahua.* I am happy to know the beautiful flowers of Honokahua." Kale nodded as the girls burst into giggles again. "Come, let's go to work and you show me where to dig." There was a bit of tugging to determine just who would show Kale where to dig, and discussion about which two girls would work on either side of her, but soon they settled into a good pace, digging out big tubers with their hands and filling the basket.

Just before sundown, Kale, her hands, feet, and knees red with Honokahua soil, rushed back down to her hale. The hills of Honokahua resounded with chattering birds, crowing chickens, barking dogs, and the "ump-ump" of hogs. In the distance, the *Ka'ahumanu* gently rocked in a pink bay with gold lights dancing on her masts and rigging. The red-orange sun was setting and the sea in Moloka'i's shadow was indigo. As Kale neared the fishing village, a familiar smell of imu ground ovens baking vegetables and fish filled the air. Kale was happy to have a little daylight to find her way to the beach and bathe.

Now in the grove behind the beach, Kale saw five hull-shaped loads of sandalwood ready for the tax collector's inspection, but the men were nowhere in sight. She left her pā'ū on a flat rock in the estuary, ran to the inviting clean surf, bathed and swam along the beach. Women and children collecting seaweed watched their new Aliʻi Wahine with guarded curiosity, ready to turn away before she might see them watching. Kale was used to being a curiosity with her pale golden hapa haole skin and less than wavy hair. She already felt comfortable at Honokahua but she missed Alika after only a few hours and wondered how she would ever get along when he sailed back to Honolulu. *Maybe he will come to live in Honokahua.* When she swam back into the estuary to rinse off the salt, the cold mountain water chilled her and she quickly got up on a flat rock to dry off. For a brief time she watched the last purple lights in the western sky, but soon she heard men's voices in the distance—singing a rhythmic song as they carried the heavy wood down the steep trail on their backs. She wrapped her pāʻū and scampered back through the dark thicket to her hale as the chorus got louder:

> My sails are all filled to my dear,
> What tropic bird can swifter move?
> Who, cruel shall hold his career
> That returns to the nest of his love?
> Ye sailors, I'm bound to my love,
> Ye sailors, I'm bound to my love,
> I've done with the toils of the seas
> Ye sailors, I'm bound to my love.

Kale peeked at the grand procession as they marched by. Kaholo was in the lead with the first load. Adams brought up the rear of the second, with eight men carefully negotiating the trail under the weight of each huge load. The sailors' shirts were rolled up for padding on their shoulders. The Hawaiians used wads of grass to soften the load. Bark dust and soil stuck to the men's sweaty faces and torsos. With a great shout, they set down their loads in the grove and ran for the beach, tossing their clothing and malo as they ran. The Hawaiians were in the water first. From her hale Kale grinned at their boisterous whooping and splashing. Little kids ran down to the beach to watch and the elders Keahi and Umuwena lit a bonfire to signal that dinner was ready.

After dinner when ʻUlumalu came to get Kale, the kūpuna and sandalwood crew were lounging around the big fire, sipping ʻawa. Kale joined women gathered in a separate eating group to one side, and managed both to listen to men's spirited conversation (especially Alika's) and to converse with the women too. After the women ate, they joined the men and listened to workday stories embellished for the benefit of their new audience.

The sailors were not used to hiking and complained about sore feet. Honokahua men mocked them, advising them to learn how to weave lauhala sandals. The sailors had great respect for the amount of weight the Hawaiians could lift and described them like giant mythical figures, but the sailors figured themselves the heroes of the day for showing the Hawaiians a rapid knot to lash wood together, called the "bowline." The Hawaiians insisted on calling it "ka boleno" because all words in Hawaiian must end in a vowel, and the sailors had great fun protesting the pronunciation. Together they managed well and determined they could bring down the remaining cut wood in one full workday. Adams was in his glory leading his men to triumph, acting as translator for both groups, and turning a rough job into fun.

"This evening's prize for the best story, however," announced Adams "goes to Mr. Fairbairne!" Fairbairne threw back his head and laughed with the two Hawaiians to his right. "It seems he was particularly fond of the roasted meat tonight and gestured to these two fine fellows, inquiring what kind of meat it was. To be clear he made some grunting sounds like a pig. Limaha'i and Kapuni'ai looked at one another, shook their heads, and barked back at him, "Wo! Wo! Wo! Wo!"—to Mr. Fairbairne's great horror, great dog fancier that he is." Adams bellowed with laughter. Catching his breath, he said, "But this is the best bit—he immediately grabbed another handful and gobbled it up!"

"Tell them I said it is delicious!" yelled Fairbairne

"*Ua ha'i 'oia, 'Ono loa ka 'īlio kālua,*" said Adams.

"Kapuni'ai patted Fairbairne on the back and said, "*Aloha 'o ia nā mea 'ai 'ono o Hawai'i.* He likes the delicious things of Hawai'i."

Not all the crew was laughing heartily at the news about the main course, and Fairbairne had the last laugh. Kapuni'ai and Limaha'i reckoned the joke was not on them and kept barking, "Wo! Wo!" to everyone's delight; soon all the sailors were doubled up with laughter.

Adams finally stood up, bid everyone a good night, and ordered his crew back to the ship. In a flurry of alohas and mahalos and hugs he whispered to Kale that he would join her later at the hale. Kale instinctively nodded for 'Ulumalu and told him to accompany the captain.

Adams nodded gratefully. "You are ahead of me again, my love." A quick kiss and he was off herding his men to the tender at the beach.

Some time later, Alika called out softly as he approached Kale's hut, "It is your Rover!" He was still animated from the day's activities and planning for tomorrow's work. The sight of Kale stretched out on her sleeping mats made him pause at the door. In the dim light of the oil lamp, Kale's golden eyes sparkled and highlights shimmered on the naked curves of her body. Without a word, he slipped off his trousers and hung them on a twig left on a cross hatch to serve as a hook. He knelt beside Kale and began to trace the lines of her body with his hands. "You are the most beautiful woman I have ever known," he said.

She guided his hands as she spoke to him in Hawaiian, "Do not delay. Honokahua is out of breath from the journey of her lover." She petted him. "Stones roll downhill before the evening rain. And the pili grass of the kula collects dew but longs for the torrents of life giving-rain." Adams knew this was not a young girl's curiosity or aimless passion. She spoke to him in her native tongue and called him kāne, husband.

Adams gave himself to Kale as he had never done before, consumed in his passion and forgetting all but the oneness of their beings and bodies, not knowing where he ended and she began. Kale responded again and again, drinking him to the last drops of consciousness. "Ku'u kāne, My beloved husband," she whispered. All that went before seemed a rehearsal for this moment.

CHAPTER 4

Life Begins at Honokahua

Gold reflections from kukui torches danced on a wet rock temple terrace, and, from a blazing fire pit, hot cinders and smoke pushed up through twirling misty rain. The eyes of two kahuna glowed through the eyeholes of their gourd masks, as they stood on a small raised altar terrace behind the exalted high chief in his yellow-feathered cape and helmet. He was tall and tattooed on face, arms, and legs. His palaoa, ivory hook pendant made his neck appear very large, but not out of proportion with his huge muscular arms crossed over his chest. Surrounding the entire heiau temple area were several hundred people, both women and warriors in full battle-dress with spears at their sides. Everything beyond the fire's canopy of light was pōʻeleʻele–the darkest night.

Rhythmic drumbeats echoing off valley walls reverberated in the bellies of on-lookers. From the right side of the heiau, a huge rough-hewn image of war god Kū looked down with demanding fiery eyes, its gaping toothy snarl warning of Kū's unbridled power to destroy and plunder humankind. Inside a tall three-tiered lana nuʻu manaʻo oracle tower, more priests prayed and chanted the gods' mighty virtues.

From the outer court came two warriors and a mū, executioner dragging by the feet a bloody corpse, a small offering to appease Kū's wrath and assure victory. The mū never kills the mōhai sacrifice in the image's presence, but brings it to the altar dead, prepared as Kū demands. Then a second drum began and one kahuna chanted over the body. The hushed crowd moved in and Kale stood on her toes to see the sacrifice—her heart skipped—the smoke and misting rain were not enough to obscure her view of familiar pale skin and blond hair tied back in a sailor's tail—"Uwēēēē!!! ALIKA!!!!!"

To utter even a whisper during the offering is kapu. The rite is broken! All eyes immediately focused on her. Drums stopped and an angry high priest pointed at Kale, shouting: "*E hāʻawi mai iaʻu i hoʻokahi mōhai hou!* Bring me a new sacrifice!"

"ʻAe!!" The warriors yelled back, and they rushed her.

Kale tried to run, but all around women were yelling, blocking her way, and pushing her toward the executioner. Only one way was open—Kū! She dashed up on the altar and threw her arms around the ugly image. "*Ua hoʻomake ʻoukou i koʻu kāne, naʻe ʻaʻaole e hoʻomake iho ana ʻoukou i kāna pēpē!* You kill my husband, but not his child!"—sneering warriors ripped her hands away from the wooden image and dragged her away—Kale's screams could not be heard above the riotous crowd shouting louder and louder—And suddenly—darkness.

She focused on a door's outline visible in the faint moonlight. Was it her hale? Kale was sitting straight up, crushing her kapa moe bedding in her arms, gasping for breath and shaking. A salty tear trickled from her upper lip and she groaned in horror at the fading nightmare. A stiff breeze was whipping around her hale, making trees and bushes whisper. A mud hen clucked and Kale shuddered. *The dream was so real. What does it mean? Is Alika dead? Is there going to be another war?* Kale got up, drank from a water gourd hanging beside her sleeping mat, and splashed a few drops on her face. *Kahakai—I can always collect my thoughts at the beach.* She wrapped her pāʻū, found her kīhei, and stepped out into the wind.

The moon was low over Molokaʻi but still some time from setting. Rumbling waves sent arcs of foam up the wet beach. Above, limbs of kou trees clacked together. Hala trees and fronds of bowing coconut palms sawed against one another, hissing at every gust. Kale wrapped her kīhei to the shoulder for warmth, but kapa is little protection against salty gusts and blowing sand. It was the Makahiki season, when it is better to stay inside.

She faced the wind and breathed deeply, allowing the enormity of sea and sky and land to put her nightmare in perspective. Alika was gone just three days but already she was weary and heartsick for him. She yearned for Alika and tears began to flow again. *This is not the loneliness I knew in the years after Papa's death. That was a dry wandering that held me back from getting close to anyone. I should have loved the Youngs for being so kind to me, but all I could muster up was respect. And even with James, there was that part of my heart that I never opened to him—a lonesome part that was my constant companion. Alika is different. I did not hold back and now I belong to him freely the way I belonged to Papa…this kind of loneliness hurts. I cannot return to Honolulu now that I have given my oath to Keopuolani…He will be away just two moons.*

Hauling goods during Makahiki season was Alika's biggest undertaking of the year. A picture of Alika focused at his work, strong and confident in his skills and knowledge, tempered her thoughts. Until the end of the Makahiki the *Ka'ahumanu* and all the king's fleet would be busy taking Kamehameha and his priests back and forth from Kailua to all the islands, collecting 'auhau tribute taxes and warehousing or distributing them to king's favorite chiefs and warriors. With the wind in her ears, Kale walked the strand toward Makāluapuna Point; sea foam lapped around her ankles and softened the sand under her feet.

Already I feel revived, she thought. We have tallied all Honokahua's tribute items, and in three days, on the kapu of Hua, King Kamehameha's Governor of Maui, Ali'i Nui Ke'eaumoku, will come to Honokahua with his priests and Manakū, his tax collector. Manu will help me be a worthy chief of the Makahiki celebrations and Alika will be so proud of me.

Again her longing welled up and Kale turned back up the beach. It was quieter with the wind at her back and she remembered the concerned look on Alika's face as he gave Kaholo instructions to prepare a hideout where Kale might flee lest lawlessness break out during the Makahiki celebrations. Whenever kapu are suspended during Makahiki or after a great chief dies, drunkenness and abandon may break out into violence and plunder. In her youth, whenever the kapu were lifted in Kawaihae, Mr. Young boarded up the windows of his stone house and bolted the doors with his family safely locked inside.

Kaholo dutifully found a lava cave under a rock escarpment three anana, fathoms up a steep wall in Mokupe'a Valley. Its interior was high enough to stand in and the opening small enough to cover easily with large rocks. He personally stocked it with firewood, tools, and mats. If danger should arise, Kale would go directly to the cave and Kaholo would bring her food, water, and kapa. Once secluded, Kale would not respond unless she heard a secret call known only to Kaholo and Alika. *I hope I never have to use it.* She remembered her own words when Alika suggested stowing a musket in the cave: "There has been too much killing and I will never kill anyone."

Alika's fears for her safety touched Kale's heart but she was puzzled by his reluctance to leave her behind with young Kaholo. *Does he think I have no honor or loyalty? Surely he knows that 'Ulumalu would never let me out of his sight.* The memory of Alika calling 'Ulumalu "my lady's shadow" made her giggle out loud. She scanned the beach and out of the corner of her eye spotted her "shadow" sitting on a rock near the fishermen's boathouse. *I am so grateful my husband loves me and my servant is faithful.* Kale knew Alika had nothing to fear, but saying adieu was hard for them both. She kept listening to Alika's words in her mind and they warmed her heart. "My bride, you are the woman of my dreams." *I hope you are having better dreams than I, my dear husband.*

For fishermen, women are bad omens, so Kale turned up the dune to avoid walking by her fishermen, Kapuni'ai and Shaw, loading their canoes before sun-up. As she did, she beckoned to 'Ulumalu, who came running.

"*O 'oe kekahi ka mana'olana. Mahalo nui loa no ko'u kia'i 'ana ia'u.* You are a faithful one. Thank you for guarding me," said Kale. 'Ulumalu looked down, waiting for some instruction, and, when it did not come, he looked up at Kale with wide questioning eyes. Kale smiled. "*Eia ka'u makemake. E hele aku 'oe i ka hale ā hiamoe 'oe!* Here is my wish. Go home and go to sleep!" 'Ulumalu smiled and ran back to his hut. Kale strolled behind, praying that her fishermen would have a good catch, and the fisherwomen would find all the shellfish needed for the Makahiki feast.

Back in her warm cozy hale, Kale smoothed out her mats, leaned back on her lauhala pillow, and snuggled under five soft layers of sleeping kapa. She prayed to Kanaloa for Alika's protection and decided her vigorous work of the last ten days, uneasy anticipation of her first Makahiki at Honokahua, and sadness over Alika's departure had produced her nightmare. But the vivid visions of Alika, Kū, and the warriors made her resolve to ask Manu to interpret her dream. The roosters were already crowing when Kale finally closed her eyes and slipped back to sleep.

As he had done for seventy years, Kamanu-kapalulu-o-ka-pua-'ohai, bird chatting in the 'ohai tree, Kahuna of Lono, the god of the harvest and fertility, began his morning prayers by incanting the rising sun and the ancestors of Honokahua. The name given him by his grandfather is a sacred name never to be used for anyone else. It is a name repeated in the genealogy chant of his family extending back to the ancient Pāliko Priests of O'ahu. From his māpele heiau, a temple of Lono perched high above Hāwea Point, he sounded the pū with a sustained deep tone that resonated through still pre-dawn air to all of Honokahua, from deep fishing grounds up Honokahua Valley as far as the woodlands. It signaled Manu's morning prayer for the people. Throughout Honokahua Valley and across the broad mountain slopes, families were rising and praying with Manu at their personal shrines.

Manu looked southwest toward Lana'i and spotted a golden plover. Its solitary call echoed off the rock cliffs, "kōlea! kōlea!" Manu called back to the bird, "Kōlea! *Ke kōlea e ha'a nui ihonei 'oe i kou inoa!* Kōlea! You just boast your own name!" Manu loved to watch kolea hunt in graceful swooping arches at dawn and dusk, and he knew kōlea's return meant winter rains would be coming soon. *You are just a visitor, but you are reliable.*

In the western sky a waning moon and navigational star Hōkūle'a, Arcturus began losing their luster to early rays of sunlight. Cumulus clouds hugged the left faces of Moloka'i Mountains across the channel. It was a windy Kona day, he thought—winds from the southwest. Soon golden rays of sunlight filtering through kou trees on the ridge gave his white malo loincloth a yellow glow. Manu chanted to Lono and Kamapua'a, patron gods of farming, and prostrated himself in the dew-covered grass in front of a large vertical stone that represented his fishing god, Kū'ula Kai.

North in the valley, 'Ulumalu had started a fire, had brought two calabashes of water up from Honokahua Stream on his carrying pole, and now began to prepare Kale's morning meal. When Kale heard the pū she told 'Ulumalu, "*E ho'omau 'oe ma'ane'i,* Continue here," while she went to see the kahuna. Kale walked south on the broad Alaloa path that crosses all of Honokahua just above the shore. Where the path started across Hāwea Point, she climbed a narrow stone path up the cliff. At the top Manu was praying.

Kale quietly knelt, watching her kahuna laying face down on the ground. After some time, as if given permission to rise, Manu pulled himself up to his knees and placed before Kū'ula Kai an offering: a bit of baked pig and a few bananas. Kale wondered how old her kahuna was, this small man with knobby joints and a bent back. His wooly white hair and wrinkled skin were rewards of a long life, but dark shiny eyes still focused clearly and penetrated all he saw, searching out the hidden wisdom. Manu slowly straightened up, and, standing square to the sun, petitioned rain and good crops from Lono and supplicated himself to Kāne, Kanaloa, and Kū, on behalf of the chief and people of Honokahua.

Manu did not allow Kale's presence to interrupt his ritual prayers for the good of the people. "*E hō mai*…Reveal to us the knowledge that comes from above and beyond, of the hidden wisdom of the land. Reveal to us; reveal to us; reveal to us. You mighty ones have protected Honokahua all my life. You protected it all the generations of the ancients who came from Hava'iki. When my stewardship is over may you, most honored ones, continue to protect the generations of Honokaua people yet to come."

Then Manu placed a bit of sea salt in a koa bowl with some water and paced the perimeter of the mapele heiau, using a handful of tī leaves to sprinkle the entire stone platform and two boulders in front that represent the relative positions of Moloka'i and Lana'i in relationship to Honokahua. He sprinkled the Kū'ula stone, his small lama-wood ti-thatched ko'a, the ti-thatched towers on either end of the heiau, and then he sprinkled all four points of the *ke kūkulu o ka honua,* the compass of the earth where the ancestors live. He chanted a blessing and ended by turning to Kale who responded, "'*Āmama,* Let it be so." The Kū'ula stone, wrapped in red kapa, guarded Manu's ko'a, a two-pace square hut just tall enough to sit in. He dropped to his knees and crawled in, sweeping the floor with a small bundle of dried grass as he went.

For many years, Manu had prayed alone in his ko'a, but the gods had blessed him with a righteous chief who now prayed with him for good fishing at Honokahua. Today he also prayed for the new growing season, protection of last year's harvested Makahiki tribute, and, with gratitude, he prayed for his chief, that she might be blessed with increased land and many offspring. After some time he emerged from the ko'a, stood up, and scanned the channel for schools of fish. Dark churning water to the south of Hāwea Point caught his eye and he smiled. Still facing the sea, he spoke to Kale: "*E Ku'u Ali'i, he aha ane'i kāu makemake no kēia lā?* Beloved Chief, what is your desire this day?"

Kale responded, "*E Ku'u Kumu, makemake wau e 'ike i ke kaona hune o ko'u moe 'uhane i ka pō aku nei.* Beloved Teacher, I want to know the hidden meaning of my dream last night."

"Let us listen to the dream. Then we will listen to our gods and ancestors. May they choose to reveal to us the hidden wisdom."

"Let it be so," said Kale. Then she told Manu her dream.

Manu was listening but also keeping watch of the fish like a heron spying a shrimp. After many minutes of silence he said, "You are a brave woman. You defy the gods for the love of your husband." Then he beckoned Kale to his side. "Come and see the school of akule fish our gods sent us today." Kale looked at a purplish churning spot out in the channel, like the shadow of a cloud where there is no cloud.

"See the birds diving over the fish? They tell us there is plenty fish. Manu stretched out his aged arm toward the school, with his palm out. "When the fish pass Pua ka Huahua Rocks north of Hāwea Point by a distance of one hand, I will call out the people. Come and sit."

Kale knelt down next to Manu who continued watching the fish as he spoke.

"The haole captain is your husband?"

"Yes."

"He will return to you?" asked Manu.

"Yes, after the Makahiki. He must take the king's 'auhau from all islands to Kailua."

"He is a warrior?" asked Manu.

"No," said Kale. "He never fought."

"Ah! Then," said Manu, "your father—he is a warrior."

"Yes…" Kale was trying to understand. *Is Papa angry at me and Alika?* But questions are very impolite, so she kept quiet.

"And your baby?" Manu probed.

The question hit Kale like a dagger. She had forgotten to tell Manu what she called out as the warriors grabbed her, "You kill him but you will not kill his child!" *How did he know?*

Manu asked gently. "Are you pregnant?"

"I don't know." Kale's heart was racing. *Alika's child!*

Manu went on. "Tell me, what color were the kāhuna kīhei and malo?"

Kale raced through the pictures in her mind. "Black."

"And the assembled people were men?"

"No, they were women."

Manu silently watched the sea, while Kale's heart pounded. Finally he announced, "*He noa 'ia!* It is freed! You took a husband, but you did not humble yourself before your gods and ask for their blessing. Neither did you ask your parents for their blessing. These two things our gods and ancestors require before they deem your union righteous." Kale nodded.

"Black is Lono's color. The image you mistook for Kū was Lono, god of the Makahiki and fertility. He does not ask for human sacrifice, but he revealed this dream because he is a jealous god. Your husband will not die, but enjoy long life." Kale took a deep breath of relief.

"Lono has blessed you with a child. Go and celebrate Lono's Makahiki as a thanksgiving for his harvest gifts to the people and his gift of life in you. After the Makahiki, you and your husband must go and ask your parents' blessing. You and your husband must humble yourselves before the gods."

Kale looked down. "My husband does not believe in our gods. It is a problem."

Manu smiled again. "Ask him which god he prays to when a storm is swallowing his ship. Have him pray to that god. It is sufficient."

Manu patted Kale's hand. "Lono does not leave his children alone. Other women of Honokahua carry babies now as you do and they will teach you. Pray for them and for yourself."

Kale was weeping. "Let it be so," she whispered.

Manu waited a moment and said, "My chief, this school of fish is very large. We must only take as much fish as we can bake and salt in the three days left before the Makahiki. The rest must be let go to feed other villages."

"I understand," said Kale. "I will tell Kaholo to take only as much fish as we can prepare before the Makahiki begins. Thank you, my Kumu." Manu smiled and nodded, his wrinkled face still turned toward the school.

Soon the school was in the entrance to Oneloa Bay and Manu sounded the pū; one long low tone, two short low tones, and then one very long high pitched tone. In a few minutes canoes were on the beach. Manu spoke aloud to his gods. "It is a good morning. My Ali'i Wahine is with child and there are plenty of fish for Honokahua. It is like the old days, when the chief always lived on the land. Lono, you have blessed us with a good chief who loves the land, the sea, and the people."

Kale felt a sudden peace fill her heart and mind, as if a heavy burden were lifted. She knew that she did not arrive at Honokahua by default or serendipity. No, she was here by the choice of the gods and the kūpuna. She got up, headed straight for the beach and told Kaholo to instruct the fishermen to net just enough fish to be baked and dried in three days, and to let the rest go. Then she stood on the beach, not only watching the catch, but standing as the gods' representative interest and care for the people. Manu's words repeated over and over in her mind, "Lono has blessed you with a child"—*Alika's child—just hours ago I was fearful and now I can hardly contain my joy! I want to tell Alika. I want to tell baby sister Peke and the Youngs. Oh Māmā, did you feel this joy when you found me in your belly?*

She thought, if only I knew how to write I would send ʻUlumalu to Lāhainā with a letter for Alika and put it on a ship to Honolulu. I will send ʻUlumalu to find Alika and tell him.

All of a sudden, a wiry little four-year-old boy pushed in front of Kale to get a view of the fishing canoes. A moment later, his older brother came and pulled him away from Kale, begging her to excuse the intrusion. Kale giggled and took the little boy's other hand.

"*ʻO wai kou inoa?* What is your name?" she whispered.

The big brother whispered back, " *ʻO Waenaʻieʻie kona inoa ā ʻo Hakakau kēia, E Kuʻu Aliʻi;* My brother is the 'middle vine' and I am the 'tall thin one,' beloved chief."

"What beautiful names and fine healthy boys. Will you keep me company until your parents arrive?"

"Why are you whispering?" Waena asked in a loud voice.

"Because if the fish hear us they will go away." whispered Hakakau. "You have to be quiet."

Waena looked up at Kale. She nodded and whispered sweetly, "Waena, there are rules we must keep for fishing and silence is the most important rule of all."

Waena stomped his feet, looked back at Hakakau, and whined, "I DON'T WANT TO BE QUIET!"

"*E hāmau!* Be still!" Hakakau put his finger to his lips and turned little Waena's shoulders toward the beach as he whispered in his ear. "This is the place where the boy died. If you are not quiet, I will throw you off the pali too."

Before Hakakau could clamp his hand over Waena's mouth he wailed, "Don't push me off the pali! I don't want to drown!"

Kale bent low and whispered, "You are under my protection and no one will let you drown here. We love you. But right now you must be quiet."

Hakakau whispered, "If your yelling ruins the catch, you'll get a beating all the way home from all these families! Shall I have Papa tell you to be quiet?"

"No-o-o," Waena whispered slowly with his head down. Kale bit her lip to keep from laughing and winked at Hakakau.

Hakakau petted Waena's wavy black hair, "When the fish are in the baskets, then we can talk as loud as we want and think of other things. Hiki no? Okay?"

"A-a-e Hiki…n-ō-ō, O-k-a-ay" little Waena whispered with a pouting lip.

Kale wondered who drowned at Makāluapuna Point, but decided to wait and ask Kaholo.

A huge crowd was assembling. Netting fish means full bellies; delicious raw fish tonight and bonfires to heat earth ovens for baking tomorrow's fish dinner. Twenty or more families on the strand watched twelve lawai'a fishermen haul a 20 anana, 20 fathom-long rolled-up koko seine net. Each man held a section of the long net bundle on his shoulder, moving along together like a forty-yard centipede to the center of the beach where three round-hulled wood canoes were ready to go. Six more lawai'a fishermen were carrying two chase canoes on their heads to the south end of the beach.

The steersman and kilo i'a, fishing expert was Maunahina, "Gray Mountain" an athletic fifty-year-old who lost an eye defending Kaeo's fleet from Kamehameha's guns at Ke-pu-waha-'ula'ula in 1791. His wound prevented him from throwing spears and shooting guns, but still there was none better at hand-to-hand combat. He would be Honokahua's champion at the Makahiki boxing competition.

Slow, the current—easy the catch. Despite some chop, an inshore current flowing lightly to the northeast was pushing the akule slowly from left to right across Honokahua Bay. Maunahina pointed to the south, directing the two chase canoes to set up behind the school. When he lightly tapped once on his calabash the three net canoes pushed off. Smoothly and silently they moved as a single unit, two men in each canoe holding the rolled net, and four others paddling straight out in front of the school. A pale moon sat in the morning sky and kona winds blew cool on Mauna's left side. As he did so many times in battle, Mauna ignored his own hunger in anticipation of the job ahead. He focused on calculating the exact moment to stop forward progress and begin surrounding the fish.

Mauna tapped his calabash again. The paddlers dug in and held their position. One more tap, and, in unison, six men holding the net slowly let it unroll, as river-rock weights tied to the net's bottom edge sank out of sight, stretching it two anana below the surface. Soon all that could be seen of the huge net stretched between the canoes was a string of bobbing wiliwili wood floats slowly forming a crescent-shaped trap in front of the school. Now the end canoes pulled closer to the school.

"What if the fish turn away?" whispered little Waena, now sitting on Hakakau's shoulders and very interested.

"See those other two wa'a canoes coming in behind?" asked Hakakau. "If the fish try to go away, they will beat the water with their paddles and chase the fish back into the net."

As the dark churning school moved into the trap, both end canoes carefully brought the ends together and a fisherman from the lead canoe slipped quietly, feet first, below the surface, sewing the net closed.

"Won't any of those poor fish get away?" asked little Waena.

Kale smiled at Hakakau. "Your free-spirited brother feels like those trapped fish, doesn't he?"

"*I kēia wā, 'a'ohe!* None this time!" Hakakau chuckled, swinging his kid brother off his shoulders and holding him tight. Waena squirmed free without a peep and scampered quietly down the beach, to his parents.

Kale patted Hakakau on the back. "See how quietly he went? You taught Waena good lesson today." Hakakau blushed and grinned, but Kale knew he wanted to leave. "It is a big catch. The men need your help. Go now." Hakakau smiled shyly at his chief, thanked her, and went to join other young men at the water's edge.

By now, the shore was crowded with every able-bodied person in Honokahua but only sounds of shallow rolling waves and murmuring hala trees met the ear. Mauna tapped his calabash three times and together the five canoes silently pushed the fish-filled net for shore where Oneloa's sandy bottom would box in the fish for good.

When the net bottomed and Mauna called the crowd to come unload the net, Oneloa Beach exploded with whooping and shouting as fishermen, farmers, women, and children waded out and surrounded the net, older men directing the work and younger men and women steadying the net as fish strained against its bulging sides. Mauna's canoes pulled away and everyone joined in scooping up flapping pink and silver akule, pouring them into large baskets, and throwing back small fry and kapu varieties.

Mauna humbly presented the first fat big-eyed akule to Kale, who gave it to Manu. He chanted a prayer of thanksgiving and took a small basket of fish to his heiau for an offering. As soon as Mauna presented Kale a big basket, young men began carrying loads of fish up to the black rock drying flats on Hāwea Point. A few luahine, old women stayed on the shore sorting and preparing fish for eating raw that day or baking the next, dividing them among the families.

It was a good catch, and early morning is the ideal time to split, gut, salt, and dry fish at Hāwea Point. The day's Kona breeze would keep flies away and fish salted by noon would be dry enough by evening to hang in mesh bags. After twenty baskets of akule were taken, the net was let down, allowing the remaining fish to escape in the surf.

Kale walked up to Hāwea where a young fisherman, Kapuni'ai and his father Umuwena were busy overseeing the fish-drying operation. While women kaha, gutted each fish into a flat butterfly with one stroke of a bulky handle armed with a sharp 'opihi shell, kids pulled out the innards and threw them in calabashes to feed the hogs and dogs, carefully reserving the prized roe in a calabash of salt water. Cleaned fish were thrown in a deep rock pool to soak. Kale joined the wahine who then shook off the seawater, rubbed the meat with sea salt, and laid the fish meat side up in neat rows on the hot rock flats to dry in the sun. Soon the whole north side of Hāwea was pink with drying fish and Kale rejoiced at the beautiful sight.

During the awakea, noon rest time, Kale walked back to the fishing village to review the day's work with her foreman, Kaholo. In the hālau were many spools of rolled olonā cordage to weave nets, and rolls of wauke fiber to make rope. As they sat and talked Kale spun the wauke fibers on her thigh and weaved the rolled strands into thin rope to lash canoes and build hale. Kaholo gave her an accounting of everything in their hale ho'āhu, storehouses: 100 large coils of olonā cordage, 30 coarse lauhala mats and 20 fine mats; 100 large net bags of dried pili grass wrapped in tufts and four loads of naio wood for house building; 40 bundles of dry wauke bark strips for kapa production. Finished kapa cloth, stored in a separate hut, consisted of 100 malo and 40 long pā'ū. There were 40 large covered calabashes filled with dried sweet potato pudding and 100 medium size net bags of fresh sweet potatoes. In addition, there were 25 throw-nets and 4 seine-nets, each 5 anana, fathoms in length, 50 net bags of dried 'ōpelu, and 20 small net bags of dried octopus.

"I am impressed at the amount of goods Honokahua amassed this year," she said.

Kaholo explained that the total represented a small increase over what was given to the king the previous year. "However, what was acceptable last year is not necessarily enough this year, as you know." He referred to the capricious governor, whose reputation for exacting more taxes than the ali'i can use was well known.

"Some of our young men are now thirty years of age and our tax collector may expect more production. Therefore, if you permit, I will hold some extra items in farmers' storehouses deep in the valley in case our tax collector asks for more tribute. Here is the risk: if he finds a farmer holding back a substantial amount of goods, the tax collector will plunder everything we have, leaving us destitute and unable to farm next year."

Kale continued weaving, considering the request. "If we are required to give everything to the king for his court and are not allowed to have stores of our own, are we not at great risk of famine in times of draught or pestilence?"

"Ae, very true, my chief."

"This is why I would take the chance to hold back any goods."

Kale put down her weaving, went to the edge of the open-sided workhouse, looked up the mountain at Eke Crater. "It is the right thing to do--to insure the future safety of the people of Honokahua. Hold some stores…but we must also increase the production of the land as our men continue to grow to maturity." She turned and looked at him, "What are your thoughts about the future?"

For a moment Kaholo just stared; his eyes seemed to focus somewhere behind her and then he looked away. "I have thought long about the future and how production may be improved."

"Good, good, good!" said Kale. "Let us put our heads together and make a plan for the coming year. She sat down at her weaving again. "First, we must bring in more men to harvest sandalwood."

Kaholo smiled. "Perhaps Captain Adams can find some cutters who would like to come and live here."

"I will ask him." Kale's mind was running now. "We don't have a canoe-builder. I am going to visit Mr. Young during the next moon and I will ask him to find a canoe-maker to settle at Honokahua to make use of our high forest."

"Ae, my chief, it would be a great advantage to have a canoe craftsman and sandalwood men here and allow our fishermen to return to full time fishing and net production."

"What can be done for the farmers?" asked Kale.

"More fences to keep hogs away from the sweet potatoes will be a great help."

"Can fences be built during the Makahiki season?"

"Yes, my chief. It is a good time—before the spring planting."

Kale saw that Kaholo was more comfortable, so she asked, "What is your dream of the future for Honokahua?" The moment she said it she sensed him tightening up again. "Do not be afraid to tell me your thoughts. Together, you and I must help Honokahua prosper. I do not know the answer to this question, but I believe you do."

"Forgive me, my chief. I have never counseled a chief before. Here are my thoughts: If we grow things the whalers desire, we will prosper." After a moment he continued, "I used to sail, and foreign crews want Irish potatoes, beans, cabbages, and melons. In Honolulu, they even grow oranges and lemons that keep sailors from getting scurvy. I see more and more whaling ships come to Lāhainā Roads every year, and whatever we barter with them can be used to acquire the tools and provisions we lack."

As Kale listened, Kaholo's ambling style of speech reminded her of someone in her childhood, but she could not recall whom. She clearly understood his idea. "We will do it! It is a good plan. We have to find other farmers who will give us the seeds and cuttings to get started." She put down her cordage. "Kaholo, I am fortunate to have you as Konohiki. You are a capable manager and your heart is warm for the people. It is a good thing too, because we have so much work ahead!"

Kaholo laughed. " 'Ae, my chief. Much to do…When you arrived, we were on the brink of losing the land because of the sandalwood tax. After just a short time under your rule, already we have hope for the future. The Honokahua people are happy to have an Ali'i 'Ai Ahupua'a who is kind and loving and has the blood of the land in her heart. It is a blessing."

"And you, Kaholo? Are you willing to continue here with me and help me grow up Honokahua?"

"Yes, my chief, I will humbly continue as long as you want me."

Kale smiled. "Good. Together we will do good for the people and they will do good for the land."

CHAPTER 5

The Makahiki

The time of taxation had arrived. It was the evening of Laʻaukūkahi, and Kale nervously waited in front of the ahupuaʻa shrine marking the boundary between Napili and Honokahua, a low area just above the coconut grove at Kapalua Bay. Atop the shrine's boulders was a block of kukui wood roughly hewn into a pig's head and ceremoniously daubed with red mud on snout and ears. It represents the pig demigod Kamapuaʻa, a visible life form of invisible Lono, lord of harvest, fertility, and the Makahiki festival. From the shrine Kale could see south to Napili, out across Kapalua Bay, and north up the paved and boulder-bordered Alaloa footpath as far as the crest of Hāwea pali. King Piʻilani built Alaloa centuries before to unite the entire island of Maui. Lonomakua, the big image of Lono that circles the island at the Makahiki, will enter Honokahua right here in six day's time.

Awe and pride filled her heart when she saw Kaholo appear at the top of the hill, dressed in white kīhei and followed by two lines of farmers, all in white malo, carrying shoulder poles loaded with the produce and crafts of a full year's work, the annual Hoʻokupu tribute tax for Lono and King Kamehameha. Family haku leaders followed by their kin filed over the crest behind Kaholo like an endless strip of lauhala. Men carried poles on their shoulders, hung with brown net bags of dried fish and sweet potatoes and tan calabashes of shellfish and poi; groups of young people bore palatines piled high with bulky but light loads of naio sticks and pili grass thatch; farmer women proudly carried woven mats, bundles of precious red feathers, kapa garments, and olonā cordage; wives of fishermen shouldered their fine nets and lures.

On Kale's left stood High Chief Ke'eaumoku, Governor of Maui, in a yellow and red feathered helmet and cape, ready to receive the land's waiwai, wealth on behalf of King Kamehameha. He fought with Kale's father 'Aikake at the battle of Nu'uanu in 1796 and became the ruling chief of Maui in 1805 at age 28. His reputation for extracting as much tax as the commoners could bear led to his nickname Pu'u Nui, "Great Pile," referring to the rotting piles of excess goods outside his storehouses. In true Hawaiian double entendre, the name also accurately described his physique.

Ke'eaumoku was the same height as Kale but heavy, with jowls that met his wide neck folds. The feather cape of his slimmer days draped open in front of a protruding belly, but his very broad frame was well supported on huge muscular legs that served him well in battle. Black tattoos circling his eyes and full lips created a fierce countenance and the large palaoa ivory hook on a thick braid of black hair around his neck gave him divine and absolute authority over everyone on Maui. On his arm was tattooed "George Cox," from a time when he and his brothers all decided to impress foreign traders by taking British names. Ke'eaumoku called himself Cox, after the first British sea captain to befriend him, and George after King George IV.

Standing behind Ke'eaumoku were two Mo'o Lono Kahuna, High Priests of Lono, dressed in black malo and kīhei with lei of lehua entwined with gray 'āhinahina moss. Manakū, tax collector for Kā'anapali Moku district, stood to one side, dressed in white, looking like a bird caught in a snare—very still, but ready to escape at the first opportunity.

Kaholo bowed before the priests and ali'i and took his place to Kale's right. His people continued to file over the hill, deposit their goods in the designated kapu area in front of the ahupua'a shrine, and sit down on the grass until all of Honokahua was seated in a semicircle, waiting for a word from the governor. In a loud voice Kaholo announced to Kale, "Here is the gift of our land, O Heavenly Chief!" and enumerated every item. All Kale could think of were the extra goods hidden up in the valley.

When he was finished, the people all lifted their hands and responded, "The gift of your people!"

Then Kale took a deep breath and raised her voice to present the tribute to Ke'eaumoku, "O Heavenly One! Here is the royal offering of your land from me," and she repeated the list of items.

The people proclaimed, "The royal offering!"

Keʻeaumoku did not respond, but waited in silence as tax collector Manakū walked up and down rows of produce and goods, looking at quantity and quality, feeling the kapa texture and testing cordage strength and flexibility. For Kale, the process was endless. When he finished, he shouted to the High Chief, " ʻĀpono ka hoʻokupu! The tribute is acceptable!" Kale breathed easily then and cut a glance at Kaholo, who was smiling.

Then the kāhuna began to chant in unison:

> Your bodies O Lono are in the heavens,
> A long cloud, a short cloud, a watchful cloud,
> An overlooking cloud in the heavens;
> From Uliuli, from Melemele, from Polapola, from Haehae,
> From ʻŌmaʻokūulūlu, from the land that gave birth to Lono.

> Behold Lono places the stars that sail through the heavens.
> High resplendent is the great image of Lono;
> The stem of Lono links our dynasties with Kahiki,
> Has lifted them up, purified them in the ether of Lono!
> Stand up!
> Gird your selves for play!"

> The people stood, raised up their arms, and responded: "*Hiu!* Gird
>   yourselves!"
> The kāhuna cry: "O Lono!"
> The people shout: "The image of Lono!"
> The kāhuna shout: "*Aulu!* Hail!"
> The people cheer: "*Aulu! E Lono!* Hail to Lono!"

Then Keʻeaumoku announced, "People of Honokahua, Our heavenly King is pleased to receive your tribute. Go now and prepare enough food for the feast of Lonomakua and Kamehameha's gods and the four kapu days after the Hiʻu Kai, cleansing rite, when all work is forbidden."

By this time Kale was beaming, not only with thankfulness to Lono and her gods for such a fine harvest, but with appreciation for her capable Konohiki, who had the courage and foresight to protect Honokahua from famine. She caught Kaholo's eye, and, without a word, their partnership of trust and respect was sealed.

Keʻeaumoku, accepted honor and thanks from Kaholo, exchanged pleasantries with Kale, and indicated his intent to return to Honokahua after storing the tax goods in Lāhainā. Kale knew members of court hated to be away from Kailua Kona, the gaiety and luxury of Kamehameha's entourage, and nightly feasts at tribute time. Being relegated to Lāhainā was bad enough, but, as Cox and his kahuna continued around Maui, they would eventually be too far abroad to return to Lāhainā and be required to overnight in a remote country district—a great discomfort and sacrifice.

The people immediately began to carry Kamehameha's goods down to Oneloa Bay and load them in canoes for transport to Keʻeaumoku's bark. The tall ship's crew was already busy loading longboats with sandalwood and dogs and hogs not brought to the shrine. It would take two shiploads and a day-and-a-half of handling to get all the tribute to Lāhainā, where some would be stored and distributed to Kamehameha's Maui chiefs, and the remainder sent to the king's storehouses in Kailua and Honolulu for trading with foreign ships. When the hauling was done, Honokahua men would return to their earth ovens to bake enough food for a village Makahiki feast and four more days of leisure. After the kapu days, foot-bearers carrying the Akua Loa, the large image of Lonomakua and smaller images of Kamehameha's feather gods would complete their rites at Nāpili and formally enter Honokahua on their tour of the entire island. For the first time since her arrival, Kale realized she was tired. *Tonight will be a welcomed rest.*

Pilialoha was a tall, buxom, and very fit makaʻāinana commoner who farmed sweet potatoes in Honokahua Valley. Her coffee-colored skin was remarkably clear after 36 years working the earth. After her first child she cropped her hair short like the aliʻi, and, like them, she always wore fresh kapa and fragrant lei. On Maui where taxes were levied on both women and men, Pili was a luhi, a single head of family who never fell short on her obligation to the king. She was her mother's last living child, the bright pretty one who bore the jealousy of her sisters but outlived them all.

Pilialoha stood on Makāluapuna Point, watching large covered calabashes full of her fine kapa cloth and bundles of her processed wauke bark being hauled up on the king's ship. When she saw them safely on board, she began hiking up to her farm. Behind Honokahua Stream estuary two streams fork out creating a broad flood plain completely cultivated with kalo. A small valley to the northeast is called Mokupeʻa, but Honokahua Stream cuts a larger well-populated valley to the east. Further uphill Honokahua stream breaks into rivulets and every bit of land between them is cultivated with kalo loʻi paddies or ʻuala sweet potato terraces. Farmers take advantage of every bend in Honokahua Stream and dig ʻauwai ditches to redirect water to their crops.

Pili met other farmers on the path, laughing and chatting as they hauled firewood, banana leaves, and tī leaves back to their ovens. Makahiki was a joyous time when common people anticipated games, feasting, dancing, and traditional Makahiki delicacies like fermented sweet potato beer and baked sweet potato, kalo, or arrowroot pudding made with coconut cream.

Soon she came to a row of kalo loʻi northeast of the stream, each bordered by a river-rock wall sealed with mud to form a watertight dike. On the dikes grew tī plants, wauke paper mulberry trees, and banana trees. Clear water diverted from Honokahua Stream slowly percolated through the loʻi and back into the stream, feeding the kalo corms and keeping them free of pests. The late-morning sun dried a last drop of dew from proud, velvety green, heart-shaped kalo leaves standing as tall as a man's shoulder above the water. They bowed gently as valley updrafts passed through their perfectly spaced rows. Gratefulness filled Pili's heart when she stopped to look at the many huli shoots around each robust plant and she thanked Lono for nourishing her kids and all of Honokahua.

Upland beyond the loʻi stood three tall kukui nut trees. Their pale green leaves shaped like pigs' ears provided welcome shade from the equatorial sun. Underneath the trees, specks of filtered light danced on Kuʻoiʻoiwahine's homestead and her patch of dark green lauwaʻe fern. The thigh-high shiny-fingered ferns beckoned Pili to rest and savor their sweet fragrance. A large triangular boulder formed one corner of Kuʻoiʻoiwahine's house, and the rest of the walls were stacked gray river rock. Its hipped roof was thick pili grass thatch. Adjacent to her main house was a mua men's house and a large fire-pit that her grandchildren were busy lining with porous lava rocks.

"Hui!" called Pili as she moved on. "No time to stop and wala ʻau, chat now—too much work to do." The boys waved and called back.

Kuʻoiʻoiwahine peeked out from her workhouse with her new grandson on her hip and waved too. Like so many Honokahua women, Kuʻoiʻoiwahine was head of the family since her husband died in the wars. After many years of hardship, her sons and daughter now planted, dug, and weeded while she took care of their small children.

"*He aha ana 'oulua?* What are you two doing?" asked Pili.

Kū'oi'oiwahine laughed. "*Ke ho'omākaukau mai nei māua no ka Makahiki, akā piha 'eleu kēia pēpē kolohe! E 'ike ana wau iā 'oe i ka lū'au!* Getting ready for the Makahiki but this rascal baby is so active! I'll see you at the feast!" Kū'oi'oiwahine wiped her forehead and ducked back inside.

Pili thought, Kū'oi'oiwahine was lucky to have a husband, if even just for a few years. I will never have one.

Just uphill from Kū'oi'oi's property was Pili's place, behind Pōhakulua o Kāne, Rocks of the god Kāne, two magnificent boulders on an elbow bend of Honokahua stream. Her land was not as rich as Kū'oi'oi's, but Pili and her kids made it grow fine 'uala sweet potato and plenty of wauke, paper mulberry, and 'ōhi'a'ai, mountain apple. A small dam in the stream formed a pool near the house for bathing and reflected in it were the pale pink blossoms of morning glory dodder vines covering her thatched hale. Her hālau workhouse, where she and her family stripped bark from young wauke trunks, was thatched on one side and open to the front. She built a mua for her boys when they were too old to sleep with her and Māmā and planted a big banana patch beside the mua to grow cooking bananas and large red sweet bananas for trading. The only sounds were the rushing stream and hidden birds calling and echoing their tittering chants.

"Hui!" she called. Up in stone-walled terraces above the house, Pili's four children and Māmā were digging sweet potatoes by hand. They waved and called back and she beckoned them to lunch. "*Hele mai e ho'omaha kākou. Kau ka lā i ka lolo.* Come in and rest. The sun is high."

Last fall Pili's mother and kids dug a large circular pit, lined it with river-rock, and filled it with kukui nutshells and leaves. By spring, the compost was soft and Māmā planted two 'uala sweet potato vines. The tubers easily pushed through the soft compost and grew into giants, as heavy as Pili's seven-year-old girl. Pili would dig one out by hand and bake it for the Makahiki feast, along with kūlolo poi pudding, several varieties of sweet potatoes, and Pili's share of akule big-eyed scad from the catch. The kids were excited about Makahiki and so was Pili.

Pili's wonderfully full white pā'ū skirt was ready for the feast. She scented the kapa with fragrant mokihana berry juice and printed a ma'o green diamond pattern border on the bottom edge. While her sweet potato pudding baked, she would render some ripe coconut meat in the sun to oil her hair and strip fragrant maile vine lei and anklets to wear to the Makahiki celebration. She imagined the high chief gazing amorously at her; watching herself in the dark pool, she struck inviting poses and remembered an old adage. *Haiamū ka manu i ka pua o ka mamane.* The birds gather around the mamane blossom. *I shall be the blossom and next summer perhaps I will have fruit.*

The days of preparation for the feast of Makahiki were complete. Kamehameha's feather gods and wooden gods had paraded through Honokahua for the past two nights and on 'Olepau, the 23rd day of the moon of Welehu, Kale and all of Honokahua were gathered at the beach, watching a blushing sun sink into a cobalt sea. Alika's concern over rioting at the Makahiki was still on Kale's mind, and her own attitude about her well-being changed the moment Manu told her she was pregnant. She would be cautious tonight and would send 'Ulumalu for Alika after the first wild Makahiki days were over and she could assure her husband that she was truly safe. Now that the taxes were paid, her main concern was reuniting with the Youngs and with Alika, so their baby might grow in righteousness.

Kale delighted in the gala appearance of her people, well dressed in fresh kapa and decked in their finest shell and garland ornaments, laughing and teasing like a flock of warblers. Already young men were standing in proud stances to show off their physiques and calling attention to themselves by mock wrestling and playful teasing. When a promising mate passed by, they loudly spoke of her beauty in flattering poetic phrases. The young women pretended not to hear, but sneaked glances at their favorites.

The evening was calm but small gray pig-shaped clouds, harbingers of rain in the days ahead, floated up the channel. Makahiki was the one time of the year when commoners could mingle with the divine ali'i without fear of breaking kapu and being sentenced to death, and many people came to share honi with Kale and greet her as they wished to when she first arrived in Honokahua. The three little farm girls she helped dig potatoes brought their mother U'i, a plump thirty-year-old with 'ehu red hair and shy smiling eyes, to meet Kale and offer her a lehua blossom lei.

"*E 'olu'olu 'oe e kalai, e ku'u Ali'i. Ua hana wau i ka hale i kou hele 'ana i kō mākou mahi 'ai. A'ole hiki i'au ke hana i ka māla no ka mea hei keiki ka'u.* Please forgive me, my chief. I was working inside the house when you came to our farm. I was unable to work in the field because of morning sickness."

Kale instantly knew that Uʻi was her ukali hānau, birthing attendant promised by the gods. She took Uʻi's hands in hers and held them to her breast. "*Ua kanaka wau ke kahi. He hoʻokahi nō hoʻi wau i Honokahua. E Uʻi, ʻoluʻolu ʻoe e kōkua ʻoe kou Aliʻi Wahine ā aʻo mai iaʻu i nā mea nui o ka hānau kama ʻana.* I am pregnant too. I am so alone at Honokahua. Uʻi please be kind to your chiefess and teach me the important things of child bearing."

Stunned, Uʻi caught her breath at such a request and quickly fell to her knees before Kale. "*He kāu kauwā wau e kuʻu Aliʻi Wahine.* I am your slave, my beloved chief."

Kale gently pulled her up. "*He kauwā kaʻu. I ka wā kēia, pono au i hoʻokahi hoaloha wale nō.* I have a servant. Right now I need just one close friend."

" *ʻOia hoʻi, oia nō hoʻi!* Of course, of course," said Uʻi as she hugged Kale. Kale could not hold back tears of joy, and tenderhearted Uʻi patted her back and wept with her. "Do not be afraid. This is a time of great joy when the gods bless us with babies. You will love it."

The next moment hollow tones of the pū brought everyone to silence and they turned to Manu, who beckoned his chief to join him. When Kale stood beside him he prayed:

> Oh Lono tender shoot of deity
> Oh Lono consort of ʻUli
> Oh Lono-ʻUli, the heavenly pair;
> Oh Lono comforter of this fleshly temple,
> Oh Lono the discerning one,
> Oh Lono who abides with us to the last sand,
> Turn to us O Lono…

> Pardon the sins of the chiefs…
> Pardon the sins of the Kāhuna
> Pardon the sins of the boor, the plebian…
> Send gracious showers of rain, Oh Lono,
> Life-giving rain, a grateful gift,
> Symbols of Lono's blessing,
> Lono-a, the mighty god.
> ʻĀmama. It is free.

All the people raised their hands to heaven and chanted:

> The bodies are purified,
> Your temple is kapu, oh god.
> Purification for the multitude.
> Purification, Purification.
> Salvation by Lono, the mighty god!

Then Kale certified the rite, " *'Āmama!* So be it!"

For the duration of the feast and cleansing rite, all of Honokahua was free from kapu and the happy crowd began moving to the torches, fires, and feast of Lono in the coconut grove at Honokahua beach. Governor Ke'eaumoku had returned for the feast and when he caught up with Kale he was out of breath from walking further than his bulk would allow. Kale politely paused, giving him time to recover. He raised a fragrant hala key lei to place around her neck and when they shared honi, he said, "*Aloha wau i kou maka ā honi wau i kou iho waliwali.* I love your eyes and I kiss your soft nose." It was an inappropriately intimate greeting that only made his damp mushy caress more distasteful.

"*Aloha mai,e ku'u Ali'i.* I feel your love, beloved chief," Kale replied flatly. Then she smiled and asked, "Will you see my husband soon?" Ke'eaumoku was a friend of her father and she was hoping to give him a way to back down from his obvious amorous intention.

If Cox could have pulled his chin closer to his neck, he would have. Instead his eyebrows shot up. "Did you not leave your husband James when you came to Maui?"

"Yes, it is so. And with the blessing of Queen Keopuolani, I took Captain Adams as my new husband. Will you see him soon?"

Cox could not help but suck in his breath as he realized his blunder. A smooth operator, he covered the misstep by puffing, "Hu! I am out of breath from this marching around." He wiped his brow. "Such good news—I am happy for you. Captain Adams is a great friend of the Kingdom." Then he looked at her with one eye squinted. Reconsidering Kale's question he said, "You should know that Alika will be in Lāhainā during the rising moon of Makali'i. Why do you ask me?"

"Yes, of course…" Kale lied, but now she knew exactly when to send 'Ulumalu to Lāhainā. Then she added, "Some questions are for the speaker, some for the listener."

Cox might have retorted, had he heard her remark, but he was intently watching each woman passing by, so Kale released him. "Please excuse me while I give some last minute instructions to my foreman. We are honored to have you join the festivities and enjoy yourself in Honokahua."

"Yes, yes," said Cox who was firmly focused on a tall, well-built woman in a green-bordered pāʻū sallying up to him with a lei. Any other day he would accept a lei from a commoner in his hand, but it was Makahiki, so massive Keʻeaumoku grinned and opened his arms wide, allowing the commoner to approach and place her lei on his neck. As he bent down to receive it, the woman seemed to trip forward and her full breasts pressed against his face. She giggled, begging forgiveness, and recovered her footing, but when their noses met Cox put his hand on the small of her back and pressed her body to his for more than just a moment.

Kale, who was watching the encounter, shook her head and said under her breath, "*Auwē, Kīkoʻolā!* How rude!"

A voice behind her said, "A little bit of stickum catches a big bird." She spun around to find Kaholo and ʻUlumalu snickering at the suddenly revived governor, proud as a rooster strutting down to the beach with statuesque Pili.

"Now I understand my husband's concern for me," said Kale. "I think I shall need your protection tonight." Kaholo and ʻUlumalu flanked her and the three slowly followed the crowd to the Makahiki feast. Three bonfires glowed in the growing darkness. The grassy knoll behind the beach was full of people seated around a long string of mats filled with platters and bowls of lūʻau, fruit and raw shellfish delicacies. At the edge of the grove, under the coconut palms, a line of kukui nut torches flickered in the damp breeze. Above, just over the eastern mountains, a rising half moon illuminated thick dark clouds building over the top of Eke crater.

After feasting to the full on meat, fish, seafood, poi, greens, and sweet potato, it was time to honor the king, governor, and Lono so Manu recited a name chant for Kamehameha that told of the great king's pedigree and ancestral lands. The mele also spoke of his conquests over the islands and his favorite queens, Kaheiheimālie and Kaʻahumanu. Several times the chant praised Keopuolani, his most sacred piʻo queen. At every mention of her name, everyone removed everything worn above the waist and bowed as a tribute to her sacred kapu.

When it came time to honor the Governor of Maui, Kale, Kaholo, and several haku family leaders stood and recited glowing tributes to Keʻeaumoku. He smiled, nodded, and seemed satisfied. Pili was seated next to Keʻeaumoku, feeding him bits of food and attending to his every word. She planned to engage him sexually before the heavy drinking began and now she made her move. Pili stood up and began to move away, but Ke'eaumoku slipped his hand up her skirt and grabbed the inside of her thigh.

"Where are you going?" he asked.

Pili could hardly believe her fortune. *He has taken the bait and now all I must do is let him win me.* She ran her fingers through his hair and looked down at him. "I am going to chant your virtues, O Governor...Where are *you* going?"

Ke'eaumoku grinned. As he released her thigh and tried to reach higher Pili slipped away and sashayed to a spot beside the flickering torchlight. She faced Ke'eaumoku, threw back her shoulders, and began to chant. She called him, "*He mamo na Kamapua'a,* a child of Kamapua'a", the pig demigod and fervent lover of Pele, goddess of the volcano. At the reference Ke'eaumoku jumped to his feet and struck a fierce beastly pose like Kamapua'a; the crowd began to cheer. Pili continued singing of Ke'eaumoku's battle prowess, and he fought an imaginary foe. At every gesture, she stepped closer and closer to him, cocking her head to one side and the other but never losing eye contact.

Then she paid him the greatest tribute of all to an ali'i, singing of the strength of his progeny. When Pili sang poetic pictures of his strong and sacred genitals, Ke'eaumoku jumped, spread his legs wide, and beat his chest. The crowd whooped and cheered.

For her finale, Pili moved closer to him, chanting:

> Climb! Climb! Red are the uplands!
> Where the weed-entangled waterway shines like pearl
> The pit where the fisherman drops his hook
> Now looms the mount Pu'u Kukui.

By the end, she was right in front of Ke'eaumoku who picked her up, threw her over his shoulder, and carried her off into the darkness.

A hooting went up from the crowd, aroused by the sexual play and intent on their partners. Sweet potato beer and 'awa flowed freely, and, before the hula of Kamapua'a began, nā mākua grandparents rounded up the children and took them to the beach for their ceremonial Makahiki swim. Kale and her bodyguards joined the kids and old folks splashing one another in the sea and drying off by the big bonfires. From the beach, they heard the rising frivolity back at the feast and saw couples walking here and there in the dark, looking for love nests. Kale noticed Keʻeaumoku and Pili bathing at the far end of the beach.

When Kale got back to the grove, Uʻi's husband Limahaʻi was sitting on a large mat with three other musicians with their large double ipu calabash instruments. They began pounding the calabash on the ground and tapping it with their fingers and palms in complicated rhythmic patterns designed for the sacred hula of Kamapuaʻa. Honokahua's young men were adorned in bushy woven tī leaf head lei and kūpeʻe wristlets. Around their calves were kūpeʻe ʻilio buskins decorated with thousands of dog teeth. Their dyed black malo represented the demigod Kamapuaʻa, the sacred black hog. The mele spoke of the pig demigod's clever seduction of Pele, drawing her away from her caldron of fire with teasing and taunting as he changed into his various life forms. Curious Pele followed him all the way to the sea where he mated with her. In the light of kukui torches, athletic dancers beat their chests and cut the air with their outstretched muscular arms, depicting the various forms of Lono and Kamapuaʻa, keeping time to the powerful kepakepa mele. Young women watched and play-acted Pele's reactions, spurring them on. When the men twisted their bodies and cocked their heads in taunting expressions, the women pretended to resist; when the men bent backwards until the tips of their malo touched the ground, the women squealed with great delight.

At the end, the crowd became respectfully quiet as women dressed in white pāʻū and maile kūpeʻe and lei performed a seated hula with bamboo pūʻili rattles. Just past midnight, Manu called the start of the Hiʻu Kai, a ceremonial cleansing in the sea continuing until dawn when the sea would become kapu for four days. Kale joined Manu at the largest bonfire and he sounded the pū. The people gathered around and he prayed:

> …Oh Lono, the discerning one;
> O Lono, who abides with one to the last sand;
> Turn to us O Lono; Forgive us O Lono…
> This is a petition to you for pardon, O Lono
> Send gracious showers of rain; Life-giving rain, a grateful gift;
> Symbols of Lono's blessing; Lonoʻa the mighty god

Kale certified the prayer. " *ʻĀmama. Noa ʻia.* Amen, It is free."

The people all shouted:

> The bodies are purified;
> Your temple is tabu, oh god;
> Purification for the multitude;
> Purification, purification;
> Salvation by Lono, the mighty god.
> *'Āmama!*

Everyone removed their kapa and ran into the sea, splashing one another and washing each other's bodies. Kale watched their revelry and her heart swelled with joy. She thought of her moonlit swim with Alika and prayed that her people too would be blessed with love and babies. Soon chilly swimmers began to huddle together at the bonfire to warm themselves, laughing and calling to others, " *'O ke ahi, ka lole o ka wela!* Fire is the garment of warmth!" Kale asked Kaholo and 'Ulumalu to escort her home.

Filled with the freedom and mystic passion of the rites of Lono, lovers and chance partners alike found expression for their hearts' desires. It was the Makahiki, and Lono, the god of fertility, was blessing his people.

The next morning Kale arose early to join Manu on his heiau. As the first rays of light came out of the east, he sounded the pū and chanted:

> *E ala e*
> *Ka lā hi kahikina i ka moana*
> *Ka moana hohonu*
> *Pi'i ka lewa*
> *Ka lewa nu'u i ka hihina*
> *Aia ka lā?*
> *E ala e!!!*

> Arise
> Sun from the East of the ocean
> The deepest ocean;
> Ascending
> To the highest summit of the East;

Where is the sun?
Arise!!!

Kāloa-kū-kahi was the first of four kapu Makahiki days when the sea is kapu and nobody may fish or bathe. The mandatory leisure time fell on the half moon when the women were fertile, and the lifted kapu allowed men and women to sleep together and have meals together with no work responsibilities, but with plenty of games, athletic competition, wagering, and fun!

Manu stayed on his heiau, away from the people and even donned a blindfold so he would not see the people's hewa, transgressions. Kale would remain at the heiau to pray with Manu for most of the day, and the people for whom they prayed stayed in their homes and rested after the previous night's celebration. The old men, Umuwena and Keahi, were busy making two Akua Pā'ani, images of gaming gods, to be born around Honokahua and to officiate over all athletic competitions and games later in the day. There would be wrestling, bowling, holua sledding, games of chance, and surfing competitions; but foremost was the mokumoku fisticuffs competition to decide the greatest fighting champions of Honokahua.

Shouting broke the early morning quiet and Kale winced at rude taunts the people of one homestead were yelling at their boxing foes in the neighboring clan.

"You should stay in bed today, you worthless weakling! There will be no triumph or honor in your house—prepare for defeat and change your malo, you defecating sack of fear!"

Immediately the insult was returned. First, a male voice wailed, "A dog returns to its vomit as you return for a good beating." Then a whole chorus yelled: "He takes more than his share of fish and robs children of their food! But he is *still* a weakling!" Raucous laughter ensued.

Kale shook her head at the crude references, clearly meant to stir up competition for the day's games. She remembered her childhood days when her father participated in the Makahiki games, to all the people's delight. It was not the winning, but the chance of winning, that made the fun. *My people are anxious for the games. This year my people will see their ali'i at sport too.*

Pili arrived back at her kauhale well after dawn and Māmā was relieved to see her smiling.

"*Pehea 'oe? Ua ho'olapalapa 'ia ka'u kaikamahine malalo o ka Pu'u Nui?* How are you? Was my daughter flattened under the Big Heap?"

"O Māmā, he is not as he seems. He was so gentle with me. When I told him I want a baby, he took me to hi'u kai, gave me his seed again, and made me lie quietly afterward under the warmth of his feather cloak, so the baby may take root. He was so pleased with me that he asked me to go with him to Lāhainā!"

"Auwē! O dear! I do not want that one for a son-in-law!"

"Māmā, it will never be that way for us. We are commoners, and he is a high chief. I will always be a luhi, burdened and lonely. If a baby comes, it will be mine alone to raise. But last night I was happy in his gentle protection and forever I will treasure in my heart those sweet hours." Māmā hugged Pili and two sets of eyes drew tears.

Pili looked at her mother. "I tell you this that you may know my happiness, but it is my secret. Others may guess, but they will never know my secret."

"*Ua poina 'ia.* It is forgotten," whispered Māmā. "Come, let us take the children down to see Lonomakua."

Before awakea, all of Honokahua was again together at the ahupua'a shrine awaiting the arrival of Lono. The tall god Lono Akua and Kamehameha's gods Kapuni, Oulu, Ka'ohumalu, and Kahoali'i, making the journey around the whole island of Maui, were arriving any moment. Soon children set as lookouts on the ridge above Hāwea began to shout, "Lono's white flowing kapa is coming up from Nāpili!" Shouting and laughter crescendoed among the people as they pressed in to get a good vantage point.

Suddenly, a great clamor arose as Lono Akua reached the shrine, and the crowd pressed in to see the ritual. 'Ulumalu helped Kale away from the excited crowd and back to her hale to await Lono's approach to her house. Lono Akua was borne on a staff as tall as three men, carved at the top with a small tiki likeness of Lono. From a long kea cross-bar flew giant sails of white kapa, adorned with feather lei, pieces of green pala fern, and the dried white feather carcass of a ka'upu bird stuffed with moss. The image still faced back to Nāpili and the districts already blessed and freed from kapu by Lono. The people fell silent when Manu began to chant:

> Strangely lofty is this heaven
> The very heaven which separated the seasons of heaven
> Turned is the face of the god toward the visible heaven

Extended be the sacred worship of Lono
Turn hither the image of Lono…
Bending low is the glory
Covered is the god by the sky
Crackling is the voice of the thunder
Crackling within the shining black cloud
Broken are the mountain springs below
The god returns and dwells in the clefts
The god returns and dwells in obscurity
The god Lono returns and dwells in the softened soil
May I be saved by thee, O Lono my god!
Saved by the supporting prayer!
Saved by the burgeoning waters!
Saved by the chanting to thee, O thou god!
Here is the chant, the voice is the offering.

Then the young image bearer turned to Manu who chewed some baked dog offering and carefully fed it to the image-bearer. Then he fed him an offering of sweet kūlolo poi pudding.

Another bearer held up Lono Poko, a walking-stick-sized version of the Lono image, and together they bore the two images, side by side, up the Alaloa with all the people following. Makai, downhill from the path to the sea, was kapu wherever the big god passed. Mauka, uphill of the path was kapu where the small god passed. All of Honokahua processed behind the two gods on the only free ground left, the Alaloa path.

As the procession came to Kale's kauhale on the hill above Honokahua Stream, the image-bearer stopped and Manu went inside. Then he called out, "*E weli iā 'oe, Lono ea!* Welcome to you now, Lono!"

The image-bearer did not go in, but begged a better invitation. The whole procession answered: "*Nauane, nauane*, Moving on, moving on."

Manu called out again, "Welcome to you, O Lono!"

But the people joined in the banter and answered, "*Nauane, nauane.* Moving on, moving on."

Finally, Manu pleaded, "*Hele mai ā komo! Hele mai ā komo!* Come and enter! Come and enter!"

Then the image-bearer went into the house, and, after a short prayer, accepted hand-fed Makahiki delicacies from Kale. The bearer came out with Kale, and, after Manu prayed she performed the kai ʻoloa rite, tying a fine white malo around the main pole of the image. Then the gods continued to the end of Honokahua at Mokuleʻia Bay, where the big god Lonomakua stopped again and the High Kahuna prayed to free Honokahua lands of kapu before entering Honolua.

The bearer of the short god, Lono Poko, turned uphill to begin his journey back across Honokahua along the mountain path with farmer women following behind, collecting pala fern, famine food that Manu and Kale would eat at the heiau in the coming days of the bonfires of Pueo.

In the ʻauinalā, after the heat of the day, Nā Akua Pāʻani gaming gods images were set up, face-to-face taunting between contestants escalated, and wagering on the mokumoku matches began in earnest. In Mokumoku, punches are warded off with the fist, and the first match ended with a broken arm. Despite the fact that expert fisherman Maunahina was reigning Mokumoku Champion of Kāʻanapali District, pecking order and bragging rights among the families of Honokahua hung in the balance of every heated match.

Kale and Kaholo were ready to officiate at the final match of Mokumoku fisticuffs. Taunting cheering consumed the crowd. Mauna went to war as a young boy and lived to tell the story of losing his eye to a spear thrown by Kekūhaupiʻo, Kamehameha's famous warrior. This evening in a circle twenty paces across, surrounded by a huge crowd, old Mauna faced thirty-year-old Pupue, a round-faced stocky fellow with a barrel chest and very well-developed biceps.

Trim and wiry Mauna sized up his young, inexperienced opponent, well proportioned and not likely to topple easily. As Pupue swaggered around the circle of onlookers, boasting and flexing his muscles, Mauna thought the neck a bit too slender and that perhaps Pupue's bulk came more from ancestry than from training. Now and again, Pupue fell into a casual stance that Mauna read as a lack of training in footwork. In the old days, youths received battle training and learned never to take all their weight on one foot, not just in battle or competition, but at any time. Now there were no wars and young men fought for fun, not for their lives. *The old man has a fighting chance.* Pupue's fans shouted about his youth and strength and Mauna's clan countered with Mauna's conquering spirit and quickness. Then Mauna slowly moved around the circle, rushing at an occasional fan with a great growl and sending the crowd into frenzy.

When Kaholo shouted to commence the contest, Pupue rushed at Mauna, apparently trying for a speedy victory by aiming a flying blow to the head, like a children's fight. Mauna ducked to the right and the blow fell on one of Pupue's fans, to the delight of Mauna's side. Red-faced Pupue came back at Mauna again and Mauna caught the blow with his left fist while his right knocked the young man's chin and sent him to the ground. *Lazy, that footwork.*

Pupue was up in a flash swinging at Mauna's blind side. *Do you think no one ever tried this before?* Mauna jumped and as his feet left the ground he swung his lower body around his torso, landing on the opposite side of Pupue and using the momentum to deliver a pounding head blow that cracked aloud like an adze on a tree trunk. The bulky contestant went down again but he was not coming up; he was out cold. Mauna's side cheered but no bets were paid, because only a fool would bet against the great Maunahina, Mokomoko Champion of Kāʻanapali.

The next day, Kāloa-kū-lua, everyone in Honokahua joined in the games: athletic events, war games, games of skill, and games of chance.

Young men were up early laying a thick mat of grass on a very steeply graded holua slide constructed above Kahua Hill and stomping down the long grass in front of the slide to make a track as wide as a man's arm span, all the way down to Oneloa Bay. Now, with a running start, they fell belly-down on a narrow double-runnered sled with a base only as wide as a man's hand, balancing and gliding all the way to the beach. The ocean was kapu and going into the sea, even by mistake, was punishable by death, but Halemano narrowly escaped the water on his longest glide and won. This was just preliminary to the games next week when the kapu days would be over. Then, Kahua Hill sledders would challenge surfers in Oneloa Bay. At the sound of a pū they would both make for the beach and the first one there would be Honokahua's champion.

On a terrace right above Makāluapuna Point was a pounded-dirt kahua track for ʻulumaika bowling where people tried their luck at rolling biconvex maika stones on edge for the length of the forty-pace course, aiming to land the maika between two stakes at the end. Long lines of players waited for the chance to throw the longest roll for one point, and two extra points for rolling the maika between the stakes. Bets flew and when old man Kānehailua won the first game by accumulating ten points, a new game began immediately.

Wherever Kale went, a growing pack of little girls followed, headed up by Uʻi's girls. It was as if she had been adopted by a great large family. She happily accepted the warmth and the feeling of true belonging her people extended, and she looked forward to raising her own children here. When the Keʻa Pua competition began, Kale and her "little flowers" were atop the sand dunes at Honokahua beach. Wagering among the adults was brisk when they discovered Kale was in the game. As chief, Kale was allowed to compete first, but she chose to go last so she could size up her competition. The Keʻa Pua darts were as long as one's arm and skillfully made from the dried tassels of sugar cane plants. The thicker front end of the dart was ground to a point and dipped in red clay for added weight. Kale watched her competition take their short runs, throw their darts off the dune, and sail them along Honkahua's long sandy beach.

Kale's brother Hūʻeu was the best Keʻa Pua thrower in Kawaihae—not just because he was athletic like Papa, but because he took all the insults before the game so seriously and his anger seemed to improve his performance. The clear memory of red-faced Hūʻeu glaring back at the kids mocking his haole blood, chanting, "*Keʻa Pua, Pua Kea, Pua Kea!* Dart, white flower, white flower!" still made Kale smile. Huffing Hūʻeu would push out his bottom lip, run, and throw so hard that nobody ever came close to his mark, except maybe his older sister.

Now Kale took her turn. She coiled up, ran six paces and planted her left foot, pulled her torso forward and down, and released the dart with a quick flick of her wrist at just the right moment to send it high into the wind. The weight of the dart's head eventually brought it down, and, as it caught the dense air near the ground, it scudded along the beach like a flying fish, sailing well past the other marks. The crowd cheered; those who had bet on their chiefess cheered loudest.

After four kapu days of leisure and games, Kale and Manu lit the bonfires of Pueo for four more nights, and sent out fishermen to catch deep-water fish for Kale to eat with the pala ferns gathered in the mountain forests. Meanwhile, the common people of Honokahua made offerings to the gods of their personal worship: Kāne, Lono, or Kanaloa. The fish caught were good omens for the provender of the coming year, and winter rains came early. Lono showed his abundant pleasure with the thanksgiving and tribute of Honokahua by sending thunder, lightning, and rain to soften the soil for spring planting. Kaholo, ʻUlumalu, and Manu continued to faithfully serve and protect their fledgling chief. By Huna, the eleventh day of the moon of Makaliʻi and the successful observance of the Kala Hua, removal of the kapu rite, a confident chief, with increasing love for her people and growing new life in her belly, sent ʻUlumalu to Lāhainā to intercept Captain Adams and ask him to come to Honokahua.

CHAPTER 6

Reunion

Kale stood in bewildered silence, and rushing fear made her legs weak as she stared into Alika's blue eyes, looking for a happy glitter that did not come. "Oh my God, no!" was what he said. Four hundred times, she rehearsed this moment when she would reveal the secret of their child, offspring of his family line and gift of the gods. Her handsome proud Captain in his gold-trimmed uniform would cry with delight and scoop her up in his arms, smothering her with his love, kissing her belly. It had been a month of anxiety since she sent 'Ulumalu to find Captain Adams in Lāhainā. "Come to Honokahua," was the message. She waited until Makahiki transport work was over and he could sail home. She read his return love-note over and over again, planning how she would surprise him. Now, face to face in her hale, he stood staring at her like a fish caught in the jaws of a moray eel—stunned. *He does not want the baby.* There were no tears. Her heart slammed shut.

"I did not want this right away. Are you certain you are pregnant?" he finally whispered.

"Yes…" She could hardly breathe. She pushed past him for the door.

Alika grabbed her hand. "Please don't go."

His round blue eyes begged, but already a familiar calm loneliness shielded her. She was motionless as he pulled her close; Alika's strong arms held her gently but she could not accept the comfort of his embrace. She said nothing—there was nothing more to say. She was his. The baby was his. Alika stroked her hair and studied her face.

"I am sorry, Kale dear. I hoped this moment would not come so soon. Not because I do not wish to be a father, for I do very much…and not because I do not want you to be the mother of my children, for I have thought of nothing else since we came together. I love you as I love my own life…" He struggled to hold in a sob. "I am afraid for you and the baby because I lost my first bride in childbirth—and I cannot face the thought of losing you."

Afraid to lose me! As suddenly as fear and disappointment had choked her soul, Alika's tears revived her deep love for this curious tenderhearted man. "*Auwē Alika, ua maopopo ia'u.* Oh Alika, I understand…I did not consider your fears for me because I am not afraid for myself. Since age seven, I took care of George Hū'eu and Peke. I saw Grace Kamaiku'i born, and, at fourteen, I attended Ka'oana'eha with the birth of Keoniana. I have been a mother all my life. Should I not now be blessed with my own child?"

Alika stepped back. "I envy your courage, my dear, but the evils of this life have left me wounded. After many years of grieving and pining over my first wife, I have come to know unspeakable happiness with you…but lurking in the depth of my mind is the notion that you too will be swept away from me. This is my weakness and I am ashamed."

"You seek to hold the future? The future belongs to the gods alone and all we can do is be grateful for this moment. Alika, let us not fret about the future but be happy now."

"How do you do it?"

"Worry will not change what the gods have chosen for us. I must trust every day for your safety at sea. Now you must trust that our baby and I will be safe. Please—be happy with me." Kale wiped his tears, kissed his hands, and pressed them to her heart. "You give me great joy…to be the mother of your child is the greatest joy of all."

He embraced her again. "I do not want to cause you any pain."

Then Kale leaned back against his arms and played with his blonde hair. "I have a question: did you first come to my bed, dear Captain?" The broad warm smile she longed for all these past days slowly emerged like sunshine after a shower. She touched his lip before he could reply and teased, "No, you did not. Sweet Kale came to prim and proper Captain Adams' bed first. So when the pains of labor come, I am the cause of them."

"I hope this little one is just like you—Oh My God, I love you!" Alika swept her up in his arms and carried her outside, yelling from the bottom of his gut, "*Ua hāpai ke Ali'i 'Ai Ahupua'a! Ua hāpai Ku'u Ali'i Wahine i ke Kāpena!* The Chief of the land is pregnant! The beloved Chiefess is pregnant by the Captain!" From the fishing village, shouts went up and mothers sent their children running to tell neighbors. Soon news was buzzing up the valleys and over the kula. All of Honokahua rejoiced with their righteous Aliʻi Wahine, blessed by the gods.

It seemed a lifetime since Kale first sailed into Honokahua on the *Kaʻahumanu*. Alika was eager to have Kale reunited with her stepfamily in Kawaihae so he arranged to have other ships take his cargos for eight days. Kaʻaumoana and the crew were happy to see Kale, and, after long weeks of hauling tax goods between the islands, looked forward to a day or two of rest in Kawaihae; as well as on the return voyage, an overnight in Honokahua, where food and women are plentiful. After two day's sail, they rounded ʻUpolu Point and headed south along the Kohala Coast. Between the Kohala Mountains and snow-topped Mauna Kea, Waimea Pass cuts a green path down barren ʻaʻā lava kula and near the sea, perched on a dry flat above Makeāhua Gulch and overlooking Kawaihae Bay, was the Young Homestead. Despite Kale's anxiety about this reunion, the "white house," surrounded by beautifully thatched hale, and whitewashed stone fences, was a comforting sight. It was here at Kaʻoanaʻeha's side that Kale learned to be a woman.

Below the Young homestead, by a small coconut grove and salt pond, stood Kawaihae village, a string of tiny thatched hale on a parched desert coast. To the south are the great stone terraces of Puʻu Koholā, Kamehameha's biggest luakini heiau temple built for his war god Kūkāʻilimoku just before he united the Hawaiian Islands.

"Oh Alika, I must tell you I am shy about this visit," said Kale.

"There is no need to be nervous, my darling…" She knew that tone. He was teasing and her eyes flashed. She was also accustomed to a slight bob of Alika's head whenever he was particularly proud of himself. "You see," he said. "I already told ʻOlohana that we are married and there is no doubt in my mind that he and Kaʻoanaʻeha will be delighted to hear we are expecting their first grandchild." She could only laugh to watch him beaming as he declared his wonderful news. He was waiting for a kiss and Kale obliged.

"You rascal! You never told me you spoke to Mr. Young! What did he say? Was he not annoyed that I took a husband so soon?"

Alika delighted at her reaction and the opportunity to reveal the details of his brilliant coup. "Well, my lady, I told him I was enchanted by you for some time and took the opportunity to woo you the very minute I heard you and James were separated."

Kale looked askance. "It's not true, is it?"

"I cannot tell a lie. The thought came straight to me when Boki booked your passage. But 'prim and proper' as I am, I quickly resigned myself because of my deep respect for Young. That is what I told him—-I said, 'I planned to wait a bit and give her more time but the attraction was mutual; and at our age we cannot pass up the perfect woman for us when she casts an eye our way.' Young understood because he took a second wife in his later years and also because we are trusted friends."

"Did he give his blessing?"

Alika was beaming now and rolling his r's like he was back in Forfarshire. He paused and cleared his throat to deliver la pièce de resistance: " 'Olohana—that is Mr. Young to you—said he is sorry for what you endured with James and he happily gives us his warmest blessing…weepy again my love?"

"But of course! You should have told me so I would not worry!" Kale was clearly delighted and much relieved that her homecoming would be warm and joyous.

"I thought it would be a nice surprise. Really, my dear, I never knew you to worry about anything; of course, with me at your side, you never will." Kale kissed him again and beamed with pleasure as she once again reflected in wonder at her handsome and clever husband. "Will you tell them about the baby too?" Alika nodded and kissed her forehead.

By the time the *Ka'ahumanu* dropped anchor 'Olohana was abeam in his canoe with Kale's seventeen-year-old brother Hū'eu, fourteen-year-old sister Peke, and his own little girls Fanny and Lahilahi. The girls were excited to see big sister and most curious about her new husband. Mr. Young had called the family together to explain how Kale now had taken Captain Alexander Adams for her new husband. Their sadness at James' dereliction continued, but Olohana encouraged them to be happy that Kale was safely settled with a man of good character. Hū'eu had good memories of Captain Adams carrying him on his shoulders and playing roustabout. Peke was too young to remember the captain but, not to be left out, she said that he gave her sweets.

"Ahoy! 'Olohana!" yelled Adams.

"Coo!" answered Olohana. "All ashore that's comin' ashore!—Kale and you in my canoe. All hands follow in the tender—all are welcome at the Youngs!"

Fairbairne thanked 'Olohana for his kindness to the crew and Ka'aumoana offered to keep watch but Adams ordered him ashore too.

"At Kawaihae everyone goes ashore," Adams laughed. "If anyone tries to take the ship, 'Olohana will open fire from the white house!"

Back at the homestead, Ka'oana'eha was waiting with eldest daughter Grace, little Keoniana'opio, her only son, and her servants who had prepared a huge feast for the family and sailors. For the first time Kale had to look up to her little brother. Broad-shouldered Hū'eu was a man now and proudly showed Kale his new goats and a canoe he made himself.

"Oh Hū'eu, the canoe is wonderful! I have missed you and now you are a man and I must get to know you all over again."

"I thought I would follow you to Honolulu, but I fell in love with a Waimea girl and I've made up my mind to stay here at Kohala. Her family has a fishing operation."

"Who is it?" asked Kale

"Kaha'anapilo." He grinned.

"Oh my! She is a pretty girl and very righteous. I am so happy for you!" She hugged her brother for the first time in over three years. "It is a good match."

"And you, are you happy now?"

"Yes, Hū'eu. I tried my best to get James away from the rum, but I was not able to do it."

"We are all happy for you, Kale. When I heard that James beat you, I wanted to come to Honolulu and protect you, but Mr. Young wouldn't hear of it. Said he would take care of it himself. I probably would have killed him."

She hugged him again. "It's better that you didn't kill anyone, but thank you for being a good brother."

Back at the white house the little girls were sporting shell lei that Kale brought them and asking the sailors all about Lāhainā and Honolulu. Ka'oana'eha presented Kale with a beautiful hand-held feathered kahili that she and the girls made from Kamuela feathers. The small kahili scepter was an emblem of chiefly rank only used by ali'i wahine at ceremonies, a valuable and most thoughtful gift that Alika insisted on calling "the flyswatter."

Alika brought Ka'oana'eha a bolt of red cotton fabric and a plow blade and harness for 'Olohana's horse. The handsome iron blade promised to cultivate soil as fast as ten men did. 'Olohana was very pleased. Ka'oana'eha just shook her head and smiled, saying, "It will give that horse something to do besides eat the little grass we have left."

After dinner, Alika stood and proposed a toast. Everyone lifted a water cup for there was no alcohol at the Young's home.

"First to the Youngs: 'Olohana, my trusted friend and father-in-law, and Ali'i Wahine Ka'oana'eha, *Pali ke kua, mahina ke alo i noho ai ma ka ua Paliloa o Waimea, mahalo nui loa no ko'u ho'okipa'ana 'olu'olu.* Stature like the cliffs, face like the moon who lives in the high cliff rains of Waimea. Thank you for your kind hospitality. Here! Here!"

"And to my beautiful bride, the sweet fragrance of Honokahua, whose golden eyes I see in every wave and every cloud at sea. You are the blood of my heart. Here! Here!" Kale blushed, waiting for Alika to tell everyone about the baby, but he sat down.

Then 'Olohana stood and all hushed. "We are thankful to have Kale home with us again and to greet her new husband Captain Adams, dear comrade and friend of the Kingdom. May they be blessed with steadiness, affection, long life, and prosperity. But most of all, we are pleased to announce to our family and all gathered here good tidings—of great joy—the Adamses are expecting their first child. Here! Here!" A big hoorah burst out and Alika's crew jumped to their feet to congratulate their captain. The girls were dancing with excitement and Kale, of course, was weeping and hugging Ka'aona'eha. The sweetest surprise was 'Olohana putting his arm around Kale and kissing her cheek.

Later after playing games and joining in sailors' songs, all pitched to cook's accordion, Alika and Kale sat up late with 'Olohana in the white house. In the dim lamp light, it was just as Kale remembered: a hard stone floor and whitewashed walls decorated with oily muskets and daggers. Under the window looking out to sea stood 'Olohana's desk with ink well and quill, Bible and journal. Besides one rocking chair, seating was hard koa wood benches.

'Olohana was a short, slight Lancashire man with swarthy skin and warm brown eyes that always seemed a bit mournful, as if longing for bygone happiness. He was a careful listener, studying every detail and taking into account every opinion before speaking his mind. For the last twenty years, Kamehameha consulted his trusted foreign companion John 'Olohana Young on nearly every decision, with Young acting as a foreign trade minister and minister of defense. Kale never knew him to show any emotion. The only indication of his approval was a nod or a blink of those big brown eyes. His word was never questioned but if one of the children misbehaved he brooded for many days, even when Ka'oana'eha intervened.

Tonight Mr. Young seemed different to Kale; at seventy, his hair was more gray, and, while still a man of measured words, Kale detected warmth and even a touch of humor she never knew. *Did he change? Perhaps I see his love for Alika.* Alika and Young discussed Kingdom politics and Kale was happy to listen and learn all she could. At a lull in the conversation she recounted to Mr. Young how Ke'eaumoku levied a new sandalwood tax on Honokahua just days before the Makahiki tribute was due and how Alika and his crew saved the day. 'Olohana knew the story from behind the scenes and explained why the tax increase was necessary to pay off the debts run up by Boki, governor of O'ahu.

"I told the King to restrict his chiefs' expenditures before they buy so many foreign goods that all the sandalwood of Hawai'i will not pay their bills. I got Kamehameha involved in sandalwood, and it is a good commodity, but look at this land—without a sandalwood forest and undergrowth it supported, Kawaihae has become a desert."

"Oh dear, we must be careful not to ruin Honokahua land as we cut down our forest…" said Kale. She looked at Alika who jumped in.

"We understand the sandalwood tax will continue and we are prepared for it—but Kale is uneasy with the Governor. Is Ke'eaumoku trustworthy?"

"I find him to be so," said 'Olohana. "He was with us at Nu'uanu and fought bravely. And when those treacherous O'ahu chiefs plotted to poison King Kaumuali'i at Waikahalulu and divide up Kaua'i lands among themselves, Ke'eaumoku helped your father get King Kaumuali'i off O'ahu. When the conspirators found Kaumuali'i had escaped, they poisoned poor Isaac instead— Ke'eaumoku did not band with them, but risked his own life trying to save Isaac. Yes, he is a good man like his father. Old Ke'eaumoku and his brother were the ones who nursed Isaac back from death when we were first captured. That whole family has been very good to the Davises."

"Well, I may have misjudged him. Papa never told me about Ke'eaumoku but he used to talk about your capture. He said the true story would never be told until Simon Metcalf was in his grave—now can it be told?" Alika's eyes lit up.

'Oholana laughed. "Yes, I will tell you, but when anyone asks you, please cover my sin!" The smile quickly faded. "Metcalf was a talented but vicious master. May God have pity on his soul. After I saw him turn the *Eleanor's* guns on 100 innocent Hawaiians at Olowalu I could no longer suffer his command. We sailed to Kealakekua to meet up with *Fair American* where I planned to jump ship and sign on under different colors. You see, once we anchored at Kealakekua, my old friend Mackee and his friends convinced Captain Metcalf they had control of the village and that if he sent the bo'sun ashore, they would take him to natives who knew the whereabouts of his son."

"You were about to jump ship?" A shocked Alika leaned forward.

"Yes...I am not proud of that plan—a desperate conspiracy with beachcombers, at that. However, I did not know—and Mackee did not tell me—Kameʻeiamoku had already killed Metcalf's son and the crew of *Fair American*. Once I was ashore, all hell broke loose. I never deserted because I was grabbed up by Kamehameha's men and restrained from returning to my ship by Kamehameha's taboo."

"When did you find Papa?" asked Kale

"The next day...all night in the hands of a fierce warrior like Kamehameha was frightful—especially with me not knowing the language. Thank God, Isaac was strong enough to survive the deathblows they dealt him. He had stab wounds and fractures—eyes swollen shut and black and blue all over—but at the sound of an Englishman he smiled." ʻOlohana stopped and grieved silently for his dear friend. Alika patted Kale's hand as a tear ran down her cheek.

A gust of wind pushed through the room and ʻOlohana began again. "Isaac somehow pulled through...he and I were able to comfort and encourage one another and carve out decent lives. As captives, we wore the malo and had to accompany Kamehameha everywhere, and all we thought of was escape. But soon we got hold of the language and he learned we were pretty good marksmen. Within two months, we were practically running his army, giving him more loyalty than some of his own warriors. I thank God Kamehameha turned out to be a just commander and trusted friend."

"Papa said the wars were terrible."

"Hawaiians are the best warriors I have seen. Devastation of the enemy is efficient and complete...but they were outgunned by Kamehameha. I will never outlive the nightmares of bloodshed at ʻĪao Valley and Nuʻuanu Pali." Again he was silent.

ʻOlohana continued. "Even so, the wars were easy compared to our service as governors of Kamehameha's monarchy." Kale looked puzzled. "Kale, you cannot serve the king as Isaac and I did without making enemies. Peace prevails now only because the people love Kamehameha and the Aliʻi are dead afraid of him. Without the king's continued protection, disgruntled chiefs would kill me off as they did Isaac. And again, without his kapu, these islands would revert to civil war inside of a month." ʻOlohana's sad brown eyes looked down for a moment and his words echoed in the silence. Then he looked Kale in the eye.

"Hear me well; you must be very careful to consider how your decisions at Honokahua affect those in power." Kale's eyes grew big and she tried to think if anything she had done might bring retribution. 'Olohana stood up, walked over to his desk, and looked out the window. "Since you went to Honokahua, you have not asked me for any help, but I am still here if you need me."

"I do have a request, Mr. Young…"

"I prefer my married stepdaughter and fellow landlord call me 'Olohana." Alika laughed and the pall over the room was broken.

Kale stammered. She could hardly put her lips around the O. "—'Olohana," she started, but the sound of her own voice saying it made her balk. "'Olohana… One thing we desire. We have plenty of high forest with big trees for canoes, but no canoe builder. Do you know a canoe builder willing to come and live at Honokahua?"

"Not offhand. Why don't you send me a young man and I will teach him to make canoes?"

Kale was a bit disappointed. "It is a problem. We don't have many young men. If I can find one, what kind is best for the job?"

"Steady hands, stubborn and quiet. A canoe hides in the wood; the work is long and monotonous and one who hurries will ruin the wood, but a determined fellow will stick to it and find the canoe."

"I understand…stubborn," said Kale. "I see why my brother is good at it!" This time 'Olohana laughed too.

I would send your brother Hūʻeu, but he wants to live on Hawaiʻi and my new policy restrains me from making decisions for my grown children." 'Olohana gave Kale a knowing look.

Kale smiled and went on, "Two other things we can use: salt to process our fish and seed for the crops I see growing here. Honokahua has hard poi, sweet potatoes, or olonā cordage to trade you in return. You see, Kaholo and I want to plant the beans, Irish potatoes, and melons to sell to the whalers in Lāhainā.

"Coo! Alika, you have a clever chief on your hands!"

"She definitely has an aptitude for ruling!" said Alika. "And she does get on famously with her konohiki." Kale tried to disregard the remark. *He is jealous of Kaholo and me!*

'Olohana went on. "Kale, your Papa would be proud of you. This is exactly how to improve the lot of Honokahua. Grow what you need for taxes, but also grow or fabricate whatever else you can sell. Otherwise, in times of famine you will lose your land."

I knew that. Suddenly it occurred to Kale that she was in a conversation among equals. 'Olohana did not say he was proud of her, but Kale knew it because he spoke to her as he did to his trusted land managers. *He has not changed. I have changed.*

The next morning the sun rose late, as it does in Kawaihae. The sea was rough and 'ohukai mist filled the air with salt, giving every vista a far-away softness. Down the hill in Ka'oana'eha's hale kua, thatched workhouse, Kale could hear tak-tak-tak-tak, tak-tak-tak-tak, the rhythm of several i'e kuku kapa beating sticks being struck on kua anvils. Māmā and the girls were flattening out water-soaked and fermented wauke bark into felted cloth, as Kale and Māmā had done so many times. Outside, dry banana leaves covered a large area where soon they would spread out the finished wet kapa cloth to dry in Kawaihae's intense sun. As Kale got closer, she heard happy female voices behind the energetic tapping. When Peke, Fanny, Grace, and Ka'oana'eha saw Kale, they greeted her but never stopped working. There, next to Māmā, was an empty spot, a prepared mo'omo'o bundle of once-beaten bark and tools just for Kale.

"*E Keamalu! Ke kali nei ka Hakaio iā 'oe!* Hey shapely one, your magical kapa beater awaits you!" sang out Ka'oana'eha. The girls giggled. Kale patted her tummy, walked over to her place between her regal stepmother and sweet sister Peke, and sat down to work her section of the large kapamoe sleeping blanket. It was as if she had never left.

Ka'oana'eha was fond of yellow and wore a deep gold pā'ū imprinted with a black "kōnane" checkerboard border. Her dark short hair, bleached to a reddish tan at the hairline, framed her fine features and accentuated her deep brown eyes. Kale always loved the pink tone of Māmā's dark skin, preferring it to her own pale sallow tone. She was full Ali'i blood and spent her days instilling her children with the history, lore, and traditions of Hawaiian royalty.

"*Ua māluhiluhi 'oe i ka pēpē?* Are you tired because of the baby?" asked Ka'oana'eha.

" *'A'ole i luhi au. 'A'ole i ōma'ima'i me pū.* Not tired or sick either," said Kale. But my breasts are very tender and I long for my husband. The kapu requires us to sleep apart until after the baby is born and my purification is completed."

"*E pili'ana kēia kapu*…Concerning this kapu…I think it is not a good thing to leave your haole husband alone with his desires."

"What do you mean?"

"These haole men are not aliʻi. Aliʻi men satisfy themselves with other women during the kapu of pregnancy. Our husbands are like makaʻāinana commoners who only have one woman and never take their eyes from her. It is not good to leave them for so long. Did you know Alika has asked ʻOlohana to keep you here with us until the baby is born?" Kale's eyes opened wide and she stopped working.

"Auwē, Māmā! I know I am safe here in the presence of your love but I made an oath to Queen Keopuolani to serve my people at Honokahua. I have come to love them too. They have been alone and needy for so long."

"I do not think Alika understands your love for the land, or your duty to your people; and he seems to be jealous of Kaholo. For my part, I would love to have you with me, but I do not think it is right. Here is my thought: you should be with your husband. When carrying Keoniana I traveled with ʻOlohana on his trips and he was happy knowing I was safely by his side. He did not grow to resent the baby, but loved it as I did. Perhaps you stay at Honokahua and sail with Alika. It will be good for him and it will allow you to serve your people. Then in the last moon, I will come to Honokahua with Peke and Grace and attend your birthing. This will make ʻOlohana happy."

"Oh Māmā, it is a good thought! It is very good!"

"I will ask ʻOlohana, but be prepared to stay if he decides on Kawaihae. Do you have a midwife at Honokahua?"

"Yes, Kekahunawahine is her name. Very few babies die during birthing at Honokahua. Her father was a Kahuna Hoʻopai birthing priest and expert—and Māmā, I am not alone at Honokahua. There are other pregnant women who are helping me on my journey."

"I see you have touched the hearts of your people as they have touched yours. I am very happy with you and your mother would be proud." Kale welled up and Kaʻoanaʻeha smiled. "Is the kapa not wet enough for you?" Peke and the girls giggled.

"Māmā, I want to go to Honokahua, too," said Fanny.

"Hush now. Everyone get to work before the day is too short for drying. I want to teach Kale about the greens and herbs she must eat now as the baby grows."

At awakea high sun Peke and the girls began drying their grand glossy white kapa sleeping blanket, well-shaped and imprinted with a diamond-patterned watermark. Carefully they spread it out on banana leaves and placed stone weights on its delicate cropped corners and sides so ocean breezes would not pick up the nearly dry edges. Kale could still feel the slippery wauke juice on her hands as she rubbed her puckered finger pads together. It was a wonderful kapa moe; a fine supple blanket to be put away as a dowry for Peke or Grace.

Two days in Kawaihae were not nearly enough for Kale to learn all she wanted to know from the Youngs, but Alika had to get back and the sail to Honokahua would take four days into the wind. Before they paddled out to the ship, 'Olohana counseled Alika to take Kale with him on his assignments and to use Honokahua as a home base to allow her to continue managing Honokahua. Alika agreed, so long as Ka'oana'eha would attend the birthing, and everyone was satisfied.

Just as the crew began weighing anchor, it came over Kale—blood drained from her head and her stomach clutched against her chest. Saliva filled her mouth. Every thought she ever had was gone save one—she ran to the rail, hung over, and retched. 'Ulumalu ran for a bucket and Alika tried to give Kale his pocket hankie, but it was too late. Alika wiped tiny beads of sweat from her brow and 'Ulumalu brought her a cup of water. When Kale looked up again she saw her family on the shore. Ka'oana'eha was scolding Peke, Grace, Fanny, and little John. Hū'eu still had a big grin on his face. Then he cupped his hands and yelled, "Good fishing today, Kale!" and the girls began laughing again. 'Olohana shook his head and waved.

Kale could only smile and wave back as the *Ka'ahumanu* set sail north out of Kawaihae Bay. Nausea gave way to hunger as quickly as it had come. Kale turned to Alika. "Will cook please make me something to eat? This baby is hungry."

"Yes, certainly my love, but I am afraid it will have to be haole food today."

"That is good—some oatmeal porridge please."

Alika grinned. "You don't like oatmeal!"

"I don't, but your baby does." Alika laughed and escorted his mother-to-be to the mess.

In Honokahua Valley, Pili rolled over when she heard the footsteps coming up the path to her hale. Moonlight was shining on the banana trees outside, casting short shadows, and she knew it was au moe, the middle of the night. The footsteps stopped. She peered out the door, but saw no one. She waited, holding her breath and listening through the familiar sounds of Honokahua Stream. A twig snapped and she spotted two men standing far down by one great boulder of Kane. Māmā and the girls were asleep and not a sound came from the boy's hut. Pili slowly gripped an adze she kept by the door, and waited. She heard the men whisper. Then as she watched, they moved up the path toward her homestead. *Should I wake the children? Will they pass by?* She sat silently and watched.

The first one was definitely a stranger, dressed like a warrior in malo. They stopped again and the unmistakable soft whistle of an ipu hōkiokio gourd whistle floated to her ears. *Is one of them signaling a lover?* When they moved again, she saw the broad fellow behind with the whistle to his nose—*Keʻeaumoku!* Pili put down her weapon, smoothed her hair, and ran to her lover. He embraced her and Pili wrapped her legs around him.

"Since the Makahiki you are the sum of my thoughts," he whispered. Give me back my heart or come back with me to Lāhainā. I want you for my wife." Pili's heart swelled in her bosom as he kissed her neck. She took his hand and led him to her workhouse.

"My Chief, I am a common farmer and a mother of young boys and girls. My days of running away are gone. I yearn for you and my heart blesses the memory of your sweet touch and tender words. Joy now overwhelms me as I look at you. I desire you for my husband…but I cannot go to Lāhainā."

"Then sleep with me here until the bright light of day—let everyone know I will have you even if I have to come to Honokahua!" Pili carefully pulled out her stored mats and finest kapa blankets and spread out a wedding bed in her workhouse. While her family slept, she entertained her lover; and he came to her softly saying, *"Kaukahi e ke aloha lawa ʻia. Hōʻā ʻia i paʻa o kuʻu ipo ka manaʻo.* Persevering love is sufficient to itself. My thoughts are firmly emblazoned on my beloved."

When the first roosters crowed, Pili did not rise as she usually did; instead she nestled peacefully in the arms of Keʻeaumoku until the full light of day filled Honokahua Valley, indicating to Māmā and the children that the governor had taken her for his wife.

Kaholo met the *Kaʻahumanu* with news that Governor Keʻeaumoku visited Honokahua and was disappointed to find Kale and Alika away. "I offered him my hale, but he preferred to stay in yours," said Kaholo.

Alika set his jaw. "What the devil! He knew I was going to be away in Kawaihae!" Was he thinking to press himself on my wife whilst I was away?"

"Oh no! Alika, he does not desire me!" said Kale. "He loves Pilialoha…" Kale was smiling at Kaholo. "Remember those two at the Makahiki?" Then she turned back to Alika. "That rascal knew we were away and came to see Pili again—he just told Kaholo he was here to see us to protect Pili—or protect himself, in case she would not have him."

Alika calmed down and Kaholo was nodding. "Yes, My Chief. Now I understand why he stayed two days…and it explains recent rumors of Night Marchers in the valley. People must have seen the governor and his servant walking up to Pili's farm and thought they were the ghosts of ancient warriors."

Alika grinned, "So the governor is in love. Honokahua will certainly be better off now."

Kale ignored his remark and instructed Kaholo, "There is no harm in lovers meeting at Honokahua. If Keʻeaumoku comes again while we are gone, please offer him our home. He is a friend of the Davis family and is always welcome here."

For six months Kale sailed with Alika all eight seas of Hawaiʻi, returning to Honokahua each month before the new moon, to pray with Manu on the nights of Kāne, Lono, and Mauli, and to oversee new crops and industry at Honokahua. Under the care of midwife Kekahunawahine, Kale suffered just a few weeks of morning sickness and her energy never waned. Every morning Alika brought her mamaki tea and fresh ʻilima blossoms to eat with her breakfast, and every night he read her to sleep with poetic visions of Scotland from the hearts of Sir Walter Scott and Robert Burns.

Of all the Kingdom's ports of call, Līhuʻe's Nāwiliwili harbor left the most welcome impression on Kale. From the ship she would gaze up the Huleʻia kahawai watching the morning mist form into tiny clouds and climb up the mountains. Reflections of beach palms in the mirror of Alakoko fishpond at the bottom of the river gently rippled as Haʻikū fishermen poured in fresh fish. Alika took her to see the waterfalls of Kalalau and sailed her up past the flat sands of Keʻi and blue knife-edged Kahelu Ridge of Nāpali. Back at Honokahua, Kaholo supervised the sweet potato planting in soils left soft and moist by ample winter rains.

By March all the planting was done and *Kaʻahumanu* was hauling sandalwood from east Maui to Kamehameha's Kailua storehouses. The great waonahele forests of East Maui used to grow down to the beach. Now, from the sea, new grass on the denuded lower flanks of Haleakalā looked like pale green moss. It was the first time Kale saw the battlefields of Wailuku and ʻĪao Valley, where her father and ʻOlohana helped Kamehameha win Maui. When she first felt the baby move in her belly, the *Kaʻahumanu* was anchored overnight in Hāna beside the blood red pali and red sand beach of Kaihalulu, where the deep blue ocean and red cove waters join at the reef. The winter months passed with frequent opportunity to visit the Youngs at Kawaihae. When Kale finally got back to Honokahua, Kaholo proudly showed her vigorous plantings of melons, Irish potatoes, and beans on the lepo red earth kula above Honokahua Beach.

The Adams spent much more time at Honokahua in April and May and they were able to properly entertain Keʻeaumoku on his visits to see Pilialoha. Pili miscarried their first child, but was happily pregnant again. Keʻeaumoku indeed became a benefactor of Honokahua, recruiting four young men to live at Honokahua to cut and haul sandalwood. Honokahua was on its way to a very prosperous harvest.

Alika took Kale to Oʻahu twice, once to Honouliuli in the Waiʻanae mountains of the windward coast and another time to Kaneohe Bay. She delighted in the sweet pungent fragrance of the hala grove at Kekele, nestled under the majestic splendor of Nuʻuanu pali where sky and earth meet in the longhouse of the wind. It was hard to imagine that so many warriors fell to their death at this beautiful place when Kamehameha took Oʻahu. Kale mourned for them and their children.

When they stayed at Alika's home in Honolulu, memories of her life with James preoccupied Kale's mind and she feared seeing him again. Alika filled her nights with joy but when he was working at the harbor, she secluded herself like a child awaiting punishment. Alika showed her the charm of Ahuimanu where his Scottish friends the Campbells lived, and he made her a beautiful lūʻau at Limaloa spring and coconut grove. While the Adams were visiting Uʻilama, Alika was called back to Kailua Kona and Kale stayed for ten more days with the Campbells rather than return to Honolulu.

"My darling, how did you enjoy your time on Oʻahu?"

"Oh Alika, I did not know how deeply James wounded me. You call me fearless, but I still cannot find any peace when I am here. The Campbells are very nice, but all I could think about was Honokahua and how I will manage with the baby."

"I was hoping to ask you to live in Honolulu. This deep harbor will eventually be the hub of the Kingdom, not Lāhainā. I have invested heavily in the growth of this place, and if I play my cards right, Kamehameha will give me land here. I can afford to get you a wet nurse or kahu for the child and you could be free of all that work at Honokahua. Kaholo is an able konohiki; he doesn't need you there all the time. Look how nicely things have gone this year."

Kale stared at him in disbelief. "Have we been together all these months and still you do not know my heart? Honokahua is not work—it is my duty and privilege. It is the heritage of my mother to rule. It is the inheritance of my father to preserve. It is my duty to my king and my people to take care of Honokahua and prepare my children to take care of it when I am gone." Alika had that same look he always had when Kale did not comply with his wishes. "I want to be with you," she said, "but my kuleana is to rule Honokahua."

"But you have only been there less than a year. You're correct, my dear. I don't understand your obsession over a backcounty fishing village!" He was agitated and pacing. He checked himself, turned to her, and gently took her hand. "Darling, I want you to be here with me."

"But Alika, what if Honolulu doesn't grow? What if the King does not give you land to rule here? You could run a shipping business from Maui today and live on your own land at Honokahua. Instead, you rent a small yard in Honolulu like a foreign trader, work in a port smaller than Lāhainā, and visit me only once a month. This I do not understand." She held her belly. "The baby is rolling around!" She laughed. "I wonder where the baby wants to live?"

"I give up," said Alika. "I am torn between my fortune and my deep love for you." He put his hand on her belly and felt the tiny movements.

Kale smiled and kissed him. "This time together is very good, but you ask too much when you ask a Hawaiian to leave her land."

In June, Kale and Alika sailed again to Hawai'i. By now, the midwife was restricting her intake of food to a few greens, poi, and a small piece of raw fish every other day to reduce the intake of salt. In July, a second crop of sweet potatoes was planted at Honokahua and while Kale was in Kaua'i, U'i delivered her first son, Leowaipahē.

A month later, at the north end of Honokahua Bay, Kale was on the Birthing Stone of Haumea, in the presence of her midwife, stepmother, two sisters, priest, husband, and dear friend U'i. In the afternoon when labor pains were far apart, Alika walked with Kale on the beach. Now, as the shadows grew long, her water had broken and she was sitting in a depression at one end of the birthing stone boulder that allowed her to assume a sitting squat. As Alika paced in the sand, helpless and sweating profusely, Kale focused on Kekahuna's instructions and managed to keep calm and not to whimper. Ka'oana'eha called Alika and gave him a moist wad of olonā to cool Kale's face. She handed Kale a piece of stripped hau bark to bite on when the pain got intense.

"I cannot tell when one pain ends and the next begins," whispered Kale.

Kekahuna quickly answered, "I will tell you when to push. Drink down this hau sap to hasten the birth."

"Ugh!—oh!" Quickly she grabbed the hau bark and bit down.

"Push now!" The pains were deep and Kale felt them in the small of her back. To cry out is shameful for one's family and the child, so she suffered silently.

"*Kū! Kau ka po'o.* Stop! The head is showing," said Kekahuna

The head is a good thing, thought Alika. He tried to smile and wiped Kale's brow again. Kale squeezed his hand so hard it tingled.

"*I lalo ke alo me pū,*" said the midwife.

Face down too. That is good, he thought.

"Wait now," said Kekahuna firmly. "Don't push. Allow the shoulders to slip first. You must hold back this time." Kale hardly sighed before the pain was upon her again and Alika saw her suck up her breath. The golden eyes grew big and round and blood trickled down his fingers as she broke the skin. She swallowed a muffled cry and he thought he would die himself until the midwife said, "Good, good!—Push next time and the shoulders will come easily."

This time when the pain came, Kale met it head on and pushed her back against the cool rock, grabbed the sides of the rock with both hands, and bore down with all her might. Suddenly the pain was gone. *What happened?* "What happened?"

Kale craned her neck to see and Kekahuna rolled a tiny warm slippery body on her belly. "It's a boy," said Kekahuna.

"A son!—is he healthy?" Alika was shouting.

"Healthy and long, this baby," said Kekahuna as she supervised Peke washing the small arms and legs. The child did not cry but just gurgled and shuddered as he stretched up his legs. The stress was over and the midwife had to shush Alika, who was crying and giggling like a lunatic.

Kekahuna quickly tied the cord in two places and Manu stepped forward, cut the cord, and chanted as he cleansed the wound:

> Cleanse the red blood from the stump
> Cleanse it from the cord
> Bind up the cord

It is for the god to safeguard this child
To make him flourish like a well-watered plant.

Kekahuna took the loose end of the cord and gently pulled, releasing the afterbirth, which she rinsed with seawater, slapped in a calabash and handed to Alika. Before he fainted, Ka'oana'eha took it from him and sat him down. Then Manu used a piece of 'ie'ie sweet potato vine to slap Kale's breasts, chanting to Hina as he slapped the left and to Kū as he slapped the right, asking the gods to make her milk flow abundantly. Kale snuggled little Isaac to her nipple and he suckled, never taking his eyes away from the sweet voice saying, "O Kū, O Lono, O Kāne, O Kanaloa, deal kindly with our first-born son, 'Aikake Ke'eaumoku Adams. Give him long life. Protect him until the last sleep of unconsciousness. 'Āmama."

Kekahuna placed fresh herbs on Kale's belly and Grace Young wrapped a malo over them to hold them in place. Ka'oana'eha gave Kale a warm herb tonic to drink and 'Ulumalu helped Alika bury the placenta under the Tree of Hulu. When Alika came back, the family walked Kale and Isaac to her hale pe'a, where she would remain secluded for 10 days, sustained on broth and herbs until her time of purification was complete.

Alika looked at his tiny pale son and beautiful healthy wife and wept, grateful to whatever providence that brought him to this joyous moment.

"I love you, Kale. You are my life…I love you, wee little Isaac," he whispered.

Kale whispered to Alika, "Please come and live with us at Honokahua. You will not regret it."

CHAPTER 7

Dearly Departed

Isaac Adams was just ten months old in May 1819, when King Kamehameha became ill and none of his kāhuna could help him. When they suggested human sacrifice to the gods for his recovery, he forbid it. His trusted companion 'Olohana, who faithfully attended Kamehameha's bedside in his illness, sent word to his own family at Kawaihae, to Kale at Honokahua, and to James in Honolulu, warning them of the King's impending death and violent mourning to follow.

Kale consulted all her family leaders and they decided that the greatest threat to Honokahua was from outsiders, plundering bands from other valleys or islands, or foreign traders looking for women.

"My chief, I have prepared your hideaway with kapa, mats, and lamps. When you decide to enter, I will bring water and food, and 'Ulumalu will stand guard," said Kaholo.

"A chief should not hide behind her people. A good chief stands in front of her people, even in danger. I will do it because I must protect my child, but first I must provide protection for my people. All must be able to defend or hide themselves."

"It is done," said Kaholo. I have assigned men to act as guards at all entries to Honokahua. All lookouts have pū for signaling, weapons, and a good supply of stones to sling. All the lawai'a and mahi'ai are ready to defend their families and homesteads. When the King dies, a herald from Kailua will go first to East Maui and then the news will come around to us. Before anyone can get to

Honokahua, we will hear distant drums and there will be plenty of time to assure everyone's safety."

"What do you think of a high forest camp for all the women and children?" asked Kale.

"Yes, it can be done and it is a good thought," said Kaholo. "I will tell the family leaders to manage it."

"Good."

Two weeks later King Kamehameha I died at the age of 69 and great wail arose over the Hawaiian Islands. The King's kapu died with him and would not be reinstated until a new king took the throne, after ten days of mourning. In Kailua and Lāhainā sincere traditional expressions of deep grief—burning the skin, shaving of heads, and knocking out of teeth—escalated to drunkenness, looting, and plundering. Soon lawlessness ignited family feuds. Ensuing thefts, beatings, and vengeful murders unleashed fear and frenzy in the whole population.

For the first time in her life, Kale was afraid. Everything she was, everything she had ever known, was connected to Kamehameha the Great. Her father had been his captive haole gunner, trusted warrior, and governor. Her stepfather 'Olohana was respected in the entire kingdom as the King's companion and counselor for trading and governing. By Kamehameha's favor, Kale and the other chiefs ruled parcels of his land, harvested his crops, and fished his fishing grounds. All rights and powers were vested in the king and he was their protector. What would happen now?

At Honokahua, work ceased and all the families mourned in their men's houses and at their shrines. On the paepae, Kale and Manu wailed and made offerings for the people and the land. In the valley and on the kula, sadness and uncertainty sat on the ahupua'a like a heavy blanket. Kaholo set up his watch guards at the Nāpili and Honolua borders of the Alaloa road and mountain paths. Others watched Honokahua's shoreline from the paepae and the bluff high above Mokulē'ia Bay.

Kale and Isaac went to the hideaway, and the other women and children went to a hidden camp in the high forest. After five days, when Kale courageously went back to her hale, the other women returned to their husbands and Honokahua continued to grieve peacefully. Kaholo ventured out to Lāhainā and discovered that, after a crescendo of rioting and violence, the village had returned to order, as if to honor the king who gave them the first lasting peace in centuries.

After ten days, a herald came to Honokahua with startling news. Keopuolani's eighteen-year-old son Liholiho had assumed the throne with Queen Ka'ahumanu as his Regent, and, at the bidding of his mother, Regent and Highest Kahuna Hewahewa, King Liholiho did not reinstate the king's kapu.

By the time King Liholiho released Alika from duty at Kailua, and the *Ka'ahumanu* sailed to Honokahua Bay, farming, fishing, and family life was the same as it had been for a millennium. Peace prevailed.

"Liholiho sailed into Kailua, went up to his mother, and sat to eat lunch with her in front of everyone! It was an incredible sight! Women are eating with their husbands and sleeping together on all the kapu nights because there are no kapu nights!" Alika was addressing a council of Honokahua's family leaders, who sat in a large circle, and listened very carefully but were skeptical about this new style of living.

"Are all families doing this?"

"No, not all," said Alika. "Some are continuing to worship the kapu gods and keep the old ways."

"Then, what is the difference?" asked Shaw

"The difference is life and death, said Alika. "The ali'i cannot punish anyone for breaking the kapu because the kapu is lifted. You may pray as you wish, but there are no kapu to break."

Shaw looked puzzled. "What about the kapu on fishing? It is a good kapu that allows the fish to multiply for next year's catch. If we fish aku all year, soon the aku will all be gone."

"We have choices at Honokahua. You and your chief must decide how you will fish. You may keep the old kapu, but if someone fishes aku out of season, he will not be killed."

"Oh…" The family leaders began to nod.

Kale watched their expressions. To be free of fear was obviously good for the commoners, but, like her, they believed in the gods and wondered why the gods would relent so suddenly. She guessed Honokahua people would keep the old kapu for a long time, not trusting this change until they saw transgressors of the old kapu go unpunished. Still, the Honokahua leaders clearly wanted Alika's news to be true.

After the council, Alika and Kale had their first dinner together at Honokahua.

"Did you know that 'Olohana was the only one of Kamehameha's companions who did not attend his funeral?" asked Alika.

"I suppose I could have guessed. Was he afraid to show his emotions?"

"No. Not at all. He was afraid the kāhuna would kill him and bury him with Kamehameha as a death companion. Remember, he was concerned that a disgruntled chief might take the opportunity to murder him if Kamehameha died. He just went up to Kawaihae and boarded up the house until things settled down."

"Was there a lot of violence in Kailua?" asked Kale.

"No. Many mutilated themselves and there was sincere grieving, but no rape or murder. The most incredible news was the dissolution of the kapu. You know, my dear, Kamehameha's own practices undermined his kapu."

Kale thought for a minute. "You mean by bringing peace?"

"Well, he first achieved peace by killing off his enemies. That was nothing different from the old chiefs. But, later on, Kamehameha stopped killing his enemies. Instead he began his policy of keeping his enemies close to him, just as he made your father live with him night and day, before making him a warrior and a chief. He never gave his chiefs two parcels of land next to one another—he spread out their lands so they could not build a rebellion without his knowledge. What I was really thinking was that Kamehameha denied himself the privilege of executing and sacrificing his subjects to the gods. He did very little of that after the wars. He would not allow the chiefs to murder commoners who broke the kapu. Then, at the end, he refused death companions for himself. The fall of the kapu was inevitable."

Kale mused, "It is a marvel that he devoted his life to the gods who made him King, but he spared his people from his own gods' demands…" She paused. "I remember when you told me Keopuolani was responsible for peace in Hawai'i…"

"And I still believe she influenced him in these things—Keopuolani, 'Olohana and your father."

Kale smiled when she thought of her father. Then she thought of Keopuolani. "Alika, I understand the isolation Keopuolani suffered because of her pi'o kapu and why she seeks to be free, but why would Ka'ahumanu give up her divine right of kapu?

"That's simple!" he laughed. "Now the playing field is level. The male chiefs she competes with always had the advantage of private meetings while they dined or on kapu nights, when Ka'ahumanu had to sleep apart from her husbands." Alika roared. "Now they will never have a moment alone to conspire against her!"

Kale shook her head. "Very good, but now *why* does Hewahewa go against his own gods? This puzzles me."

"I, too, cannot figure how the two Ali'i Wahine convinced him to give up all his power…and in this life we may never know the answer, my darling, but I am happy to be done with the kapu and ready for an evening swim with my bride.

"That is a wonderful idea. Shall I bring the baby?"

"Let him sleep and have 'Ulumalu watch him while we two enjoy ourselves."

Kale giggled. "Oh Captain Adams, it is the Hōkū Moon!"

In September 1819, Hewahewa and Liholiho systematically closed all the luakini heiau devoted to human sacrifice, and the commoners began to believe that the kapu would never come back. Throughout the kingdom, all temple images were taken down and burned, and rites to the gods were openly broken by the highest ali'i to dispel the fears and superstitions of the people. And peace continued. The last luakini heiau dismantled on Maui was Kā'anapali's Ma'iu Heiau at Honokōhau.

When the King Liholiho's brig was spotted north in the channel, everyone at Honokahua knew he had come to close Ma'iu Heiau. Kaholo prepared three canoes to take Kale, Manu, Kekahunawahine, and two family leaders around Lipoa Point to Honokōhau.

The north-running offshore current helped them up to Lipoa and the paddlers went against the current for a short time until they made Punalau, where another current pushed them into Honokōhau Bay. The tall steep red cliffs on either side made the canoes seem small and insignificant. Their landing point was a narrow beach at the base of Honokōhau Valley, where Honokōhau River's rushing water had deposited a natural foundation of gray high-mountain rocks it had smoothed and rounded on their trip to the sea. Deep in the clear water of the bay, a big parrotfish flashed its sparkling blue side toward the surface as it pursued a mountain shrimp.

"I expected to hear drums," said Kaholo.

"No," said Manu. "They will not sound the drums of Kū today. This is a funeral."

Kale understood. Without a rite, the only thing to do was to prepare the gods for burial…salt and fire.

By the time they landed and climbed the eastern side of the valley, Liholiho and his chiefs had already built a huge fire, taken the wooden images from inside the temple grounds, and toppled the large tiki surrounding the main terrace. A huge crowd of people from the whole of Kāʻanapali looked on as the chiefs cut a gash in each image. Then High Kahuna Hewahewa pressed salt into the hole, and the chiefs leaned it into the bonfire. There was no rejoicing, no excitement like the old times when the kapu was lifted and women entered the heiau or laughed and ate kapu foods on the terraces—just the silence and crackling fire, as flames blackened and distorted the images.

"I have seen it," said Manu. "Now we may go." His face had a calm peaceful expression as usual. Kale wondered if he grieved the passing of the gods, and how they would pray in the future, but she did not want to be impolite. "These are just images. The gods were never in them." Kale smiled. She knew the gods were invisible and Manu aimed to continue his prayers to them. She would be with him, praying for the good of her people. But the sacrifice of humans to the gods was over.

In March 1820, the *Thaddeus* sailed into Kealakekua, and Alika and John Young convinced Liholiho and Kaʻahumanu to allow eight New England missionary couples to live in Hawaiʻi for a probationary period of one year to demonstrate their intentions. Nā Kāhuna Haole, 'the foreign priests' were inspired to come halfway around the world to preach the Gospel by Henry ʻŌpūkahaʻia, an orphan of the civil wars in Hawaiʻi. Until that time, the teachers at Yale Divinity College thought aboriginal people were incapable of learning to read and write. Henry excelled in all his studies and begged his teachers to send missionaries to Hawaiʻi. Henry died in Cornwall, Connecticut before he could return to his motherland, and the first American Mission Board was formed to send missionaries to Henry's home and tell his people about Jesus Christ, as he had wished. Seven other Hawaiians, educated at the Foreign Mission school in South Ferry, Massachusetts, accompanied the missionaries as interpreters. It was not until they arrived that the missionaries discovered that Hawaiʻi's civil wars were over and human sacrifice had been abandoned.

"Oh Peke, I am so happy for you!" Kale hugged her little sister.

"George Humehume is his name. He is not a missionary, but an interpreter. Oh Kale, he is so handsome and the son of King Kaumualiʻi of Kauaʻi. Isn't that amazing, that the son of the king Isaac Davis saved would fall in love with me, his daughter?"

"It is incredible fortune! Come and tell me more as we have our lunch. I am so happy to have you here with me at Honokahua—and you delight me with such happy news!"

"Isaac is so precious and such a big boy. I cannot stop hugging him. Kale, his skin is so pale and rosy."

"Poor thing. He is such a curiosity here." Kale asked Isaac, "Where is Papa?"

"Brig! Mama," said the toddler.

"Yes, my sweet boy, Papa is on the brig. And what does Papa say?"

Isaac stood up straight and put out his arm and shouted "Heeeeee Hooooooh"

Peke swept him up and squeezed his face next to hers. "Yes, Heave Ho! Oh Isaac you are so smart!"

"You will have a Christian wedding, I suppose," asked Kale.

"Of course. My witness has to be a member of the Sandwich Isles Mission Church, so I may not have you stand with me as I wish, but you must be there with me, even so."

"And you are a member of the church?"

"Oh yes. Mr Young made us all recite our verses for the missionaries—me, Grace, Fanny, and Keoniana. Then we were baptized."

"It is good to have a husband who prays to the same god you do. Isaac and I will be there for certain. Perhaps you will marry when Alika may come too."

"Oh yes! Mr Young has already thought of that. And my George thinks very highly of Alika. He said it was through Alika's and Mr. Young's intervention that Liholiho and Ka'ahumanu allowed the missionaries to land."

Kale beamed. "I hope your husband is just as wonderful as mine. He always makes me so proud. If only he would come to live at Honokahua, I would be completely content…where do you and George plan to live, Kailua?"

"Oh no. George does not share the missionaries' zeal. He wants to live on Kaua'i, in Waimea with his father. You told me Kaua'i is beautiful."

"Aside from West Maui, Līhu'e is my favorite place. It is not dry like Kawaihae and Kailua, but lush, green, and cool with grand pali and valleys. Your big sister will be a frequent visitor!"

"Oh, Kale, I am so happy…"

George and Peke were living at Waimea in 1821 when Liholiho sailed into Nāwiliwili Harbor, invited King Kaumuali'i on board his ship, and kidnapped him to O'ahu where Queen Regent Ka'ahumanu took him for a husband. A month later she took George's half brother and heir to Kaua'i's throne as her husband too, placing control of Kaua'i firmly in her hands. The Kaua'i chiefs were incensed and looked to George Humehume for leadership. Ka'ahumanu needed a strong Governor she could trust so she installed her brother Ke'eaumoku, who dutifully moved to Kaua'i but pined for Pilialoha until his health failed. Pili finally took their son Huluoha'ae to Kaua'i and stayed with him at Waimea until he died in May of 1823. Kale made sure Pili's family was well cared for while she was gone. When Pili returned, all of Honokahua mourned with her the death of Ke'eaumoku Kahekili, Governor of Maui and Honokahua's benefactor.

After the end of kapu days, Keopuolani blossomed in the nurture of her family, friends, and community. The deep wounds of her heart seemed to heal. When Reverend Richards came to teach in Lāhainā, her sad resignation turned into a joyous passion for the missionaries' savior, Jesus Christ.

"My queen, I am so sorry that you are not feeling well," said Kale. Keopuolani had lost a third of her weight and gasped for every breath. Beside her chaise was a well-worn leather covered Bible that she often patted as she quoted passages from memory.

She smiled. "I only regret that cannot study more." She waited for her breath to return. "You have been faithful to visit me every month." She paused again and Kale waited. "You are a good daughter." Kale bowed her head and tears fell on her pā'ū.

"My queen, if I pray to Jesus, will you recover?"

"Pray and see—" She shook her head and pointed to her chest.

"I will go and let you rest," said Kale, but Keopuolani grabbed Kale's hand.

Soon the breath came back. "Jesus is alive in heaven. He is waiting for me. I am happy."

Keopuolani held on to Kale, and Kale patted her hand. "May the blood of Jesus...cover your sins...and make you whole." Then she smiled, let go, and closed her eyes. Kale tried to keep from crying as she left and got almost to the front porch before sobbing. Taua, Keopuolani's Christian teacher from Tahiti, was there.

"Are you all right, Mrs. Adams?"

"Yes, thank you, teacher. Is she dying?"

"I don't know how long she can continue."

Keopuolani held on until September 1823. No violence or rioting erupted. The wailing and grieving was intense because the people, chiefs, and missionaries alike deeply loved Keopuolani, but what impressed Kale was the dignity and orderliness of the solemn procession of mourners walking before the casket, dressed in rags and with ashes on their heads. It was noble and grand.

Kale and Alika joined over a thousand persons dressed in black walking behind the casket, borne by Liholiho's five queens and Hoapili's daughter, Lilihā. Alika's ship's bell tolled and minute guns fired as her body was deposited in a tomb at Sandwich Isles Mission's Waineʻe Church. Then, mourners carried stones from the old heiau on Mākila Point and piled them into a wall around the tomb. At Keopuolani's house, Alika flew the Hawaiian flag he had designed for Kamehameha. Reverend Ellis offered prayers and preached, saying Keopuolani was alive in heaven with Jesus, "rejoicing with the multitude of God's children and angels." Kale wept with joy that her beloved queen, tortured by a solitary life, would never be lonely again.

By 1824 Kale was used to her own loneliness. Alika worked more at Honolulu Harbor than ever. A fortnight between visits stretched to a month and sometimes two. Kale longed to have another baby, and planned to sail with Alika on one of his trips so they could spend some needed time together. There were not enough hours in the day to take care of Isaac and do all she could to help Kaholo manage Honokahua's expanding farming operation, which paid an increasing tax obligation. The population of Honokahua was also growing.

Kaholo and ʻUlumalu were paddling Kale to Lāhainā on trading day. Following them were four large canoes loaded high with Honokahua produce.

"Kaholo, I am so thankful that you got us started in Irish potatoes, beans, and melons. Just look at all the whalers anchored at Lāhainā Roads! Let us see if we can find some more Chinese sailors to hire. Ying Fat and Yee seem to fit in very well and they do good work."

"Yes, my chief. Do you like the new canoe that Makauli made for you?"

"It is a fine canoe. I like it much better than I do Makauli."

"Hū! Why don't you like him?"

"There is just something about him that is not right."

"We have three more orders for canoes—everyone likes his work."

"ʻOlohana sent him, so he must be all right, but I would keep an eye on him if I were you."

"I will do it, my chief."

Kale thought for a minute. 'Ulumalu was nearly 20 and Kale wanted to reward him for his service by releasing him. If she sent him to apprentice with Makauli, he could report any pilfering, and learn a trade at the same time.

" 'Ulumalu, would you like to learn how to make canoes?"

"Yes, chief."

"I expected you to say 'yes'. But you must know that I intend to release you from being a servant. I want you to be free like the farmers and fishermen. Do you understand?" He nodded. "If you say yes, then I will send you to Makauli's camp and you will live there and make canoes—no more work for me." She looked him in the eye. Still 'yes'?

"Yes, chief."

"I will never know!" she laughed. "No matter—Kaholo and I will keep track of you. If you are not happy, you can work at farming or fishing." 'Ulumalu grinned and Kale nodded.

Isaac was six years old–a tall strong boy with blond curls and pink cheeks whose skin was so fair that he had to wear a small sailor's shirt and cap when he played in the sun. Kale had nursed and weaned him herself. And now that he was old enough to understand, Kale saw to it that Manu circumcised Isaac and taught him the ancient prayers, while she patiently taught little Isaac sharing, cooperation, love for others, and love for 'ohana, as her mother taught her.

"Mama, when is Papa coming to see us?" asked Isaac.

"Not for eight more days. You watch the moon every night and when it is in the shape of an egg, he will come. Do you have something happy to show him?"

"Yes, Mama, come inside and see the lure I made. Papa said he would take Hulu and me in the longboat so we can catch he'e octopus and Keahi helped us make lures."

Kale laughed. "You are just like your Papa with your big plans and surprises." When he gave her the shiny cowrie shell with a bone hook and stone lashed to the bottom, she smiled and looked at Isaac. "My son, this is the most beautiful lure I have ever seen! It is very, very good!"

Isaac was grinning and looking it over as he fidgeted with his hands, "Will Papa like it?"

"Oh yes, he will love it."

"See right here? This is my dog bone hook. And this is the sinker that holds it down near the hole, where the octopus is hiding. And this is my blood-red leho pāuhu shell, so beautiful that the he'e cannot resist. And Mama, this is the place where I will tie tī leaves to make the tail and on this other end is where I will tie my line…and when the octopus wraps itself around my lure I will PULL and hook him!"

Kale giggled. "It is perfect! You will catch a big heʻe with this lure. How will you know when to pull up and hook him?"

"Oh Mama. I will watch him. I will chew some kukui nut and spit it—pchoooo! Right on the water and the water will become flat and so-o clear."

Kale was grinning with pride and nodding her head. "You know more about fishing for octopus than Papa does! He can hold the boat still while you and Hulu do the fishing. And I will show you how to salt and dry your catch."

Isaac was jumping up and down with excitement. "Maybe we will catch two or three, Mama!"

At the window, hidden by banana trees and vines, Makauli silently watched Isaac and Kale giggling, and being so close to her made him tingle. He backed silently away from the window and carefully made his way up through the rows of wauke. Then he darted out to the kula trail and switched back past Kale's kauhale on the path. His heart was beating fast. Today was not as satisfying as when she was alone, asleep. I am the octopus and she is the blood-red lure, thought Makauli.

Kaholo was on his way to Kale's hale. He stopped to talk to Makauli until he saw Kale and Isaac coming out into the pā yard.

"Hui! Kaholo!" sang Kale. "Come and see what Isaac has made."

"What is that boy up to now?" Kaholo said as he strolled into the pā.

"He and Hulu made leho heʻe and Alika promised to take them fishing for octopus."

Isaac proudly handed Kaholo the lure. "Maikaʻi…Good…" Said Kaholo as he inspected the lashings and tested the hook. "I think you will get a big octopus with this one. Very, very good."

"Isaac, put your lure inside and go and tell Auntie Pili that Mama wants her family to come and eat with us tonight."

"He is a good boy," said Kaholo as he watched Isaac scamper up the shady valley trail. "My chief, I had word in Lāhainā that the cattle will be coming soon."

"The cattleman who will rent our land, Pāhaʻaikaua, is a very nice young man. I like him. He is for Honokahua. He came to tell me his plans and has made friends with some of the men already."

"Yes, he is a nice fellow and plenty smart too."

"And handsome too." She laughed. "I am surprised that my jealous husband sends such a handsome one to me! Now you won't be the only one he is jealous of."

Kaholo blushed. "I have never given him any reason to be jealous."

"Nor I. But that is his way. Pili and the family are coming down. Will you stay and eat too?"

"Thank you, my chief. Perhaps we can plan how to keep the cattle in their grazing land and out of the farms."

There was much for which Kale was thankful. In Honolulu, Alika had met Pāhaʻaikaua, a low-rank aliʻi from Molokaʻi, who bought some of Don Marin's cattle when Marin's business failed. Alika suggested he graze them in Honokahua's cleared sandalwood forest land. The cattle would bring in rent and Kaholo would sell cow's milk to the whalers. Pāhaʻa would give Kale calves as rent so Honokahua would eventually have its own herd.

George Humehume's father, King Kaumualiʻi was in poor health after three years of exile with Kaʻahumanu, and he formally ceded Kauaʻi to Liholiho, on the condition that his Kauaʻi chiefs would remain in place as stewards of the land. By May 1824 he was dead and Oʻahu chiefs were eagerly seeking Kauaʻi land from the Kaʻahumanu. While Kaumualiʻi was being buried at Waineʻe Church in Lāhainā, George Humehume's uncles and disgruntled Kauaʻi Chiefs conspired to take back Kauaʻi and install George as King. Peke feared for herself and her infant daughter, Puaonaona, as the threat of violence in Waimea became inevitable.

July 8ᵗʰ, 1824 Honokahua

Dearest Peke,

Fanny is visiting me and writing this letter as I speak it to her. It was good to see you, even if in sad circumstances. We have heard rumors that Kaʻahumanu will give Kauaʻi land to any Oʻahu chiefs she can control. ʻOlohana expects a war. We are concerned for your safety. Please come with little Puaonaona and stay with me until Humehume gets things settled on Kaua'i? Alika spends much more time in Honolulu and I am here in Honokahua like a widow. Yet, he is jealous and worries I will take another husband. I will never understand him.

You asked if I go to church. Since Keopuolani passed, I have not gone to a single meeting in Lahaina. I hope you will still love me if I do not become a Christian.

'Olohana sent us a canoe builder from O'ahu and Alika rented our uplands to a Hawaiian rancher from Moloka'i named Pāha'aikaua, to graze 8 cows and a bull. With so much forest gone there is plenty of room for them and the whalers will buy the milk. I am helping him to get settled. Laura Konia was here last week. She flirted all day with my handsome cattleman and tired me out talking all night of her passion for Pākī, who plays hard-to-get at court. Do you think she will ever marry?

Isaac is a good boy, very curious and busy. Does that sound like anyone you know? He is growing up so fast it breaks my heart. He and Ke'eaumoku's son Hulu are great friends and 'Olohana says when they stand side my side they are a picture of King Kahekili! Isaac often asks for Anakē Peke. Please come soon.

Fanny sends her warmest regards and I my love,

Kale

CHAPTER 8

Courage at the Crossroads

Two days after Fanny went back to Kawaihae, a canoe came into Honokahua Harbor with a lone passenger. 'Ulumalu was the only person who recognized James Kānehoa Young, Kale's first husband. Instead of greeting him, he ran to warn Kale, who went to the beach so she would not have to receive James at her hale.

By the time she got there, Kaholo was talking with James and pointing at Kale's hale up the hill. The handsome dark young man she left seven years ago was now skinny, and his hair was long and greasy. His British-style waistcoat, trousers, and stockings, so fashionable at court, were dirty and they hung from his bony limbs in deep folds. Under a white panama hat, his blotched skin and pale lips gave him a deathly look and Kale's fear dissolved into pity.

"*Aloha e Kānehoa,*" said Kale

"*Aloha iā 'oe, e Kale,*" James said with his hands in his pockets, without an attempt to honi or even look her in the eye.

"Kaholo, this is my stepbrother, James Kānehoa Young. Please make him a place to stay at your kauhale and ask Umuwena and Keahi to prepare an imu for three of us. I will join you later."

"Yes, my chief." She waited and James said nothing for an uncomfortable moment until he realized he was not going to be invited to her hale, and he looked at Kaholo, who said, "Please follow me."

They walked away and a memory of James in an angry stupor, swinging his fists at her head, shot through her mind—followed by a vision of Alika's stern set jaw at the very mention of James' name.

I can afford to be merciful as long as I do not let him near me or my boy, she thought. If James drinks at Honokahua, I will have Kaholo remove him.

When ʻaina ahiahi, dinner was ready, Kale went to Kaholo's kauhale. James had obviously bathed and Kaholo had given him a fresh malo.

"Kale, thank you for receiving m…"

"I did not receive you. I have given a lone traveler food and shelter. I will not receive you unless you tell me why you have come."

"It was the only place I could think of. I have nowhere to go." He looked down.

"You cannot go with the hangers-on at court in Lāhainā?"

"I want to give up the rum."

"Then give it up—I cannot give it up for you!"

"Kale, I cannot do it in Honolulu…may I stay here in Honokahua until I am sober and healthy?"

"No! Alika will not allow it and I will not risk having you get drunk here. I cannot let you stay here."

"I promise I will stay away from you. Just give me a laborer's job and a place to stay. I cannot go home to Kawaihae—at court in Lāhainā and Honolulu I am a disgrace. Please don't turn me away."

Against her best judgment, Kale let James stay for three days until Alika was due home. James' transformation was remarkable and when she sent him off to a small pāhale homestead in Lāhainā that Peke owned, he was smiling. She instructed Kaholo not to mention James' visit to Alika, and Isaac never saw him at all. All mouths kept silent and Alika sailed back to Honolulu never knowing Kale's first husband had been there. The following day James returned to Honokahua and Kale had Manu bless him and treat him with lomilomi and herbal cathartics. James worked in the fields, and, as the time drew near for Alika's return, James was gaining weight and confidence.

When the Kaʻahumanu sailed into Honokahua Bay three days early Kale immediately sent Kaholo to warn James and lead him down to Nāpili on foot. From there, one of Laura's men could paddle him down to Lāhainā. Kaholo ran to his place and removed all evidence of his houseguest while Kale collected Isaac and walked to the beach to greet Alika.

"My love, where is Kaholo?"

"He must be up the hill. We did not expect you for several days. Isaac has been so lonely for his Papa."

"Alika swept the lad up in his arms and Isaac said, "Papa, the man ran away when you came." Kale held her breath.

"What man is that?" Alika looked at Kale and knew immediately that she was lying to him. She looked down. "What man, Kale?" She felt blood run to her face.

"James." Alika's face turned red and his teeth clenched as he scanned the hillside.

"The man who drove you away from Honolulu now comes here and you receive him? Have you gone mad? Where is he?" he snarled.

"He asked to stay at Honokahua to recover from alcohol and I allowed him. He had nowhere to go. When your ship came in, he fled."

"Of course he fled! And you lied to me because you knew I would never allow him to set foot in Honokahua!" She had never seen him like this. His lips were pale with fury. His voice was measured and halting as he held back his full wrath in front of his boy.

"How can I trust you anymore, now that you have lied to me?" Panic froze Kale as she counted the enormous cost of helping James. Her mind went blank. "Is this what you teach our son? To lie?" Kale trembled with remorse.

"Please forgive me..."

"Come Isaac, my lad. You and Papa will have an evening swim and let Mama rest. She has been so busy with the MAN."

Alika spent two days controlling his rage and quizzing everyone he could find about the "man." Finally convinced his wife was still faithful to him, he asked Kale to come for a walk on the beach. She knew better than to start the conversation.

Finally, he said, "Next month King Liholiho and Queen Kamāmalu leave on a voyage to England to see George IV. While they are gone for two years, I will be needed full time at Honolulu Harbor. The Kuhina Nui has commissioned me as pilot of Honolulu Harbor. I will no longer be master of the *Ka'ahumanu*...Kale, I have asked you to come and live with me in Honolulu many times. Now I am permanently stationed there and Ka'ahumanu has given me the Ahupua'a of Niu and acreage in Kalihi to rule. My darling, I beg you to come with me to O'ahu."

Kale just stared at him and tears filled her eyes. She knew this moment would come.

His eyes begged her. "If your answer were yes, you would tell me straight out." A tear dribbled down his cheek too and he looked out to the Bay. "To be given a lofty position like this and kingdom land is everything I worked for—a great honor and this should be the happiest day of my life…but in gaining it, I have lost you, haven't I?" He turned back with an expectant look that quickly faded.

"Just as I lost you years ago…After Isaac was born, when you didn't come to live at Honokahua. My hope returned when the royal court moved to Lāhainā; but you still did not come to live with me…and I knew we would never be together." She was astonished at her calm. "We are alike. You are an important man, and the King needs you in Honolulu. I am chief and my people depend on me to be here. It is not a matter of love, for I love you deeply."

"As I ever will you, my dear." Alika walked away a few paces and Kale sensed he was struggling with what to say next. "I was jealous of James—forgive me. I understand you pity him. I don't think for a moment you can dry him out, but I know you will die trying…is he coming back?"

"I don't know."

"It is your choice to take him in, but if he lays a hand on you, I will kill him—Young or no Young. Do you understand?" He paused and looked down for a moment. "I don't want Isaac around if James gets drunk and violent—the fear of it will make me distraught…please let me take Isaac back to Honolulu." Kale's heart sank.

"Please don't take him, Alika!" she held on to his arm and pleaded. "I cannot bear to lose my baby and my husband. He is your son and you may take him, but please have mercy on me—not now."

He took her hand. "Keep him with you for now, but promise me that you will bring him to me if James returns."

"I promise." He held her in his arms and she remembered the first consoling embrace. She looked at him.

"I know that look," he said. "It is the piercing gaze of your uncanny wisdom. You know me better than I know myself…"

"Do you not long for companionship as I do…someone to be at your side all the time? These years have turned your hair white. I am a friend of loneliness, but separation has been very hard on you."

"Have you taken another husband, Kale?"

"No. I have been faithful to you. Now that you are leaving, I will allow myself to look at other men. Please take another wife in Honolulu. It is not good for either one of us to be alone."

"Oh God, I pity the girl. I have given my heart away twice and there is little left to give."

Kale smoothed his hair. "How did you say it? 'There are many fish in the sea and you are wonderful bait'—especially now that you rule Niu." His broad smile flashed but his eyes were sad.

"Isaac is fearless like you, Kale. It is a gift."

"And he is a picture of you. If you ever regret these seven years, just look at him."

They strolled back to the hale, and, when they peeked in, Isaac was fast asleep, stretched out on the sleeping mats with arms flung wide, golden locks framing his pink-cheeked, peaceful, innocent face.

"Kale, you have raised him well with little help from me."

"He is a good boy and clever. He is keen on athletics like my father, and he works unselfishly at his chores. He casts a net as well as boys twice his age and he has a kind heart like you. The kids here tease him because of his white skin, but he never holds a grudge. I have taught him nearly all I can." She began to weep. "I have so many dreams for him...and he wants to be like you. You are right. He needs to be with you now, to learn how to read and write...and how to be a man...Alika, if you take him with you, you won't let him forget his mother, will you?—" She burst into tears and he held her tight.

"Neither Isaac nor I will ever forget you...if it were not for Honokahua..." Kale looked up at Alika and he stopped. It was a stalemate, and they both knew it.

Kale touched his cheek. "Please let us not fight when it may be our last night together."

"It would be easier for me to fight than to face the final parting. But I do want you to remember me with fondness." Alika looked at Isaac. "Kale, just think how surprised he will be when he enters Foreign Mission School and sees all the other haole children."

Kale smiled. "It is a good thought. He will not be alone...will you take Isaac fishing for octopus before you leave? I want to see his face when he shows me his catch..." She wept again. "Please hold me. I need to not be alone tonight."

Kale missed her boy and regretted her circumstances, but filled her days helping Pāha'aikaua settle at Honokahua and enjoying the company of someone her own age and rank. In the evenings she sat with U'i or Pili and in the daytime she prayed with Manu and worked with Kaholo. Pāha'a was from Kalama'ula, Moloka'i and his large family had Maui roots. His deep bronze skin reminded her of Ka'oana'eha and his facial features were so fine

Kale thought he must look like his mother; but his big frame was strong and muscular, with broad shoulders and perfectly proportioned arms and legs like the old warriors. His playful disposition and dimpled grin lifted Kale's spirits. Pāhaʻa gave tools, hogs, and chickens to all the Honokahua farmers with land abutting his pasture. In return, on appointed days, they cooperatively built a stone wall across the kualono broad plains between Honokahua and Moku Peʻa valleys to contain his herd in the uplands. It offered the extra benefit of keeping wild hogs out of their sweet potato patches, and, when the fence was completed, Pāhaʻa held a huge lūʻau to celebrate the farmers' fine work and released his cattle to graze.

Under clear skies on Akua night in March, when the moon is full and lights the land, Kale could not sleep. She was thinking about Isaac and listening to swishing banana leaves twirling in the breeze and the rhythmic pounding of small waves on Honokahua Beach. Holding her breath, she listened between the waves for the sounds of koholā, the humpbacked whales; Soon she heard a loud double thud—and another. Koholā were slapping the face of the water. Kale grabbed her kīhei and pāʻū and walked down the beach path. In the intense moonlight, Molokaʻi's saddleback topped with a single cloud looked close enough to touch. Up Kahua Hill behind her, every kukui tree reflected pale gray moonlight and the streams sparkled.

Three koholā played close to the beach and one continued to slap the sea. First his huge black shining tail arched into the air and uncurled. When the monster contracted his belly and pulled his tail down hard, foam sprayed high into the air and a loud pa-poom echoed up the kula. Kale decided to walk out Hāwea Point to get a better view. Halfway out the north side of the point a muffled moan made her stop. She did not see anyone, but heard it again—the eerie sound of a tiny blowhole, expelling air whenever a wave filled the underwater cave below. Kale knew blowholes and underwater caves where sharks live are very dangerous, so she ran ahead few paces. When she looked up again, a strange old man stood in front of her and a startled cry escaped her lips before she could control it. "*E kala mai iaʻu, e makua. ʻO Kale, ke Aliʻi Wahine o Honokahua.* Excuse me, elder. I am Kale, Chiefess of Honokahua."

The elder wore a simple malo and kīhei, and he leaned his huge frame on a walking stick. His long gray hair and beard shined in the moonlight.

"*Mai hoʻokolo aku ʻoe, e Kale. He kaha luʻu ke ala o kēia pali.* Don't run there, Kale. That path goes to this cliff's diving place.

" *Mahalo, ku'u kupunakāne. 'O wai kou inoa?* Thank you, dear grandfather. What is your name?" asked Kale

" *'O Hewahewa kēia.* My name is Hewahewa." Kale froze. She had seen the great high priest of Kamehameha only once, when the kapu gods were burned, and she knew about his powerful mana. He laughed at her reaction. "*E weliweli 'oe i ko'u inoa?* So you are frightened by my name?" She did not answer. "Do not be afraid. I know about you, too. I had great respect for your father and I know you are a righteous chief." His countenance and words were not fearsome, but kind.

"I am sorry if I have trespassed on your land," said Kale. "I do not allow my people to disturb you and I have broken my own kapu. Please forgive my presence here. I only came to see the whales."

"Since you have come this far, let me show you my favorite place to watch koholā. Come. I cannot sleep either."

Kale laughed. "The full moon always wakes me up."

He led her to a flat overlooking a place where the surge of the Pailolo Channel spills into Hāwea's tide pools. Out of habit she turned and looked for 'Ulumalu, but remembered she was alone. Hewahewa sat on a rock. "Sit down and tell me your story." Kale sat on another rock and began a short version of her life story, hoping Hewahewa would do the same. "I have often thought to go over to Honokahua to meet you, and now my god brings you to me. You know I am kahu of the 'iwi at Honokahua?"

"Yes. We do not plant near the gravesites. If we find any bones in the dunes, my people know to bury them where we found them. Manu prays over each burial."

"Good. When I am gone, you will be kahu of the ancestors' bones."

"How can I serve as kahu? I am not a kahuna."

He laughed. "Neither am I." *What is he saying? He is the Kahuna Nui!*

"You call me 'Kahuna'. I am expert in the rituals of Kū, Kāne, Kanaloa, and Lono, but I have no mana." *Is he mad with fever or is this a riddle for me to solve?* Kale's mind began to run as she listened intently. "I have known for many years that these gods were just stone and wood barriers set up by ruling chiefs and priests to keep commoners under their control. My only answered prayers were those I prayed to 'Io and I believe he is the only real god in heaven." Kale was dumbstruck. Seeing her puzzled look he asked, "Do you think it is by chance that we meet tonight?"

"No," said Kale. "My life is in the hands of my gods."

"You speak correctly, as you have been taught. But, if that is so, what do your gods accomplish by allowing you to hear Hewahewa, their highest kahuna, defile himself and blaspheme them?" Kale did not answer. "What I tell you tonight I was telling Kamehameha and his priests for years and still I am standing here, unpunished."

"Why do you say you are not a kahuna?"

"If the gods are not real, then their priests are not real. This is why I counseled Liholiho to abolish the kapu and the gods of the kapu."

After a moment, Kale said, "Beloved Kahu, we still keep the rituals at Honokahua," said Kale. I made an oath to Keopuolani to keep the old ways. Do you say I do wrong?"

"There is no harm in it as long as you know the truth and do not punish your people harshly when they break the kapu. But why waste your time praying to gods who do not answer; better to pray to the god who does. I counsel you for the protection of the sacred gravesite of Honokahua and for the good of your people. Send Manu to me and I will teach him about 'Io, the god worshipped here before my ancestor Pā'ao came from Tahiti."

"Hū!" cried Kale as a long shooting star grazed the summit of Moloka'i. Hewahewa laughed. "It is a sign. Righteousness is served and now you will sleep well. And I tell you—do not delay to take a new husband." Before she could ask him whom she was supposed to take for a husband, Hewahewa pulled himself up on his staff and the encounter was over. She watched him slowly walk down to his camp at Kapalua Bay; she sat a while longer, watching the waves and pondering all that he said.

"*E Ali'iwahine! Ua mākaukau 'oe?* O Chief, are you ready?" Pāha'aikaua's deep resonant voice softly called from outside Kale's hale. It was first light, but Kale was dressed. She picked up a water gourd, slung it on her shoulder, and stepped outside. Pāha'a carried a net bag on his shoulder and a lei ali'i of tī leaves to ward off evil spirits in the uplands. He handed Kale a similar lei. "*E mālama 'ia māua ma nā waonahele āpau.* May we be protected in all the forests."

"'Āmama, Let it be so," answered Kale.

Pāha'a smiled and started up the kula trail and Kale followed. "*Pehea ku'u Ali'i Wahine i kēia kakahiaka?* How is the beloved chiefess this morning?"

"*Māluhiluhi paha au, akā hau'oli e hele holoholo aku me ka'u kahu pipi. 'Auhea ka wahi i hele ai?* I am a little tired but happy to go exploring with my rancher. Where are we going?"

"I told you it is a surprise. But it is a long way—are you sure you want to come?"

"How long do you say?"

"To the top of the pasture and the edge of the high forest. It would be easier if we had horses, but if you can keep up with my pace, we will be there before awakea." Kale could not see his face, but she could hear a smile in his voice.

"You will be panting before I will," said Kale, and Pāha'a laughed.

"I am panting already. Do you think I am tired?"

Kale laughed. "*E kolohe 'oe!* You rascal! I cannot say yes and I will not say no!"

"Then I will tell you. My heart pants for Honokahua." Kale found herself disappointed he did not say he panted for her.

There was a long time of silence as they passed above the wet basin of Honokahua Valley and the last kualapa ridge homestead. Then Pāha'a said, "Now there is no one to hear me but you. I pant for Honokahua and for you." He did not stop walking or turn around. Kale's heart beat harder and she blushed, but said nothing.

As they passed U'i and Limaha'i's homestead on the edge of the low forest, long rays of sunshine cut the summits of Eke and separated Honokahua's misty hills into blue shadows and yellow blotches of dewy vegetation, and the hard-packed red clay earth under their feet was slick and oily. When they stopped to rest, Honokahua Bay had become a small scooped-out section of an arched Kā'anapali coast, punctuated as far north as Kale could see with black cliffs stretching out into an azure sea. Pāha'a squatted down to rest. Kale drank from her water gourd, offered it to Pāha'a and sat down on a fallen tree.

"Have you ever drunk rum?" she asked.

"Once. It made me sick. It is not good for me—or for the Hawaiian people. It is a curse the haole bring to us. I take 'awa for the gods, but not for me. Why do you ask?"

"I have a stepbrother who is a drunkard; that is all. I do not want any drunkards at Honokahua. Do you mean to make Honokahua your permanent home?"

"For now, yes. My 'ohana is large and there are plenty of brothers and cousins to manage the Moloka'i land. It will take a few years to grow this herd; If I am successful, perhaps the queen will give me some land to rule."

At least he loves the land and not the sea. They continued uphill through the forest where kupukupu ferns formed a feathery green blanket under the black lama and 'ōhi'a 'ai mountain apple trees. Kale grew tired but focused on Pāha'a, his black wavy hair hanging down the broad back, his easy gait, and the sound of his feet on the path. They passed fourteen other homes in the low forest before reaching open grasslands where Pāha'a's herd was lying down. At their approach, the cattle raised themselves up, ready to flee, but when they recognized Pāha'a's voice they anxiously stood their ground, looking at Kale and Pāha'a, flicking their tails and twitching their ears. He threw some salt on the grass and patted several cows on the ears and nose, calling them by name. Kale stood back and watched the big brown animals maneuver into a small tight herd around the salt, lapping it up completely and then licking their noses clean.

"They are beautiful animals," said Kale.

"Yes, they fit well in beautiful Honokahua with her beautiful chief," said Pāha'a

Kale rolled her eyes and lifted one eyebrow. "You think to flatter me into buying you a horse?"

"Auwē! May I not compliment you in truth?" His eyes smiled and Kale put her head back and giggled like a little girl.

"I will give you a horse—not because you flatter me, but because you convince me that this is too far to walk every day. I cannot believe the sandalwood men never complained. They must be stronger than ranchers." She grinned at him. He cocked his ear toward her, and his dimples gave away the grin he held back.

"Did I hear you say stronger? We ranchers are thinkers, not sweaters. The odor of those sandalwood men still lingers, do you smell it?"

"I can smell those cows!" Kale giggled again. "How do you stand it?" She turned to walk away.

"—watch out!" Before she could react, Kale's left foot was ankle-deep in manure.

"Tschaa!" she yelled and as she pulled back, the gooey pile released her foot with a loud sucking noise. Pāha'a tried to contain himself, but burst out laughing. His big grin showed his pearly teeth, curled dimples into his cheeks, and made his eyes smile. Kale laughed at herself for the first time since Alika and Isaac left. "When it comes up through the toes, it is like the bottom of a kalo patch on a hot day!" cried Kale as she rubbed her foot across the grass. She could hardly get her breath. "*E Pāha'a—hō'ike 'oe ia'u i ke kula holoholona, ā nā pipi. 'Anō, hō'ike ia'u pehea e ho'oma'ema'e ai i ke kūkae pipi mai ko'u wāwae!* Hey

Pāhaʻa—you show me the pasture and the cows; now show me how to clean dung off my foot!"

"There is a small stream just over that hill. Come follow me and watch where you walk." Kale sat down on the bank of the kahawai stream and dangled her feet in the cold water while Pāhaʻa stood in the water and gently bathed her feet until all the manure was gone. Kale enjoyed the gentle strokes of his big hands carefully rubbing her feet as if he were washing a baby. She admired the deep rich color of his skin next to hers and without thinking; she pushed his shiny black wavy hair out of his face.

He looked up, slowly taking in all her features, and Kale sucked in her breath as their eyes connected…"*Ua maeʻmaʻe ka wawae.* The foot is clean," he said and the tension broke. Pāhaʻa pulled himself up on the bank, offered Kale his hand, and pulled her up but did not let go of her hand. Her breath rose in her chest when she looked up into his dark brown eyes, expecting him to kiss her. Instead, he said very seriously, "If you think I brought you up here to ask you for a horse, you are mistaken." Kale blinked. *What? Is he offended by my teasing?* He led her by the hand into the pasture. "Oh No!" he yelled up the mountain. "I brought you up here for a cow!" Pāhaʻa was gleeful as he led Kale under a large ʻōhiʻa tree where a lone cow lay on her side, lowing. He began whispering. "We are going to attend the birth of the first Honokahua cow!"

Between the cow's legs was a tiny nose and hoofs covered with a pale membrane, and the cow lifted her head to look at her calf just starting to drop. It is a precious moment for a rancher when his herd increases and Pāhaʻa was excited. In a short while the calf was born, the mother licked it free of its membrane and gently nudged it to stand up on spindly, wobbly legs. The female calf, a beautiful image of the mother, suckled at her mother's great udder.

"It is a good birth and the calf is healthy. Will you name her?"

Kale thought for a minute. " *ʻO Hamowaipahē kona inoa*," said Kale. It had a double meaning "courteous flattery" or "gentle stroking," commemorating their teasing conversation and Pāhaʻa's washing of her feet.

"Good, good, good!" Pāhaʻa petted the mother. "Have you ever seen such teats on an animal? After the calf is weaned she will continue to produce milk like a wet nurse—as long as I harvest the milk—for three years!"

"It is wonderful," said Kale. "The whalers desire cow's milk. How do you take the milk?"

He petted the cow and spoke gently to her as he squatted by the udder and gently took a teat and kneaded out a squirt of milk. The cow did not seem to be disturbed. Kale tiptoed over to get a better look and squatted by Pāhaʻa. He squeezed again. Then he aimed the teat at Kale and squirted warm milk in her face. She cried out, sputtered, and jumped back. Pāhaʻa patted the cow to steady her and laughed.

"Can you imagine haoles desire cow's milk?" he said.

"No. It is most disgusting! Now you have to wash me again." He poured some water from his water gourd into Kale's hands; she splashed her face, and smoothed her hair.

"Your face shines pale like the moon…" said Pāhaʻa. When she looked up he placed an ʻōhiʻa lehua lei on her neck and pulled her head close. They exhaled and breathed deeply. He whispered, "I desire your breath in me." Kale tingled with excitement. He exhaled very deeply again and she followed him until all her breath was gone and then they inhaled deeply again, but he did not embrace her. Instead, he held her shoulders and said, "If you think I brought you here for a cow, I have misled you."

What is he doing? She sighed and watched him open his net bag. Pāhaʻa pulled a lauhala mat out of his net sack, spread it out under the tree, opened up tī leaf wrapped baked sweet potatoes and a small calabash of fresh salted ʻopihi.

"I brought you up here for lunch!" he announced. Kale shook her head, sat down and smiled. She was hungry.

From the pasture, Honokahua fishing village was not even visible. Beyond the broad green slopes stretched the deep blue Pailolo Channel and three islands: Molokaʻi, Lanaʻi, and Kahoʻolawe. Pāhaʻa chatted about his family until Kale leaned back against the tree. He knelt beside her and, touching her thigh, said, "If you thought I brought you up here for lunch, I have misled you."

Kale removed his hand. "You tire me out with these riddles. Why <u>did</u> you bring me up here?"

His expectant look collapsed and she thought he would cry. "I have planned this day for so long…how I would impress you and make you desire me…but in your presence I am awkward…for fear you will reject my love."

Kale smiled. *How innocent—he jokes to hide a trembling heart.* "How can I reject what is not offered? Did you dream that with a wink and a smile I would throw myself at you like a silly young girl?"

"No…I prayed to my god for restraint—to do nothing to offend you, and for wisdom—to speak the perfect words to touch your heart." *I am touched but you must make your move.*

" 'Āmama, Let it be so." whispered Kale. She pushed his hair back, looked at his beautiful face, and prayed too. *'Io, if you are a true god and this union is righteous, give him the words.* Her heart pounded with expectation and she searched his dark brown eyes and full lips.

Pāha'a's eyes began to gleam and he said, "A farmer picks up the soft wood of his digging stick, and loosens the moist earth and plants his seed..." Kale smiled. She knew he spoke of making love. Now the supple smooth skin of his chest was full of tiny bumps and she knew the poetry of his own words was thrilling his heart. He ran his hand over her thigh and she did not remove it. "And a fisherman follows his fish to the hook hidden in the deepest ko'a fishing hole..." She closed her eyes and her thoughts floated on his words like leaves in a whirlwind. He drew her close, kissed her neck and throat, and whispered, "But a rancher climbs the mountain, wary of every danger. He denies himself until he is sure his cattle are safe and fed. Then he searches out the place where the sweet grass is deep and moist and finding the spring hole, he drinks deeply." A tingling sensation swept through Kale's body from the crown of her head to her toes and she thrilled to his every advance.

At the edge of the meadow, behind a tree just twenty paces away, Makauli, the canoe builder watched Pāha'a and Kale. It was not the first time he watched Kale. Whenever 'Ulumalu was busy up in the forest, Makauli went down to the village to spy on her, but today she came to his woods and this idea excited him. *She does not know I want her.* She would know, but there were some people in the way, some obstacles. *I will get them out of the way. She does not love this boy. He makes her a shame, a prostitute.* Maka was aroused thinking of Kale and he breathed hard against the bark of the tree and pressed himself into it as he would her.

He watched Pāha'a gently explore Kale. *That is not what she wants. I will press the full measure of her flesh—squeeze, pull, stretch...*

He watched Pāha'a make love to Kale. *I will not hold back. I will thrust into her until she cries out in pain, in pain, in pain—*

Maka was suspended in silent climax, chafing his thighs and belly against the koa tree trunk and rubbing moss and bark into the sweat running from his face and down his arms. He shuddered and breathed out. A twig cracked behind him and he turned to see 'Ulumalu, frozen with disbelief and fear. Without a word, Maka wearily shook his head, rubbed the sweat out of his eyes, picked up his adze and motioned to 'Ulumalu to return to camp. 'Ulumalu hesitated as if he would run away, but as always, he followed instruction.

"Did you hear that cracking noise?" asked Pāha'a.

Kale smiled. "It's just a hog or 'Ulumalu. He was my servant before I released him to apprentice with the canoe builder. They have a camp nearby. If 'Ulumalu saw us here he would stand in the forest and guard us—he is so accustomed to guarding me that he does it without thought." Kale kissed him again.

Pāha'a flashed his dimpled grin, pulled Kale on top of him, and held her tight. "I'm going to hold you until the stars come out. Shall we stay here until morning?" It was a proposal of marriage.

"Kaholo will find me missing and cause a terrible stir in the village. We have to go." Pāha'a rolled to his side and got on his knees. He looked disappointed. Kale asked, "Why are you sad?"

"Kale, this is not a passing desire for me. I want to stay with you forever."

She touched his face. "Do you love me?"

"Yes." He had a tear in his eye. "I have never known love before and if you turn me away my heart will choke with grief."

"You have captured my heart. Take me down to my hale and stay with me until the sun shines on us tomorrow and I will take you for my husband." Pāha'a closed his eyes, breathed deeply, and sighed.

"I love you," he whispered as he kissed her. Then his dimpled grin appeared and he said louder, "I love you!" Kale giggled and he jumped up. Pulling her up and containing her with his big arms he leaned his head back and yelled from the bottom of his lungs, "I LOVE YOU!" and Honokahua Valley echoed back his deep voice—"love you!"

By the time Kale and Pāha'a returned to Honokahua the warm kona winds of morning turned strong and swirling, carrying the smell of the land. Dogs were barking and hogs running around and grunting in anticipation of a storm. The air was thick with Kilauea's ash; sea spray and imposing triangle-shaped banks of dark gray clouds poured over the top of Pu'u Kukui, making Honokahua dark. Waves thrashed the points, chop on Honokahua Bay was backwards, and sideways swells of a kona storm broke waves in odd places. As fishermen pulled up their canoes into the longhouses, terns floated overhead in the updrafts and whistling winds sneaked up the valley, bending kukui limbs and exposing the matte undersides of shiny-fingered 'ulu leaves.

When the rain came, it was black and heavy, a *pe'e pōhaku* "hide behind rock" rain of Kā'anapali. Pāha'a and Kale pulled off their kapa and let the dense rain bathe their bodies. Back inside Kale's cozy hale, they dried off and explored the treasures of their spiritual and physical union with a freedom Kale had never known.

The kona storm whistled and beat Honokahua all night. Early in the morning it was still raining hard when Kale heard sloshing footsteps approaching her hale. It was Kaholo and Maunahina. Their faces were grim.

"*E ku'u Ali'i Wahine, hele mai 'oe wikiwiki!* Chief, come quickly!"

"*He aha kō 'oulua pilikia?* What is the trouble?"

"*Ua loa'a iā mākou ke kupapa'u o 'Ulumalu i lalo o Makāluapuna.* We found the corpse of 'Ulumalu at Makāluapuna."

"*Uwēē!*" Kale screamed and collapsed. Pāha'a caught her.

"What do you want me to do?" he asked.

"*Uwēē*...tell the men to run and get Manu! Find out who touched the corpse and send him to Manu, but do not let him touch any one else or anyone in his 'ohana until Manu cleanses and frees him. Manu will give the men instructions. Please, my husband, stay with me."

Pāha'a did exactly as Kale wished, returned to her side, and mourned with her. Pili and U'i came to weep with her.

Manu sent word with Kaholo that 'Ulumalu's body was being prepared for burial, and he was postponing the interment and funeral offering until the storm passed.

"What happened to him?" asked Kale.

"His skull was broken. Makāluapuna is a very dangerous place in high seas. Many people drowned there over the years. When a surge washes a man off this point, the waves beat him dead against the rocks."

"He was like a brother to me. I will miss him the rest of my days. I declare this point kapu to everyone except the fishermen. Go and tell everyone."

Manu buried 'Ulumalu with the kūpuna of Honokahua in the sacred burial ground. Kale wept for many days and news of the drowning spread all through Kā'anapali and Lāhainā. Slowly Kale released him from her mind and began to think of him in the spirit world, at rest.

Pāha'a took care of Kale and thanked his god every day for his wife and his herd. Kale finally told Pāha'a about her meeting with Hewahewa and asked Pāha'a if he knew about 'Io, the god of Hawai'i nei before Pā'ao.

"On Moloka'i, where the priesthood of 'Io survived, we do not dare to speak this god's name at all. There was a time when to speak his name meant certain execution by the priests of Pā'ao. Now that the gods of Pā'ao and their kapu are gone, I suppose there is no harm. My 'ohana prays only to 'Io; but I never told anyone this before."

Kale was amazed. "Hewahewa knew! He told me to take a husband quickly because he knew you would soon woo me. "You are a gift to me from 'Io."

"No, you are the gift—I am an offering." He smiled and kissed her fingertips and for the first time since 'Ulumalu died, she responded to her fine-looking gentle husband. With him, she returned to the comfort of her mother tongue and the relaxed freedom she knew as a girl. Pāha'a was at her side every evening and she grew confident in the depth of his love, not said in words, but demonstrated in unrestrained devotion.

One gnawing feeling preyed on Kale's mind. She still imagined 'Ulumalu waiting in the dark, watching her.

CHAPTER 9

Good Waterspout of Heaven

Kale was 27 and happily married to Pāhaʻa. She and Kaholo continued to improve the lot of Honokahua farmers by converting sweet potato kula to Irish potato fields, planting gardens of French beans that were in great demand at Lāhainā Roads, and timing their crops to ripen during the two seasons each year when whalers took on provisions, spring and fall.

Queen Kaʻahumanu chose James Kānehoa Young, to accompany King Liholiho and Queen Kamāmalu on a voyage to London, acting as interpreter for negotiations to bring the Hawaiian Kingdom under the protection of Britain. The expedition would take two years.

Kale's sister Peke's first son died shortly after birth, and her second son, in the ancient tradition of Hawaiian royalty, was given to Chief Niʻau of Kauaʻi to raise. When a daughter, Puaonaona was born, Peke insisted on keeping her. Ever since Kaʻahumanu kidnapped George Humehume's father, King Kaumualiʻi, she kept him close by her side in Lāhainā and he grew steadily frail. On May 26th 1824 King Kaumualiʻi died, and Kauaʻi mourned him by scarring their bodies and abandoning all constraints. Commoners plundered farms and fishponds and violence erupted.

While King Liholiho's court buried Kaumualiʻi "at the feet of Keopuolani" in Lāhainā, Prime Minister Kalanimoku sailed to Kauaʻi to proclaim that no ruling chiefs of Kauaʻi would be replaced; but Hawaiʻi chiefs were already in Waimea, vying for Kauaʻi land. An eclipse of the sun seemed a sign of impending disaster to grief-ridden Kauaʻi chiefs fearful of losing their lands and in desperation they attempted to take the Fort at Waimea. They found it held by Hawai'i chiefs, who fought them off and killed several chiefs including Chief Ni'au.

When news of a revolt on Kaua'i came to Ka'ahumanu in Lāhainā, she charged Hoapili, Governor of Maui, to command Maui and O'ahu cohorts in a swift attack to crush the rebels. 'Olohana was too old to fight, but he counseled Hoapili on the mission and pleaded mercy for Peke and George. War canoes and tall ships with cannon sailed for Kaua'i in early July and Kale could only pray that her sister's family might be spared.

In late July Kaholo returned from his weekly trading trip to Lāhainā and Kale heard the answer to her prayer: "*Ke ho'i mai nei nā koa mai Kaua'i!* The warriors are returning from Kaua'i!" yelled Kaholo. *Ola kou kaikamahine a me kāna kāne!* Your sister and her husband live!"

"*Paulele ke aloha o 'Io.* Faithful is the mercy of 'Io," said Kale as she helped pull up his canoe up the beach. "*Ua 'ike 'oe iā lāua?* Did you see them?"

" *'A'ole i 'ike iā lāua. 'Akā, Ua ha'i ho'okahi koa ia'u, e hele a'e ana lāua i Lāhainā mai Kaua'i i ka lā 'apōpō.* I did not see them but one of the soldiers said they will arrive in Lāhainā tomorrow."

"*Nolaila e hoe wa'a ana'oe i Lāhainā me ia'u i ke kakahiaka 'apōpō!* Then you will paddle to Lāhainā with me tomorrow morning!" As they walked up to Kale's hale, Kaholo told Kale all the news from Lāhainā, including his sale of three more canoes.

"I have not seen Makauli since you left. Do you still think he fits in at Honokahua?" asked Kale.

"His work is good. He finished three canoes last month and now he is cutting trees for three more. Perhaps this is why you did not see him."

"Perhaps…How does he get along with the lawai'a fishermen?"

"No problems, my chief; he keeps to himself."

"I don't like the way he stares at me—what do the women say?"

"They are afraid of him. They say his 'aumakua is a man-eating shark." Kale shuddered.

"One thing, there is a dispute between him and Limaha'i that you must settle."

"Bring them both to my pā yard and I will hear them out."

In the afternoon Limaha'i came down with two neighbors as witnesses and Makauli showed up alone. Manu began the judgment by praying for ka mikimiki "free talk" and ka pono "righteousness." Kale affirmed the prayer and Limaha'i began by saying one of three white pigs in his pen disappeared the same day his neighbors saw Makauli near the pen. They claimed Makauli stole the hog, but when they went to his camp, they found no hog.

Makauli stood silent for some time. He always looked out from under his brow as if painfully shy, and Kale thought his face would be pleasant except for the semicircular scars on his cheeks, the marks of mourning. Geometric tattoo patterns covered nearly all his body, even his chin and tongue. He calmly said he never stole any hog, nor did he take any hog up to his camp. Kale intently scrutinized and questioned both parties, but neither side backed down, so Kale called for a calabash of truth.

Each man took his turn holding his hands over the water. When Makauli's hands passed over the water, ripples broke on the surface, indicating he lied. Staring at the ripples Maka calmly said, "I did not steal his hog."

Then an idea came to Kale. "So you did not steal; but did you kill Limaha'i's hog?"

"Yes," he said. The farmers were astonished at the admission.

"If you did not steal it, what did you do with it after you killed it?" she asked.

"I watched the other hogs eat it."

"Why did you kill the hog?"

Maka's gaze slowly rose to meet to Kale's. "I wanted to hear it squeal." Evil and fear hit her with a chill and immediately turned to loathing. She scowled back but Maka did not look away. As the farmers watched the confrontation, they gripped their digging sticks. Kale immediately stood up to deliver her judgment and quell the growing tension.

"What Maka has done is hewa, wrong. We do not torture our animals at Honokahua, nor do we sacrifice our precious livestock for evil sport. This is my judgment: These animals have tasted flesh of their kin and may now attack other hogs. Therefore, Kamanu will offer the two remaining hogs to Lono to atone for this hewa sin. Makauli will repay Limaha'i with enough goods to trade for three new white hogs, each an arm span in length. It is finished." Without a word, Maka walked up the mountain path, leaving the farmers talking among themselves. Kale went straight to Kaholo's hale.

"I want to know this man's background! He is not for Honokahua, but this is not reason enough to banish him. 'Olohana surely made a mistake sending him here. Please go to O'ahu tomorrow and find someone who knows him or his family. If he is hehena insane, I will turn him over to Ke'eaumoku. Assign one of your men to keep an eye on Makauli and warn the farmers and fishing families not to let him on their property without questioning his intentions. I do not like this man."

The next day Kale went as far as Lāhainā with Kaholo and Lahela, fisherman Shaw's wife, to see Peke and Humehume. Kaholo sailed on to Honolulu on the *Pōlua*. Outside the King's court Kale spotted red haired Peke in a handsome orange cloth pā'ū and Humehume in a waistcoat, pantaloons and stockings like a true Kamehameha courtier.

"I see Ka'ahumanu is treating you well," called Kale

Peke ran and hugged her and shared honi. As she did she whispered, "Please walk with me. I need to talk to you."

Under the 'ulu trees and out of earshot, Kale asked, "O Peke, I have been so worried about you. Are you and little Puaonaona all right?"

"Those drunkards got George involved in a coup to take back Kaua'i. imagine a band of farmers with clubs and spears against ten shiploads of Kamehameha's Battalions—it was disaster! Hoapili and Kalanimoku showed mercy and nobody fell in the skirmish at the Fort, but the greedy Hawai'i chiefs saw opportunity to kill off some of our ruling chiefs and take our land. They hunted down and killed the Nāpali chiefs and their women and children, leaving the corpses for pigs and vultures. We escaped on horseback to the Kalalau mountains with Puaonaona. "Kale, we nearly died in the mountains by the time amnesty was declared, and we are still sick from the ordeal." She held Kale's hand and wept, keeping her back to the palace so no one could see her distress.

Kale's heart broke for her. "Peke, what may I do to help?"

"Kale, we are prisoners! We will never be let go from this place. Ka'ahumanu named my daughter 'Wahinekipi', 'rebel woman', and now my sweet Puaonaona will carry our shame her whole life. I wish I had died on Kaua'i!"

"Oh no Peke! It is good you are alive. You do not know what may happen tomorrow. Remember how Papa endured so much…"

"—and they killed him!"

"Yes…but he survives in us. And he survives in little Pua too. You must tell her about him and about all the good things her grandfather, King Kaumuali'i did for Kaua'i."

"Kale, I begged them to let me to come to Honokahua but Ka'ahumanu would not allow it."

"I will come to you. Your husband needs you with him and Pua needs you too. There is a new school here and Pua will learn to read and write. Some good will come of it. You will see."

Kale faithfully went to Lāhainā every week to visit Peke, and soon Peke accepted her confinement and found great solace in Reverend Richard's sermons at Waine'e Church. Queen Ka'ahumanu went to the services too, but Peke suspected she came to keep an eye on her.

The weather was unusually cool for late August and a storm came in from the northeast with little rain, but with seven days of high winds and large swells breaking and pounding on the reef and filling Honokahua Bay with breakwater and 'ehukai salt spray. Everything at Honokahua was tied down or inside for the night and Kale anxiously waited for Pāha'a, who was unusually late returning from the high pasture. When the wind died for a moment, she thought she heard his horse on the path, but the clip-clopping stopped and her husband did not come. Honokahua winds will trick the most careful listener by making sounds miles away sound close, so she looked for him from the door; and in the dark, out of the corner of her eye, she thought someone moved.

"*Hui! Aia kā'u kāne ma'ō?* Hello! Is that my husband there?" No response. Kale watched but did not see anything but blowing trees and shrubs. It is the wind playing tricks, she thought, and she went back inside. Then she heard footsteps. "Pāha'a!" she called and went to the door. She halted and gasped. Standing in front of her in the gale was a tattooed figure, Makauli.

He stared at her as he did at the judgment and calmly said, "*Ua loa'a ia'u kāu kāne i ka waonahele. Ua make 'o ia.* I found your husband in the woods. He is dead."

"Uwēēē!" Kale screamed. The room seemed to close in on her. Her knees buckled and she held the doorpost for support, crying " 'Ā'ole! 'Ā'ole! No! No!"

Maka could not have wished for more. She wailed and cried in exquisite pain and the thrill overtook him. He grabbed her, hugged her tightly, pinning her arms to her sides and pushed her up against the wall of her hut. Her wet shrieking face pressed against his chest. "Yes, Yes!" he whispered and panted as he pulled her body up the wall, crushed her back against the cross-latched rods, and forced himself into her. He dug his fingers into the flesh of her buttocks and let her hands go free—and she followed his lead, hitting and scratching as he rammed and pounded her into the wall. He pressed his head into her collarbone and neck until her clutching gasps rang in his ears. Then she stopped fighting. *You need a rest.* He threw her down on the matted floor. Blood ran from the gashes on her back. Kale caught her breath and let out a whimper as she tried to crawl away. But Maka pulled her head back by the hair and she screamed in anger. He mounted her and shouted, " *'Alalā! 'Alalā mai noʻu!* Cry! Cry for me!" He climaxed and fell limp on her, pinning her to the ground. "I love your pain," he whispered in her ear. Then Maka was suddenly calm again. He stood up. "Get up," he said calmly. Then he pulled her up and threw her a piece of kapa. "Gird yourself. You are too good to kill. Come, I want to show you your boy husband."

Kale was at the backdoor of fear, where emotion dies and consciousness looks through a cool dark veil that softens the light of right now…and 'I am' becomes 'it is'; when the heart beat slows and time stretches out, bending back on itself. She focused on one thing: *I will not cry.*

Maka covered her back with the kapa, pulled her outside, and told her to get up on Pāhaʻa's horse. Like a kauwā outcast, she got on the horse and when, in the corner of her gaze she saw blood running down her bruised leg, she just gripped the saddle horn and stared straight ahead. Maka jumped up behind her, took the reins, and started the horse up the mountain path. "Do not cry out for your friends," he said quietly. "If they get in my way, I will kill them as I killed ʻUlumalu and your boy husband." Kale heard, but she could not find her feelings.

Don't cry.

The gale howled and blew the tree limbs together so hard that sparks flew in the darkness. When they had gone a short distance Maka pulled up the horse and got down to relieve himself. Kale kicked the horse hard, and when he bolted, the reins slipped out of Maka's hands. As she galloped the horse up the trail, she heard Maka running behind, laughing and yelling, "I will find you! You will cry for me when I find you!" Up, up the trail she beat the horse, straight into Maka's forest. *The hideaway!* Honokahua valley was below her on the left and she knew if she could get down to the valley, she could find the way to her hideaway. Kale slipped off the horse and slapped him hard. He ran up the trail and Kale quickly started lowering herself down the valley wall, hanging on roots and tree limbs as she went. When she reached the riverbed she cut back down to the halawai, where Moku Peʻa stream cuts off to the northeast, and she ran up the trail to the spot below her secret cave. She stopped and listened…*No footsteps.* She began climbing up the valley wall, choosing her footholds, careful not to release an avalanche of rocks and give away her location. With her last strength, she pulled herself up to the cave's opening and crawled inside. Beside the entrance was a pile of rocks that Kaholo put there when Kamehameha died. One by one, she dragged them over and closed the entrance. Inside there was no wind, no light, no sound but her breath and heartbeat. She shook and tears streamed down her face but she did not utter a sound.

The blustering winds continued the next morning when Manu and the elders missed Kale and Pāhaʻa. They went through Honokahua asking everyone, but nobody had seen them. After Uʻi's boy Leowainahē found a bloodstained kīhei on their farm, the hunt began in earnest, and Manu sent word to Kaholo and Alika in Honolulu. Kaholo had already confirmed that Makauli had killed a man named Waipālua and his wife. They immediately sailed back to Honokahua, arriving six days after the aliʻi were discovered missing.

Kaholo, Alika, and four sailors with muskets rowed ashore in the longboat. As they neared the shore, stern-faced Alika yelled to Manu, Maunahina, and a small group of young men on shore, "Did you find the aliʻi?"

"No sign of them," Maunahina called back.

Once on shore, Kaholo asked, "Where is Makauli?"

"At his camp," said Mauna.

"Where is Kalāhei, who was sent to watch him?"

"Missing too."

Kaholo addressed all the men. "Makauli is a murderer and he may have killed our aliʻi. Kalāhei may be dead too. Maunahina—you and Shaw get your weapons. We will go up to get Makauli, bring him down, and tie him to the ʻulu tree at the beach."

Manu grabbed Kaholo's arm. As I was praying I saw a vision of the Aliʻi Wahine alone in the dark, crying. I believe she is alive."

Kaholo and Alika looked at each another and both said, "The hideaway!"

"Kaholo, you go with Maunahina and my men to bring down Maka. I am going up to Moku Peʻa Valley. My God, she has been there a week! Manu, give me some drinking water and food. Send up two men and Kekahunawahine with a palanquin, in case she's alive."

At the bend in the stream Alika looked up. The cave entrance was covered with rocks and nearly invisible against the valley wall. He whistled twice, threw a rock against the opening, and whistled twice more. After a long moment, the top center rock moved and fell inward; and Kale's hand reached through the hole and then disappeared inside again.

"Kale! It's Alika! I am coming!" *She was supposed to whistle back once.* He scrambled up to the escarpment, pulled away enough stones to squeeze inside, and gasped, "Oh My God!" His strong spirited bride was curled up against the cave wall like a dying bird, exhausted from pulling down one rock. The old bruises on her face ran in dark blue streaks down her cheeks and chin. Her parched lips trembled, and her body quaked with fever. He knelt next to her, gave her sips from his water gourd, and held her.

Alika looked around and spotted all the undisturbed provisions Kaholo had carefully stacked in the back of the cave years ago. "Hold on—" He grabbed a fine mat and some kapa moe and wrapped them around Kale to keep her warm. As he did he saw the inflamed gashes and bruises on her back and his courage failed him; he wept.

"Who did this to you?"

"Maka…" She whispered. "He killed ʻUlumalu and Pāhaʻa…"

"Oh, Dear God—and Kalāhei is missing. He must be dead too. Thank God you are alive!"

"I would prefer to die…he raped me." Alika's eyes reddened with anger.

"The devil! Kaholo and his men are taking him into custody now…how did you let this happen? Oh my poor darling, why did I ever leave you in this place…"

Alika's words snuffed out the small light of his presence and Kale quietly shut her eyes for the first time in six days. Alika held her until Kekahuna and the men came and carried Kale back down to her hale on a litter made out of two long ʻohe bamboo poles and a sennit net. Before they took her inside, Manu exorcised all four corners and sprinkled inside and out with ʻolena turmeric and kai seawater to remove all evil.

Maunahina, Shaw, and the men found Makauli at his camp, honing a canoe. When he saw the guns, he knew they finally had the courage to serve him his rightful punishment. He laughed at them. *Come. Make me sorry.*

They were poi in his hands. They tied him up and the pressure of the cords thrilled him. He taunted Maunahina, who demanded to know where Pāhaʻa and Kalāhei were, until finally, Mauna cracked Maka's head with his club but the canoe builder only recoiled and grinned.

"Your man cried like a baby. He made me love him."

Mauna raised his dagger but Shaw held him back. "Look, this long-legged fish desires to be gutted! Do not do what he wants!"

Suddenly Maka spit on Shaw. "Leave him alone. He loves it. I love it!" Shaw looked at Mauna.

Maunahina pulled his chin up and stared at Maka, took a step back, put his dagger away, and turned to the four sailors. "Shaw and I will take him down to the 'ulu tree at the beach. You haul down this roughed-out canoe and meet us." Then Mauna turned and grinned back at Maka. "Don't worry, we will not hurt you."

Kekahuna bathed Kale and dressed her back with fibers rubbed from the shiny side of many la'i tī leaves and crushed naupaka leaves. Then she wrapped fresh fine kapa cloth around Kale's midriff to keep the poultice in place. She carefully treated Kale's abrasions with aloe sap and drew out her bruises with slices of kalo. Then she fed Kale 'ilima blossoms, mamaki tea, and dog broth. U'i sat by Kale's side and watched her sleep.

While Kale slept, two outrigger canoes made their way out of Honokahua Bay into the channel, with a third rough-hewn canoe lashed between them. The inside canoe contained Maka, lying face up, bound, and weighted with heavy stones. When they were halfway between Honokahua and Kaunakahakai Moloka'i, Mauna motioned the paddlers to stop and unlash the dugout canoe. Alika stood up and aimed his Brown Bess. With a thunderous "crack" the musket discharged, cleanly missing Maka and blowing a hole the size of a man's fist through the bottom of the doomed canoe. The sea poured in and Maka was not smiling when the water rose up over his nose. His last cry was a rush of bubbles.

"May you rot in hell!" shouted Alika. Mauna, Kaholo, and Shaw nodded and smiled at one another. Silently, the casket of Maka's own making quickly sank, becoming darker and darker blue until it disappeared in a fishing ground well known for manō sharks.

"*He moe wa'a o Honokahua*, A death canoe of Honokahua." said Kaholo.

It took a long time to push for shore against the swell. When they finally landed, Kaholo and Alika rushed back to check on Kale. Alika asked, "That devil killed three men and raped your chief right under your nose. Didn't you suspect anything?"

"Captain, we still have not even found the bodies of the men he says he killed. This man was very clever."

"That may be so, Kaholo, but I cannot understand why you left Kale unprotected! You have a share of the blame along with her!"

Kaholo turned squarely to Alika, blocking his way to Kale's door. "I will take the blame. Perhaps I should not have followed her order to go to Honolulu; but if I had not, you would not be here. Do not blame her."

"She should have been more careful! I begged her to keep a weapon at the hale, but she would not and then she sent all her guards away!"

"Captain, please; it is not Kale's fault."

"And now you refer to her by a familiar name? Perhaps she has taken you for a husband too—that is another problem!"

Kaholo's nostrils flared and he spoke through pursed lips. "I am not her husband. But if she took me for her husband, I would never leave her side!"

The words fell on Alika's soul like a pile of rocks and his anger fled before a rush of shame. He swallowed hard, looked over Kaholo's shoulder, and realized Kale was awake. His chin dropped. He turned and walked down the beach path and Kaholo went inside.

"My chief, all is peaceful now. Maka will never hurt anyone again. The captain sends his aloha, but he must return to Honolulu."

"I heard the argument. Do not be too hard on Alika. I blame myself too."

Kaholo knelt by her side. "Forgive me. If I had been here perhaps…" Tears filled his eyes and he struggled to speak, "I will die before I ever let anyone hurt you again."

"Kaholo, I do not blame you. You have always protected me and I thank you for your deep loyalty. I am tired. Will you stay with me while I sleep? Perhaps when I am feeling better you will take me to see my sister in Lāhainā?"

"I will guard you and I will bring your sister to see you here. Everyone in Lāhainā knows the pilikia, trouble at Honokahua. May Queen Kaʻahumanu be merciful and allow her to come."

" ʻĀmama," said Kale and closed her eyes.

The following week, Peke brought Kale a *Hawaiian Reader*, the first written primer for Hawaiians from the mission school in Lāhainā, and a large bag of loke rose flowers that they sewed into long lei. Kale was very interested in the book and asked Peke to drill her as she memorized each page.

"Kale, do you remember what you said to me the day I arrived in Maui after the revolt?"

"No."

"You told me that something good would come of my confinement. You were right. I could not see at the time, but now I am content and Kaʻahumanu has become kind and merciful, and she dotes on my daughter like a makuawahine mother. Now I tell you that something good will come from this terrible tragedy you have endured."

"I hope you are right. Everything I see is spoiled by the sadness in my heart. My Pāhaʻa made me Hawaiian again after so many years of living a haole life. I cannot tell you the freedom and pure joy I shared with him. I will not accept that such a good and kind person died before the dreams of his life were fulfilled. If it was not his hewa sin, was it mine?"

"Perhaps it was nobody's hewa. Perhaps his righteousness was complete and there was no more for him to do in life."

"Yes, perhaps. It is a good thought."

Kalāhei's funeral was a blur. Kale insisted on officiating with Manu, but she had to be carried to and from the dunes. It was many days before Kale mustered courage to venture out of her hale alone. When Pāhaʻa's remains were finally found in the wao wild forest, Manu purified them and prepared them for burial in a sennit basket. Kale was still weak, but Kaholo took her to Molokaʻi to return Pāhaʻa's bones to the land of his kūpuna. Kale stayed with his ʻohana two weeks, mourning and cleansing her memories in the righteous, peaceful homeland that Pāhaʻa loved.

When Kale returned in August, King Liholiho's herald came to Honokahua and all the people gathered at the sound of his drums:

> People of Honokahua, The Kuhina Nui Kaʻahumanu and King Liholiho Kamehameha have declared these laws for the all the Kingdom:
>
> You shall not commit murder; he who puts another to death shall die himself.
> You shall not commit adultery; he who commits this crime, man or woman, shall be banished to Kahoʻolawe
> You shall not practice prostitution; anyone guilty of this shall be imprisoned and beaten across his back with a rope and if he fails again to keep the law shall be banished to Kahoʻolawe.
> Natives and Foreigners are forbidden to manufacture, sell, or drink liquor.

The laws were the result of Kaʻahumanu's response to Christian teaching, and of her desire to stop the wanton abuse of her female subjects by businessmen who made their money sating the foreign traders' lusty desires. Kale rested on the idea that Alika and Kaholo had carried out the queen's law, just a little earlier than it was declared, and she let go of her guilt for Maka's death.

As her strength improved, Kale spent much time praying with Manu. On a September evening, after they had offered thanks for the harvest and the sun had set between Molokaʻi and Lanaʻi, Kale asked, "Why has so much innocent blood been spilled here at Honokahua? What have we done to deserve so much sorrow?"

"My Chief, I have made offerings and prayed much. I have asked the ʻaumakua and I do not think it is our hewa, our sin that brought us this sorrow. I do not think an enemy put a curse on us. Pray to your god and ask for an answer."

Kale lifted her voice, "*E ʻIo, Ka ʻĪ Mākuaʻole, Ke Akua e ʻike ai āpau*, O ʻIo, the all-sufficient parentless one, the God who sees all, what good can come from the death of righteous Pāhaʻa, who was faithful to you? What do you gain by making Kalāhei's wife a widow and his children fatherless? And please, why do you allow me to live?" She bowed her head and wept silently. Manu prayed too.

That night, Kale dreamt she was high on the northern flank of Mauna Kea, looking down at the hazy light blue ocean and at Maui in the distance. Suddenly a bolt of lightning struck Maui and all the lizards jumped off the cliffs and into the sea. Thunder rolled and another firebrand struck the island; a million centipedes crawled from the forests to the shores, and schools of big aku fish swallowed them all. Then rain fell like a waterspout from heaven, washing red soil down the mountain into the sea until the whole ocean was red. When the rain stopped, the island sparkled green and gold in the sun; rising to her ears were children's sing-song voices and giggles—from so many children that the island vibrated with their laughter.

The dream was so beautiful that when the animals of Honokahua welcomed the day, Kale stayed tucked under her kapa moe, remembering the profound images and sounds.

When Kale told Manu her dream, he said a vision of blood came to him in the night too and he recognized the cleansing blood of offering, not the sinful blood of murder.

Then Kale remembered. "Pāhaʻa once said he was 'the offering' and I was 'the gift'. But I do not understand."

"To cleanse evil a sacrifice always must be offered."

Kale thought of all the rituals she knew. "Yes. And the offering must be righteous."

"*Pololei*. Correct." said Manu, smiling.

Kale understood and wept for Pāhaʻa and herself. "And what is required of me?"

Manu's pinpoint stare met Kale's questioning eyes and she wished she had not asked. He said, "You must lead your people in righteousness—put fear aside and take courage."

"I am an empty calabash; I have no strength and I don't know where to lead them."

" 'Io is close to you. He answers your prayers. He will supply strength, but you must take courage. I say this to you now because you are pregnant."

Kale knew too, but she had avoided the thought. "Pāha'a or Maka?" is all she asked.

"It is your baby. Both fathers are dead. It will always be your baby and no one will ever take it from you."

" 'Āmama," said Kale.

Kale continued to grieve but prayed to 'Io for strength every day and somehow made it to the next morning prayer. She prayed for courage, held her head high, and led her people by example, working hard and carrying a child that fear would destroy, but that Kale nourished with love.

One day U'i drummed up courage to ask Kale, "Who is the father?"

"It is mine. There will be no father to claim it."

Then innocent U'i asked what Kale asked herself only in her darkest hours, "What if the child is evil like Maka?"

Kale resisted the temptation to fear and took courage. "I have prayed to 'Io to make the baby pono and 'Io will make it so."

U'i smiled in admiration of her chief's bravery. "How nice to have your baby in the spring. I always became pregnant at the Makahiki and delivered at harvest time when Limaha'i needed me in the fields. Some farmer women kill their babies in the womb or even after birth, so they can bring in the harvest and keep the rest of their family alive. Since the end of the kapu, men sleep with their wives when they please and the babies are born all year long."

Kale smiled. "It is good. We have had enough killing here at Honokahua."

"U'i whispered. " The women thought you would kill your baby. They marvel that you dare to keep it."

"Good."

U'i chattered on. "I am so happy that you are here with us. I often thought that you would move to Honolulu with the captain."

"I thought about going there, but it was not right for me. My heart is bound to Honokahua and the blood of the land flows in me. I made a vow to Keopuolani to do good for Honokahua people and she said if I did that, Honokahua people would do good for the land."

"She was right. Our land has prospered ever since you came. We have many more workers, such fine crops, and so many babies. The fishermen say you brought plenty fish to us too, and now we have those pua'a pepeiao hao, 'pigs with iron horns', those cows. And I have a friend closer than a sister."

"I, too."

One morning Kaholo heard the pū sound and saw a brig coming into the bay with Alika and little Isaac at the helm. He ran to get Kale and escort her to the beach. Just the mention of Isaac brightened her spirits and she hurried to see her boy and Alika. As she waited expectantly at the shore, Kaholo paddled out to get them and Kale saw two more people appear on deck...the Youngs. Guilt pulled up old memories of 'Olohana's brooding face and Kale turned inward to confront her shame again. She wanted to return to her hale, but she could not turn her back on little Isaac. She focused on him alone, watching the blonde fringe of hair below his cap. She waved to him and the sound of his voice, calling "Mama!" warmed her heart.

Ka'oana'eha and 'Olohana stepped on to the beach first, but Kale was still looking past them and it wasn't until 'Olohana hugged her that Kale realized he was not angry. His big brown eyes looked sadly at her.

"We came for Ho'oponopono," he said. She opened her arms and hugged him. His frail body shook as he wept. "O Kale," he said, "I am so sorry I sent that madman to Honokahua. Please forgive me!" She could not find words. It was too much. She kissed his cheeks and hugged him.

"Mama!" said Isaac. Kale bent down, held him close to her, kissed his sweet pink cheeks, and breathed in the fragrance of his skin.

"*Ku'u 'Aikake, aloha nō ho'i wau iā ko'u hi'ilei makamae. Ua kali wau iā ko'u ho'i 'ana i kēla i kēia lā*" "Beloved Isaac, I love my precious baby so much. I have awaited your return each and every day."

"Let us go to the hale," said Kaholo.

Ka'oana'eha grabbed Kale's arm and held her tight to her as they walked up to the kauhale ali'i. They all sat down and Ka'oana'eha never let Kale free from her touch, holding her hand, rubbing her back, or smoothing her hair. She encouraged Kale with soothing talk of past happy times and blessed her with bright visions of the future.

Alika had rehearsed his words, and everyone listened quietly as he spoke. "Kale dear, please forgive me for leaving you alone so much these seven years. From the start, I knew I could not give up the sea and live here, but I did not have the courage to tell you, for fear of losing you. It is my fault that you became accustomed to being alone and I hate myself for it." He looked at Kaholo. "Forgive me for being jealous of you and Pāhaʻa; you gave her the protection and comfort I denied her." Then he looked at Kale again. "Imperfect as I am, I will always love you."

Her golden eyes had a faint sparkle. "Your love remains in my heart and you are always welcome at Honokahua." He bent over and kissed her and then hugged Kaholo.

"Where is Isaac?" asked Kale.

"I sent him up to play with his friend Hulu—he wants to stay here with you for a while, if that is all right with you." She could hardly believe what she heard.

"What about his reading and writing? Is he in school?"

"Yes, he is a good student at the foreign school, but he misses you. I will come back for him in a month. Can you manage it?"

"Oh yes!" Kale wept and Kaʻoanaʻeha held her. "But please, before all things are set right…I must tell you that I am pregnant." It was as if everyone went deaf—no reaction, no signs of recognition, not even a breath was drawn. Before they could form questions Kale said, "I do not know if the father is Pāhaʻa or Maka…But here is my thought: the baby is mine and it shall remain mine since both men are dead. No one will ever claim it or take it from me. It is not a burden; it is life within me that I accept from my god."

Kaʻoanaʻeha held Kale close, looked at ʻOlohana, and finally said, "We are with you. It is our grandchild too."

Alika smiled. "And Isaac will have the little brother or sister he wants."

ʻOlohana stood up and said, "*Ua pono āpau. Noa ia.* All is set right. It is freed"

Everyone said " ʻĀmama!" and Kale sighed.

Umuwena and Keahi prepared a delicious lunch of shellfish and poi. For the first time since Pāhaʻa died, Kale felt hungry and a small hope dawned in her heart.

Her month with Isaac went quickly, with mother and son studying their reading and writing together. Hulu and Isaac surfed and fished every day, and Kale taught them how to throw keʻa pua darts. When Alika came to get

Isaac, Kale was sad, but Alika assured her there would be many more cheerful reunions ahead.

Kale wanted to keep Pāhaʻa's herd so Kaholo went to Waimea to learn the dairy business from John Palmer Parker, who was ranching one of the large royal herds. ʻĀwaʻa, one of Parker's limahana, hired hands, wanted to go out on his own so Kaholo rented him the Honokahua pasture in return for running the dairy. He was a young broad-backed Kaʻu man with a hearty laugh, pleasing round face, and curly dark hair that stood up on his head. He joked that his horse was just wide enough for his bowed legs. ʻĀwaʻa quickly made friends with the farmers and lawaiʻa and began courting one of Kalāhei's daughters.

It was a fine September harvest and later, in November, Kale presided at all the Makahiki events. It was not the same as in the old kapu days, but the taxes were extremely heavy and Honokahua was happy to feast and play when the tribute was complete. Sporting and athletic events were much larger now that there were more men at Honokahua, and the Chinese farmers and ranchers joined in the gaming and fun, enjoying the affection and care of their neighbors and chief.

For Kale, it was a matter of endurance. She missed Pāhaʻa. Her morning sickness became afternoon sickness before she regained her strength; every night she prayed between her short periods of sleep and awoke tired every morning. She forced herself to eat even though she did not desire food, and every day she doggedly ate ʻilima blossoms and ʻalaea red earth minerals scraped from the red-veined cliff at the south end of Honokahua Bay.

Winter rains came in January when Kale was six months pregnant. Day after gray day Kale relied on Kaholo and Uʻi for companionship. She focused her attention on ʻĀwaʻa's herd and winter deep-sea fishing, building larger pens for the cows and assigning farmers to help pull in the catches.

When March planting time came, the whole community—ʻo kō auka, uplanders, and ʻo kō akai, lowlanders—joined in planting the sweet potatoes. Early in the month, they burned the fields to kill all the weeds. At the quarter moon, in another cooperative effort, farmers spread mulch of dried kukui leaves, decayed kukui nutshells, and cinders on the kula and tilled the moist spring soil with their digging sticks. On the day of planting, after the night of Akua full moon, all the farmers arrived early in fresh malo and short maile lei. They formed a line across one field, each carrying a net ʻeke bag of slips to plant. In perfect formation, they dug a hole with one hand, placed a slip in the hole with the other, tamped the slip in place with their feet, and moved on in unison like hula dancers. The planters moved across one field after another, chanting, until the whole kula was finished. Kaholo and Kale beamed with pride at the precise, energetic plan and at the joy with which they worked.

Afterward, the elders dug open earth ovens and the planters made an offering to Lono and feasted to commemorate the beginning of kau, summer:

> Pause and give thanks to god; O Kāne, O Kāne of life giving water.
> Here is the lūʻau, the first leaves of our kalo; turn back and eat o God;
> May our families also eat, the pigs eat, the dogs eat.

By May, the sweet potatoes were maturing with long green vines raked into high mounds. Kale felt labor pains, and when Kekahuna palpated her stomach she declared the baby was head-down and ready to be born. Kale's water broke while Kekahuna was still at Kale's hale. By the time they walked to the birthing stone at the beach, contractions were close together and the baby came fast. The tiny girl that Kekahuna pushed up on Kale's belly cried until she heard her mother's cooing. Kale drew the black-haired beauty to her breast saying, " *ʻO ʻUwaikīkīlani kou inoa. E Kuʻu keiki wahine, e ola ʻoe i ke aloha o ʻIo, ka makua o nā mea lani.* Good waterspout of heaven is your name. Beloved little girl, live in the love of ʻIo, the father of heavenly things."

Her baby suckled and closed her little eyes and long eyelashes. Kale touched her tiny chin and the baby smiled. "*Ka minoʻaka!* The dimpled smile!" Kale whispered. "Your father Pāhaʻa lives in you! Your auntie Peke said something good would come, and she spoke of you. I will tell you about your Papa and your grandparents and all the good that is in you."

May 1825's news was devastating. King Liholiho and Queen Kamāmalu's bodies were returned to Hawaiʻi from London where they succumbed to measles during a trip to visit King George. His Majesty's Ship *Blonde* sailed into Lāhainā Roads covered in black bunting, and Hawaiian people began to mourn once more. The Royal Throne went to Liholiho's younger brother Kauikeaouli, who was just twelve years old, assuring Kuhina Nui Kaʻahumanu full governing power for many years to come. The old ways of kumākēnā aloha aliʻi mourning continued in some outlying areas; at court and at Honokahua, there was sincere grieving, but no lawlessness.

Soon after Kauikeaouli took the throne, James came to Honokahua, dissipated again. After he spent several days with Kaholo, Kale invited him to come to her pā, where she received him. When he saw the baby, his eyes lit up.

"Kale, she is beautiful! I am so sorry about your husband, Pāha'a. Kaholo told me what happened and I was so sad. I never had a chance to meet him."

"When you see this baby, you have seen him. She smiled at 'Uwaikīkīlani. You would have loved him—such a joyous person. How long will you stay with us?"

"I want to make Honokahua a permanent base. It is the only place I can stay sober and find any peace."

"I will allow it as long as you don't drink here. Do you promise?"

"I promise."

"I will ask Kaholo to build you a hale of your own."

"You are not ashamed to have me here?"

"Should I be?"

"You do not know that I accompanied King Liholiho to England as his interpreter?"

"Yes, I know. 'Olohana was so proud. So what?"

"I missed the ship when she sailed from Rio de Janeiro—drunk again." Kale shook her head. "I hopped another ship but by the time I arrived in London the king and queen had died from measles. Nobody even claimed their bodies at the morgue. They got halfway around the world without an interpreter and King George never even saw them before they died. Boki was useless because he knows only the language of barter. 'Olohana's dream was to have Hawai'i under British protection to keep out the French and Russians...I failed him and disgraced my King and my Country before the entire world."

Kale's face grew sad. 'Olohana's shame and disappointment were bad enough, but all she could picture in her mind was the fear and humiliation Liholiho and his young queen must have felt as they lay dying in a strange land. She looked James in the eye. " 'Oia mau nō. It's always the same." James began to cry silently, his head shaking as his chest heaved under him. "You chose rum over your father's wishes and over duty to your king and queen, the same way you chose rum over me." Kale stood up to take the baby inside. "Yes, you may stay. You are my stepbrother and you are welcome here as long as you do not drink. We do not have rum at Honokahua, but if I find you are drinking sweet potato mash, or 'awa, or anything intoxicating, I will banish you and you may never return. It is your choice and I pray you choose well." She put her hand on his shoulder. "I will pray to my god for you and he will help you."

CHAPTER 10

The Living God

When it was time for ʻUwaikīkīlani to be weaned, Kale offered her two bananas and the baby took one and ate it. Kale prayed and dipped her baby's little hand in the poi bowl; ʻUwaikīkīlani licked her fingers with great pleasure, and then fell asleep. Kale watched her twitch in her sleep and memorized her fine features, long eyelashes, and tender brown skin; then she kissed her soft forehead and shed a tear that this most precious infancy was at an end.

"Aloha e Kale!" *Peke came to visit!* Her sister's sweet voice was a welcome distraction any time.

Kale waved from the door of her hale and ran out to greet her sister whispering, "*Aloha nō! Pehea ʻoe? Ua hiamoe ka pēpē i ka hale.*" And love to you! How are you! The baby is sleeping in the house."

Peke gave her a big hug, and presented Kale a net bag with a canvas sack inside. "Fresh off the ship from America. Something you will love!"

When Kale took it, she felt the bag move. "Oh my goodness, is there an animal in there?"

"Look."

"*Auwē...He popoki keiki kēnā...Mahalo piha e Peke.* Oh my…It's a kitten… Thank you very much Peke." She carefully picked up the orange tabby, whose little claws seemed to catch on anything within its grasp, and looked at its wide green bewildered eyes and pink nose.

"Isn't she pretty?"

"Oh yes, she is a pretty cat, and we have plenty of work for her." Kale laughed. "We just had our first rats not a month ago. It did not take them long to make their way up here from Lāhainā. What a thoughtful gift...what shall we call her?"

"It's your cat."

"How about 'Po'i'? May she pounce on all the rats and keep them away from our storehouses."

"Yes! Look, she wants to get down and get to work already," said Peke. Kale let her jump down and explore her new home.

Peke and Kale sat down in the yard under the shade of the banana trees, and Keahi was already on his way up from the bay with lunch for Kale and her guest.

"How are you and Wahinekipi?" asked Kale.

"We are good. When Humehume died, I did not think I could go on. I felt so alone and daily life seemed like a terrible task. Influenza is a terrible plague on the Hawaiians...but I think he might have lived if we were not under house arrest. When Kalanimoku divided the lands among the Hawai'i and O'ahu chiefs, leaving landless even those who did not revolt, Humehume bore the guilt of their destitution. The sorrow and humiliation just wore him down..." Peke began to cry and Kale held her in her arms.

"Yes, Humehume was an easy excuse to gather in the rich Kaua'i lands. And he was too lofty a thinker to understand the wicked treachery he faced. I do not know why a man of 28 dies and another lives on to old age. It is such a terrible shocking loss...Manu told me some die because their righteous work is done."

"It is a good thought. He was the only one of his brothers who even tried to redeem his father's throne. Maybe that was his work..."

"How do you like Kapewakua?"

"Oh, it is lovely. The garden that your men planted for me is growing plenty of food, and since we are near Māla, I trade vegetables for fresh fish. The other two houses on the land are rented and the income is enough so I can give money to the mission."

"I notice that you dress like the missionary women. Your holokū is very pretty."

"Would you like me to make you one?"

"Me? Oh no. I keep the old ways and I do not like to be confined..."

"It is confining, but I teach reading and writing at the mission nearly every day and they demand teachers wear modest clothing."

"I think the missionaries are silly to insist on hot, uncomfortable clothing, but I understand you do not wish to offend. For me, a pāʻū is fine. How is Queen Kaʻahumanu these days? Does she still spend time with you since she released you?"

"She would, but she has been traveling through all the islands teaching about Jesus Christ and about her laws. She picked up where Queen Keopuolani left off as a champion of the faith. Next month she and Prime Minister Kalanimoku will be baptized at Kawaihaʻo Mission on Oʻahu with eight other chiefs—Kale, Christianity is growing among the chiefs and the commoners."

"Oh the whalers are not going to be happy about that!" Kale laughed. "We have trouble enough from just one drunkard in the family. Kaʻahumanu will be up against thousands."

Kale was right. The day Kaʻahumanu and her chiefs were baptized, Christianity went from a minor irritant to a major threat for the traders catering to the baser needs of foreign sailors. Governor Hoapili, the late Keopuloani's husband and the trusted counselor who hid Kamehameha's bones, now applied his new faith in Jesus Christ to governing Maui. As a proud Hawaiian and father, he loathed the ever-growing epidemic of untreatable venereal disease, infanticide, and barrenness produced by prostitution of Hawaiian women to foreign sailors. As a Christian, he felt compelled to take a stand against sins that would bring God's wrath upon the people under his stewardship. In the high-ruling aliʻi style to which he was accustomed, Hoapili made a sweeping judgment and outlawed prostitution and alcohol consumption on Maui. The law was of little consequence in outlying country areas like Honokahua, where rum and prostitution were never a problem; but at Lāhainā Roads, where whalers were used to buying grog and sleeping companions while in port or for the months at sea, protests against the new law were vicious.

In 1825, Captain Buckle's men attempted to kill Reverend Richards at his house, but Hawaiian warriors guarded him. Kaʻahumanu supported the law, and sailors stormed her prayer meeting at Kalanimoku's house on Oʻahu, threatening the Queen Regent with violence unless Hawaiian women were released to them. Governor Boki, who owed fabulous sums to Oʻahu's foreign businessmen, continued to sell women and rum in Honolulu so the ships went there, but Lāhainā protests continued.

On September 14, 1826 when Kaholo came back from his weekly trading trip to Lāhainā, Kale and all the family leaders were waiting to find out the cause of the cannon fire the night before.

"All Lāhainā is in a stir and Governor Hoapili has armed warriors on the streets, at the harbor, and all along the strand. There is a curfew at sundown," said Kaholo

"And the cannon?" asked Kale.

"Captain Clark's ship fired on Lāhainā—men began to riot early last evening, so he sent some of his men to pay women large ransoms to break the prostitution laws and secretly come aboard his ship."

Halemano jumped in. "That is what happened at the Mauae homestead. Sailors came up after dark and offered the father some iron fittings and a knife for his daughter! He told them to get out of his house."

"Well, some families gave up their women, because they were seen going out in the longboats. Governor Hoapili took Clark into custody and demanded the girls' release—and Clark's First Mate, who was on the ship, fired his 12 pounders on Lāhainā."

Kale's heart sank. "Was anyone hurt?"

"No. He intentionally aimed high as a warning, but he still singed some breadfruit trees and damaged the property next to Reverend Richard's house.

"*Nā mea kuko ʻino*, The lustful ones, will attack anyone who favors Hoapili's laws—even Kaʻahumanu," said Kale.

"She is right," said Kaholo. "They were desperate to find any women at all, because most of the women were hiding up in Kauaʻula or Kahoma valleys."

All the family leaders began to laugh. "Those Lāhainā people are smart. Just take the women away and let the sailors squirm with their desires!"

Kaholo did not laugh. "It was a game played with rascals. Clark said he would give back the women, but instead he sailed with the girls on board. Their families may never see them again."

It was a sobering picture for every family leader as they thought of their own wives and daughters at the mercy of a shipload of sailors. Kale welled up with pity and anger. That was the day Kaʻahumanu ordered heavy guns installed at Lāhainā Fort. No ship's captain would ever plunder Maui women again.

In the end Hoapili's Laws were enforced and those who infracted them, including aliʻi, were sentenced to lashes, hard labor, or exile on Kahoʻolawe. Despite the outrages of a few, the majority of whaling captains taking on provisions in the Hawaiian Islands took advantage of the temperance and morality in Lāhainā, where they did not have to look after drunk and riotous crews. For a time, Maui families escaped the deadly diseases and the demands of haole sailors.

Later in1827 the new paniolo, ʻĀwaʻa, married Kalāhei's daughter Nālehu and started his own herd of children. The dairy herd tripled to 24 cows, creating a need for more pasture. Cattle roaming upland forests began killing off small trees, allowing easy access to the remaining large trees, so Kaholo set his men to cutting and selling Honokahua hardwood to carvers in Olowalu.

When Kale's childhood friend, Laura Konia, fell in love with chief Abner Pākī, she began spending time at Nāpili, because Pākī ruled nearby Honokowai, Mailepai, and Mahinahina ahupuaʻa. Laura grew up at court and her young adult years with King Kauikeaouili were filled with amorous adventures and drunken capers that defied Kale's imagination. Even her crush on Pākī developed into a deep romance after she won him in a match of Kilu, an aliʻi-only game with sexual stakes.

Now Laura was following Pākī into the church, a journey that influenced her behavior in ways that her dear friend Kale welcomed. Every morning after Kale prayed with Manu, she walked Oneloa beach with Laura, collecting tiny shells for a lei pū, shell lei.

"I used to hate coming to Honokahua and never understood why you loved it so, but I have come to love it too," said Laura.

Kale gave her a skeptical eye. "Oh Laura, now you like coming here to spend time with Pākī, away from the prying eyes at court. Once you marry him I will never see you again!"

"Kale, you break my heart." She feigned a pout. "Are we not like sisters, you and I?"

"Yes, and that is how you know what I say is true."

"I will not deny that I come to see Pākī, but I do not stay on my own land, Nāpili—Kale, I come here to be with you. Tell me, are you going to let the teacher Kānekuapuʻu come here and teach the people?"

"I will allow it. I held a council of the haku family leaders and they want to learn to read and write. They also are willing to hear the Bible lessons from ke kahuna haole, the foreign priest. Tell me, where does this Kānekuapuʻu come from?"

"From Maʻalaea." said Laura. "His grandfather and father were chiefs down there. His mother was makaʻāinana, so he has no land. His wife died with the cough and he was baptized shortly after I was in 1824, and then trained in Lāhainā by Richards and Taua."

Kale bent down and sifted a handful of sand at the high water mark, pulling out a few very tiny shells. "It is very strange to hear such a dark-skinned man talk like a haole. I think that when he took up the haole god he lost his Hawaiian heart. He is too solemn and serious, but there is still softness to the eyes."

"He is definitely not for you," said Laura.

"For me!" Kale raised herself up to her full height and pointed at Laura. "You must marry one time before you make me a match for my fourth husband!"

Laura grinned. "Yes, you are much more passionate than I. But me…" She put her head to one side. "…I had so many suitors I had trouble making up my mind."

" 'Āpiki!, humbug!" said Kale. "You just wanted to try them all first, at kissing games!"

"Kolohe wahine! I should never have told you any of that!" Laura kicked sand at Kale and Kale quickly put down her treasured shells and ran into the surf with Laura in pursuit. They splashed one another and giggled like little girls until they wore themselves out.

"Oh I will miss you when you go back," panted Kale "When will you take Pākī for your husband?"

"Reverend Richards says he will perform the Christian ceremony in the month of Makali'i."

"Why do you wait? Do you need permission from your teacher to take a husband?"

"It is a part of the Christian rite—to test the strength of our intentions and to seek God's blessing first, before we marry. And the new Kawaiha'o Church building will be finished then."

"Laura, you are so changed…I think it is good to go slowly. Your teacher is right."

"Auwē, it was more fun before," said Laura. She did not have to wait long for Kale's reply, which came as a big hug as she dunked Laura and the laughter started again.

Kaholo was assigned to help teacher Kānekuapu'u locate a meeting place in Honokahua and to set meeting times convenient for the people. Lāhainā meetings began with sacred hula and 'oli chant, lasted as long as the teacher's voice held up, and concluded with a lengthy prayer. Kaholo knew that

Honokahua people would think it rude to leave until Kāne told them to go, so he instructed Kāne to dismiss them at the first hāmama, yawn.

"Kaholo," asked Kale. "Laura Konia and Peke think highly of this Kāne; what do you say?"

Kaholo smiled. "A good man, but too serious. He did not eat the whole day—that is why he is so lanky. Is he hapa haole?"

"Kale giggled. If he is, I cannot see it—he just has haole ways. Just be certain that the people know it is their choice to attend this meeting. They have no obligation to you or me."

"Yes, my chief."

The first meeting held late one afternoon in Kaholo's pā was so well attended that people filled the yard; behind those seated on the wall stood more people craning to hear. Kāne was dressed in a black coat and high collared shirt like the missionaries. His, long gray pants and leather shoes were not at all like the rich finery worn at Kamehameha's court. His Bible lesson was entitled "Seek the Lord," and began with a verse from Isaiah, "Seek the Lord while he may be found; call on Him while he is near," which he repeated several times. The listeners repeated the verse; at intervals in his lesson, he referred to the passage and asked the assembly to chant back the verse to him again. Kale remembered being bored at "the white house" Bible lessons, but Kāne's lesson caught her interest and the sight of her people nodding and memorizing the words gave her great joy. He is a good teacher, she thought.

After the meeting, Kale asked Kāne to come back to Honokahua and teach the people again. Kāne suggested that he teach weekly, and Kale agreed, so long as the people eagerly continued to attend.

The farming operation now required more workers. Every week when Kaholo went on his trading trip to Lāhainā, he solicited all who were down on their luck to come to Honokahua. Some were widowers or orphans. Some were women spurned by their families after returning from the whaling ships. Anyone who was willing to work hard and to give up alcohol was welcome.

James Kānehoa Young took over Honokahua's canoe building. He still had commitments in Honolulu, but Honokahua was his safe haven and his trips to Oʻahu were occasion for much prayer. Temperance and hard work suited him and soon his body regained its youthful tone.

"James, will you be with us all this month?" asked Kale.

"My next trip to Oʻahu is scheduled in two weeks."

"I want to invite our parents to come and see ‘Uwaikīkīlani and to have Alika and ‘Aikake join us too. They are the only grandparents he has. ‘Olohana is elderly and won't be with us forever."

"Do you really think I will ever be free from him?"

"No. You never will. Even when he is gone, you will carry his name. Now is the time to make things right." She touched his arm. "Oh, James, I know ‘Olohana has been hard on you, and my heart breaks that he will not receive you at Kawaihae. But if he could see how healthy you are now—how sober and reliable—I believe he would show you his love again."

"Again? He always treated Robert and me like his sailors. Robert got away, but I stayed and watched him be fatherly to you, Hū‘eu, and Peke, and then shower affection on his second family. I am to blame too; I have caused him so much disappointment and humiliation and he will never forgive me."

"He has forgiven me many times and I know he will forgive you too—when you are ready to be forgiven." Kale saw his cold expression and gave up the argument.

"I see that I cannot entertain the Youngs while you are here, so I will take the baby to Kawaihae and have Alika and ‘Aikake meet us there. Will you write me a note to Alika asking ‘Aikake to join me at Kawaihae?"

"Certainly, as long as I don't have to go."

Kānekuapu‘u, or "The Book Man," as the people called him, became a familiar figure at Honokahua's meeting place. So many people attended every week that Kaholo was obliged to construct a large open-sided hale hālau in the center of a large yard enclosed with a stone wall. On meeting days the new pā soon was filled, not only with Honokahua's farmers and lawai‘a, but also with many relatives and friends from Honokōhau and Kahakuloa.

After a teaching about "The Sower and the Seed," Kale asked Kaholo and Kāne to come back to her hale and watch the sunset. As they sat in the pā, toddler ‘Uwaikīkīlani played quietly.

"Kāne, Kaholo, and I do not know how to write, and we wish the people to learn too. Will you teach us?"

"Yes…I will require these things: a meeting time, separate from prayer meeting, Spanish dollars to purchase writing slates and chalk, and the number of students you wish me to teach."

"Kaholo, me, and the haku of every family…that makes 28."

"28 students! I thought you would start with 6 or 8!"

"If that is all you can manage, then 8 students to start now, and more later?"

"Yes, I recommend 8 now, and 8 more when they are proficient."

"Good, good, good. Kaholo will give you dollars."

Kāne was elated. He had been praying that Kale would come to know Christ and he took her enthusiasm as God's immediate answer. A shy smile broke his solemn demeanor. He blurted out, "Thank you!" but immediately regained his serious face. He struggled to hide his enthusiasm and stammered, "I thank God for you—and for Honokahua's thirst for learning."

'Uwaikīkīlani toddling into her arms distracted Kale, and she smiled at her daughter as she said to Kane, "If you can teach me to write, I will be thankful too." 'Uwaikīkīlani fell into her mother's lap giggling.

The vision of Kale and her baby reminded Kāne of Mary tending baby Jesus and he wondered at her beauty, as if he had never before seen her narrow nose and soft golden eyes or small chin and lovely full lips in a perfectly bowed smile. She held petite pretty 'Uwaikīkīlani in her arms and kissed her. The baby pulled back her head, looked into her mother's face, and touched her lips. Rays of red sunlight light traced across Kale's hair.

"Kale looked at him curiously. " Is anything wrong?"

"No—no," he stammered. "I was just observing what a good mother you are."

Kale smiled again at her daughter. "Thank you, teacher, but it is easy with such a good baby. She is my treasured lei."

"I wish Lāhainā women could see how the mothers of Honokahua dote on their children. It is a great tribute to God."

After a moment, Kale asked, "Do you think my God and yours are the same?"

Her question begged Kāne to tell her about Jesus and he jumped at the opportunity. "I do not know your god, but there is only one God, Iehova, and He is Lord of all."

"But everything you say about your God is true of my God too."

"Then perhaps they are the same—but how do you know your God?"

Kāne expected her to answer that she did not know her God at all. Instead, Kale said, "I have never seen him, but I know he is real because he answers my prayers—for me *and* for my people."

Kānekuapu'u suddenly recognized the presence of God; his spirit soared as it did when he fasted and prayed alone. He longed to cry out in praise and thanksgiving, but a tiny fear made him think about the cost of offending Kale, and he dropped back into the carnal world like a shot. The anointing was gone. He sought something spiritual to say and finally parroted a stock answer he had given to a hundred students, "Just keep praying. God's Word says, 'The fervent effectual prayer of a righteous man availeth much.'" He stood up. "Dear chief, I must leave now and report to you next week when reading and writing classes will begin. *Ā hui hou, e pōmaika'i 'ia Ke Akua.* Until then, may God be praised."

"Thank you, teacher. *Ā hui hou.*"

As Kāne left, he rebuked himself. *God was about to do a marvelous work and I got in His way.* He prayed: "Dear Heavenly Father, please forgive me, and continue to send the light of salvation to this woman. As she prays, please reveal Jesus Christ to her. And if you give me your words to speak again, I promise to take courage and not turn away. Amen."

As headman of the ahupua'a, Kaholo had become an influential person in Kā'anapali, but he never used his power for personal gain or recognition, preferring to live a humble, quiet life. His pleasant round face inspired trust and his shy habit of looking out from under his brow caused uninitiated traders to try their luck at cheating him. Once tried, they never again mistook his kind demeanor for weakness or indecision. Under his short curly hair Kaholo's ears stuck out a little, just enough to make his hearing acute, and he used this gift to great advantage when hunting in the uplands or listening to scuttlebutt in Lāhainā. But most of all he loved to surf.

Kaholo liked "the book man" and enjoyed his teaching; even more, he found in Kāne a friend who did not live at Honokahua and did not have anything to trade but companionship. When Kāne was teaching at Honokahua, the two spent the noon hours surfing, fishing, or hunting birds.

One morning, big waves crashing on Honokahua Beach awoke Kaholo and he thanked God it was the day when Kāne was coming. By the time he prepared an imu earth oven full of sweet potatoes and bananas, and took down his koa long board and Kāne's board, it was time to make his morning rounds. He began with the fishermen. Maunahina and Shaw were deep-sea fishing and their 'ohana women and children were busy repairing nets. Up Honokahua Valley, past Pilialoha's place, Halemano and his 'ohana were diging an 'auwai, and planning to harvest kalo in the halawai bottom land later in the day. When Kaholo got to Limaha'i's homestead on the kula, his crew was digging out one side of each row of sweet potatoes, leaving the rest of the tubers in the ground for next month, with their vines piled high above them. Last, he went to see how 'Āwa'a was doing with the dairy. All his haku had good reports.

Kāne arrived at awakea and Kaholo put his responsibilities aside for the noonday hours. The two thirty-five-year-olds walked up the dusty alaloa to Honolua Bay where the dark blue northerly swell was drawing up into frothy walls that swept toward the rock shore, curled over into rolling tubes, and crashed into billows of churning white foam and spray, sending deafening thunder up the cliffs to Punalau. Kaholo and Kāne were not alone. Many families lined the beach to cool off in the sea and watch their bravest members he'enalu, surf and hide in Honolua's waves.

The two took their time choosing when to paddle out between breakers and negotiating their heavy long boards through the crests to a place beyond where the waves break. There they sat on their boards, rested, and waited for a swell to carry them back to shore.

Kaholo saw his wave and paddled fast until he knew he had joined the wave and he felt it lift his board and carry him forward. He knelt, taking weight off the back of the board and allowing the front end to cut into the wave crest at an angle, and the wave was his. Kaholo lifted himself to his feet in one motion and leaned back into the wave; as it swept him toward Honolua's rock cliffs, he slid down the face, free in the breeze but a prisoner of the sea, a master powerful enough to take his very life. He touched the wave with his hand and when the aqua crest became transparent and thin enough to curl and fall, he kicked his board back, jumped down behind the crest, and watched the collapsing demon pound into the rocks. "UIHĀ!" he bellowed and the excitement of victory shot through his body as he paddled out again to his next ride. After several strenuous rides, he traversed a long cresting wave all the way to the foamy shallows near Honolua's rock beach and then took his board in. Kāne, who was not as strong as Kaholo, was already waiting on the shore where kids were playing, netting uhu parrot fish and catching 'a'ama crabs.

Soon the surfers were back at Honokahua, enjoying lunch.

"I love to come to Honokahua," said Kāne. "With no wife or family, I work at my ministry and forget to rest and have fun. I was sad when I was not assigned to the Olowalu mission substation close to my home in Ma'alaea, but God had pity on me and sent me you, my friend."

"It's good for me too. I look forward to going holoholo with someone who is not under my stewardship at Honokahua. Do you have a big lesson for today?"

"Very big—Acts, Chapter 17, 'These times of ignorance God overlooked, but now commands all men everywhere to repent'…Kaholo, I have to tell you I had a vision last week, concerning your chief and her child. I know she is a widow. But what happened to her husband?"

"She took Pāhaʻaikaua, a cattleman from Molokaʻi, for her husband and less than a year later he was murdered by a worker here. Pāhaʻa's memory lives in his child."

"It is very sad…and she is still young. Are her parents living?"

"Her father was ʻAikake, the warrior Hūʻeu, Kamehameha the Great's companion, who died when she was thirteen. Her mother died in the ʻōkuʻu plague and she is hānai to ʻOlohana Young."

Kaholo sensed his friend might be falling in love with Kale and his instinct was to protect her. "Her first husband, James Kānehoa Young lives here part-time and attends Kauikeaouli's court. Her second husband, Captain Adams lives in Honolulu with their son, ʻAikake."

"Hū! I thought this was her first baby. She is young to have so many husbands."

"She is a beautiful woman and a righteous chief who is loved by her people."

"And you, you have never thought to woo her?"

"Auwē! I am her konohiki, chosen by ʻOlohana to manage her land and protect her. I do not have a bloodline fit for the husband of a chief. If she chose me for her husband I would gladly go to her, but to 'woo' her would be most disrespectful to her and a shame to me."

"In God's eyes chiefs and commoners are alike and free to marry as God provides mutual love."

"Maybe, but here on earth I am konohiki of Honokahua and I am *not* free to marry whom I please."

"You say, then, that you love her?"

"I say I am her konohiki and to think such thoughts comes to no good end."

"Well, if you are not going to woo her, I will. I believe God has chosen her to be my wife."

Kaholo did not show any reaction, but a pang in his gut surprised him. He pictured Kale in Kāne's arms and "The Book Man" sitting in Kale's pā, giving out orders.

"How do you come to this? You do not know my chief. You do not rule any land."

"My family has land, but I do not rule; you are right. And I do not know her, but I had a holy vision when I spoke to her last week. If God has chosen for us to be man and wife, he will work out the details."

"I don't know about visions," said Kaholo. "My chief is a good woman, who has seen much disappointment, yet she loves her people and the blood of the land flows in her heart. You are a good man, but I must know; if you win her, will you stay at her side and never leave her lonely?"

"You speak like a father. You *do* love her."

Kaholo looked out from under his brow. "*Will* you stay by her?"

"Yes. I will love her as Christ loved the church and lay down my life for her—now it is time for the meeting. Are you coming?"

"I will join you later."

Kaholo watched Kāne walk over the kula before he returned to his hale. Inside he knelt and began to moan as he mourned his low birth. He clenched his teeth and pounded the mats with his fists until they bruised. Exhausted, he asked God to forgive him for holding on to a deep love for Kale all these years. "Please remove it!" he cried, "or else take me away! I will look for another konohiki position—ask the governor to reassign me." Before he even finished the sentence, he thought, what will I tell Kale?

"*Hui! Kaholo?*" Kale was calling outside his hale. He got up.

"*Eo, ku'u Ali'i Wahine.* Here, beloved chiefess." He rose and collected his thoughts but did not go to the door.

"Are you all right? It is time for the lesson. Please come and walk with me to the meeting."

He tied his malo and kīhei and went out. When he saw her smile he knew he would never leave her. "I must have fallen asleep. Forgive me."

"Forgive you? No need. You could never offend me."

After the meeting, Kāne asked Kale to stay behind and go over plans for the new reading and writing school. But he also wanted to evangelize her so that she would be a suitable missionary's wife. After reviewing his school plan he said, "Chief, I want to tell you more about Jesus Christ. If your God and my God are the same, then I must teach you about God's son who died as an offering for our sins." Suddenly Kale began crying. "I am sorry, Chief, What did I say? What did I do?" He handed her his handkerchief

Kale regained her composure and told Kāne how Pāha'a called himself an "offering" and called her a "gift." She told Kāne about her dream of Maui and the blood running into the sea, and of the waterspout that came down from heaven, the inspiration for ʻUwaikīkīlani's name.

Kāne listened intently and finally said, "God has shown you these signs for a reason. I believe he was teaching you how serious an offering Christ made for you, not just for others, but also for you. When a good man like your husband dies, it is a great sacrifice. But consider the magnitude of Jesus' sacrifice; the perfect and sinless Son of God, died for you."

After a moment Kale said, "Teacher, after Pāhaʻa died I wanted to die too. I could not accept him dying and me being spared—I felt so guilty and worthless. Why would God let his son die for someone so worthless?"

"You may feel worthless, but is it the truth? Kāne felt God warming his spirit and he spoke freely. "I look at you and at what Jesus did for you and conclude that God does not think you are worthless, but very valuable—so valuable that he chose to give up his only son for you."

"I don't know…"

"Look around! Look at the work God has given you to do here at Honokahua. And how he has blessed Honokahua with increase, and how he has given you children to rear. Did you become a chief or a mother by working hard, or did God give you these things?

"Yes, God gave me Honokahua and my babies…"

"He places great value on your person and your deeds. You are *not* unworthy! God chooses to love you and he is not wrong in his choice!"

Kale's eyes focused on Kāne as if she were trying to memorize every word he was saying and he instinctively repeated his last point. Then he said, "I believe God knows you, and you know him. If you read the Holy Scriptures, God will teach you more about Jesus and himself."

"I did study the scriptures when I was young, but I never understood them."

"That may be, but you are an adult now. Read them again now and see if I am right"

"Yes, teacher."

"Start with the Gospel of John. I will be reading along with you and if you have questions, I will answer them for you."

"One thing, teacher. How am I a gift?"

"God's offering was his own son, Jesus. God's gift is his love. God's love flows through you to others—you probably knew that already." Kāne smiled. "Shall I escort you back to your hale?"

"No, teacher. I want to walk on the beach and ponder what you said. Thank you."

The next day, Honokahua's Kahuna, Manu, fell ill and Kale had him brought to her hale so she could care for him. They prayed together every morning as usual, and he told Kale many stories of his family and the old days of the warring chiefs. He recited his mele inoa and his genealogy that came down from the Pāliko priests.

"These are the important things I would have passed on to my children, but I had none. I am the last kahuna of Honokahua and soon I will die."

The next morning she brought him his food. "*E ku'u kumu, 'a'ole anei e 'ai?* Beloved teacher, will you eat?"

" *'A'ole i pololi a'e.* No, I am not hungry."

"*Pehea ka'ōpū?* How is the stomach?"

" *'Eha.* Sore"

"*Ka wai?* Water?" He took a sip, but, unable to swallow, he dribbled it down his chin. Kale gently wiped his face.

"*Hele kokoke mai.* Come close. Come and receive my breath that I may die… Pray for the people and do not forget the ancestors. We are one…Take care of their bones and the land."

Kale remembered Hewahewa telling her she was the next kahu of nā 'iwi. "Yes, my kumu. I will do it."

"Maunahina," he whispered.

Kale called for Maunahina and his lawai'a fishermen. When they came in, Manu called them to his side.

"I have no son. You must carry on without a kahuna. Pray with your chief. Her god will answer. Pray for fish and pray for the chief." He blew on them with his last breath.

Kale lifted her voice and wailed. The fishermen wailed too, and soon the grieving rose up the valley and over the kula, as Honokahua mourned their last Kahuna Pāliko. Kale prayed, "O God, receive him in your bosom. Reward his faithfulness with eternal life." It was the first time Kale felt at peace in the presence of death. She knew Manu's righteous heart, and believed he was with Jesus, Keopuolani, and Pāha'a. She asked Maunahina and Shaw to help her prepare the body as Manu wished, in the ancient tradition.

That night Kale saw the many faces of God on a fiery throne above Honokahua's green hills and tree-lined riverbeds. Surrounding the fiery godhead were Honokahua's kūpuna, thousands of smiling faces, young and old, too many to count. Before the throne was a small man who stood erect and God called out his name…"Kiaʻi Pono", "Righteous Guardian." When the kūpuna bid aloha to the man he turned, and Kale saw that it was Manu. He was looking down at Honokahua's people. A few people were furiously preoccupied with work, but many others were looking up at the kūpuna and lifting up their babies to see them too. When Kale looked up again, she awoke and saw streams of light coming in her doorway. It was the day Manu's bones would rest with the kūpuna, but Kale knew he was already with them.

When Kāne heard about Manu's death, he wanted to have a Christian funeral for him but Kale declined. "It would not be wrong," she said, "but it would not be pono, right. We will bury him as he wished, in the ancient traditions he was faithful to until his last breath. You may come and offer a prayer if you wish." Kāne declined and Kale, Maunahina, Kaholo and the entire ahupuaʻa interred Manu, the last Kahuna, in the dunes. When the last chant ended and the last earth covered his bones, Kale looked up to the sky and smiled.

CHAPTER 11

Love Knots

Laura and Abner Pākī were married at Kawaihaʻo Church in Honolulu on December 5, 1828. Kaholo escorted Kale to Honolulu. Peke gave Kale a western style dress to wear, beautiful lavender peau-de-soie with seed pearls at the neckline, but terribly confining and uncomfortable. She gave Kaholo one of George Humehume's casual suits and they looked, for all purposes, like members of the high court.

All Kamehameha III's high chiefs were there, including pillars of the church, Kaʻahumanu and Hoapili. Laura's childhood playmates, including Ruth Keʻelikolani, Harriet Nahiʻenaʻena, Kinaʻu, Lilihā, and other members of the court—Kuakini and Kekauʻonohi, sat on chairs in the front rows. Even Boki risked being seen in church.

Alika came with his new young wife, Charlotte Harbottle, daughter of harbor pilot John Harbottle. Even James attended because he was in Honolulu at the time. First, a group of eight men and women sang hymns of Zion. Abner Pākī and his witness, John Papa Iʻi, stood at the altar, which was adorned by two large brass candlesticks and three red kahili; Laura, dressed in a white satin and embroidered silk gown and wearing a lei poʻo of pale yellow feathers, came down the center isle followed by her witness, Kapiʻolani, and Kale. Kale did not qualify as a witness because she was not yet baptized, or formally received into the church, but Laura insisted she stand at the altar. Reverend Hiram Bingham conducted the ceremony and Kale wept for joy when Laura and Pākī repeated their vows of devotion. Following the rite of holy matrimony was a simple reception. Kaholo stayed at Kale's side wherever she went.

"Charlotte, may I introduce 'Aikake's mother, Kale Davis, and Kaholokahiki," said Alika, who was dashing in his formal uniform and plumed black beaver top hat. It was the first time Kale had seen his new wife, and she wanted to show Alika that she was truly happy for him. Nevertheless, her mind nearly went blank.

"How do you do," said Charlotte, a very lovely hapa haole young woman with dark eyes. She smiled warmly, and Kale wondered what she was thinking.

"It is a pleasure to meet you," said Kale. Kaholo smiled and nodded. "I wish you every happiness," said Kale. "You and Alika are always welcome at Honokahua."

"I thank you for your graciousness. You are welcome too, at Niu."

Before the moment could become uncomfortable, James came up behind Kale, nearly shouting, "Kale, you look stunning in a dress!" Alika laughed and looked like he would chime in with a remark but checked himself. Kale blushed. She did look wonderful with her waist cinched in and the cleft of her breasts pressed up against the low neckline, but it was dreadfully hot in the new stone church building packed with royalty; all she could think of was getting the dress off.

"James, if you could know how uncomfortable these gowns are, you would never encourage women to wear them! I wore it only to please Laura. Excuse me, Charlotte, this is my stepbrother James Kānehoa Young." Then she pointed. "Oh, look how Laura glows with happiness. It was a beautiful ceremony." Turning back to Charlotte, she said, "Please excuse us. James, will you take me outside to get some air?" Kaholo knew Kale had a letter for James so he held back, and Alika immediately engaged him in conversation about Honokahua.

As they moved toward the exit, Kale whispered, "Oh James! I don't like it when my mind runs wild and I start to chatter like a bird."

"I know when you're uncomfortable. That is why I jumped in and saved you. Don't worry, Charlotte looked uncomfortable too."

Outside in the churchyard, Kale reached into her satin bag. "I have brought something for you." She smiled and handed him a sealed envelope. He recognized his father's scrawling handwriting.

"What have I done now?" he asked as he unsealed the note and began to read. Soon he was blinking to hold back his tears. "He asks my forgiveness and tells me he is proud to have me as his son."

Kale hugged him. "James, 'Olohana loves you and it is time to make amends. He wants to see you and tell you face to face."

"Thank you, Kale."

"Come, let's stroll in the garden." She led him away from the chattering crowd.

James was silent for a while and then he said, "I don't deserve my father's love or your attention." Kale could tell he spoke from his heart. "I have been drinking again…every time I go away from Honokahua, I drink, because I am weak. You do not understand because you have always been strong." He paused and then blurted, "I didn't just come to Honokahua to stop drinking. I still love you and I came back to see if you would take me back—that's why I do everything you say." He looked relieved at first, but he looked also for a response; getting none, he hung his head. "But I failed at that too. I regret what I have done and I am afraid of what I might do. In the middle of all this, I am a failure."

Kale wanted to hold him and console him, but she could not foster false hopes of a renewed marriage so she took his hand. "Oh, James! Please do not overlook all the good that is in you and the good you have done…You and I are different, yes, but not because I am strong. I am weak too…I never feel as though I belong anywhere—except at Honokahua. Look at me; I am strange here with all these fancy people, in this church building, and in this dress. I married you so I could belong to Honolulu society again but I failed at that. I fell in love with Alika, who reminded me of Papa, and nearly destroyed him trying to lure him away from the sea. I failed; when I set him free, I lost my boy…And dear, sweet Pāha'a loved the land as I do and devoted himself to me, but that brief taste of happiness and belonging made my widowhood the worse. I felt such shame that I did not protect Pāha'a and myself from Maka. It is a miracle that I am still alive…The reason I am different from you is that I find strength in God and he has always been with me."

"I wish I believed in God," said James

"Do you *really* do what I say?" He nodded. "Then come to Kāne's meetings, learn about God, and see what happens. I cannot explain it, but God takes away my fears and I know he will take your fears away too."

James did not know exactly what Kale was talking about, but listening to her there in the churchyard he felt a little expectant, a bit hopeful. He could not remember being hopeful since his youth, before the drinking began. Calm came over him and he sighed. Before he could think, he heard himself say, "I'll go to your meetings. I have nothing to lose."

Kale smiled. "I have prayed for you and God is answering my prayers."

At the close of 1829, Oʻahu Chiefs and Governor Boki in particular, were so indebted to foreign traders that Kaʻahumanu decided to pay the notes on the chiefs' behalf in return for their promise to refrain from further wanton spending of the king's money. In the bargain, she bought back the power of the throne from Oʻahu businessmen. It was a bold move, at a time when the sandalwood forests of Hawaiʻi were gone, and no new cash crop had emerged. The only chief who failed to accept her offer was Boki, the most indebted of all. He bet on more sandalwood windfall to cover his debts, rather than accept any favors from Kaʻahumanu.

He and his brother Manuia organized a sandalwood gathering expedition to Nānāpua, New Hebrides Islands, with over 400 crewmembers, and many prominent warriors and chiefs. Boki's ship, *Kamehameha*, was lost and all but a few men on Manuia's ship survived a deadly fever. The needless loss of hundreds of young Hawaiian men of rank ended the sandalwood era, and Hawaiʻi mourned again. Nevertheless, Kaʻahumanu regained the throne's power, and soon she was replenishing her treasuries with profits from the whaling industry.

The day after Kāne baptized Sarah Kale Kaniʻaulono, he came to her hale.

"Hello teacher. Is there a meeting today?"

"No meeting. I just came to see you." He looked down and fumbled with something in his coat pocket. Then he said, "I have been quite attracted to you these last months…"

Attracted? Oh dear!

"…and I believe that God has chosen you to be my wife." He looked up and smiled. Kale tried to smile back to be polite, but her eyes were round with shock.

"How do you know this?" she asked.

"When I first came to Honokahua I saw you one evening playing with ʻUwaikīkīlani, God gave me a vision of you as the Madonna–Mary with the baby Jesus, with your hair glowing. It was as if I was seeing you for the first time, beautiful and holy."

"That is the way you see me, holy?" The thought was absurd.

"Yes. I cannot get the vision out of my mind. I am here to ask you to marry me."

Married? She tried to be calm and polite.

"I cannot marry you, Kāne. I do not know you, and while I am fond of you as my teacher, I do not love you as one loves a husband."

Kāne looked surprised. "Perhaps you need some time to think about it—pray about my proposal."

"No, I do not need more time. I cannot marry you. Please do not embarrass us both by going on. Because I want you to continue to be my teacher, I will forget this visit. Perhaps you misinterpreted the vision."

"Yes, perhaps I did. I am sorry. Good day." He backed out of the pā, turned, and ran down the path to his canoe at the beach.

Kale watched him go and felt pity for him. It was difficult for him to ask. She considered going to Kaholo and telling him about Kāne's visit. *I did catch him staring at me—and now he shows up at my hale…*the thought kindled a familiar trembling fear, but she caught herself and consciously decided Kāne was not dangerous. And she had all but promised him not to tell anyone about the incident. *However, I will not allow him to be alone with me.*

On the next meeting day, the sea was an unusually calm for winter, so Kaholo and Kāne went deep-sea fishing. As they paddled around Makāluapuna Point, they saw the square "oven" at the end of the point. The six-pace square indentation did not look dangerous, but when a swell rushes against the rock point the surge flows up the "oven" with great velocity, pulling unsuspecting fishermen to their death. After an hour's paddling to get to Kaholo's secret fishing ground, Kāne steadied the outrigger canoe and maintained their position until Kaholo had finished releasing their very long coiled line into the water. Tied to the end of the main line was a large stone sinker. Six feet from the stone, Kaholo had lashed in a short bamboo cane crossbar and from it hung four short lines, hooked and baited. After the sinker dropped out of sight, Kaholo waited to feel it hit bottom. Then he pulled it back a bit off the bottom and waited, keeping the line just taught enough to feel the fish bite. When the bite came, he gave a quick tug on the line, released the slipknot on the sinker, and slowly pulled in the line. For their work, Kaholo pulled three kāhala out of his "calabash," his deep sea fishing ground.

On the way back into Honokahua Kāne suddenly said, "I asked Kale to marry me."

"And…" Kaholo's neck stiffened.

"She said she cannot marry me because she does not know me and she is not attracted to me in an amorous way."

Kaholo released the breath he was holding. "That is my chief, brutally honest. She broke your heart."

"Oh, no. I have not allowed myself to brood over her. I have to be about God's work and I will take whatever he gives me. If not now, then perhaps later; but I believe she will be my wife."

"Believe me," said Kaholo. "If she wanted you for her husband, she would say 'yes'. You have your answer."

The Bible lessons continued at Honokahua with two small changes: James Kānehoa Young became a new student, and Kale asked Kaholo to attend whenever Kāne gave her private lessons. Even so, Kāne kept finding opportunity to remind Kale that she would one day be his wife. Every time the answer was "No."

With much practice, Kale satisfied her lifelong dream to write her own letters.

Dear Isaac,

I hope you are able to come to Honokahua soon. I love you and pray for you every day. Do not despair that you cannot do everything you wish. It is a good thing to be fearless and continue to take courage. But your papa and I want you to be wise and consider the cost of what you do. Before you try something new, observe the risks of danger or failure, and decide, "what will I do if something goes wrong?" Grandfather 'Olohana never went to war without counting all the risks and planning a way of retreat. This is your heritage and you have it in you. Papa treats you like a man because he left home to sail the seas at your age; but you are still a boy, and your job is to watch, listen, and learn. Do as your father says now, and when you are big like Uncle Hū'eu, then Papa will be taking orders from you. Tell him I said so. Hulu asks for you and wants you to know he surfs Honolua now. Soon he will write to you himself. The rainy season is continuing and the hills are very green. Come soon.

Love to you,

Mama

Kale was also learning to read Hawaiian but there were only a few verses translated, so she studied Papa's English Bible and she was astounded at what she read. Now Keopuolani's words and blessings became clear, and Jesus' great commandments to love God and love one another rang true. The light of Christ did dispel her darkness and the deep wounds of her heart began to heal.

One day James asked her to forgive all he had done to her and stolen from her.

"I forgave you long ago, but, so you understand, I tell you I forgive you. But what did you steal from me?"

"Remember the dream you had to be happy together forever in Honolulu? I stole that from you and I am sorry."

Kale smiled. "I look back and I am grateful to be right here where I am. Why do you think of these old things now?"

"I am going to Kawaihae tomorrow and I want things to be right between you and me before I go. Will you pray for me?"

"Oh, yes!" She hugged him. "I pray for you every day, but tomorrow I will pray harder. May God give you courage and peace."

For two years Kānekuapuʻu taught two days a week at Honokahua and never gave up asking Kale to marry him. She warned him that she did not have amorous feelings toward him, but that protest did not quell his zeal. As she learned more about his determined character and his endless patience to teach her people to read and write, she grew fond of him and finally agreed to marry.

Kāne suggested that, as a missionary's wife, Kale should not "entice men to sin" by revealing her still-youthful curves, and she agreed to wear modest dresses, not fitted ones like the westerners, but loose-fitting flowing muʻumuʻu made from the kapa cloth of Honokahua and sewn together with cotton thread from England. But she refused Kāne's request to adopt dress codes for Honokahua. "If you have done your work and the people have Jesus Christ in their hearts, they will choose modesty as I have. Honokahua's righteousness comes from the heart—it is not laws but the blood of the land and the Spirit of God that keep us."

Laura Konia Pākī spent considerable time with Kale, enjoying the cool breezes and lush hills of Honokahua and visiting the court at Lāhainā, where Laura's dear friend, Queen Kinaʻu was raising Laura and Pākī's daughter Bernice Pauahi.

"I told Kānekuapuʻu I will marry him." Laura just stared back in disbelief. "He pledges his love to me every week!" protested Kale.

"But do you love him?" asked Laura.

"Yes, I love him…but if you mean 'do you yearn for him' as I did the others, no."

Laura shook her head. "Then I am not for it. What if you do not grow to love him but instead resent him? Then you will shatter the life of yet another man."

"Laura, I followed my passion into three marriages and look at me, I am alone. I plan to live out my days with Kāne. He loves my people as I do and he agreed to leave the Sandwich Isles Mission, come to minister at Honokahua full time, and stay by my side. I am willing to sacrifice passion for the deep needs of my soul, and in return, I will be a good wife to him."

"You talk like the missionary women, as if passion does not exist. If all you want is someone at your side, why don't you just take Kaholo for a husband? You know he will never leave you."

"I tell you I have considered it, even years ago. His kindness and strength are exactly what I look for in a husband. He has never touched me except to offer me his arm or help me get in the canoe. If he loved me, he had many opportunities to express his love but instead he pledged his dutiful loyalty to me—no more. He does not have amorous feelings for me. If *once* he ever had hinted at love, the flame I hold for him would have ignited."

"Why do you think he never took a wife for himself? I have never seen him in the company of any woman, here or in Lāhainā?"

"I don't know. But I do know that if I called him to be my husband he would come to me, but I would never know if he agreed out of love or duty."

"So you choose a loveless marriage for yourself, but another may not choose the same?"

"They may, but not at *my* bidding. I want all my people to be free, and most of all dear Kaholo."

"You are a better woman than I am, my righteous friend. I would have brought Kaholo to my bed as soon as I got here…but those were the old days." She grinned at Kale and Kale threw up her hands. "All right," said Laura. "If you think this is what you want, I will be your witness to marry Kāne. And may God help you."

In April of 1830, Kānekuapuʻu and Kale Kaniʻaulono were married by Reverend Richards at Honokahua Meeting Pā in front of all of Honokahua.

Kale felt the love of her people and her family who all came to bless her: Peke and her daughter Wahinekipi, James and his new wife Haʻale, Fanny Young, Grace and Dr. Rooke, Keoniana, Laura and Pākī, Alika and Charlotte Adams, twelve-year-old ʻAikake and six-year-old ʻUwaikīkīlani. Mother Kaʻoanaʻeha stayed in Kawaihae with ʻOlohana, who was too frail to travel.

Kāne's father Waʻapāʻoniʻole and mother Ahonuilani sailed up in a ferryboat from Maʻalaea with fifteen brothers, sisters, and cousins and eighty-year-old kupunawahine grandmother, Maʻolanalana. Kaholo stood up with his best friend Kāne and it was a blessed day.

What Kale failed to anticipate were deep-seated fears that pushed her to tremors at Kāne's embrace. From their first night together, she realized that she could not keep her end of the marriage contract.

"Forgive me," she sobbed. "I did not know the depth of my wounds. At your touch…fear and shame of that horrible night overtake me and all I can think of is running away. Oh Kāne, I want to be a good wife to you, but I am tortured by these memories as if they are happening again!"

"I do not know how you survived such an ordeal, Kale, but I know God put us together and he will heal your wounds. I pray he will grant me wisdom to minister to you. I have waited for you and I will continue to wait until you are ready."

Each night Kāne held her hand to his heart and gently petted her, whispering sweet words of love. When the tremors came, he let her go, saying, "Rest in God's love and trust me." And slowly, Kāle learned to endure, then accept, and finally enjoy intimacy as a gift of her husband's love; but never did she find the passion of her younger days. There was a calm resolve to her marriage. Precious to her was Kāne's continuing pledge of love and she came to rely on his constant presence.

When Kaʻahumanu died in 1832, after 36 years beside or behind the throne of Kamehameha's Kingdom, all Hawaiʻi mourned the passing of their most powerful beloved Aliʻi Nui Wahine. Her death left nineteen-year-old King Kauikeaouli to explore his rebellious years in relative freedom and opened an excellent opportunity for foreign businessmen, many of whom failed in their own countries before sailing to paradise, to whet the appetite of Hawaiian people for luxuries and vices of the great Western nations. With the most effective protector and champion of Christianity gone, Honolulu traders hoped to surpass the power they wielded when Governor Boki was alive. Kinaʻu was made Queen Regent.

By 1834, Honokahua's growing population produced record crop harvests and its fishermen netted storehouses full of salted fish. The hala groves in Kahauiki Gulch and alongside Hāwea Point gave enough lau hala leaves to make many mats, baskets, pillows, and hats, and the dairy was thriving. Cattle were now the most profitable product Honokahua ever had, at $2 per hide plus the salt beef and tallow, and demand kept rising.

After four years, Kale and Kānekuapuʻu had three children of their own: Amelia Nākai, Mele Kuamoʻo, and Fanny Kanekuapuʻu; all Kale's days were spent with toddlers. Ten-year-old ʻUwaikīkīlani learned mothering from Kale as she had learned from Kaʻoanaʻeha.

"I will tell you a story, but then you must go right to sleep. Do you know the eight winds of Maui?"

"Yes Māmā.," said ʻUwaikīkīlani. *Ka ʻAi Maunu,* the bait-eating wind of Hāna…*Ka Moae,* the customary tradewind…" She stopped when Kale looked at her, and motioned to let the younger children answer.

"…*Ka Nau, nā makani ʻanuʻanu o nā kula ma uka,*…The Nau, the teeth-grinding cold winds of the upland hills" said Nākai.

"*Ae,* yes," said Kale.

"*A me ke Kaumuku, ka makani o Maʻalaea, i ka home o Pāpā!* And The Kaumuku, the squalling wind of Maʻalaea, Papa's home!" cried Fanny

" *'Ae, Pane! E 'ike 'oukou i hoʻokahi aʻe?* Yes Fanny! Well, do you know one more?"

"The Oʻopū wind of Waiheʻe," said Kuamoʻo

"*Ka Kahalalele*…the dry, jumping wind from the south," said Nākai

"'*Ae. ʻO 'ehiku keia…a me ka hope loa, Ka…m-m…*Yes this is number seven, and very last…the…m-m," Kale cued them.

Kuamoʻo began and the other three joined in, "*Ka Māʻaʻa o Lele!* The reaching wind of Lāhainā!"

"*Maikaʻi nui loa!* Very, very good! Now here is my story: In the days of old King Hua, a very, very long time ago, the people were grumbling, and the namunamu grumbling caused the king great trouble. It seems a kolohe rascal wind was destroying crops and swirling red dust into high plumes around the houses, spoiling everyone's food and clothing. All the pigs and dogs were red. And even the children were all red…"

Kāne wisely left all of the farming operations to Kaholo and Kale and focused his time and effort to building a schoolhouse, north of Honokahua

Bay, above the estuary. The 1832 mission census counted the population of Kāʻanapali at 3200 persons, and 233 of them lived in Honokahua. Since Kāne was teaching at Honokahua, the mission built a church further north at Honokōhau Valley, the major population center of Kāʻanapali, where the Word of God was taking hold. This greatly decreased the number of persons coming to Honokahua services every week and took the pressure off Kāne. The literacy level of the ahupuaʻa was soon sixty percent. When the mission's new high school, Lahainaluna Seminary, began publishing the first Hawaiian language newspaper, *Ka Lama Hawaiʻi*, the Honokahua's Meeting Pā became a favored channel of information from the Hawaiian Kingdom and the world.

When Kaholo brought the monthly edition of *Ka Lama* back from Lāhainā, a line of people waiting to read the news would stretch up the kula. Wahine Haʻili was the keeper of *Ka Lama* and hung each page on a line between two posts so one group of four persons could read the front of the page, while another four read the back. When they were done, Wahine Haʻili would call up two more groups and move the first ones on to the next sheet. Like any good event on Maui, reading news became sport.

In the spring of 1834, Kale received a letter from Governor Hoapili requesting her to look in her ahupuaʻa for children adopted after the Kepaniwai Battle at ʻĪao in 1790. His younger brother, Kaiʻehu was born in the mountains during the battle and their father, Kameʻeiamoku gave him to some Kāʻanapali men to bring down out of the cold mountain air. Only two men from Honokahua survived the battle, the two kūpunakāne elders, Umuwena and Keahi. Kale went to them, and asked if they knew anything of this incident.

Umuwena said, "My chief, I am old and dying. I have but one son and he is the one you search for."

Kale was shocked. "Kapuniʻai?"

"Yes. When we were bringing Keopuolani down from the Mountains of Eke to sail to Molokaʻi, a high chief had the baby in his arms, but he had to return to the fight. He asked us to take the baby down, but not to send it with Keopuolani to Molokaʻi because the baby belonged to a Hawaiʻi chief and he feared she might kill it. The chief said he would come back for the boy. We saw Kamehameha's canoes sail away to Molokaʻi, and, when no one came for the baby, my wahine raised him as her own. When she died, I taught him to fish with me. I have the token of his birth the chief gave me, but I never knew that chief's name…Are you going to take my boy from me?"

"Not until I am sure he is the one they seek. Give me the token and do not speak of this to Kapuni'ai until Hoapili identifies the token. Until then Kapuni'ai is your son."

Kale and Kaholo went to Lāhainā to see Governor Hoapili. Lāhainā had become a bustling whaling town with more than a dozen western-style buildings, including Kamehameha's brick longhouse and watchtower, Reverend Richards' frame and stucco home and garden, Dr. Baldwin's coral stone house, the tall rock walls of Lāhainā Fort prison, and broad lawns of Waine'e Church. Storehouses and grog shops lined Front Street, a dirt road where sailors walked in the shade of the 'ulu trees, and the commerce of Maui was transacted.

"I am Kale Kani'aulono, Ali'i 'Ai Ahupua'a of Honokahua, and this is my konohiki, Kaholokahiki," said Kale. She put a lei 'ilima in the Governor's hand and he drew her to him and shared honi.

"Love to you, Kani'aulono. Why do you come to me?"

"I bring a token of your younger brother who was lost at 'Īao. A fisherman at Honokahua received it with a baby boy. Can you tell me of the token?"

"Auwē! I did not think the boy could still be living all these years. It was the palaoa fishhook of my father, made from the tusk of a walrus. The hair of the lei is ruddy 'ehu color because the boy, Kai'ehu, was ruddy like my father."

"Your brother lives," said Kale, as she handed him the palaoa.

Hoapili wailed and tears filled his aged eyes. "Tell me, where is he?"

"He is with me at Honokahua. My fisherman, Umuwena and his wife raised him as their own son and taught him to be a fisherman. He is called Kapuni'ai. Now Umuwena is dying and the boy cares for him. Shall I send Kai'ehu to you?"

"No. Send him when the old man dies. How may I thank him?"

"He loves Kai'ehu. Allowing him to die in his son's arms will be enough."

"How may I thank you?"

"I am just happy to see you reunited with your brother."

Kale embraced him and kissed his cheek. "Love to you and our God."

"And may he give you the desires of your heart, Kale."

CHAPTER 12

A Matter of Wills

In December 1834, Grace sent a ship to collect Kaʻoanaʻeha and ailing ʻOlohana at Kawaihae and transport them to Honolulu so her husband, Dr. Rooke, could administer a new heart medication and keep him under observation. True to his methodical attention to detail, ʻOlohana insisted on bringing his own coffin with him. "When I die, I don't want to leave any question about how I wished my body to be treated," he said. Fears of being murdered and having his body treated for burial in the old tradition, with chiefs taking his bones to make icons or fishhooks, plagued his pain-filled days and nights. Two weeks after his arrival in Honolulu, John Young breathed his last; while the Oʻahu chiefs planned his funeral, Grace sent for all the family.

Peke and Wahinekipi arrived at Grace's grand wood-frame home on Union Street in downtown Honolulu with Kāne, Kale, and her children: ʻUwaikīkīlani, Nākai, Kuamoʻo and Fanny. James and his new wife, Haʻale, and John Keoniana and his wife, Julia Alapaʻi, were already there. It was a very large two-story house with a wide sweeping veranda across the front of the building and four pillars that went up to the roof. The bottom floor was a clinic and dispensary. On other days, the sick and infirmed lined the walk, waiting to be examined by Kauka Luka, Dr. Thomas Charles Byde Rooke. Today, the lower level swarmed with mourners paying their last respects to John ʻOlohana Young. Grace and Thomas lived upstairs in British manor house style, with red Kashmir carpets, mahogany and dark oak furniture, and framed oil paintings on the walls. Kale's children were fascinated with everything and most fond of the grandfather clock that tick-tocked loudly and rang out a resonant gong every fifteen minutes.

The following day, seven-month-pregnant Fanny Young arrived from Hawai'i with Kale's brother Hū'eu, his wife Kaha'anapilo, and their two sons, George and Isaac. The last to arrive were Jane Lahilahi and her husband Joshua Ka'eo. Jane immediately retired to bed, suffering from morning sickness. Kale was pregnant too, but beyond her fourth month and feeling energetic. After all the family arrived, Thomas sent for Alika, who walked up from his home on Fort Street with tall, handsome, seventeen-year-old Isaac, who immediately came to sit next to Kale, put a lei on her neck, and kissed her.

"Let me look at you," she said, cradling his face in her hands. His long blond hair was tied back in a sailor's tail. He had Alika's thin nose and dancing blue eyes, but Kale's full lips and perfectly bowed smile. " 'Aikake, you have grown into such a handsome man!"

"Now that we are all assembled," said Dr. Rooke, "I will begin by telling you that 'Olohana prepared his last will and testament last year and named Alika and myself executors. To the best of our ability, we will administer his last wishes concerning the distribution of his lands and wealth. First, I shall read the will to you and later you may study it if you choose. Mother Ka'oana'eha is provided for first, and the remaining lands are divided equally among the Young and Davis children. Therefore, all of you will have to decide which lands you will live on or work."

Alika stood and addressed the family. "It is very important that these lands be managed properly so they are kept in the family. The king will confiscate lands that do not meet their tax obligations, and redistribute them to his cronies. Moreover, this year the tax burden is greater than ever. 'Olohana has responsible konohiki taking care of all parcels, so your role will be one of supervising the konohiki. I suggest that those with ability and resources stand forward and take what they can handle."

Dr. Rooke chimed in. "And if you wish to live on more than one of the properties in the future, take it to manage now."

"I will continue to live at and work Honokahua," said Kale. "If there are any parcels that are not of interest to other family members, I will oversee them until they may be of interest to the next generation."

James spoke up. "I live at Honokahua too, but I have no interest in or ability to manage land. The only land I would like to have is the small 'ili of 'Ula'ino in Hāna, where 'Olohana first stepped on Maui. It was his trophy and of little worth to anyone but Kamehameha's gunner and advisor."

Fanny said, "I, like James, have never successfully managed anything." Everyone laughed and the tension broke. "But I think it is good for the women of the family to have a piece of property that they may retreat to if they divorce or lose their husbands. I am divorcing Naʻea..." Kale drew in her breath and saw the shocked looks on all the faces around the room. "Behind closed doors he is not the public man you see—enough said of this." She looked at Grace and smiled. "Since Grace and Thomas have not had any luck having a child, I have decided to give the baby to them to raise as their own." Her announcement brought nods and smiles and tears of joy from the whole family, pleased that Grace, who had the desire and means to raise a child, would have this precious gift.

Grace just said, "Thank you, my dear sister."

The room got very quiet and Fanny went on, "I would like to live at Pahoehoeiki, Kona, near Māmā and George, and they can help me manage it."

Now everyone looked to Keoniana. "I am the youngest boy and it is my kuleana to take care of mother's needs, so give me the land where I live in Kawaihae. And like Kale, I will help oversee unclaimed parcels."

"Then I will take Waikoloa where my fishing business is located," said Hūʻeu.

Peke said, "I wish to live on Maui at Kapewakua where I now live and that is all I can handle."

"And I will take the Ewa land on Oʻahu, since I am living here," said Grace. "There is another parcel here at Waikīkī that I think Keoniana should have. Thomas thinks it is likely that Honolulu will become the future seat of government and since Keoniana is pursuing a government career, he should have some land near town."

"Well, it is a start," said Alika. "As time passes, lands of no interest to the family may be let go, but that will have to be decided by a majority vote of family members. Is that agreed? All those in favor say, "Aye.""

All said "Aye."

John Young's funeral was a dignified procession of Kamehameha's old chiefs and warriors who served with ʻOlohana, traders and businessmen, and a line of mourners that stretched over several hundred yards. As Kale and the family walked behind the casket from Rooke House to Kawaiahaʻo Church, minute guns discharged uphill at Punchbowl, downhill at the Fort, and in the distance from tall ships anchored in the harbor; the last of ninety three shots, one for every year he lived, echoed in the profound silence. Kaʻoanaʻeha and all the children held back their emotions, as he would have wished, but his comrades-at-arms wailed and gave him the full respect due a life-long trusted friend. Hiram Bingham preached a short message from the 90th Psalm, and Mr. Tinker prayed as Kamehameha's companion and gunner, foreign minister, and counselor was laid to rest at Pohukaina Mausoleum with highest honors.

Kale and Kāne followed the family back to Rooke House and a lūʻau luncheon on the side lawn under the huge old kou trees. The young cousins amused themselves at play and there was much reminiscing about ʻOlohana.

"He made my dream of being a ship's captain come true," said Alika. "When Kamehameha wanted to buy the *Forester*, ʻOlohana insisted that the purchase include someone who knew the vessel and could command the crew. I, the first mate, was 'bought' and pronounced 'Captain', a position I would never have attained on British or American merchant ships. To him I am forever grateful."

James was looking at the ground and then he said, "I ruined his dream of having Hawaiʻi in the British Commonwealth. For many years I drank myself nearly to death and caused him such humiliation but he forgave me...he was a great man and I wish I had come to know it sooner." He began to weep and his wife Haʻale put her arm around him.

"James," said Fanny. "He had such grand plans for all of us...in some way; we could do nothing but let him down. I know I never measured up to his ideals, and I thank God he is not here now to know I am divorced again."

"Oh, he *knows*, Fanny!" said Hūʻeu, and everyone snickered.

"You are right! He's up there with the high kūpuna aliʻi, isn't he—business as usual."

Kale patted Fanny's tummy. "I know he is as happy as we are that your child will have a good home. It carries royal blood, enough to be in line for the throne."

Keoniana jumped in "And it has enough white blood to survive the western diseases. Doctor, I think intermarriage with the whites is the only hope for the survival of the Hawaiian race—what do you think?"

"Well, I do not know if I would go so far as to say that is the only hope, but the hapa haole seem to be very hardy and to fare much better in the epidemics. Nevertheless, we have not seen the pox here yet and there is no reason to believe that hapa haole will survive better than other populations around the world, including whites. Grace and I see much suffering every day, and our idea is that better hygiene and less rum will have a much greater impact than breeding. One thing is certain: venereal disease *will* eventually kill off everyone unless we stop gratuitous sexual intercourse. I cannot tell you how many barren women there are now in these islands. Everyone with syphilis and gonorrhea will die a young and terrible death. Guard your children or there will be no grandchildren." Everyone soberly considered his remarks. Kale looked at Alika and they both shot an eye at 'Aikake. Kale thought, I hope his father has kept track of 'Aikake and his girlfriends.

The afternoon was pleasant and Kale took a walk with 'Aikake. He was a full head taller than Kale, with broad shoulders like Papa Isaac's. She locked arms with him and beamed. "Your father is so proud of you and when I see you, my heart swells so I can hardly breathe. Tell me how you like land management."

"Māmā, I love it. We have fruit trees at Niu, and I am learning how to produce good crops. You taught me so much, and I remember all of it, even though I was little. So many times the people think because I am white, I am ignorant. But thanks to you, I speak Hawaiian and know farming and fishing. I didn't know the Niu land, but I knew enough from Honokahua to figure things out. *He Hawai'i ha'aheo wau.* I am a proud Hawaiian."

"You were smart from the first breath, my son, but your best quality is your good heart. You were always kind and never rude or hateful. These things will endear you to your people. Don't ever let anything take you away from the land and your people."

"Māmā, Papa asked me to talk to you about my marriage." *Marriage! Oh No!* Kale was too slow hiding her reaction. "He said you might not like the idea."

"Like the idea…I cannot even begin to think about the idea, let alone *like* the idea!" She began to laugh at herself. Then 'Aikake laughed and they giggled themselves to tears.

"Oh, my son, forgive me." She hugged him. I see you are a man, but I think of you as my baby boy!"

"Māmā, I love a girl named Keli'iopunui Kalanikaukeha, and she reminds me of you."

"If Papa told you to say that, he told you well."

"No. I say it. She is beautiful and graceful, and her heart is Maoli. She is not afraid of me, or Papa, or anything. And she loves me the way you used to love Papa—we laugh and spend hours together and time passes before we know it…Māmā, are those your happy tears or the sad ones?"

"Happy ones," she blabbered. "If you love her, take care of her, protect her with your life, and never, never leave her. The one thing you must do is stay together. Are you prepared to do this, even when circumstances make life difficult?"

"Yes, Māmā."

"Come to Honokahua. Bring Keliʻiopunui to me and I will give you my blessing. Go now and tell your father I want to talk to him."

After a few moments, Alika came out to the garden grinning. Kale smiled at him and then the tears came again. He embraced her and said, "My dear, our son is a man and it is time to give him a good send off."

Kale laughed and pulled out a hankie. "First the christening, and then the launch! Just yesterday he was a baby and today I welcome his bride..." She looked at Alika. "He said she loves him the way I 'used to' love you, as if love comes and goes. For Charlotte's sake, I did not protest and tell him how I still love you. But you must tell him that once he gives his heart away, he may never claim it back. Please tell him love remains even after loved ones are parted or passed away. Otherwise he may not stay married."

Alika blinked, breathed in deeply, and exhaled before he spoke again. "Kale, you are just weepy because of your delicate condition, the funeral, and now this wonderful news. Shall we take a walk?" He offered her his arm.

"Yes, Captain Adams, make me laugh."

"I shall do my best, Sarah Kale Davis Young Adams Pāhaʻaikaua Kānekuapuʻu." She flashed her eyes at his teasing and he laughed. Kale watched Alika work his charm. His blue eyes twinkled under his snow-white eyebrows and the familiar smiling creases around his eyes reflected back her joy. His pilot's uniform complete with gold braid, brass buttons, and medallions reminded her of the day they fell in love.

Soon they were half a mile away from Rooke House, sitting on a hill overlooking Honolulu and the harbor. From above the treetops, Kale only saw corners and rooftops of the many homes, shops, and warehouses of Honolulu and she thought of her childhood days when just a few grass huts dotted the shore. How grand the fort seemed then. Now it was just one feature in a landscape full of man-made objects that nearly obscured the view of the shoreline. In the harbor, more than 40 ships flew their colors at half-mast for ʻOlohana. It was the end of an era.

Alika took off his jacket and looked out at the harbor. "Kale, I have always been honest with our son. I tell him how I love you and miss you and he knows love does not die...but until today I did not know you still love me...I waited such a long time before remarrying..."

His eyes welled up and he looked down, wiping them. Kale touched his shoulder and her heart broke for him again. She drew a breath. "I am so sorry that I hurt you. My thought was that I had caused you enough pain and further contact would only keep you from the happiness you deserve. Please tell me you are happy."

"As happy as I suppose you are," he said flatly. Then he searched her golden eyes.

He sees my unhappiness... She asked, "Do you remember the day you came home and I was hiding James at Honokahua—and you knew by just looking at me that I lied to you?"

He snickered. "Yes...you're not going to lie to me again, are you?"

"No." She leaned over and kissed him and he held her gently in his arms for a moment and then kissed her deeply. A thrill radiated through her body and danced on her skin as she let him kiss her neck and she pressed herself close to him. In the next moment, she knew she had made a mistake.

She pulled away, "Please—My love for you remains in my heart...but this can go no further."

"For God's sake, Kale, have pity on me! We should be together. Is not constant love enough?"

"For *God's* sake, I cannot break two more hearts...my husband, your wife— and my children—I will not risk losing my children, or Charlotte losing hers. No. At this moment my heart aches for you, but this is not right..."

"All these years I pined because I thought your heart had gone cold and today, you reveal your enduring love for me and give me hope anew—but for nothing?"

She looked up at him and saw his pain. "After Maka raped me, my heart and soul *were* cold. I could not love anyone but my children and God—I thought you would be happy to be free in Honolulu." He looked down and shook his head. "I did not think I could ever love again. Kāne wore me down with marriage proposals and I allowed him to marry me so I would not be alone."

Alika looked again. "And he gave you the one thing I could not..."

"Yes. Kāne has been at my side, faithful, and kind—and I was contented until I kissed you today..." She stood up. "But it is done. I will return to him knowing that I am capable of passionate love, but denied it...worse off than before...I have paid dearly for companionship."

"And I have paid dearly for position and wealth. I was a fool to leave you."

"Alika, don't make the same mistake again. Build your life around Charlotte and never leave her alone...I am supporting Kāne in his work. I will never interfere with his dreams as I did yours. Forgive me...."

Alika turned to her again. "I have lost you for the last time then…" Their eyes tried to hold the moment, knowing the inevitable answer.

Finally Kale whispered, "Please go back to your wife and pretend today never happened."

"It did happen. I will never forget that you love me, my dear, and I will always love you."

Kale watched Alika walk down the hill and she sat for a while, trying to focus on her children. Pretty ʻUwaikīkīlani is petite, but even so, she looks older than her age. I must talk to her about protecting her heart, body, and soul by choosing wisely when young men woo her.

Sweet Kuamoʻo, grandma's namesake, the dark-skinned beauty with my eyes, she is so easily hurt, and so loving. How can I protect her from heartbreak?

I will never have to worry about Nākai. She is tall, athletic, and a leader. When the children play games, she always wins. She never ventures into anything without full assurance that it will be righteous, and that she will come out ahead.

And little Fanny is still my baby. How I love her!

Finally, Kale prayed to God: Please forgive me for putting myself in a position of temptation. I came so close to committing adultery and I thank you for giving me a way of escape—but Lord, I am suffering and I feel so unworthy of your love and kindness. Please find the hurtful ways in me and cleanse me. Do not let me hurt my husband. Please give me as deep a love for him as I have for Alika. And please let Alika forget me…" The finality hit her like a cold wind.

Then she remembered her precious son. "And bless ʻAikake and Keliʻiopunui with affection and steadiness and long life. Amen"

Kale returned to Honokahua sober with the reality of her commitment to Kānekuapuʻu and her children. She prayed every day for strength and kept busy with details of farming, fishing, and the slaughter of steers for hides, salt beef, and tallow.

With the help of Kānekuapuʻu's friends in Olowalu, James expanded his canoe business into a small barrel works, keeping Honokahua self-sufficient, a strategy that Kaholo insisted would best preserve the land and the village.

Kāne was as serious as ever, intently focused on Honokahua School, a beautiful wood-frame building set up on pilings four feet off the ground to protect it from flooding. The front had a wide veranda and the steps passed between two large river rock pillars. The farmers insisted on thatching the roof, since Honokahua was famous for its thick pili grass, and soon trailing morning glories covered the roof. Every morning the children under ten attended school, and Kāne taught them to read, write, and calculate.

ʻAikake, Keliʻiopunui, and her family came to Honokahua in February and Kale and Kāne gave them a big reception lūʻau. Keliʻiopunui was a lovely girl who was very much in love with ʻAikake.

"Oh ʻAikake, I love your bride. I thought I might be jealous of your attention to her, but she has a good heart and she loves you dearly. It is a good match."

"Māmā, I knew when you talked with her you would love her too. Her mother and aunts were so surprised to see my Maoli family. You were the main topic of conversation and they love you."

The couple was married in Kāneohe in March and the Kalanikaukeha clan's large family and lavish hospitality was a perfect setting for Kale and Kāne to interact gracefully with Alika and Charlotte.

High Chiefess Kinaʻu's first action as Queen Regent was to shut down Oʻahu's stills and destroy the rum. King Kauikeaouli and his retinue of young chiefs and chiefesses, called The Hulumanu, continued to amuse themselves with drunken outings and licentious living in the countryside, to the consternation of the older chiefs. A major scandal was the day the King divided Molokaʻi lands among the Hulumanu, leaving the Molokaʻi chiefs landless.

After Kaʻahumanu had converted to Christianity, many of the highest chiefs joined the church and practiced the temperance, morality, and self-control of Jesus' teachings. But the makaʻāinana were slow in joining a church that taught the sanctity of marriage but did not denounce adultery and incestuous marriages of the aliʻi, marriages that commoners always considered sinful, even under the old religion. Finally, missionary teachers took a stand against incest and excommunicated Princess Nahiʻenaʻena, who was cohabiting with her brother, King Kauikeaouli. From this time, conversions among commoners tested the ability of the church to receive the multitudes.

Hopes for an heir to the Kamehameha throne withered when Kauikeaouli and Nahiʻenaʻena's infant son lived only six days and by 1837 Nahiʻenaʻena herself was laid to rest in Mokuʻula Lahāinā, in the "calm of Hauōla." Kauikeaouli mourned his sister and seemed despondant until he announced his marriage to Kalama.

Queen Kalama was soon pregnant with Keʻaweʻaweʻula. While she was in seclusion, Keoniana ʻopio, Kale's little step brother, was found sleeping with her and the King sentenced him to death. The laws against adultery were clear and high chiefs of the court met to discuss how to carry out justice. Hoapili finally interceded with the king and Ka'oana'eha's only son escaped an early death. The experience caused him to stop drinking and begin a responsible role in the King's government, and the Young and Davis family rejoiced.

By her 8th month, Kale became increasingly uncomfortable in the summer heat, and finally gave up her frantic work schedule for mornings of weaving with the old farmer women and afternoons with the children at the beach, collecting shellfish and salt. It was a time that she treasured, teaching little Fanny to swim and showing the girls how to fish.

Now that the school was well-organized, Kāne and Kaholo built a proper church over the Meeting Pā area, a huge thatched hale with windows all around and an overhanging hipped roof supported on heavy poles, so overflow crowds of worshippers could stand outside and hear the message, protected from the elements. Kāne selected two men and one woman from Honokahua as deacons: Halemāno, Limaha'i, and Lahela Shaw. Soon they were conducting three services every Sabbath, and Kāne was teaching a choir to sing the hymns of Waine'e Church. When Kale heard broad mellow voices singing God's praise, ringing up the valley and over the kula, her heart filled with thanksgiving. *God, you are indeed giving me the desires of my heart!*

Kaholo had traded for two more horses, one for Kāne, and one for Kale. He spent most of his days riding around to his haku, keeping track of the mauka, upland operations, and makai, lowland industries. One afternoon he was helping Makekau resolve a dispute with a farmer whose bean patch became prime fodder for a wandering steer. On the way back down to the fishing village, Kaholo saw Kāne's horse tied to a tree at the edge of the lower forest. As he rode closer, the sound of his horse disturbed some lovers and his eyes burned with anger when he recognized Kāne and a young farmer's daughter behind a rock outcropping, pulling on their clothes. If it were anyone else, Kaholo would have ridden away and forgotten the incident, but betrayal of his own trust and the honor of his chiefess were at stake. Kāne was his chief, but Kaholo's rage burned as he galloped toward them. Kāne was shaken and speechless. The young girl hid behind him.

"Please, Kaholo, do not harm us," he stammered.

"Can I harm you more than you have just harmed yourself? You teach morals but you yourself are an adulterer! You call me your friend, but you lie to me and betray my chief. Adultery is a crime punishable by death at Honokahua. That is what YOU teach!"

"And *you* are konohiki. *I* am your chief and I can banish you from Honokahua for talking to me this way." The girl shivered.

"Do what you want to me, but do not do any further harm to my chief. She has been a good wife to you. She carries your baby while you fornicate with this young girl!"

"Kale does not love me!"

"She loves you enough to bear your children! And she believes you love her—but now I know the truth."

"I beg you not to tell Kale! Do not tell anyone!"

"I will not tell my chief because she is ready to give birth and I would not upset her or risk her health. But I will be watching you and if you betray her again, there will be no words between us. I will crack your bones, you and your lover, and leave you both for the wild pigs!" He pulled his horse around and rode down to the village.

When Kāne got home, Kale greeted him cheerfully and obviously knew nothing. Kaholo had not been at the hale. Kāne trembled with remorse, fear of discovery, and impending loss of his life's work. He walked to the beach and fell flat on the sand. "Oh God, forgive me."

Just after sunset, an eight-foot tide swept down the Pailolo Channel, ripping boats from their moorings at Lāhainā and all along west Maui's coast. The next day news came that a kai e'e, tidal wave hit Ma'alaea, and swept away the entire village of 26 huts. First the sea drew out 75 to 100 paces, leaving fish flapping on bare sand, and then a wave formed into a steep precipice, rushed the beach, and pushed people and property into the Kanahā Pond behind Pu'unene, many furlongs away.

Kāne immediately ordered two fishermen to paddle him to Ma'alaea to see about his family. Kale said, "Please take two more canoes filled with food, kapa cloth, and drinking water to give to the people—and bring back your family to Honokahua to live with us until they can rebuild their homes." Kāne turned back to Kale to say a word of parting but shame and grief left him speechless. To Kāle he just looked as serious as he always did, so she hugged him, kissed him, and wished him a safe journey as he left Honokahua.

What used to be the busy village of Ma'alaea was an empty mud and sand plain, completely razed except for a few banana tree and coconut palm trunks. The tidal wave carried all 150 persons of the village the length of the isthmus to a place below Wailuku, but only two elderly women perished. The local fishermen said everyone just swam and floated until the water returned to the sea. Maʻolanalana and all Kāne's family were safe, and they rejoiced. Kāne secretly thanked God for not punishing him as he deserved. For two weeks, he and the five Honokahua fishermen built new hale for Kāne's family. For Kāne, the time was filled with remorse and fear.

When Kāne returned, Kale greeted him and asked him to sit down for hoʻoponopono.

"What is it? Did Kaholo come to you?"

"Kaholo? What does he have to do with Māhuaʻai's daughter, Kalei?" Kāne hung his head. "The girl came to me with her father and told me she tempted you and caused you to sin with her. What do you say? Did you make love to this girl?"

"She is not to blame. She is just a girl. I saw she was attracted to me at school and I took advantage of her. She tempted me, yes, but I sinned against you and against God."

"I have had two weeks to think about this—as you have. What do you want to do now? Do you love this girl?" asked Kale.

"I want to be your husband. I do not want the girl."

"And if she is pregnant, then what?"

"I will not take the child from her if she wants it."

"And what of me? Will you abide by my wishes too?"

"Yes."

"Then this is what I want: repent of this sin and after you have prayed, if you believe you will not stray again, come back to my bed. However, if you think to come back to me out of duty or need of wealth, do not come back. I will release you or give you the money you need to live elsewhere."

Kāne wept. He started to leave and turned back. "Kale, have you been faithful to me?"

"Yes…I have been tempted, but by the grace of God I escaped. That is how I can find mercy for you."

"I doubted your love because you never seem to desire me as I desire you."

"Kāne, I told you I could not give you amorous love and you insisted that we marry without it. I love you, but I am sorry the love I have for you is not the same love you have for me." Kale waited a moment then she asked, "Tell me, is your love stronger or weaker than mine?"

"Weaker." He wept again and she held him in her arms like a child.

"I forgive you for taking the girl, but I will not suffer such a betrayal a second time. Perhaps God will give me passion for you but if he does not, you must decide if the love I can give you is enough."

"I do want to stay with you."

"Good. Then go to Māhua'ai and have ho'oponopono. If Kalei has a child, tell Mahua'ai we will support it. Tell Kalei that if she wants to put the baby away, she should give it to me. I will raise it."

"I will go to the family but I cannot face the Church. I will give up my ministry."

"Please pray about this, Kāne. We are all sinners, and we must all accept forgiveness. I believe if you take courage, confess your sin before the Church, and ask forgiveness, they will shower you with love. After Maka raped me, the women of Honokahua thought I would kill the baby. When I did not, the women took courage too and the practice of killing newborns stopped. If you show them that God forgives even his preachers, it will give the people courage to repent and seek forgiveness for their own sins."

Kāne looked into Kale's eyes. "I am the minister, but you walk with God. I saw that in you at the start."

"I love God and he is always with me but you have been called to teach, and this I cannot do. Please, take courage and teach the people repentance. I will stand by you, and God will make something very good come from this trouble. You will see."

In two weeks, Kale delivered her second son, James Kānehoa Young, named after her stepbrother, who had no children. JY was big and plump, with a round face like Kāne's mother, Davis square shoulders and broad back, and sweet folds at his wrists and ankles. James wanted to adopt him but Kale refused, "I will raise him, but you may spend as much time with him as you wish. He will grow up knowing how much I love him."

In 1838, Queen Regent Kina'u died of mumps and was succeeded by Miriam Kekauluaohi. Reverend Richards left the Sandwich Isles Mission and went to Honolulu to teach Kauikeaouli Kamehameha III and his court a course on Political Economy, so they could decide what kind of government would best apply to the Hawaiian Kingdom. Fed on the Magna Carta, Jefferson, and Descartes, Kauikeaouli chose liberty and inalienable rights for his people and on June 7, 1839 enacted a Declaration of Rights including property ownership, universal suffrage, trial by jury, and a uniform system of taxation.

Kāne's confession and repentance in front of the church and Honokahua village shocked the people, but they were hesitant to judge him harshly because they too could count their own hidden sins. By 1839, the Meeting Pā was just not large enough to accommodate the many Christians at Honokahua, where love and forgiveness were taught and practiced. Kāne and Honokahua's men built the first church in Honokahua, a wood-frame building facing the sea over Oneloa Bay, large enough to accommodate all the newly baptized Christians thirsting for the Word of God and making a joyful noise of praise and thanksgiving to *Ke Akua a ke aloha*, the God of Love, with music that filled the Honokahua breeze like fragrant perfume. Throughout Hawai'i nearly 80 percent of native Hawaiians attended weekly services and the literacy level of the Sandwich Islands was the highest in the world, including England.

CHAPTER 13

Upheaval at Foundation Bay

The crashing waves of change in Hawai'i were not followed by a drawing-out, a time of quiet recovery; instead, a surge of whaling, mercantile growth, foreign involvement in government, cash-crop agriculture, and epidemics pounded Hawaiian shores. The waves swept away those who turned their backs.

"Mama, I love him." The words were cause for great joy any other time, for any other girl, but Kale still held 'Uwaikīkīlani too close to her heart. At sixteen, her perky petite daughter, who had Pāha'a's beautiful rich-toned smooth skin and sweet innocent dark eyes was about to embark on her life's journey with a man nearly twice her age.

"I understand." Kale stroked 'Uwaikīkīlani's long dark hair and remembered how she fell in love with Alika's confidence and savoir-faire and how she looked to him for security and approval. Kale knew. "You say he has a good reputation and he is kind to you?"

"Yes, Mama…when I am with Johnnie, I feel so much at peace. He knows so much about the world and business. He is a Christian man and he is building us a wood house in Lāhainā like the houses in America."

"Did you tell Kaholo about your plans? He thinks of you as a daughter and you should ask his blessing too."

"Oh Mama, forgive me, but I went to Kaholo first. I asked him to stand with me at the wedding. He welled up and could hardly speak. He gave his blessing. He knows Johnnie will take good care of me."

Kale smiled and took 'Uwaikīkīlani in her arms. "You are a good girl. Kāne approves because Johnnie is a church member and I think it is a good match."

John Joseph Halstead, a small but muscular man from New York, with sun-bleached hair and short beard was waiting in the pā, and as Kale and ʻUwaikīkīlani came outside he looked anxiously at them. His western clothing was brand new and fit him very well. He held his hat in one hand and a gardenia lei in the other.

"*Aloha iā ʻoe, e Ka Wahine Kānekuapuʻu,*" said Johnnie.

Kale smiled at his strange pronunciation and responded, "*Aloha nō, e Johnnie.*" He waited for her reply before he approached and put the lei in her hand.

"You are very respectful, Johnnie. ʻOluʻolu ʻoe…You are kind…" Kale lowered her head. He placed the lei on her neck they shared honi.

"I have come to ask for your daughter's hand in marriage. I promise to take good care of her. I love her deeply as she loves me."

"You were a sailor. Are you content to live in one place now, or will you go back to the sea?"

"I am a carpenter, and I went to sea for the fortune. Now I have settled in Lāhainā, where I have a good carpentry business. I will not go back to the sea."

"Do you promise to keep her by your side and never make her lonely?"

"Yes, I want her by my side forever."

"Then I say yes. It is my daughter's wish to marry you and I give you my blessing. May God bless and protect you both with steadiness, affection, and long life." It was the family blessing that ʻOlohana gave Kale and Alika so many years ago.

"Oh Mama, I am so happy!" ʻUwaikīkīlani giggled and hugged Johnnie. "I told you she would love you as I do."

In January 1840 John "Johnnie Liʻiliʻi" Joseph Halstead and ʻUwaikīkīlani were married at Honokahua. Kaholo and Kale stood with ʻUwaikīkīlani. Johnnie's partner, Samuel Hoyt, and Kāne stood with Johnnie. They took up residence in the first log home in Lāhainā, which Johnnie built for his bride. Every week they sailed up to Honokahua on Johnnie's boat, the *Jane*, for Sabbath dinner.

In May 1840 the royal sage, counselor, and defender of Christianity, Governor Hoapili, died in Lāhainā; before the time of mourning was over, rum and prostitution returned to Lāhainā Roads, ending the peaceful time of law and order he commanded. Most of the old chiefs who served Kamehameha the Great were dead, and with them died the tenets of a Stone Age culture and social system that served Pacific islanders well for millennia. Lahainaluna educators like Richards, Malo, and Iʻi focused on helping Hawaiians enter the

Industrial Age, and pressed on to educate, chronicle oral traditions, forge a constitutional government of written laws, and change hearts, but the riptide of western business ventures and foreign intrusion outran them.

Kauikeaouli Kamehameha III was a popular king and he wanted elected representatives rather than foreign advisors running his government, but chiefs, governors, regents, foreign ministers, and kings had proclaimed so many conflicting laws that confusion led to chaos. This problem of governing style was small compared to political outfall of the ali'i's indebtedness to foreign traders, and the very independence of the Hawaiian Kingdom was in jeopardy. The King dispatched William Richards and Timoteo Ha'alilio to Europe to secure treaties with Britain and France and with America, declaring Hawai'i an independent kingdom.

On a clear day in early February 1843, the *Jane* rounded Makāluapuna point, and Kale went down the beach path to greet Johnnie, 'Uwaikīkīlani, and baby William. As the small fishing boat neared shore, she saw her sister Peke, Wahinekipi, and Peke's grandchildren were huddled in the back with Johnnie's toolbox and net bags full of their belongings. This was not a family outing. Kale waved and called, "*Aloha nō ho'i E Peke! E ku'u mau keiki!* A very warm hello to Peke and my dear children!"

Their eager waving did not hide expressions of concern and Kale knew something was wrong. Kāne also saw the unexpected visitors and was on his way down the beach from Honokahua Schoolhouse. Kale called to him, " '*O Ka Lāhainā mā āpau, kēia! Kūnānā au i kō lākou hele mai 'ana.* All the Lāhainā clan is here! I am puzzled why they came."

Kāne and fisherman Ho'ohei were helping the children ashore, when Peke's daughter Wahinekipi collapsed in the boat. Johnnie and Kane lifted her up and carried her to shore.

Kale had three-year-old William and Wahinekipi's four-year-old by the hands. "Take her up to my kauhale—in the mua. Ho'ohei, go and tell Nākai to come to my kauhale. Her cousin Wahinekipi is not well."

Peke was breathless, and held her sixth-month old infant granddaughter in her arms. "We came to save our skins, Kale. Lāhainā is in mayhem! The Union Jack is flying at the harbor, all the prisoners from the Fort are roaming the streets, and the whalers have gone mad! It is the worst thing that ever happened!"

"The British attacked Lāhainā?" Kale was shocked.

"The British man-o'-war just sailed in and Captain Lord George Paulet hauled down the Hawaiian flag on the Fort, let out all the prisoners, and declared Hawaiian Law null and void. He raised the Union Jack in the name of Queen Victoria!" said Johnnie. "The King was in Honolulu, so Honolulu must have fallen."

"We had to protect ourselves and the children," said 'Uwaikīkīlani.

"Yes, yes, you did the right thing. Where is Wahinekipi's husband?"

"We do not know!" Peke began to weep. "Miki'opio sailed to Honolulu four days ago and he must have been there when the attack came."

A thought of Alika defending his Port and King against his beloved motherland quickly faded in the reality of her family's immediate needs. "'Uwaikīkīlani, please take the children up to Nākai's home. I will send up some farm girls to assist you. You are safe there. I see Kaholo coming now and he will protect us. Go on. These little ones look tired and hungry." She turned to Peke. "Is Wahinekipi sick or faint?"

"Oh, she is pregnant again and this time is the worst. From the start, she has been tired and very sick. She already has four little ones to care for, and now she is suffering so much she cannot manage at all. I have been taking care of the whole brood for months and she gets worse by the day."

"What does Dr. Baldwin say?" asked Kale.

"He says her frail body is worn out bearing children and she should not have any more babies."

"We need to have Kekahuna examine her right away," said Kale.

"I'll go up and fetch her," said Kāne.

"Thank you, my dear husband. I will help Peke and Johnnie get settled in our home and talk to Kaholo about securing Honokahua."

Against Kale's wishes, Kāne went to Lāhainā to see Dr. Baldwin the next morning. "I am just a poor teacher and of no use to the British or the whalers," he said. All Kale could think of was the hatred sailors had for Baldwin and the others who opposed prostitution and promoted temperance. "Please be very careful. I do not wish to lose you."

"As God wills. If I am successful, we will find out what is going on."

Kekahuna began treating Wahinekipi with minerals and herbs. Kale and Peke attended to her and 'Uwaikīkīlani took care of her children.

"This girl has no strength, no blood. She must rest and eat lū'au greens and 'alaea earth every day. No salt. The baby is not one, but two. I will do my best to keep them all alive."

Kale and Peke were astounded. They never knew a woman to have two babies at once and they speculated how this could happen and what it might mean.

The family rejoiced when Kāne returned that evening and announced, "There was no attack on Honolulu."

Kale sighed with relief.

"Lord Paulet came to collect payments for many debts King Kauikeaouli owed British citizens and the British government. When he threatened to fire on Honolulu unless the King paid the notes in full, the king admitted that the entire treasury did not amount to the sum owed. Lord Paulet then announced that he was authorized by Queen Victoria to receive the Kingdom of Hawai'i and all its assets to pay the debt. With no other alternative, and looking down the bore of Paulet's guns, King Kauikeaouli ceded Hawai'i to Britain. That is when Paulet raised British flags on all the islands and abolished Hawaiian Law."

"Oh my!" cried Kale. "After all Papa and 'Olohana went through to support the Kings and to build a peaceful land, what a pity to have it squandered away. Some will be happy to have us in the British Commonwealth, but not Alika."

"Why, Mama?" asked 'Uwaikīkīlani.

"He is like your grandfather. They were poor common people in Wales and Scotland. When they came here, Kamehameha gave them important jobs and he made them ruling chiefs. If we are now a part of Britain, British governors will come to rule, and in their eyes, men like Alika are commoners. It would have been better for everyone if the Kingdom of Hawai'i had remained independent. Then Alika would retain his wealth and status under Hawaiian Law. It is a shame."

"At least we hope to see our loved ones in Honolulu once again," said Peke.

Kale knew she meant John Meek, Miki'opio, Wahinekipi's husband, but Kale's mind was full of pictures of Isaac and Alika: his dancing blue eyes charming everyone, the roll of his Scottish accent describing pictures of his homeland and fantastic escapades, his proud gold-trimmed captain's uniform, and his jovial exploding laugh.

"Yes, thank God, we will see them again."

Lawlessness and violence continued for five weeks, but Honokahua was a safe haven for Kale's extended family. Treasury Minister of the Hawaiian Kingdom, Dr. Gerrit Judd, wisely hid the Kingdom's documents in the Royal Mausoleum, and by lamplight penned a formal protest to Queen Victoria while leaning on Queen Ka'ahumanu's casket. The letter of protest must have convinced

Victoria that Lord George Paulet had acted beyond his mission, because she dispatched Rear Admiral Richard Thomas who dismissed Paulet and formally returned sovereignty to King Kauikeaouli. It was over this incident that the King first spoke the motto of the Hawaiian Kingdom, "*Ua mau ka ea o ka ʻāina i ka pono*, the sovereignty of the land is perpetuated in righteousness." Soon after, Richards and Haʻalilio returned from their successful mission to establish Hawaiian independence.

Against Kale's wishes, John Meek took Wahinekipi back to Lāhainā. She was much stronger, but Kekahuna warned that she must rest every day. Peke returned to Kapewakua and continued to mind her grandchildren. Nevertheless, when the time came for Wahinekipi to deliver, the afterbirth came first and she hemorrhaged. There was nothing to do but save the babies.

"She never even saw the twins," said Peke. Her eyes were glazed and her face drawn.

"It is so sad. She was a good daughter, Peke. And you are a good mother," said Kale.

"I am glad I did not give her away as Humehume wished. She was all I had, Kale."

"I know. But look what she left you…these beautiful babies and children. You will never be alone. It is not good to be alone." She held her younger sister as she did when Papa died. "Now we are grieving and we cannot see the future, but God has more good things for you. I am sure."

Throughout the Kingdom Hawaiians died at an appalling rate. Western and Asian communicable diseases, introduced through foreign trade, overwhelmed the ability of Hawaiʻi's few Western physicians and dwindling number of Hawaiian practitioners to contain them. Measles, mumps, and influenza swept the islands like ripples in a pond. Prostitution continued to spread debilitating syphilis and gonorrhea at all levels of society. Christian pastors' morality codes had a salutary effect on the spread of venereal disease among their congregations but the barrenness it caused took a great toll on the native population. In country areas like Honokahua, strong ʻohana family ties and deep faith in Christ kept venereal disease in check, and women remained fertile.

Kale's oldest son, ʻAikake and his wife Keliʻiopunui already had a daughter, Sarah, and a son, Alexander; Wahinekipi's six children were with Peke; Grace

Young Rooke's adopted daughter, Emma, was seven years old; and Hūʻeuʻs family at Waikoloa swelled to five children and three grandchildren.

In 1844, King Kauikeoauli appointed Kale's first husband, James Kānehoa Young, Governor of Maui, and Grace's husband, Dr. Thomas Rooke, Port Physician for Honolulu. When the seat of government moved to Honolulu in 1845, the king named Keoniana Young as Kuhina Nui, Regent. Mother Kaʻoanaʻeha Young lived just long enough to see her son and stepson inaugurated into office and then peacefully went to her rest. Kale went to her funeral in Kawaihae and mourned for her precious stepmother as she had mourned for her own mother.

The January 1844, the appearance of a comet called Kokoiki just over the western horizon after sunset had caused great concern. It was the same star seen at Kamehameha's birth and right before his death. From the time of Kokoiki, rain ceased to fall on Maui. For two years insufficient winter rains failed to soften the ground. Spring planting was difficult work, and many of the slips died before taking root. In the second year, Lāhainā faced famine and the whalers went to Honolulu and Līhuʻe for provisions. By the third year, Honokahua fields were dust and there were no slips from last year's crop to plant. Farmers sacrificed their hogs and dogs when there was no food left to feed them, and for a while, the people did not starve. The life sustaining fresh water of Honokahua Stream ran one quarter of its normal flow and Kaholo feared it would dry up all together.

"How many sweet potatoes are left?" asked Kale.

"None. We have gone into the wild yams from the low forest. Just ten bags stored up in the valley. All the low forests have been stripped of iʻiʻi and ʻamaʻu shoots, ʻēkaha bird's nest ferns and pāpala beans. All we have left is hala and famine foods in the very high forest."

"Hala…the old people and babies cannot chew it anyway. At least we have the fish and seaweeds, thank God."

"Yes, but the reef fish have been fished out and the ʻopelu and akule won't be running for two more months. If the stream dries up, we will die eating fish. It is too salty."

Kale nodded and thought a minute. "Kaholo, Manu once told me the old name of the point was Makāluapunawai, and that there are spring holes out there. Is it true?"

"If Manu said it, it is true. I will ask the fishermen if they can find a fresh spring above the tidemark. It is a good thought." Kaholo paused. "There is one more thing. The cattle."

Kale did not want to hear about the cattle. Honokahua had been able to pay their taxes with hides and tallow but she knew the time would come when there was no more graze for the cattle and she would have to sacrifice the herd.

"Our cattle have grazed the hills down to red earth. When the rains do come, the soil will run down the kula and stream like thick poi. It will be big trouble."

"Nothing can be done to save the rich soil?"

"I believe if we build a taller stone wall below the existing wall, it will work like a terrace and hold back the heaviest soil."

"I understand. There is nothing else for the men to do now, anyway. If they take their time I will consider it, but I don't want the work to kill us before the rain comes."

"'My chief, 'Āwa'a says the only way to save the cattle is to graze them in the high forest, but I told him no."

"I agree. We must reserve famine foods for our people. Perhaps we should harvest the cattle now, while they are still healthy; what do you say?"

"I say yes. Harvest the steers first and save the cows that are still producing milk—it is food for the children. When the cows stop producing, we will harvest them too. The hides, tallow, and jerky will pay our taxes and feed us too, if I can do some trading on Kaua'i. If not, then the people will have dried beef, plus the ferns and wild yams of our high forest to eat."

"Just save the bullock until last, in case the rain comes."

"Ae, my chief."

"We are in agreement. Let it be done," said Kale. "Look at the mountain… nearly bare in the low forest and not a speck of green. I see rocks and gulches I never knew were there. And the high forest looks thin, Kaholo…very thin and golden…"

"My chief, it is time we send some men up to harvest the high forest. I will go too."

"Yes, it is time. Ride up with the old men. They know what to look for and how the kūpuna survived these times. While you are gone, please tell one of your men to guard my family and me. It is silly, but I am still afraid when you are gone."

Kaholo smiled. "Of course, my chief"

Kale was tired; watching the land wither and die broke her heart. "God, I know that this is just a season of drought, but you have given me these people to care for and I have done nearly all that I can. The children are skinny and listless. Please do not let their mothers watch them die. Please don't leave us helpless…"

Kale saw she was near the end of her ability to save Honokahua. The horses would take the men up the mountain, but they would not be able to make another ride. Pāhaʻa's precious herd that paid the King's taxes for twenty years would soon be used to keep her people alive for another few months. And then Honokahua would be a silent desert, no birds, hogs, dogs, cattle, or horses. One question remained, would there be any people?

In Lāhainā, angry Makani Pōkalakī winds whipped dust into horrific red storms that polluted emergency water supplies and spread disease. For weeks, people had been coming up the Alaloa from Kekaha and Honokōwai begging for food, but today there was no food to share.

It took three days for Kaholo and his men to return. Kale spotted the red dust cloud rising in the low forest and knew the men were on their way down, but she was not prepared for their report.

"The high forest is dry. The ferns and pāpapa beans are dead. The wild yams were nearly impossible to dig and when we got them they were woody and dry," said Keahi.

"We should have gone sooner. There isn't even enough up there to graze the cattle," said Umuwena.

"We cannot let the cattle trample the forest, or it will never grow back when the rains come," said Kaholo.

"Why were you gone so long, then?" asked Kale.

"We decided to let the horses eat their fill of the dried brush. Perhaps it will keep them a while longer."

Kale shook her head. "All right; tomorrow we will begin slaughtering the herd. How many shall we take?"

ʻĀwaʻa said, "A crew of ten may process five steers each day. If we take 15 now and 15 in two more weeks, then there will be just 20 left, including the bull."

"Then we will take the first 15 now and see if we can sell the hides."

"My chief," said Kaholo, "my thought is to divide the remaining stored yams, ration half to the family leaders, and bake the rest for your slaughtering crew.

The men will have life enough to get the job done well, so we can get the hides to Kaua'i before everyone else starves."

"Yes, Kaholo, I agree."

The men distributed the end of the yams and dug a ground oven to bake the last starch meal for the slaughtering crew. The smell of the baking yams filled the hot dry air and guts growled and hurt in anticipation of the coming feast.

Nothing from the cattle was lost. While the hides dried, men distributed the collected blood, joints, and innards to all the family leaders. Others built big fires to render the fat and to collect lard and tallow. Later they burned the bones and crushed them to use for farming. When the men were done slaughtering 15 steers, Kaholo went to Kaua'i with the hides, tallow, and jerky and returned with enough barrels of thick hard poi to feed Honokahua for the last month of kau, summer.

When all the babies, children, and elderly were fed, the rest of Honokahua filled their bellies and Kale set them to the task of building terracing walls on the kula.

"Kaholo, it's only a month until the Makahiki. Maybe the rains will come then. I want to let the rest of the herd loose to forage in the high forest. They will eat the dry ferns and maybe survive. What do you think?"

"We cannot use the horses to rope them in, so they will be gone until they come back on their own…or die in the mountains. If the rains do not come, we will not have hides and tallow to sell for poi. I say harvest the rest now."

"And if the rains come and we have no cattle to pay the tax and no beef or milk to sell the whalers, we lose the land or die during the winter anyway."

Kale decided to risk letting the last cattle forage in the high forest and the drought broke with "ka lani pipili" rainy season of November 1847, when more rain fell on Maui than in the previous twenty years. Nevertheless, the drought continued to take a terrible toll. By the end of 1848, three epidemics—measles, influenza, and whooping cough—had taken the lives of one in every 10 persons on Maui, and 19 at Honokahua, including aged High Kahuna Hewahewa and his daughter, Lahela Shaw. As an added insult, the dreaded easterly wind swept down Kaua'ula pass and razed a wide swath of destruction through Lāhainā town, collapsing Waine'e Church.

Even after five months, Honokahua still had daily showers, and the kula were vibrant green with new grass and a new crop of sweet potatoes mounded high. The sweet potatoes matured in three months, but it would be two years before the newly planted kalo huli would produce corms large enough to harvest so Honokahua continued to trade for poi.

In 1848 the whirlwind of government transition continued with The Great Mahele, when the crown lands of Hawai'i were divided into thirds and redistributed—one-third to the king, one-third to landlords and one-third to tenants—to be apportioned among those qualified persons who petitioned the Land Commission Board and paid a patent fee. Kale and all the Young-Davis family members had their lands surveyed, made applications, claimed lands inherited from 'Olohana, and secured Royal Patents or Land Awards, among a throng of eleven-thousand other applicants.

Peke was 45, and raising a large family in Lāhainā, with Kale and Kāne's assistance when a stonemason from Fiore in the Azores settled on Maui and fell in love with Isaac Davis's redheaded daughter. Antone Sylva pursued Peke and she fell in love with his Portuguese charm. They had a small wedding at the newly built Maria Lanakila Roman Catholic Church in Lāhainā, and Antone happily raised Peke's grandchildren as the large family he always desired.

In 1849, Laura's daughter, Bernice Pauahi, married a newcomer businessman from New York, Charles Reed Bishop, recently assigned as Collector of Customs at Honolulu Port. Dr. Rooke became Chairman of the newly formed Hawai'i Board of Health in 1850. And in Lāhainā, 'Uwaikīkīlani and Johnnie Halstead opened the doors of the Hawaiian Hotel.

Back in the mid 1840s Dr. Dwight Baldwin, Pastor of Waine'e Church, had read about smallpox inoculation technique, using dried exudates from infected patients to vaccinate healthy persons and protect them from the disease. Even though the technique was experimental, the threat of an epidemic was so great that he acquired some inoculua from America and for eight months traveled all of Maui, vaccinating thousands of people.

When the first three cases of ma'i pu'upu'uli'ili'i, smallpox were reported in Honolulu, on May 1, 1853, Baldwin saddled his horse and rode the Alaloa to every ahupua'a, instructing the people not to receive any canoes from other islands and to avoid travel to other islands. James Kānehoa enacted a law stating if anyone concealed a case of pox, their house and all its contents would be burned to protect the community. While whole sections of O'ahu were depopulated by the smallpox epidemic, Maui had only 109 deaths, and Hale Aloha monument was erected in Lāhainā to thank God for sparing Maui.

In 1853, Honokahua farming was healthy again, growing crops for whalers due in September. Johnnie and ʻUwaikīkīlani came to Honokahua and urged Kale to plant more Irish potatoes.

"But Johnnie," said Kale, "The number of whalers is down. They tell us the fishing is poor so I have cut back my crops by a third."

"That may be true next year, Mother, but this year we are looking at a great windfall. The spring rains came early in California and rotted their potato starts. Agents for Gold Rush mining camps are sending letters everywhere, trying to find potatoes for the Forty-Niners. My farming cooperative in Lepolepo has planted all the land we have, so I am offering any Maui farmer willing to plant several acres of Irish potatoes $4 a barrel for spuds delivered to us. We will ship them out to California."

Kale looked at Kaholo and he looked back, but not a word passed between them. Then Kale turned to Johnnie. "Honokahua will agree to grow eight acres of spuds. Good, good, good!" She stood up and looked around. "Where is my grandson, William? I promised him a walk up the valley to gather herbs."

Pleased but bewildered, Johnnie turned to his wife, "How did they come to that?"

ʻUwaikīkīlani giggled. "Don't worry; Māmā and Kaholo have worked together all day long for so many years—each one knows exactly what the other is thinking."

Kale and Kānekuapuʻu were busy preparing for the marriage of Amelia Nākai to George Hūʻeu Jr., Hūʻeu's son. It was one of the only times Hūʻeu visited Honokahua and Kale was delighted to have the families together. There was some discussion about the children being cousins, but Dr. Baldwin said that they were far enough removed by the fact that Kale and Hūʻeu had different mothers.

The wedding day in April was clear and bright. Happy ao keʻokeʻo white clouds on a dark blue sky reflected white patches on the sea as they danced down the Pailolo Channel in the moae breeze. The smell of baking hogs, sweet potatoes, and coconut puddings filled the air, and children bubbling over with anticipation, played at the shore. The ceremony was held at Honokahua Church followed by a wedding lūʻau at the old Meeting Pā overlooking Oneloa Bay, in the shadow of nā ʻiwi o nā kāpuna, the bones of the ancestors. Tall and slim Nākai, who looked like her father, was stunning in her white-trained hohokū gown and lei poʻo crown of gardenias.

"Nākai, you are as beautiful as your mother the day we married," said Kāne as he smiled and took his daughter's arm to bring her into church. Pastor Kauwealoha came down from Honokōhau to perform the ceremony and preached I Corinthians, Chapter 13, "Love is Kind." Kale's beaming face spoke the joy she felt to see her mother's namesake happily married to a fine young man who planned to come to Honokahua and help run the ranching operation. Nākai was like Kale in many ways; most of all, the blood of the land flowed in her heart.

Nākai's brothers and sisters all attended: big sister 'Uwaikīkilani and Johnnie came up from Lepolepo with thirteen-year-old William; Fanny and her new husband Kū'auhau came in their canoe from Honokeana; Mele Kuamo'o and her husband Mahoe and baby Alexander came up from Lāhainā; and J.Y., twenty-one and single, helped Kaholo organize wedding details.

Kale's brother and father-of-the-groom Hū'eu and his wife Kaha'anapilo were delighted with the match between Nākai and their son George Hū'eu Jr. and enjoyed themselves so much they stayed two weeks. Aunt Peke, now happily married to Pōkīkī Portuguese rancher, Antone Sylva, brought her sweet six-year-old granddaughter, Mary, to see all her Davis cousins who had a grand time surfing, riding horses, playing games, and exploring Honokahua Valley.

The big hungry crowd sat around a long line of lauhala mats covered with koa wood bowls and festive calabashes full of pūpū appetizers: limu seaweed, fresh 'opihi, cracked raw 'a'ama crab, one-day-old 'ahi tuna poke salad with 'inamona kukui nut relish, grilled butter fish, fresh poi, fermented poi, and sweet potato poi. Proud father-of-the-bride and host, Kānekuapu'u, prayed the blessing:

> E Ke Akua Mana Loa, Ka Makua o nā kumu honua, ke kāhea a'e nei mākou iā 'oe. E komo mai i kō mākou pā'ina ha'aha'a. Mahalo piha no nā mākua nei, nā kūpuna nei, nā keiki nei, mo'opuna nei a me nā hoaloha loa o Honokahua nei. E pōmiaka'i 'ia Nākai a me Keoki'opio Hū'eu i kēia lā a me kau ā kau. Ke ho'omaika'i nei mākou iā 'oe no nā mea 'ai a me nā lima i ho'omākaukau ai i nā mea 'ai. Ke pule nei kākou ma ka inoa o Ka Makua Mau, Ka Haku a me Ka 'Uhane Hemolele. 'Āmene

> Almighty God, Father of the Universe, we call to you. Welcome to our humble banquet. Many thanks for the parents, grandparents, children, grandchildren, and dear friends of Honokahua here. May Nākai and George be blessed today and forever. We bless you for the food and the

hands which prepared it. We pray in the name of the Father, Son, and Holy Ghost, Amen.

In the evening, after a most glorious wedding celebration, a bright red and orange sky streaked with lavender not only delighted sailors and wedding guests but began a season of breath-taking sunsets on Maui, caused by volcanic dust thrown high into the Pacific heavens by Krakatoa volcano in Indonesia. It was a memorable beginning for the newlyweds, who retired to their new kauhale on Honokahua's kula.

When King Kauikeaouli died in 1854, tall, handsome, and impeccably educated Alexander Liholiho Kamehameha IV ascended to the throne, and surrounded himself with native and British advisors, fearing the American bias of the Lahainaluna graduates. On June 18, 1856 he married Emma Rooke, 'Olohana's granddaughter. Kale and Kāne were among the 500 persons who attended the grandest wedding in the history of Hawai'i at Kawaiha'o Church in Honolulu. King Alexander immediately began developing Hawai'i's constitutional monarchy according to the British model as 'Olohana once wished.

In February, 1857 Kale was sixty years old, and gray hairs glittered her short dark-brown wavy locks, but her pale golden skin was clear, her golden eyes still sparkled, and her body was fuller, but still slim and fit from daily farm chores. She and Kaholo carefully watched the decline of whaling ships putting in at Lāhainā and decreased crops accordingly. East Maui was producing over 600 tons of sugar from cane plantations that made the flanks of Haleakalā an undulating bright green. Most plantation laborers came from China and the "Young" name, once owned by a few, was the most common name on Maui.

Better methods of killing whales led to over fishing and the whalers moved on to new fishing grounds in Mexico and the Artic. Provisioning in Lāhainā dwindled, and the effect on Honokahua was devastating. With no market for food crops, Kale and Kaholo could not plant, and there was no work for the laborers. For her first time as chiefess, Kale was unable to support all her people.

"It is a matter of righteousness," said Kale. "I am responsible for the people's livelihood, and I am out of ideas to put two-hundred people to work."

Kaholo saw she was upset. "My chief, these are different days; everywhere the farmers seek work, they will be well fed and protected. Perhaps you and I may help them find new positions with good Luna bosses at the sugar plantations."

"They were born here. They buried their parents here. They fell in love and raised their children on this land. How can I ask them to leave the beloved land I do not want to leave? Can't you think of some other business besides ranching?"

"I have tried, my chief. I have consulted with the family leaders and we have all reluctantly decided to move on."

"You are going too?" Kale never considered that Kaholo would leave. The thought choked her heart and she bit her lip. "Please leave me alone. I need to think." She turned and went into her Kauhale. *How could this happen? Did I preserve the land for a herd of cattle? Did I do good for the people all these years to shuffle them off to a plantation now? We should have gone into sugar too. I have failed my people. I have overlooked the one man who has always been faithful to me and now he is leaving.*

The hale interior darkened and when she looked, Kaholo was in the doorway. "My chief, I do not wish to leave. I will stay as long as you need me." She wanted to embrace him and the thought terrified her. *Oh God, please take this temptation from me! He will think me a foolish old woman.* She just stared at him.

"It is good, Kaholo. I am at the end of my wits," is all she said. He smiled and she saw his pity. *He feels sorry for me and I am a sorry woman.* "Please go outside and I will come and sit with you. My husband is not a businessman. He cannot help me, but you and I will figure this out."

"Yes my chief." Kaholo went out in the yard and sat down. Kale drank some water and went outside. The tradewind cleared her mind.

"I want to help the farmers in the valley acquire ownership of their lands. And the tenant farmers deserve the jobs we have, if they are willing to do them. At least we can do that. You ask the Chinese laborers where they want to go. Ying Fat said he desires to take his family back to China. If other families seek passage, I will buy it for them," said Kale. "If they would rather go to a Maui plantation, I will help them move there."

"My chief, I calculate that if we restrict farming to food crops for the fishermen and ranchers and also grow feed for the cattle, we will be solvent. But we cannot begin that plan until the excess laborers have found other work. We could run at a loss for the next two years.

Kale was firm. "Whatever it takes to be righteous, we will do."

In all her years at Honokahua, Kale took care of the people and they nurtured the land, but cattle do not nurture the land. They trample fragile plants, herbs, and mosses into hardpan, and eat all but the very thorniest weed. Even large trees die when their roots are trampled, until only a lone 'ōhi'a stands one corner of the pasture, where all the cattle congregate to escape the noonday sun. The pure joy of planting, watching new growth, anticipating the ebb and flow of sun and rain, pest and disease, and thrilling to the sights and sounds of harvest time would soon be just memories.

"Kaholo?"

"Yes, my chief."

"Will you stay with me? You have been my constant companion for so many years that I cannot imagine living at Honokahua without you."

"I will stay with you…"

"Will you miss the farmers as much as I will?"

"Yes. Nevertheless, I will never lose my love for this place. Some good will come of this change, you will see."

CHAPTER 14

Faithful to the End

During the summer, a combination of influenza and viral meningitis broke out on Maui and there seemed no way to stop its spread. At Honokahua, nearly half the people were sick. Kale had the fever first, accompanied by body aches, a stiff neck, and vomiting. After four days, her fever broke and she was able to attend to her children.

When Kāne fell ill, he was much worse off than Kale; on the second day, his fever was blazing. Kale put cool compresses of damp kapa on his head and neck and fed him broth.

"I am cold…" Kale put another sleeping blanket on him but his head felt red hot even though he was quaking.

"Kāne, your fever is very hot. Please try to drink a little water."

"I must build the church."

Kale was frightened. *He is delirious!* "Please drink a little water."

Kekahuna came on the third day and give Kāne some herbs. "He is not good. When I was with him, he stiffened and his eyes rolled up. It is a very bad sign."

By that night, he suffered three more seizures and fell unconscious. Kale sent Nākai for Kaholo.

"Please, go to Lāhainā and bring back Dr. Baldwin. JY is here, and Nākai and Fanny are helping me." She turned to her grown daughters and sobbed, "I tried everything I know, and nothing helps. I tried to be a good wife."

"Mama, you are exhausted. Please sit down and try to get some rest. We will stay with Papa."

Dr. Baldwin was away in Honolulu, so Kaholo scoured Lāhainā to find any ship's physicians who might help, but they were attending hundreds of critical patients in town. Before Kaholo returned, Kāne was dead.

"He's gone," said Kale. She was too exhausted to cry and just put her head on Kaholo's shoulder, closed her eyes, and shuddered.

"I am sorry," he said as he put his arm around her, walked her out to her lanaʻi, and gave her a drink of water. "So many people are sick in Lāhainā and only two ship's doctors. They said there is nothing to do but keep the fever down and drink water. It is not like the measles—this time, bathing will not hurt. And not all die; even the most desperately ill may recover." He looked back inside the hale. "Shall I stay and prepare his body?"

"No. You keep away from the sick and the dead. I have already recovered from the fever. I shall do it. I have a large bag of salt. If you can find some men who have recovered, there are graves to dig in the morning."

"The sick are everywhere, my chief. I will send a runner to all Honokahua families with the doctors' instructions; then I will get some men. Where will you bury Kāne?"

"He wanted to be with his brothers in Maʻalaea, but I dare not take him there and pass on his disease. Let us put him in the dunes, but further north than the kūpuna. I will take him to his family later. Put your men to work making a pit there, big enough for several bodies."

"Yes, my chief. I am very sorry Kāne is gone. He was a good husband and my dear friend."

"Yes, Kaholo, I am sorry for you too. He was a good husband and teacher and now he is at peace with God in heaven…" Kale sobbed and Kaholo put his arm around her again. Her burning eyes longed for sleep, but she just stared at the first glow of morning light in the eastern sky and sighed. "Go now and I will prepare him."

Kale told her children to go outside, and took down her knife. The old kahuna Manu taught Kale how to prepare the dead by cutting a long incision, removing the organs, and filling the cavity with salt. She stood motionless with the knife in her hand, looking at poor dear Kāne, who never received the love and desire he wished from his wife, and she could not tear him apart anymore. *Dear God, I have been faithful, but is this really obedience? Was it righteous to continue so long, yet never become the wife he wanted? Forgive me, Kāne; I did what I could. Forgive me, oh God, for what I have failed to do.*

When she came out to look for Kaholo, he was already waiting with Maunahina, knowing that it was impossible for a wife to prepare her own flesh and bone for burial. She looked at Kaholo and bit her lip, and he just nodded to Maunahina. Without a word, she gave the knife to Maunahina and he went inside. Nākai and Fanny made her sit down, and soon she was asleep.

Kale mourned and pitied her poor children who had to bury their father. And she pitied Kāne, but thought nothing for herself. She would never be alone because she had her children beside her, and she knew that God would never turn his back on her forever. She wondered what heaven was like and what Kāne was seeing and feeling now. *Now he knows that I loved him.*

By the end of the month, 24 people were dead at Honokahua, including James Kānehoa Young and his adopted son, Alebada, Wahinekū'oi'oi, and Pilialoha. Once James found sobriety at Honokahua, he never left its peaceful calm, faithfully running the canoe business even when he was Governor. Kale prepared a special gravesite for James and his son, on a bluff overlooking Honokahua Bay and the Valley, and mourned with his wife Hikoni, and with Grace and Fanny Young.

Kale and U'i mourned their friend Pilialoha and looked ahead to their own deaths, when their children, like Pili's, would carry on. For many days, Kale officiated at funeral after funeral where the angel of death took a mother, child, brother, or uncle; there were no more tears left to cry at Honokahua, only dry swollen eyes, deep rumbling wheezing coughs, and unending sadness.

One morning Kaholo did not show up for morning prayer, and Kale went to his hale. She called and heard nothing but a quiet groan. When she went inside, she found him nearly unconscious and partially paralyzed on his right side, burning with fever.

Kale ran to the door. "Help! Come and help Kaholo!" Then she ran back into the hut, and grabbed a water gourd off the wall. When she held up his head to give him a drink, the heat radiated from his neck and face and she knew exactly what to do. *I must bathe him!*

"I am going to get you some cool water," she said. She found a pole and two large calabashes, ran to the beach to fill them, and hauled them back up the hill. By then Maele and Ohapau Shaw were there. "Let's move him outside," said Kale.

They picked up his mat on either side and carried him out to the lanai where Kale began to pour cool seawater over his neck and chest, arms and legs.

Then she dipped a malo in the water and laid it over his forehead. "This is not working—Ohapau, can you make a palanquin with a net sling and carry him to the estuary? My idea is to dip him into the stream as far as his neck and cool him down."

"Yes. I have just what you need."

Kaholo's eyes opened and he tried to focus. "Kani'au...lono..." he whispered and he closed his eyes again.

"Go! Hurry!"

They brought back a net lashed to two bamboo poles and two more men; they carried Kaholo to the estuary in front of their longhouses and suspended him in the cold stream water until his forehead was cool, and then lifted him up on the mud bank on a soft bed of dried sweet potato vines covered with lauhala mats. Whenever the fever spiked, they cooled him down. All day and all through the night, Kale stayed at his side, forcing him to take sips of water whenever he was conscious. She pleaded with God for his recovery all night. In the torch light, she watched his every breath and blessed his strong shoulders that carried the problems of Honokahua, and blessed the square-knuckled rough hands that built the stone fences for the herds. She smoothed his white hair and white mustache that gave their youth to Honokahua's valleys and kula.

Before the morning light fell through vine-covered trees on the cliff behind the estuary and dew was hanging on the grasses by the shore, Kaholo opened his eyes, looked at Kale, and smiled.

"Take some water," she said. As she lifted his head, he groaned.

" 'Ā'īkū...Stiff neck..."

"I won't lift it again," she said. "Please drink some water. The fever is passing." He drank but when he tried to touch the gourd Kale held to his mouth, he could not move his hand far enough to reach it and a look of fear came over his face.

"He aha ka pilikia? What is the trouble?" asked Kale

" 'A'ole pono au e ka'ika'i i ka lima, I can't lift the hand." he whispered. Ohapau saw a tear well up in Kale's eye.

Paralyzed. Oh God forbid it! She found her courage and said gently, "Just rest now. Are you comfortable?"

"Ae, hō'olu'ia Yes, comfortable." And he was asleep.

"You must recover," she whispered. "I love you." Kale wept and kissed his forehead; it was warm again and she asked Ohapau and the men to ease him down into the water again.

By the next day, Kaholo's fever was completely gone. He had regained some use of his right arm, but he was very fatigued so the fishermen carried him back to his hale. His neck was still stiff and he could not sit up without getting nauseous, but he was fully conscious and able to drink on his own, using his left hand. Kale stayed with him, feeding him broth and mamaki tea.

"Thank you my chief, for staying with me."

"You nearly died from the fever. And the Shaw family helped me keep you cool in the estuary. I thank God for healing you…you called for me…"

Kaholo blinked. *Oh no. What did I say?* He searched Kale's face for a reaction, and saw tenderness.

"What did I say?"

"You called me by the name my mother gave me, Kani'aulono. Do you remember?"

"Yes…I saw you as a young girl, calling to me…thin as a reed, voice light as a kona breeze. I was drowning and I called to you…you pulled me up and took me back to shore." He watched her face as tears welled up in her golden eyes and she bit her bottom lip.

"Kaholo, I never thought of losing you until these last days…I want you near me forever."

"Have I not always been faithful these 40 years?"

"Yes, but…I want you for my husband." Kaholo heard the words he longed for all his life, but he could hardly move. *I hope it is not too late for me.* "Will you come to me now and let me continue to care for you?"

He blinked again and a tear trickled down his cheek. "Ae, my chief."

As Kale continued to speak slowly, he looked at her and listened, trying to memorize every word. "A small flame always burned in my heart for you, but never once did you blow it hot…I watched, but never once did you even look at me with yearning eyes. Back then I was shy and I did not want to force you…I wondered, if he agrees to come to me, how will I know if he comes out of duty or love? But now that I am old, my thought is this: if you say yes, then you will be happy, whether by duty or love…Kaholo, I will do my best to make you happy."

"You always made me happy, but today the happiest…Since you came to Honokahua I kept two thoughts: I have no right to yearn for you because I am maka'ainana…and I am grateful God allowed me to be at your side as your konohiki. How could I give up seeing you every day of my life for the chance to touch you once?" Kale leaned over and kissed him tenderly on the forehead, cheeks and eyes. Kaholo did not respond, but when their lips met, he touched her hair and whispered in her ear, "Let Halemāno marry us as soon as I recover, but please, let me choose the day I come to sleep with you. I promise when I come, I will never, *never* leave you."

Kale kissed him gently. "I will do as you wish and wait for you."

By sunset the next day, Kale and Kaholo were man and wife, and Kale continued to sit by his side and to nurse him back to health, but honored his wish to stay apart until he chose the day of consummation.

After three days, a letter for Kale came from Honolulu:

July 18, 1857 Rooke House, Honolulu

Dearest Sarah,

I regret to tell you that last week your brother Keoniana and dear friend Laura Konia Pākī fell victim to influenza and meningitis. They were both under our care at the clinic, but I was unable to save them. We saw to Keoniana's burial at the mausoleum and under the dire circumstances of the epidemic, we have not called together a family wake and funeral. It is our hope to have a memorial service for Keoniana when circumstances permit. We are sorry for your losses, of which we are certain there are many more at Honokahua.

Yours in Christ,

Grace and Thomas Rooke

Kale mourned again.

On August 6, Kale awoke to the soft floating tones of an ipu hōkiokio gourd whistle outside her hale. She grabbed her muʻumuʻu and crawled to the door to peek out. Standing on the lanaʻi was Kaholo wearing a white malo and two long maile lei. Beside him was a net bag on top of two wiliwili short boards; as Kale knelt in the doorway listening, he continued his serenade, smiling as he pressed one nostril shut and blew into the tiny gourd through the other.

When the music ended, she grinned and whispered, "*ʻO ka lā kēia o kou ʻiʻini?* Is this the day that you desire?"

"Ae, he lā kēia o ka wai o kāunu. E ku'u lei makamae, hele mai e he'e nalu me 'oe. Yes, this is a day of the water of love. My beloved cherished lei, come and surf with me."

"Oh Kaholo, I am too old for surfing!" said Kale.

"We missed our youth together and today we will regain it. Come along and do not disappoint me."

Kale laughed and shook her head, got up and went to him. He embraced her and quickly gave her the net bag to carry; then he picked up the boards and balanced them on his shoulder as they walked up the Alaloa.

"Where are we going?" asked Kale.

"Mokulē'ia. I waited for the perfect day when the waves will be just the right size for you. And no one will be there but us." He grinned at her. "Are you ready?"

"Ready for what?" she smiled coquettishly.

"Ready to be a child again—to play in the sea and not worry about anything all day. Are you ready?"

"I am! Sadness has drained me and I want to laugh and have fun."

Soon they were looking down on Mokulē'ia's perfect sandy cove from the pali high above. Kaholo heaved the boards, one-at-a-time, as far away from the cliff's edge as he could and they fell with thuds on the sand below. Then he turned around and let himself down the cliff, picking footholds, grabbing roots and branches as he descended. When he was on the sand, Kale threw the net bag down to him and climbed down herself.

Kaholo took off his malo and looked at Kale. She hesitated to take off her dress and he smiled. "I know we are old. Today we just pretend to be young and no one will see." He turned and walked into the water with the two boards. Kale pulled off her mu'umu'u, ran and dove in the water, and swam out to where she could just stand. It was the first time she bathed in the nude since Hoapili outlawed it in public places almost 20 years ago, and she laughed at herself and delighted in her regained freedom.

He came to her, gave her a board, placed one of his lei around her neck, and they shared breath, but he did not caress her. Instead, he patted her surfboard. "I want us to surf one wave together." Kale pulled herself up on her board and they paddled out where the waves pile up on the reef. The inshore water was clear and turquoise blue until outside the reef, where it turned deep blue. Kale turned and faced the beach, pulled herself up and straddled her board, and Kaholo came up beside her and did the same. He reached out his hand and she reached out and touched his hand, a sign that they would ride the same wave, like young lovers.

"I forgot that surfing is so much fun. Thank you for bringing me here. I have not felt so free since I was a girl! What are you holding in your other hand?"

"A good luck charm."

"You don't need luck today. I need luck! Is this our wave?"

"Yes, I think it is." They paddled to catch the pressure of the crest, cut into the three-foot wave, and rode it to the edge of the poʻana kai where the waves scoop out sand near the beach. Kale rode on her knees, and Kaholo on his chest. Kale was squealing with delight at her triumph and immediately paddled back out for another wave. This time she and Kaholo both stood on their boards and got close enough to touch hands. When Kale dove off her board at the end of the run, she was panting.

"Tired?" asked Kaholo.

"Exhausted!" panted Kale. "This old lady needs a rest."

"Then come in. I have some lunch."

Kale spread out the lauhala mat and lay down. Kaholo sat down beside her.

"You have kept so much of your beauty. I think I will stay here all day and gaze at your pale skin." Kale gave him a coy glance, but he smiled like a little boy with a good riddle. He pulled out of his net bag a cylinder of poi wrapped in tī leaves, a water gourd, and a piece of sugar cane. Kaholo untied the poi and offered some to Kale. She sat up and looked around for fish, but there was none.

"What kind of a man are you?" she teased. You bring poi, but no fish? I cannot eat poi without fish."

"I have a fish."

Kale laughed "Hū! Kikoʻolā! How rude!"

Kaholo was grinning from ear to ear. "You are my fish." He leaned over, licked the salt from her cheek, put a finger of poi in his mouth, and waited for her reaction.

Kale's skin rose up in tiny bumps like chicken skin and she sat up straight—stunned, looking at Kaholo's smiling face and expectant eyes. And suddenly she connected to a flash of memories: *Waikīkī*—the handsome young sailor. *My eyes only saw him*—surfing the same waves. Teasing about my pale skin. A thrill of holding hands. *Lunch on the beach…"You're my fish."*

"How do you know this?" she cried. She grabbed his closed fist and pulled open his fingers. In the palm of his hand was the small cowrie shell that 13-

year-old Kale brought that day to Waikīkī as a magical charm, to bring Hiki, the handsome sailor boy, to her wave. He surfed her wave and invited her to sit with him on the beach. And when he took out his poi, he licked the salt from her face to eat with it. And when they pledged their love to one another, she gave him the shell to remember her when he was far away. "It is YOU!"

"Yes, Kani'aulono; now do you doubt that I love you?"

Kale threw her arms around Kaholo. "All this time I never knew!" He kissed her, and the world around her faded from her consciousness. The sweet enticement of her gentle Kaholo fanned the passions of her heart well beyond her childhood memories and she was shaking with excitement. He rolled her on her back, saying, "Be gentle with me, my sweetheart. I have waited a long time for this moment."

Kale breathed deeply and smiled at him. "*Auwe Hiki, ke ka'a niniau nei au i ka 'eha koni nou…*, Oh Hiki, I am rolling about in the throbs of love for you…" He lay down beside her and she slowly led him to her favorite places and tenderly found the secrets of his hidden desires in the seclusion of Mokulē'ia Bay, as frothy waves lapped against the strand.

Later the lovers went back to Kale's kauhale, and even though they were already married, Kaholo was not at peace until the sun came up the next morning, when he truly embraced his position as Kale's husband and Chief of Honokahua.

Kale teased him. "Are you going to sit in the pā all day? You walk back and forth like a rooster protecting his hen!"

"If I were a rooster I would be sitting on the roof and crowing for everyone who walks by!" She giggled and walked over to him, pressing up against him. "I think it is time for lunch…" Kaholo held her close and kissed her neck. "Show me again."

One moonlit Mohalu night, Kaholo and Kale rode their horses up the Alaloa to Honolua Bay. Moloka'i looked like a giant whale in a black sea, and southward, down the coast, Makāluapuna and Hāwea points were visible, outlined in white where waves hit the rocks. Up the hills and Mountains of 'Eke, moonlight tickled the tops of the trees and shone on the grass of the lower kula. And down below them, surfers in Honolua Bay rode blue-black waves, crested in silver and white foam, as their friends and lovers waited on the shore beside orange glowing fires. Kaholo's white hair glowed in the moonlight as he tied the horses to a tree. Kale looked up at the "woman in the moon" and thanked God for giving her this most precious husband and this glorious night.

"I thought I never would see you again, and I am so happy to have you now. Papa died right after you sailed and I was taken to Kawaihae to live with the Youngs. That is why I was not there when your ship returned to Honolulu."

"I know, I know that now…The first time I spotted you on the deck of the *Ka'ahumanu* I thought you were the most beautiful woman I had ever seen." He smoothed her hair and kissed her forehead. "Then you sang out your name from the ship and my heart beat hard with the anticipation of meeting again… only to be broken when I discovered you were married. It was good you did not recognize me… One time I almost told you who I was, when Kāne decided to woo you, but I did not because I never thought you would marry him."

"It was a terrible mistake."

"I should have revealed my love."

"Forgive me!"

"Do you think God denied us togetherness for the good of the land? So many years of prosperity—

"I don't know, my dear Kaholo…" Kale breathed in the sweet night air and watched the glimmering ocean. "What did the pastor teach this week…We were predestined to be conformed into the image of Christ before the world began? That is what I think of you and me. God knew we would find each other, in spite of our foolishness, passions, or hardships. In the end nothing could keep us apart…" Kaholo squeezed her tight and she kissed him. "Do you know what else?…We are together now, at a time when there is no more hard work, no babies to raise, and we are free to enjoy the fruits of our labors together."

Kaholo just petted her hair and smiled. "Kale, it would have been nice to spend our youth together, but then, we might not be here, watching the moon over Honokahua. I am content and very thankful."

"Yes, I am very contented too…when Kāne died I was happy that I had kept my vows to him, but sad that I failed to make him happy. I did not yearn for him and it deeply hurt him. I did yearn for Alika, but his pride was his work. I hurt Alika too, by clinging to Honokahua. But you and I have always shared the same dreams and supported one another. To have you as my husband fulfills my life…

"—And you yearn for me!" He squeezed her again.

Kale giggled. "Oh yes, I do!"

Then Kaholo lifted up her muʻumuʻu, threw the fabric over his shoulders, and pushed his head up through the scooped yoke. As he fondled her, Kale pulled her arms inside the dress, unwrapped his malo and soon the giggling mākua oldsters found a soft spot of grass, where they fulfilled their childhood fantasies.

One day in early November, Kaholo looked out and saw blue-black clouds on the northwest horizon.

"A northerly storm is coming. I will tell everyone to tie down their boats and belongings."

Within hours the kaikoʻo rough seas started to pound the pali. From the paepae high on the ridge, Kale watched huge waves crashing into the points and shooting 100 pace-high plumes of spray up and over the rocks. Thunderous waves and whitewater filled the bays and above the bay hung a thick gray haze of salt; the sound of walls of water hitting Hāwea's lava tubes resonated up the hills in thunderous explosions. After three days of wind and swell pushing water down the channel, the wind turned and a kona storm surge came up from the south, creating an unusually high tide and dangerously fast offshore current.

The 122 whaling vessels in Lāhainā Roadstead yawed about their anchors; when the current pressed them broadside, they broke loose from their anchor chains and flew up the channel. Native sailors knew to keep the tall ships heading straight in the current but when the foreign helmsmen let their three-masters turn off heading, they swamped and capsized. After three days, 16 ships were lost. It was impossible for Honkahua's fishermen to rescue all the men adrift in the rough seas, but by the grace of God, only three died. When 1857 was over, 12 more whaling ships were lost in the Arctic and two more went down in Baja. It was a sad farewell to an industry that had fueled Hawaiʻi's economy for nearly five decades.

It was a great honor to have someone in her adopted family on the throne, and Kale prayed that Fanny Young's daughter Emma would have babies. In 1858, King Alexander Liholiho and Emma had a son, first heir to the throne born to a reigning Kamehameha since Kamehameha the Great. They named him Edward Albert Kauikeoauli Leiopapa o Kamehameha, but Emma and Grace never called him anything but "Baby." The death of Grace's husband, Thomas, in 1859 tempered their joy and Grace began her tireless quest to found a hospital in Honolulu dedicated to him. She called it Queen's Hospital. When four-year-old Baby tragically died of meningitis, the Kamehameha dynasty ended and the Davis-Young family mourned once more.

CHAPTER 15

Kaniʻaulono; The Silent Reed

In 1863 Alexander Liholiho Kamehameha IV died of chronic asthma at age 31 and was succeeded by his brother Kapuʻaiwa Lot Kamehameha V. Queen Emma and her family mourned, and Emma continued to be a political and charitable force in the Kingdom.

Sugar was Maui's major cash crop and there were no whalers left at Lāhainā both because Union and Confederate armies had commandeered so many ships for the American Civil War and because petroleum found at Titusville, PA in 1859 had replaced whale oil as a commodity. An ancient disease from the East called Maʻi Pākē or leprosy was further diminishing the Hawaiian population; on Maui Dr. Baldwin was reporting 60 cases every year.

Most of the people who once worked at Honokahua chose to sign on at sugar plantations on East Maui or to Baldwin's Pioneer Mill in Lāhainā, but three fishing families remained, with several farmers in Honokahua Valley, whom Kale helped get title to their land. A few newcomers, called paniolo, who rode horses and roped steers after learning their trade from Vera Cruz vaqueros, came to Honokahua to help ʻĀwaʻa and Makekau keep the herds. All but the high forest was gone, and cattle grazed down to the shore, causing fishing and paniolo families to build stone walls around their small gardens. Kale and Kaholo maintained a few kalo loʻi in the halawai, but most of Honokahua, and neighboring Honolua and Nāpili, now owned by Laura's daughter Bernice Pauahi and her husband Charles Bishop, were ranch and range.

At 70, Kale was a contented matriarch of six grown children and their spouses, nine grandchildren, and two great-grandchildren. Kaholo had convinced her to turn all the land management duties over to the children. George and Nākai lived in Kale's old kauhale near the beach and ran the cattle operations, including slaughtering, salting beef, rendering tallow, and tanning hides. William, 'Uwaikīkīlani's boy, ran the dairy, and JY managed the fishing operation, which still produced salted 'ōpelu, akule, and aku for sale on Maui. Kale and Kaholo lived at the top of Kahua Hill with JY and his family in a large wood-frame house with a deep wrap-around veranda that overlooked all of Honokahua, as far north as the chalk cliffs of Honolua, as far south as Honokōwai, and across the channel to Moloka'i and Lāna'i. Kale and Kaholo still prayed every morning at the paepae and spent the days with their grandchildren when they were not visiting 'Aikake's clan in Niu, Kuamo'o's family in Lāhainā, or the Halsteads in Makawao.

Kale viewed her extended family like a kalo patch, where huli sprout from the sides of the main stem, and, when tall strong leaves that catch the sun and rain wither, fresh new leaves uncurl to continue the work, while underneath, out of sight, the heritage and knowledge of elders nourishes the next generation. She always thought about her kūpuna elders and mo'opuna grandchildren as she padded through the rows of proud kalo, weeding out debris, or pulling corms to make tomorrow's poi.

This day, she thought first of her stepfamily, the Youngs. Dear Fanny was the only one still living; besides cousin Paul Nahaolehua, she was poor Queen Emma's only living blood relative. Like Kale, Hū'eu and Peke attained old age. Aside from Peke's girl, Wahinekipi, who died at age 21, all their children were alive and raising families. The whole Davis clan convened for Easter, sometimes at Hū'eu's place in Waikaloa, sometimes at Honokahua, reminiscing about old times and getting to know the newest spouses and babies. Kaholo treated all the little children as his own, regaling them with stories of Kamehameha the Great or Demigod Maui, and organizing outings or contests to thrill their hearts and build their strength. Kale's own children treated Kaholo like a father and genuinely loved him, but there was a special bond between him and 'Uwaikīkīlani, who looked like Kale, and who desired so much to have a Papa of her own.

In April 1867, the Davis family celebrated Easter at Honokahua. It rained for three days and Kale amused the small grandchildren with stories, games, and handicrafts. One afternoon she took them down to Honokahua Stream to show them the blood of the land, red silt-stained water rushing to the sea, cleaning the streambed and pushing mountain shrimp out into the Bay. "So, when you gaze over the rolling valleys and ridges, or walk through the valley and hear the rushing stream, if tears of joy come to your eyes, you know you have the blood of the land in your heart."

"I cry, Nana," said ʻUwaikīkīlani's chubby two-year-old granddaughter, Charlotte. Kale scooped her up in her arms and squeezed her. "Ooh, dear Charlotte, are you crybaby like Nana?" Charlotte nodded. "Well, it's not such a bad thing to be." She looked at the other kids, "Do you love Nana?" They all nodded and little Elinor said, "I do too, Nana"

Kale pointed to Elinor's chest. "Well, that love will remain forever in your heart…Once you give me your love; you may *never* claim it back…" Then she pointed to her own heart. "And I will keep your love here in my heart forever… Love remains forever." They were all wide-eyed, respectfully serious, and did not say a word. *They are so like me—memorizing every word.* She laughed. "One day you will remember my words, and you will understand completely…Now off you go! Run up to the house, but ask Papa to clean your feet before you go inside. The first child sitting on the porch wins a prize!"

It was the last day Kale walked Honokahua with the grandchildren. In May, her heart began to fail and for the next four years, she was confined to the house atop Kahua Hill. Nākai had become a skilled kahuna lapaʻau, expert in Hawaiian natural remedies, and she attended to her mother. Kaholo never left her side.

Kaholo looked out from the veranda to the north, across the rolling kula of Honokahua and up the mountains to Puʻu Kaʻeo and Puʻu Kukui. "It's a lovely day, light winds that used to blow your hair and spring blossoms on the hau kokiʻo keʻokeʻo and puakinikini—and red kou trees in the valley. Let's saddle up and take one last ride around the ahupuaʻa together and visit all your favorite places, shall we? We are free and easy now…good, good, good. First we'll stop at Kapalua Bay coconut grove, and then up the ridge to the old heiau where we like to pray. Then down the gulch and over the lower kula where we used to grow those giant red sweet potatoes, and then we'll pay our respects to all the kūpuna, and especially the ones we knew: Manu, Umuwena, Keahi, Maunahina, Limahaʻi and Uʻi, Shaw and Lahela, ʻUlumalu, Pilialoha, Kalāhei, Kāne and the others. Then we'll walk Oneloa Beach and look for your favorite tiny shells…" He took a deep breath and sighed. "It would not be complete without a visit to Hāwea to fish the rock pools and gather salt. If you are not too tired, we'll ride up the kula to the first cow pens that Pāhaʻa built and stop for a picnic lunch, just you and me. Do you think we'll have time to ride back down to the halawai and up the valley trail past Pili's old homestead and see her 'ōhi'a'ai mountain apple in bloom? Maybe there will be some bananas to pick. And maybe we can go to the top of the mountain and gather plenty mamaki leaves for tea, and maile and lehua blossoms for lei, like we did in the old days...."

He sobbed and gasped for air and held on to the porch post for strength. He turned around and through the open door he looked once more at her corpse. The high forehead, the narrow straight nose, and strong chin were still there. But how she looked at him, with tenderness and expectancy, the glow of her countenance and soft skin were gone, and the wavy hair, now silver and brown, had lost its luster. *It is not you there—Kani'aulono. You are here with me and your presence fills me, but I long for a little word, a smile, one look.* "I cannot live without you!" he cried. "I have not been beyond the sound of your voice for 50 years. Please come back! Please take me with you!" A ray of morning sun streamed through the 'ulu tree and fell warm on his hand as if she were consoling him one last time.

"*Pāpā? Mākaukau 'oe?* Papa, are you ready?" Kaholo sobbed and shook his head and JY put his arm around him. "Do you want something to eat or drink before we read the kanikau?"

"No, no, my son," he sniffled. "I need to sit down...and yes, a little water please."

Kale's niece Lucy wrote the kanikau, a poetic dirge in Kale's mother tongue that told of her life's journey, and several people were prepared to read parts of it: Nākai, 'Uwaikīkīilani and her son Will, and Alika. JY sat Kaholo down in his chair, and in the privacy of her home, Kale's family gathered and mourned as their ancestors had done for millennia. Kaholo offered a pule prayer and spoke aloud his cherished Kani'iaulono's name chant. All the family responded " 'eā-ā..." after each short stanza. Then everyone began to cry and wail.

When they collected themselves, Nākai began to read aloud all the places her mother treasured and all the things of nature that would always remind her of Mama. After a time there was silence again, and 'Uwiakīkīlani continued to speak of times and places that would never be the same without Kale, pausing twice to regain her composure. Then Will spoke of Nana's deep affection for her grandchildren and their love for her, but he could hardly finish. They all cried together. Finally, Alika, with long white beard and mustache, bedecked in his pilot's uniform that was a bit too large on his 85-year-old frame, leaned on his walking stick, set his jaw, and forced himself to read the places Kale traveled with him and the love all her husbands had for her. His wife Charlotte helped him outside for some air. After a long time of mourning and each family member saying a last goodbye, JY asked all to step outside but the pallbearers. The six men—'Aikake, Fanny's husband Kū'auhau, Will Halstead, Kuamo'o's husband Boas Mahoe, George Hū'eu Jr., and JY—stood to one side while Kaholo said his last farewell to the only woman he ever loved. When he left, they put the lid on Kale's coffin and nailed it shut.

'Uwaikīkīlani took Kaholo's arm and escorted her favorite Papa as he followed the boys carrying Kale's coffin down to the gravesite on the bluff above Honokahua Bay. The local minister, J.H. Moku, walked on Kaholo's other side and the children followed. Then came Alika and his wife Charlotte, Laura's daughter Bernice and her husband Charlie, Peke and her husband Antone Sylva, and Fanny Young. There were no minute guns or drums, just the echo of Honokahua surf pounding the shore, the footfalls of the pallbearers on the dirt trail, and tradewind blowing gently through the trees. Where the path turned downhill, the paniolo's families were waiting. Makekau, Mattias, 'Āwa'a, Mahuna, and Ka'aea, on their lei-decked horses, took up the rear; the sound of their horses' hooves on the path and soft jingle of spurs set a rhythmic pace. At the beach, the Shaw, Kekoa, and Halemāno families joined the procession with the Ha'ili and Kekahuna mā. The boys carried Kale across the halawai and up to the bluff overlooking the beach, where many former farmers and laborers who had come from Wailuku and Lāhainā waited to pay their respects to their righteous chief. The men were dressed in white trousers and white shirts, with colorful kapa sashes at the waist and some had bandanas at the neck. The ladies had white or bright pastel dresses and everyone wore lei and papale, lauhala panama hats.

'Aikake stood with his brothers and sisters, some of whom he hardly knew; when he saw Hulu in the crowd, he went and hugged him.

"I am so sorry," said Hulu "Your mother was so good to me and my family. We will miss her."

"Thank you. I am so glad to see you," said 'Aikake. He thought back on the days when Mama and auntie Pili were always waiting when he and Hulu brought back a sack of reef fish from the beach or when they came running back to the hale to be comforted after skinning a knee or elbow. And he grinned when he thought about Mama's famous kukui nut laxative treatment that they tried to avoid at all costs. The preacher started the ceremony but 'Aikake was lost in a picture of the past: the day he went to Honolulu to live, when Mama took him in her arms and told him that he was her hiapo, her first-born son and that there would never be anyone closer to her than her "precious ʻAikake."

"My brothers and sisters," said Reverend Moku, "Kale Kaniʻaulono lives. Today she is rejoicing in the arms of Jesus, her Savior in heaven, and praying for you as she always has. We talked many times about her love for you, her family, her friends, and her people. Her greatest concern was caring for us without interfering with our freedom to choose our own way. She stood before us as an example of courage and righteousness…"

JY glanced around and everyone was listening quietly. The sun was high now, but the breeze off the sea was cool at their backs as they looked across the pali and out to Molokaʻi. Kaholo looked very tired and the girls were so sad. JY remembered his father's funeral at the dunes, when Mama cried and asked God to forgive her. She put a Bible and a lei of lokelani roses in the grave with Papa and said, "Kāne, you were a good husband and a man of God's choosing." She wept and wailed; no one could console her and JY had felt so helpless. *I was little then and I did not understand death. Now I know, Mama.*

Halemāno was eulogizing Kale: "God has blessed her with children who walk in the ways of their mother, and now her body rests close to them in the land she loved, close to her family and the kūpuna she respected. Kale believed that if she took care of us, God would take care of the land. And he did. Honokahua prospered and survived hard times with our chief at our side, giving us courage."

Reverend Moku then said, "And so, God, we commit her body to the grave, but her soul to you. Comfort us you did her, and as she comforted us. Give us strength as you gave her strength, and as she strengthened us. And show us your love, Lord, as you showed her love, and she, in turn, loved us. *E Pule kākou i ka inoa o Ka Makua Mau, Ke Keiki, a me Ka ʻUhane Hemolele.ʻĀmene* We pray in the name of the Eternal Father, the Son and the Holy Spirit, Amen…"

Then Moku read Kale's favorite scripture, as Paul preached to the Romans:

> For I am persuaded that neither death, nor life, nor angels, nor principalities, nor powers, nor things present, nor things to come, nor height, nor depth, nor any other created thing, shall be able to separate us from the love of God, which is in Christ Jesus.

Then he began the Lord's Prayer, "*E ko mākou Makua i loko o ka lani, e hōano 'ia kou inoa.* Our Father up in heaven, holy is your name." As everyone joined in, the sound became fuller and richer until the valley resounded, as in the old days at the Meeting Pā. They closed with Kale's favorite Hymn, *E Jesu Ka Mohai Noʻu. Jesus our Sacrifice.*

Back at the house, there was a full lūʻau feast, as Kale had wished. While adults savored the food and comforted one another, the grandchildren went swimming and JY, Kale's executor, read Kale's will and her cherished keiki decided what to do with Honokahua.

"Papa said he did not need to be at this meeting because Mama provided for him. She tried to give him a piece of land, but he turned it down. All he wants to do is stay here with me and the family and live out his days close to her." He wiped his eyes and Fanny broke down. ʻUwaikīkīlani held her and JY slowly regained enough composure to go on. "Mama left all the land and her entire estate to us, to be divided equally, and we have to decide where to go from here."

Nākai cleared her throat. "George and I want to continue to live here and run the ranch. All of us can share in the profits of the ranch."

ʻAikake said, "I don't know about the others, but I do not feel right receiving profits from your work. I say keep whatever you make on the ranch, because the ranch makes the land more valuable for all of us. We should all pay our fair share of the taxes so we can keep our portion of land. I want to stay in Niu, but if the land is sold, which I hope it never is, then I will receive my share at that time." Heads were nodding.

"I agree with ʻAikake's thought. Mahoe and I are happy with our fishing business in Lāhainā," said Kuamoʻo. "I too would only exercise the right to my share if the land is sold."

Fanny blew her nose and wiped her eyes. "I am sorry…I can't believe she is gone…" She took a deep breath. "Kūʻauhau and I want to live here. He is a constable in Lāhainā, but I will do whatever work you have here and contribute to the ranching operation."

ʻUwaikīkīlani chimed in, "Johnnie and I have so many businesses going now—we really do not have time to be involved here, but Will and Lameka live here and they wish to continue running the dairy for George. Johnnie and I want Will to have our share of Honokahua."

JY added, "That is fine. You will have to make a will to be sure the land legally falls to him when you pass."

"Of course."

Now all eyes fell on JY, but there was no question as to his desire. "It is no surprise that Kawelo and I will continue to live here, manage the fishing and farming, and take care of Papa and the kids. If you are all willing, I suggest that we all have a meeting once a year before taxes are due to be sure that all interests are protected. All in favor?"

"Aye."

Just then, a great commotion arose outside, with shouting and the rumble of feet running up the front steps and across the veranda as family and guests tried to get under the porch eaves before a sheet of white rain, pushed in by a frisky squall, passed over the house. The wind swirled around the house and big drops of rain plopped and popped on the roof, windows, and ground all around. In a few minutes, the rain stopped and a rainbow suddenly appeared, glowing bright and arched high, looking like it touched the trees in the valley.

"It's her!" cried Kaholo. "The day she came to Honokahua was the same— the shower came and brought a rainbow just like that one!"

Alika stared…"I was there too. It is the sign of the aliʻi."

Nākai took her sister Fanny's hand. "Remember what Mama always said? 'Honokahua's rainbow has a name…'" she sobbed and could not go on.

All around the room three generations joined in the answer "*Ke Ānuenue kō ke Aloha a Ke Akua*, The Rainbow of God's Love."

Epilogue:
From Honokahua to Kapalua Resort

As was the custom of Hawaiian families, Kale Davis willed her land as a single parcel to her children:

> Isaac Keʻeaumoku Adams had five children and became the patriarch of a large Oʻahu clan. (His father, Captain Alexander Adams, married two Harbottle sisters, Sarah and Charlotte. He died at age 91, survived by 10 children and the Adams name is well represented today on Oʻahu.)

> ʻUwaikīkīlani married John Joseph Halstead, who built Hale Piule, a tin-roofed "palace" for Kamehameha III, that was eventually torn down and its timbers used to build the Lahāinā Courthouse. Their son William H. Halstead and his wife Lameka lived in Makawao. There are no Halsteads on Maui today. Their daughter Elinor Halstead married Charles Kauakahiahiakua Wilcox and had ten children. Wilcox descendants still live on Maui.

> Amelia Nākai married Kale's half-brother's son, George Hūʻeu Davis Jr., and had eight children. Kale's brother Hūʻeu had children and a large number of his descendants live on the Island of Hawaiʻi.

> Mele Kuamoʻo's Mahoe descendants still live on Maui.

Early in the 1850s, Henry Perrine Baldwin, son of Dr. Dwight Baldwin, bought Laura Konia's Nāpili land from her son-in-law, Charles Bishop. He also acquired Honolua ahupuaʻa, which Charles Bishop had sold to Taughton and

Childs. By the 1890's, Baldwin had purchased most of the Honokahua ahupua'a from Peke's granddaughter, Mary Sylva, who was a wealthy landowner in Honolulu and had acquired much of her cousins' lands.

Lameka Halstead sold the last remaining section of Honokahua to Baldwin in 1894, with the provision that the Davis family gravesite be protected. Today, after 139 years, Kale still rests in peace, overlooking Honokahua Bay

Baldwin put the ahupua'a back into one parcel again, and made Honokahua part of Honolua Ranch, which slowly went into pineapple; in 1920 when, the company name was changed to Baldwin Packers, which later merged with Alexander and Baldwin on East Maui.

In 1923, Kā'anapali became part of Lāhainā District, and the Kā'anapali name was lost until 1962, when AmFac Resort used it for their resort destination in Lāhainā. In 1969 the Cameron family bought Maui Pineapple Company from Alexander and Baldwin, naming it Maui Land & Pineapple Company, Inc., and petitioned the State of Hawai'i to change the land use classification of 317 acres from "agriculture" to "urban" in order to develop the Kapalua Resort. Previously the Kapalua name was used only for Kapalua Bay on the south side of Hāwea Point.

When many Kapalua Resort homeowners look at a title search for their property, they will see Kale Davis noted as the earliest recorded owner of their land, granted to her in a Royal Patent of Confirmation in 1855 by King Kamehameha IV.

Visit www.theloveremains.com

- View photos of Honokahua sites
- Learn more historical facts
- See additions to Kale's family tree
- Book a historical tour or lecture
- Contact Katherine Kama'ema'e Smith

Pronunciation Guide

1. Pronounce Hawaiian vowels like Spanish vowels: a = ah, as in t<u>a</u>co
   e = eh, as in b<u>e</u>so
   i = eee, as in burr<u>i</u>to
   o = oh, as in burrit<u>o</u>
   u = ooo, as in <u>U</u>ruguay

2. Hawaiian vowels are never silent, and diphthongs are rare, so pronounce all vowels as separate syllables and glide from one to the other, e.g. Aloha = Ah-loh-hah, or Maui = Mah-oo-ee, or Kale = Kah-leh

3. Unless a word contains a stressed vowel, (ā, ē, ī, ō, ū) the next to the last syllable is stressed, e.g. the name Keahi is pronounced Keh-AH-hee and Honokahua is pronounced Hoh-noh-kah-HOO-ah

4. Words with an unusual stress are marked. Therefore, the name Haleakalā, where the last ā is stressed, is pronounced, Hah-leh-ah-kah-LAH, and Hāwea is pronounced HAH-weh-ah, not hah-WEH-ah.

5. Hawaiian words may contain glottal stops, as indicated by an ʻokina (ʻ), a diacritical mark that looks like a backwards apostrophe. Here the easy glide from vowel to vowel is interrupted, as if taking a very short breath. e.g. Aliʻi = Ah-LEEʻ ee, or Kāʻanapali =KAHʻ ah-nah-PAH-lee

Glossary

ʻaʻā	Rough stony lava
ʻaʻama	Large black edible crab that runs on shore rocks
Abner Pākī	High Chief and husband of Laura Konia; father of Bernice Pauahi Bishop
ʻAe	Yes
ʻahi	Tuna
ʻāhinahina	Silversword plant
Ā hui hou	Farewell; lit. until [we] meet again
ʻAhuimanu	Land division of Kāneʻohe Oʻahu; lit. flock of birds
Ahonuilani	Character: mother of Kānekuapuʻu
ahupuaʻa	Land division managed for the king by a chief or his foreman
ʻāina	Land
ʻaina	Meal
ʻaina ahiahi	Dinner; lit. evening meal
aku	Bonito fish
Akua	God
Akua Loa	Big god image; the large banner carried around every island at the Makahiki festival
Akua Pāʻani	Game god image that oversaw the Makahiki games
akule	Big-eyed scad fish

ʻalaea	Red earth rich in iron salts; mixed with salt as a condiment
Alakoko	Fishpond in Līhuʻe, Kauaʻi
Alaloa	Circumferential footpath around the island of Maui built by King Piʻilani and completed my his son, Kihapiʻilani
Alapaʻi	Julia Alapaʻi; Keonianaʻs second wife
Alapaʻinui	AlapaʻinuiaKauaua, Famous High Chief of the Island of Hawaiʻi
Alexander	Son of Kaleʻs daughter Mele Kuamoʻo
Aliʻi ʻAi Ahupuaʻa	Chief of an ahupuaʻa land division
Aliʻi Nui	High chief
aloha	Love; used in many greetings and idiomatic expressions
ʻamaʻu	A fern; the pith was eaten in times of famine
ʻāmama	Amen; lit. let it be so
Amelia Nākai	Daughter of Kale Davis and Kānekuapuʻu; married George Hūʻeu Jr.
Anakē	Aunt
anana	Fathom; the distance from fingertip to fingertip of a manʻs armspan
Antone Sylva	Second husband of Kaleʻs sister, Peke Davis; came to Hawaiʻi from the Azores in 1846
ao keʻokeʻo	Small puffy white clouds on a fair day
ʻAuʻau channel	The channel between Maui and Lanaʻi
ʻauhau	A tax or offering of produce and provender given to a king or chief
ʻauinalā	Afternoon, from 2 p.m. to sunset
ʻaumakua	A family god that may take the form of an animal or inert object
au moe	The middle of the night

'auwai	A ditch or canal
'awa	Kava shrub; root makes ceremonial drink that contains a mild narcotic
awakea	Middle of the day; from 10 a.m. to 2 p.m.
'Āwa'a	Character: a rancher from Hawai'i
auwē	Expression of fear, scorn, pity, or wonder; Alas!
barque (bark)	Sailing ship with three to five masts, square-rigged except for the after mast
Bernice Pauahi	Daughter of Laura Konia and Abner Pākī
Boki	High chief and kahuna lapa'au; Governor of O'ahu; younger brother of Kalanimoku; married to Lilihā
Brig	Two-masted sailing ship with square-rigged foremast, fore and aft mainsail, and square maintopsails
Brown Bess	Nineteenth century British musket
calabash	Dried, cleaned and decorated gourd used as bowl or container
Charles Wilcox	Married Elinor Halstead, Kale's granddaughter
Charles Bishop	Married Laura Konia's daughter, Bernice Pauahi
Charlotte	Daughter of William Halstead, Kale's grandson
Charlotte Harbottle	Third wife of Captain Alexander Adams
Chief Ni'au	High Chief of Kaua'i, killed in the 1824 revolt
corm	Underground edible stem of the kalo plant, similar to a bulb
Dr. Dwight Baldwin	Missionary and physician for 27 years in Lāhainā, Maui
Dr. Gerrit Judd	Minister of Finance for King Kauikeaouli Kamehameha III
Dr. Thomas Rooke	O'ahu Physician and founder of Hawai'i Board of Health; husband of Grace Kamaiku'i Young
'eā	Refrain; lit. "isn't that so"

Edward Albert	Son of Queen Emma and King Alexander Liholiho Kamehameha IV
ʻekaha	Bird nest fern
ʻeke	Bag
Elinor Halstead	Daughter of William Halstead and Lameka
Emma Rooke	Queen Emma, daughter of Fanny Young and George Naʻea, hānai to Grace Young and Dr. Thomas Rooke
Fairbairne	Character: Second Mate on the *Kaʻahumanu*
Fanny	Youngest daughter of Kale Davis and Kānekuapuʻu
Fanny Young	Second daughter of John Young; mother of Emma Naʻea
Forfarshire	County in eastern Scotland, where Alexander Adams was born
George Cox	Assumed name of Kahekili Keʻeaumoku, Governor of Maui
George Hūʻeu Jr.	Son of Hūʻeu Davis; married Amelia Nākai, daughter of Kale Davis
George Humehume	Son of Kaumualiʻi King of Kauaʻi, educated in Massachusetts; returned with missionaries in 1820; married Kale's sister Peke
George Naʻea	Husband of Fanny Young and father of Queen Emma
Grace Kamaikuʻi	Oldest daughter of John Young; stepmother of Queen Emma; founded Queen's Hospital
Great Mahele	Division of Hawaiian lands from 1848–1856; the beginning of fee simple land ownership
Haʻale	Second wife of James Kānehoa Young
Haʻalilio, Timoteo	Statesman for Kamehameha III and IV
Haʻikū	Land division of East Maui
Hikoni	Third wife of James Kānehoa Young
Hakakau	Character: Young farmer boy
Haku	Lord; master

haku 'ohana	Head of an extended family unit
hala	Pandanus screw pine; leaves used to weave mats, baskets and hats; flowers used for perfume; fruits used as fodder and famine food
hala key	Sections of orange pandanus hala fruits used to make fragrant lei
hālau	Longhouse or work house
halawai	Meeting; place where two streams meet
Hale Aloha	Monument in Lāhainā commemorating 1853 when Maui was spared from smallpox
hale hana	Work house; factory
hale ho'āhu	Storehouse; shed
hale kua	Workshop for making kapa cloth
hale moe	Sleeping house
hale noho	Dwelling house
Haleakalā	Dormant volcano that formed East Maui; lit. "house of the sun"
Halemāno	Character: fisherman and minister
hāmama	Yawn
Hāna	Land division and ancient village of East Maui
hānai	Adopted; foster child; to rear; to caretake
haole	Foreigner; now connotes Caucasian
hapa haole	Half-white
Harriet Nahi'ena'ena	Daughter of Keopuolani
hau	Native lowland hibiscus; several varieties with flowers from dusty red to yellow; used as hedges
hau koki'o ke'oke'o	Native Hawaiian white hibiscus with red center stamin and delicate fragrance

Haumea	Pele's mother; equivalent of Papa; goddess of childbirth
Hauōla	Ancient surfing area of Lāhainā where a mythical woman was turned into a rock
Hava'iki	One name of the land of the Hawaiian ancestors; also called Kahiki
Hāwea Point	Large point at Honokahua, named for a sacred drum brought from Kahiki by La'amaikahiki
he'e	Octopus
he'enalu	Surfing
hehena	Insane, possessed
hewa	Sin
Hewahewa	High kahuna of Kamehameha I; from Maui
Hi'u Kai	Cleansing rite of the Makahiki, bathing in the ocean from midnight until dawn
Hiki	Kale's nickname for Kaholokahiki; lit. "arrive"
hiki nō	"Okay" or "can do"
Hiram Bingham	Pastor of Kawaiha'o Mission and Church, Honolulu
Hoapili	Counselor to Kamehameha I, II and III; Governor of Maui; husband of Keopuolani and Kaheiheimalie
Hōkū	Fifteenth night of the lunar month; a full moon night; Star
Hōkūle'a	Navigational star, Arcturus
Hōkūpā	Constellation Leo
holoholo	To go out for enjoyment
holua	Sled used on constructed slides and mountain slopes
honi	To touch noses on the side; breathe out and then in; kiss
Honokahua	Land division of Kā'anapali District, Maui; between Honolua and Nāpili

Honokōhau	Land division of Kāʻanapali District, Maui; between Honolua and Kahakuloa
Honokōwai,	Land division of Kāʻanapali District, Maui; between Hanakoʻo and Mahinahina
Honolua	Land division of Kāʻanapali District, Maui; between Honkahua and Honokōhau
Honouliuli	Land division of Waipahu in the Waiʻanae mountains of the windward coast of Oʻahu
honu	Turtle
Hoʻohei	Character: fisherman
hoʻokupu	Makahiki offering
hoʻoponopono	Hawaiian tradition of speaking freely, making amends, and forgiving; lit. "to make right"
Hua	Fourteenth night of the lunar month; an ancient king of Maui; egg; seed
Hūʻeu	George Hūʻeu Davis, son of Isaac Davis by Kalukuna and half brother of Kale; lived in Waikaloa, Hawaiʻi; lit. "witty, comical"; also the warrior and kapu chief name given to Isaac Davis by Kamehameha I
Hui!	Greeting equivalent to "Hello!"
Huleʻia	Stream of Līhuʻe, Kauaʻi, where Kamapuaʻa mated with Pele
huli	Kalo top used for planting; sprouts from the base of the kalo plant; to turn
Hulu	Feather god believed to help women in labor; also nickname of character Huluohaʻae
Hulumanu	Band of young chiefs and chiefesses who accompanied Kauikeaouli in his youthful rebellion
Huluohaʻae	Character: Son of Pilialoha
Huna	Eleventh day of the lunar month
ʻĪao Valley	Valley behind Wailuku, where Kamehameha the Great defeated Kalanikupule and conquered Maui

iʻe kuku	Wooden tool for beating wauke bark into kapa cloth
Iʻi	John Papa Iʻi; Hawaiian historian, statesman, and graduate of Lahainaluna
ʻiʻiʻi fern	Small fern used as famine food
ʻili	Narrow or small land division inside an ahupuaʻa, usually stretching from sea to mountain
ʻiliʻili	Small pebbles used in games, as teaching aids, or in dances
ʻilima	Native bush or ground cover with small orange flowers used in lei
imu	Earth oven lined with lava rock
ʻinamona	Relish made from ground toasted kukui nut and salt
ʻIo	Polynesian supreme creator diety worshipped in Hawaiʻi before 1400AD
ipu	Gourd used as a musical percussive instrument
ipu hōkiokio	gourd whistle
Ipu Pule Rite	Ceremonial separating of male children from eating with women, at age six
Isaac Davis	Warrior, gunner, Governor of Oʻahu for Kamehameha I
J.Y. Kānehoa	Youngest son of Kale Davis and Kānekuapuʻu; used the Davis surname
James Kānehoa	Second son of John Young and Nāmokuʻelua; Governor of Maui; first husband of Kale Davis
Jane Lahilahi	Youngest daughter of John Young; married Joshua Kaʻeo
John Harbottle	Harbor pilot of Honolulu; worked with Alexander Adams
John Keoniana	John Young's youngest son; Governor of Maui, Kuhina Nui for Kamehameha III

John Meek	Captain John Meek married Peke's daughter, Wahinekipi
John Palmer Parker	First rancher of Hawai'i
John Papa I'i	Lahainaluna educated statesman; Treasurer for Kamehameha III; Speaker of House of Nobles
John Young	Warrior, gunner, Governor of Hawai'i for Kamehameha I
Johnnie Halstead	'Uwaikikilani's husband; ran Hawiian Hotel, a general store in Lāhainā and a farm in Lepolepo
Joshua Ka'eo	Husband of Jane Lahilahi
Ka Lama Hawai'i	First Hawaiian language newspaper in Hawai'i, printed at Lahainaluna Seminary beginning 1834
ka lani pipili	Rainy season between November and January
Ka'aea	Character: farmer
Ka'ahumanu	A favored Queen of Kamehameha I; Queen Regent of Hawai'i for Kamehameha II and III
Kā'anapali	District of Maui between Keka'a and Waihe'e
Ka'aumoana	Character: Helmsman, First Mate and Navigator of the *Ka'ahumanu*
kaha	To gut or slash; stripe
kahakai	Seashore; beach
Kahakuloa	Land division of Ka'anapali; between Honokōhau and Waihe'e
Kāhala	Amberjack or Yellowtail fish
Kahana	Land division of Ka'anapali; between Mahinahina and Mailepai
kahawai	Stream or streambed
Kahawalu	Wife of Kauhi, brother of Kamehamehanui, who took Maui in 1738

Kaheiheimālie	A favored Queen of Kamehameha I; later married Hoapili and took the name Hoapiliwahine
Kahelu Ridge	Famous ridge of Waimea, Kaua'i on the Nāpali coast
kahili	Royal scepter of ruling chiefs, made of rare colored feathers carried on a long wooden staff
Kaho'olawe	Island used in nineteenth century Hawaiian Kingdom as a penal colony for men
Kahoali'i	One of Kamehameha I's gods, impersonated at Makahiki by a naked man
Kaholokahiki	Fifth husband of Kale Davis
Kahoma Valley	Valley behind Lāhainā where women fled from rioting sailors
kahu	Steward or administrator
kahua	Foundation or footing
Kahua Hill	Name of the broad slopes above Honokahua Bay
kahuna	Priest or expert
kahuna lapa'au	Expert in Hawaiian natural remedies
kahuna nui	High priest
kai 'oloa rite	Ceremonial tying of fine white kapa malo on an image or icon
kai e'e	Tidal wave
kai po'ana	Shallow water near the beach where waves scoop out sand
Kai'ehu	Son of Kame'eiamoku and brother of Hoapili lost at 'Īao Valley
Kaihalulu	Beach at base of Ka'uiki head, Hāna
kaiko'o	Rough seas
Kailua	Royal residence of Kamehameha I early in his reign; southwest Hawai'i
Kalāhei	Character: Mauna's man sent to guard Makauli

Kalalau	Largest valley of the Nāpali coast of Kaua'i with upstream terraces and high waterfalls
Kalama.	Queen of Kauikeaouli, Kamehameha III
Kalama'ula	Land division of Kaunakakai, Moloka'i; place of the first Hawaiian homesteads
Kalanimoku	Prime Minister under Kamehameha I and II
Kaha'anapilo	Wife of Hū'eu Davis
Kalei	Character: daughter of farmer Mahua'ai
kalo	Taro plant; grown in paddies or dry ground; primary source of starch in the Hawaiian diet
Kāloa-kū-kahi	Twenty-fourth night of the lunar month
Kāloa-kū-lua	Twenty-fifth night of the lunar month
Kalolo	Grandmother of Keopuolani
Kamāmalu	Queen of Liholiho Kamehameha II; died with him in London, 1824
Kamapua'a	Pig demigod who is a form of Lono
Kame'eiamoku	Ruling chief of Hawai'i, who captured Isaac Davis in 1790
Kamehameha I	King of Hawai'i 1748–1819; unified the Hawaiian Islands into one Kingdom
Kamehameha II	Liholiho; reigned 1819–1825; ended kapu in 1819
Kamehameha III	Kauikeaouli; reigned 1825–1854; instituted the Hawaiian Constitutional Monarchy
Kamehameha IV	Alexander Liholiho; reigned 1854–1863
Kamehameha V	Lot; reigned 1863–1874
Kamehamehanui	Ruling chief of Hawai'i, who took Maui in 1738
Kamuela	Land division of Hawai'i; eastward and upland of Kawaihae
Kanahā Pond	Salt ponds at Pu'unene Maui
Kanaloa	Major Hawaiian god of the sea and the planter of bananas

Kāne	Major Hawaiian god of the staff of life and giver of taro and ground water; short name of Kānekuapuʻu; husband; man
Kānehailua	Character: farmer
Kānekuapuʻu	Fourth husband of Kale Davis; father of Amelia Nākai, Fanny, Mele Kuamoʻo and JY
Kāneohe Bay	Bay of Eastern Oʻahu
Kaniʻaulono	Kale's Hawaiian name; lit. "the silent reed"
kanikau	Poetic dirge composed for loved-ones; read during 10 days of mourning between death and burial
Kaʻoanaʻeha	Second wife of John Young; mother of Grace, Fanny, Keoniana and Jane Lahilahi
Kaʻohumalu	God of sorcery; a god of Kamehameha
Kapalua Bay	One of five bays of Honokahua
kapa moe	Sleeping blanket
Kapewakua	Small parcel of land in Lāhainā, Maui owned by Peke Davis
Kapiʻolani	Chiefess companion of Kauikeaouli
kapu	Taboo; proscribed or prohibited
kapuna haole	Foreign priest; name used for early missionaries
Kapuni	A feather god of Kamehameha I
Kapuniʻai	Name of Chief Kaiʻehu, lost at birth and found at age 44, working as a fisherman in Kāʻanapali
Kau	Summer; place; put
Kaʻu	Land division of the southern tip of Hawaiʻi, near Kilauea; possessive, "my"
Kauaʻula	Land division of Lāhainā, Maui; destructive easterly ventura wind of Kauaʻula Valley
kauhale aliʻi	Royal homestead consisting of several buildings
Kauhi	Son of King Kehaulike of Maui; killed in the battle for Maui in 1738

Kauikeaouli	Kamehameha III
Kaumualiʻi	King of Kauaʻi
Kaunakahakai	Old name of Kaunakakai, Molokaʻi
kaʻupu	Albatross; also name of a fern
kauwā	Outcast; used figuratively as 'humble servant'
Kawaihaʻo	Early Christian mission and stone church of Sandwich Isles Mission on Oʻahu
Kawaihae	Trading port of West Hawaiʻi; home of Isaac Davis and John Young
Ke Kaumuku	The squalling wind of Maʻalaea,
kea	White
Keʻa Pua	Old dart game played with sugar cane tufts
Keahi	Character: elderly survivor of ʻIao Valley; lit. "fire"
Keʻaweʻaweʻula	Child of Queen Kalama and Kauikeaouli Kamehameha III
Kealakekua	Village of Kailua, Hawaiʻi
Keʻeaumoku	Prominant warrior of Kamehameha I; father of Keʻeaumoku Kahekili
Keʻi	Famous beach of Nāpali, Kauaʻi
Kehauiki Gulch	Gulch on Northern boundary of Honokahua
Kekaulike	King of Maui; died in 1737
Kekaʻa	Black rock promontory at north end of Kāʻanapali Beach, Lāhainā; a jumping off place
Kekaha	Old name for Kekaʻa
Kekahunawahine	Character: midwife and kahuna lapaʻau medical practicioner
Kekauʻonohi	Wife of Liholiho, Governor of Kauaʻi
Kekele	Land section at the base of Nuʻuanu Pali, Oʻahu; famous for fragrant hala groves
Kekūhaupiʻo	Famous warrior of Kamehameha I

Keli'iopunui	Keli'iopunui Kalanikaukeha Ka'ahuko'o; Wife of Isaac Ke'eaumoku Adams
Keoniana'opio	Youngest son of John Young
Keopuolani	Highest pi'o queen of Kamehameha I; first ali'i convert to Christianity
kepakepa	Spirited talking style of chant
Kepaniwai	Battle of 'Īao Valley; lit. "dammed waters," when bodies choked the Wailuku stream
Ke-pu-waha-'ula	First sea battle where cannon were used on war canoes; between Maui and Hawai'i forces
Kia'i Koa	King's guards
kīhei	Cloak; knee-length square of kapa cloth tied over one shoulder
kiko'olā	Rude
Kilo I'a	Fishing expert
Kina'u	Queen Regent for Kauikeaouli Kamehameha III after Ka'ahumanu died
King Hua	Ancient king of Maui
King Kahekili	King of Maui, Moloka'i and O'ahu before Kamehameha I
kō	Sugarcane
koa	Hawaiian hardwood tree; wood is deep red; soldier
ko'a	Fishing shrine
Ko'olau	Mountains of Honolulu
Kohala	Northern coast of West Hawai'i
koholā	Whale
Kokoiki	Halley's Comet, which appeared in Hawaiian skies in 1824, and in 1758 at Kamehameha's birth
Kōlea	Pacific golden plover
kolohe	Rascal

Kona	Village of Kailua, Hawai'i
kona	Southerly
kōnane	Checkerboard game or pattern
konohiki	Land manager or foreman
kou	Native hardwood tree with graceful branches and red-orange blossoms in spring
Kū	Major god; god of war that required human sacrifice for appeasement
Kū'oi'oiwahine	Character: a widowed farmer
Kū'ula kai	God of fishing
Kū'ula Stone	Icon and altar of fishing god, Kū'ula
kua	Back
Kuakini	Son of Ke'eaumoku; Governor of Hawai'i for Kamehameha I; brother of George Cox, Ke'eaumoku Kahekili
kualapa	Ridge between two valleys
kualono	Broad plain between two valleys
Kuhina Nui	Regent or Queen Regent
Kūkaniloko	Birthing place of kings in central O'ahu where drums of La'amaikahiki were sounded
kukui	Tree with oily nuts used for torches and ointments; leaves and nutshells used as mulch; many medicinal uses for leaves, sap, and nuts; wood used for imu fire
kula	Flat grassy lowlands used for farming or grazing
kuleana	Responsibility; authority; jurisdiction
kūlolo	Baked kalo pudding made with coconut and cane sugar
kumākēnā aloha ali'i	Ten days of mourning after the death of a chief
kūpe'e	Decorative wristlet or anklet

kupeʻe ʻilio	Anklets adorned with hundreds of dog teeth that serve as percussive instruments in hula
kupukupu ferns	Native rainforest spreading ferns that resemble "Boston" ferns
kūpuna	Ancestors or elders
Laʻamaikahiki	Ancient King from Tahiti who came to Oʻahu and brought his drum, Hāwea.
Laʻaukūkahi	Eighteenth day of the lunar month
Lāhainā	Land division and town of West Maui
Lāhainā Roadstead	Port of Lāhainā where East and West shipping lanes crossed; also called Lāhainā Roads
Lāhaināluna	First high school west of the Mississippi, founded 1831
Lahela	Wife of George Shaw of Kaʻanapali and a konohiki; daughter of Hewahewa
lama	Tree with black bark and extremely hard wood; used ceremonially
lana nuʻu manaʻo	Sacred house of oracle where priests received word from the gods
lanaʻi	Terrace; porch
lauhala	Leaves of the hala tree; dried, heated, despined and made supple for weaving mats and baskets; today used for hats
Laura Konia	Chiefess of Napili ahupuaʻa; mother of Bernice Pauahi Bishop; companion of Liholiho
lauwaʻe	Maile-scented fern with large fingered leaves.
lawaiʻa	Fisherman
Leʻahi	Ancient name of Diamond Head, Oʻahu
leho heʻe	Lure for catching octopus made from a sinker stone, hook and line
leho pāuhu	Octopus lure made with a cowrie shell

lehua	Red feathery flowers of the 'ōhi'a, found in the rainforest
lei hulu	Feather lei worn by ali'i
lei la'i	Tī leaf lei worn to ward off evil spirits
lei palaoa	Walrus tusk ivory or whalebone fishhook lei on necklace of human hair worn by ali'i
lei po'o	Crown; head lei
lei pū	Shell lei
leina	Dry plain
Lele	Ancient name of Lahaina; lit. "jumping" or "landing"
Leowaipahe	Character: Son of U'i
lepo	Dirt; soil
Lepolepo	Farming location on East Maui
Liholiho	Kamehameha II; reigned from 1819 to 1825
Līhu'e	Harbor of Kaua'i
Lilihā.	Daughter of Governor Hoapili of Maui; wife of Governor Boki of O'ahu
Limaha'i	Character: farmer and husband of U'i
Limahana	Hired hand; lit. "work hand"
Limaloa	Spring and coconut grove on O'ahu
limu	General term for seaweed
lo'i	Water-fed flooded field enclosed by stone and mud and dikes, where kalo is cultivated
loke	Rose
lokelani	Hawaiian green rose
lomilomi	Massage
Lono	God of farming and fertility
Lono Poko	Small image of Lono for the Makahiki celebration
Lonomakua	Large image of Lono with white banners floated on a tall staff

Lord George Paulet	Captain of a British Man-o'-War who "forclosed" Hawai'i for debt owed Britain in 1843
luahine	Old woman
luakini heiau	Temple where human sacrifices were offered to Kū, the god of war.
lū'au	Any of a number of edible greens baked and eaten with fish or meat
luhi	Burdened; name used for widows with families to raise alone
luna	Boss
mā	Clan; suffix word attached to identifying name or placename of the clan
Mā'alaea	Small harbor and village between East and West Maui
Mackee	Character: former sailor and beachcomber
Maele	Character: fisherman in Shaw family
mahalo	Thanks
Mahinahina	Land division of Kā'anapali, West Maui
Māhua'ai	Character: farmer
Mahuna	Character: paniolo
mai'a	Banana
maile	Fragrant rainforest vine used for lei and kupe'e
Mailepai	Land division of Kā'anapali, West Maui
Ma'i Pākē	leprosy
Ma'ipu'upu'uli'ili'i	smallpox
Makahiki	Harvest and fertility rite of ancient Hawai'i, celebrated for four months starting in October
makai	Toward the sea
Makali'i	A cluster of stars, the Pleiades; the month of December
Makāluapuna	Narrow jutting point of Honokahua where springholes may be found

Makani Pōkalakī	Name of an angry wind
Makauli	Character: canoebuilder
Makawao	Village in land section of Haiku, East Maui
Makeāhua Gulch	Gulch near Kawaihae, Hawai'i
Makekau	Character: paniolo
makua	Old person or parent
makuawahine	Female elder; any female in your parents' generation
Māla	Land division and port at Lāhainā
malo	Loincloth
Malo	David Malo; Hawaiian historian, statesman and graduate of Lahainluna Seminary
mamaki	Upland bush with fragrant leaves used medicinally as tea
mamane	The tropical almond tree
mana	Spiritual power
Manakū	Tax collector of Kā'anapali
manō	Shark
Manu	Character: Kahuna Mo'o Lono and Kilo I'a
Manuia	Brother of Governor Boki
ma'o	Green
Ma'olanalana	Character: grandmother of Kanekuapu'u
Maoli	Aborigine or Native
mapele heiau	A temple to Lono
Mary Sylva	Granddaughter of Peke Davis
Mattias	Character: paniolo
Maui	Demigod accredited with founding Maui island, raising the sky and discovering fire
mauka	Toward the uplands

Maunahina	Character: head fisherman and mokumoku champion of Honokahua
Mauna Kea	Highest mountain in Hawaiʻi; 13,796 feet high
Mele Kuamoʻo	Daughter of Kale Davis and Kānekuapuʻu
Mikiʻopio	John Meek, son of Captain John Meek; married to Wahinekipe, Peke Davis's daughter; owned a lot on Oʻahu
mikimiki	Free talking; a prerequisite to making amends in hoʻoponopono
Miriam Kekauluohi	Queen Regent after death of Kinaʻu
moʻi	King
mōhai	Offering; sacrifice
Mohalu	12th night of the lunar calendar
mokihana	Fragrant berry used to perfume kapa cloth or lei
moku	Land division consisting of several ahupuaʻa
Moku, J.H.	Sandwich Island Mission Minister assigned to Kāʻanapali
Mokuʻula	Fishpond in Lāhainā with island that was burial place for Hawaiian chiefs
Mokulēʻia	One of five bays of Honokahua
mokumoku	Hawaiian boxing, where blows were blocked with fists; fisticuffs
Mokupeʻa	Valley and tributary stream of Honokahua
Molokaʻi	Island visible from Honokahua
Moʻo Lono	Line of kahunas worshipping Lono
moʻomoʻo	Bundle of soaked and once-beaten wauke bark used in second stage of making felted kapa fabric
moʻopuna	Grandchild
mū	Executioner; also means bug
muʻumuʻu	Loose flowing dress gathered into a yoke

mua	Men's sleeping house used in days of kapu
Nāhaolehua	Paul Nāhaolehua, Governor of Maui 1852–1874
Nā Hono a Pi'ilani	Six Bays of Kā'anapali: Hononānā, Honokeana, Honokōwai, Honokahua, Honolua, and Honokōhau
naio	Tree; wood prized for making houses
nā 'iwi	Sacred ancestral burial ground; lit. "the bones"
Nākai Nālima'alu'alu	Kale's mother who died in the 'ōku'u plague in 1803; Isaac Davis's first wife
Nālehu	Character: Kalāhei's daughter who marries 'Āwa'a
namunamu	Grumbling
Nānāpua	Island of the New Hebrides where Boki ventured and was lost at sea
Nāpali head	Headland of Kaua'i's northern coast
Nāpili	Land division of Kā'anapali ruled by Laura Konia; south of Honokahua
naupaka	Succulent beach plant used by Hawaiians as an antiseptic
Nāwiliwili	Harbor of Līhu'e, Kaua'i
Night Marchers	Spirits of ancient warriors who march at night
Nu'uanu pali	O'ahu's Eastern cliff coast where Kamehameha's forces conquered Kalanipule's O'ahu chiefs
'ohana	Extended family unit
Ohapau	Character: woman in Shaw family
'ohe	Bamboo; Ancient Hawaiian variety is thick and tall, with yellow canes and green nodes
'ōhi'a lehua	Family of rain forest trees with feathery red, yellow, or white blossoms and hard wood
'ōhi'a'ai	Mountain Apple trees with hot pink feathery blossoms and pear-like red fruit
'ohukai	Ocean mist

ʻōkuʻu	Plague of 1803–4, possibly cholera; lit. "squat hunched up"
ʻolena	Turmeric; prepared from the root of a species of ginger; used medicinally
ʻOlepau	Tenth night of the lunar month
ʻoli	Chant
ʻOlohana	John Young's Hawaiian name; said to be Hawaiian for "all hands", the cry of the bo'sun
olonā	Native shrub; bark prized for strong fiber used to make fishnets and base for feathered capes
Olowalu	Southern most land division and small town of West Maui; site of 1790 massacre by Captain Simon Metcalf
ʻoluʻolu	kind, pleasant
Oneloa	One of the five bays of Honokahua; today the bay is in front of The Ironwoods
ʻōpae	Shrimp
ʻōpelu	Mackerel scad
ʻopihi	Limpet
ʻŌpūkahaʻia	Henry ʻŌpūkahaʻia, Hawaiian missionary whose death and memoirs led to the first American Board of Missions
Oulu	One of Kamehameha I's feather gods
pā	Yard
pāʻani	Game
Pāʻao	Priest of Tahiti who brought the worship of Kanaloa, Kū and Pele to Hawaiʻi in 1400s
Paepae	Platform or paved foundation for a temple or house
Pāhaʻaikaua	Third husband of Kale Davis
pāhale	A small land section just large enough for a house and garden

Pāhoehoeiki,	Land division of West Hawai'i willed to Fanny Young by her father John Young
Pailolo	Channel between Maui and Moloka'i
pala fern	Rainforest fern used for food in times of famine
pali	Cliff
Pāliko Priests	Line of kahunas worshipping Lono
paniolo	Hawaiian cowboy
pāpapa beans	Famine food
pā'ū	Very full sarong made from numerous yards of kapa cloth
Paul Nāhaolehua	Governor of Maui 1852–1874
Peke	Half sister of Kale Davis
Pele'ioholani	Warrior High Chief of Oahu, who sided with Kauhi in the battle for Maui in 1738
peleleu	Long, wide double war canoes made for Kamehameha I in 1796
Pi'ilani	Ancient King of Maui
piko	Navel
pili	To cling or cleave to; used in love songs ; used to describe close family relationships
pili grass	Grass growing in tight clumps, tied in bundles and used as thatch for houses
Pilialoha	Character: single mother farmer; lover of Ke'eaumoku
pilikia	Trouble
Pioneer Mill	West Maui sugar mill built by Henry Baldwin in 1862
pō'ele'ele	Darkest night; black
Pōhakulua o Kane	Natural double rock formation where Kāne was honored
Pohukaina	Royal mausoleum where high chiefs and dignitaries were buried after 1825

poi	Cooked kalo pounded into a smooth paste; a food staple eaten with fish,meat or salt
Pōkīkī	Portuguese
pono	Righteous, proper, virtuous
pōpoki	Cat
pū	Shell
puaʻa pepeiao	Cattle; lit. "pigs with iron horns"
Pua Ka Huahua	Rock formation at north end of Hāwea Point
puakinikini	Non-native flowering tree with fragrant white to gold blossoms
Puaonaona	Character name: Peke's daughter's name before Kaʻahumanu named her
pūʻili	Bamboo rattles used in hula
pule	Prayer
puna	Spring
Punalau	A point near Honolua Bay
pūpū	Raw fish appetizer
Pupue	Character: young mokumoku contestant; lit. "to crouch like a cat"
Puʻu Kaʻeo	Mountain of Honokohau visible from Honokahua, named after a ruling chief of Kauaʻi
Puʻu Koholā	Luakini heiau of Kamehameha I; built to his war god at Kawaihae before he conquered Maui and Oʻahu
Puʻu o ʻEke	West Maui Mountains from the Lāhainā side
Puʻunene	Plain south of Wailuku, Maui
puʻupuʻu liʻiliʻi	Smallpox
Richard Thomas	Rear Admiral Richard Thomas restored Hawaiian sovereignty July 13, 1843
Rooke House	Clinic in Honolulu operated by Thomas Rooke, M.D., Queen Emma's adoptive father

Ruth Pauahi	Bernice Pauahi Bishop's cousin; Princess Ruth
sennit	Any cordage made from several strands of natural fibers twisted and then woven together
Shaw	Character: head of fishing family
Simon Metcalf	Captain of the *Eleanor*, perpetrator of the Olowalu Massacre, 1790
taro	Kalo
Taua	Christian teacher who came from Tahiti with Rev. Ellis and taught Keopuolani the Bible
Thomas Metcalf	Son of Simon Metcalf and Captain of *Fair American*; killed at Kealakekua 1790
tī	Woody plant with elongated green leaves; used for cooking, thatching, and medicinal purposes; roots baked and eaten in times of famine.
ʻuala	Sweet potato
ʻuala ʻieʻie	Sweet potato vine
uhu	Parrot fish
Uʻi	Character: farm woman whose children befriend Kale
Uihā	Exclamation meaning "hooray"
Uʻilama	Place name of southwest Oʻahu
ukali hānau	Birthing attendant
ʻUkumehame	Land division, gulch, and stream in Olowalu, Maui
ʻUlaʻino in Hāna	Small parcel of land near Kaʻuiki Hill, Hāna, Maui
ʻulu	Breadfruit tree or fruit
ʻulumaika	Biconvex stone discus used in Maika, a bowling game
Umuwena	Character: elderly survivor of ʻĪao Valley; lit. warm oven
ʻUpolu Point	Northern most sea cliff in Kahala, Hawaii
ʻUwaikīkīlani	Kale Davis's oldest daughter, married to John Joseph Halstead

uwē	To cry
wa'a	Canoe
Wa'apā'oni'ole	Character: Kānekuapu'u's father
wahine	Woman
Wahine Ha'ili	Character: farm woman who supervises the distribution of the weekly newspaper
Wahinekipi	Peke and Humehume's daughter
Waiehu	Land division between Waihe'e and Wailuku
Waikahalulu	Pond where O'ahu chiefs planned to murder King Kaumuali'i in 1810
Waikīkī	Land division on O'ahu with flat plain and long beach; now part of Honolulu
Waikoloa	Land division of West Hawai'i; Kohala coast
Waine'e Church	First church in Lāhainā, on Waine'e Street, now called Waiola Church
Waipālua	Character: people killed by Makauli
waiwai	Wealth; money
waonahele	Inland forest
wauke	Paper mulberry trees grown without side branches; bark stripped and used to make cloth
Welehu	November
wiliwili	Varieties of trees with colorful seeds that are drilled, threaded, and woven into handsome lei
William Ellis	English missionary of the London Society; arrived in Maui from Tahiti in 1822
William Halstead	Son of 'Uwaikīkīlani and John Joseph Halstead; Kale's grandson, married Lameka
William Richards	Pastor of Waine'e Mission and Church, Lāhainā
wōwō	Sound of a dog's bark in Hawaiian; 'oau is the sound of a popoki, cat

Bibliography

Books

Adams, Alexander. *Journal 1815–1846.* Hawaii State Archives. MFL47

Alexander, Mary Charlotte, *Dr. Baldwin of Lahaina.* Privately published, 1953

Bartholomew, Gail and Bailey, Bren. *Maui Remembers.* Honolulu: Mutual Publishing, 1994

Beckwith, Martha Warren. *Hawaiian Mythology.* Introduction by Katherine Luomala. Honolulu: University of Hawai'i Press, 1970

Beckwith, Martha and Warren. *The Kumulipo.* (Public domain), 1951

Beckwith, Warren, ed. *Kepelino's Traditions of Hawai'i.* New York: Krause Reprint Co., 1971

Bingham, Hiram. *A Residence of Twenty-One Years in the Sandwich Islands, or, the civil, religious and political history of those islands: comprising a particular view of the missionary operations connected with the introduction and progress on Christianity and civilization among the Hawaiian people.* Introduction by Terrence Barrow. Rutland, VT: E.E. Tuttle Co., 1981

Buck, Peter H. (Hiroa Te Rangi), *Arts and Crafts of Hawai'i.* Honolulu: Bishop Museum Press, 1957

Cahill, Emmett. *The Life and Times of John Young, Confidant and Advisor to Kamehameha the Great.* Honolulu: Island Heritage Publishing, 1999

Chinen, Jon H. *The Great Mahele, Hawai'i's land division of 1848.* Honolulu: University of Hawai'i Press, 1958

Daws, Gavan. *Shoals of Time: A History of the Hawaiian Islands.* Honolulu: University of Hawai'iPress, 1968

Desha, S. L., translated by Francis N. Frazier. *Kamehameha and His Warrior Kekūhaupio.* Honolulu: Kamehameha Schools Press, 2000

Duensing, Dawn E. researcher and annotator, Nakayama, Mona and Strazar, Marie D., ed. *Maui in History: A Guide to Resources.* Honolulu: The History and Humanities Program of the State Foundation on Culture and the Arts in cooperation with the Maui Historical Society, 1998

Ellis, William. Journal of William Ellis: *A Narrative Tour Through Hawai'i in 1823.* Honolulu: Hawaiian Gazette Co. Ltd., 1916

Ellis, William. *Researches During a Residence of Nearly Eight Years in the Society and Sandwich Islands.* NewYork: J. & J. Harper, 1853

Fornander, Abraham. *Ancient History of the Hawaiian People to the Times of Kamehameha I.* Honolulu: Mutual Publishing, 1996

Hopkins, Alberta Pualani. *Ka Lei Ha'aheo, Beginning Hawaiian.* Honolulu: University Press of Hawai'i, 1992

I'i, John Papa. *Fragments of Hawaiian History.* Edited by Dorothy Barrère. Translated by Mary Kawena Pukui. Honolulu: Bishop Museum Press, 1993

Judd, Bernice. *Voyages to Hawai'i Before 1860.* Honolulu: University Press of Hawai'i, 1974

Judd, Bernice and Bell, Janet et al. *Hawaiian Language Imprints, 1822–1899: A Bibliography* Honolulu: Hawaiian Mission Children's Society and University Press of Hawai'i, 1978

Kamakau, S. M. *Na Hana a Ka Po'e Kahiko.* Edited by Dorothy Barrère. Translated from *Ke Au'Oko'a* by Mary Kawena Pukui. Bishop Museum Special Publication 61. Honolulu: BishopMuseum Press, 1976

Kamakau, S. M. *Ruling Chiefs of Hawai'i,* revised edition. Honolulu: Kamehameha Schools Press, 1992

Kāne, Herb. *Ancient Hawai'i.* Kailua: Kawainui Press, 1998

Kikawa, Daniel. *Perpetuated in Righteousmess.* Kea'au, HI: Ke Aloha Ke Akua Ministries, 1992

Kuykendall, Ralph S. *The Hawaiian Kingdom 1778–1854: Foundation and Transformation.* Honolulu: University of Hawai'i Press, 1947

Mack, Jim. *Haleakala: The Story Behind the Scenery.* Las Vegas, NV: KC Publications, 1979

Malo, David. *Hawaiian Antiquities,* 2nd ed. Honolulu: Bishop Museum Press, 1974

Merlin, Mark. *Hawaiian Coastal Plants.* Honolulu: Pacific Guide Books, 1999

Moke, Manu et al. Dennis Kawaharada, ed. *Hawaiian Fishing Traditions.* Honolulu: Kalamakü Press, 1992

Moffat, Riley M. and Fitzpatrick, Gary L. *Surveying the Mahele: Mapping the Hawaiian Land Revolution.* Honolulu: Editions Ltd., 1995

Pratt, Douglas H. *A Pocket Guide to Hawaiian Trees and Shrubs,* Honolulu: Mutual Publishing, 1998

Pukui, Mary Kawena and Elbert, Samuel H. *Hawaiian Dictionary,* rev. ed. Honolulu: University of Hawai'i Press, 1986

Pukui, Mary Kawena. *'Ōlelo No'eau, Hawaiian Proverbs and Poetical Sayings.* Honolulu: University of Hawai 'i Press, 1983

Pukui, Mary Kawena et al. *Place Names of Hawai'i.* Honolulu: University of Hawai'i Press, 1974

Smith, Edward and Handy, Craighill and Elizabeth, with collaboration of Pukui, Mary Kawena. *Native Planters in Old Hawai'i: Their Life, Lore, and Environment,* rev. ed. Honolulu: Bishop Museum Press, 1991

Sterling, Elspeth P. *Sites of Maui.* Honolulu: Bishop Museum Press, 1992

Stewart, C. S. Intro. by Rev. William Ellis. *A Residence in the Sandwich Islands.* Boston: Weeks, Jordan, & Co., 1939

Stone, Scott C.S. *Yesterday in Hawai'i, A Voyage Through Time.* Honolulu: Island Heritage Publishing, 2005

Thurston, Lucy. *Life and Times of Mrs. Lucy G. Thurston.* Ann Arbor, MI: S. C. Andrews, 1921

Walton, Dr. Stephen. *Gospel Hawai'i,* Series 1–4. Lahaina, HI: Steve Walton, 2004

Wenkam, Robert. *Maui No Ka Oi,* rev. ed. Deerfield, IL: Tradewinds Publishers, 1980

He Inoa no Sarah Kani'aulono Adams. Henriques Special Collection, Genealogy 24, Honolulu: Bishop Museum Archives

Holy Bible, New King James Version. Nashville, TN: Thomas Nelson Publishers, 1980

Internet Sites

Beckwith, Martha Warren. "Lono of the Mahahiki." [Excerpt from *The Kumlulipo.* 1951] <www.ling.hawaii.edu/faculty/stampe/Oral-lit/Hawaiian/Kumlipo/kumlipo-book.html>

"Biography of Founder Queen Emma" http://www.queens.org/about/queenbio.html May 2005

Emerson, Nathaniel: "The Hula Ni'au Kani." <http://www.sacred-texts.com/pac/ulh/ulh37.htm> May 2005

Emerson, Nathaniel: "The Hula Pua'a." [Excerpt from *Unwritten Literature of Hawaii: The Sacred Songs of the Hula.*] <http://www.sacred-texts.com/pac/ulh/ulh37.htm> May 2005

Environment Hawaii Inc. "The Roots of Ranching in Hawai'i: From Vancouver to Parker and Beyond." <http://www.hawaii.org/902the.html>

Greene, Linda Wedel: "A Cultural History of Three Traditional Hawaiian Sites on the West Coast of Hawai'i Island." < http://www.nps.gov/puhe/> Aug. 2005

Nelson-Burns, Lesley, ed. "Come Loose Every Sail to the Breeze." <http://www.contemplator.com/sea/loosesail.html> April 2005

"Hawaiian Kingdom Arbitration-Reestablishing the Hawaiian Government." <<u>http://www.alohaquest.com/arbitration/constitutionalgovernment.htm</u>>Aug. 2005

U.S. Dept. of Interior File Report 03-482: "Coastal Circulation and Sediment Dynamics Along West Maui, Hawai'i"<<u>http://pubs.usgs.gov/of/2003/of0482/of03-482.pdf</u>> March 2003

"Hawaiians of Miloli'i Sea Resort Threatening Cherished Traditions." [Excerpts of testimony by Uncle Wilfred Kaupiko and Uncle Walter Paulo before the Land Use Commission]<<u>http://www.environment-hawaii.org/691cov.htm</u>> Feb. 2004

"Io-Matua, The Supreme God"< <u>http://www.sacred-texts.com/pac/lww/lww2.htm</u> > March 2004

"Stories and Genealogy of Maui's Royalty."<<u>http:www.mauiculture.net/mookuauhau/index.html</u>> Jan. 2004

"The United States and Its Territories, 1870–1925: The Age of Imperialism"<<u>http://www.hti.umich.edu/p/philamer/</u>> March 2005

"The Whare-Wananga"<<u>http://www.sacred-texts.com/pac/lww/lww1.htm</u>> March 2004

Periodicals, Audiotapes, Manuscripts

Barrère, Dorothy B. "The King's Mahele: The Awardees and their Land." University of Hawaii Mānoa Special Collections, 1994

Chapin, Dr. Alonzo. "Climate and Diseases of the Sandwich Islands." *The Hawaiian Spectator*, Vol I, No. 3, pp. 260–66

Hope, Bradley and Janette. "Native Hawaiian Health in Hawai'i: Historical Highlights." *California Journal of Health Promotion, Special Issue: Hawaii.* 2003, pp. 1–9

Judd, Laura Fish. "Sketches of Life in the Hawaiian Islands 1828–1861." *Honolulu Star Bulletin*, 18 March, 1928. p36

King, Samuel Wilder. "Hawaiians as Navigators and Seamen." *34th Annual Report of the Hawaiian Historical Society.* pp 11–14, 1925

Pukui, Mary Kawena. "Audiotape Interview with Annie Ako, Minerva Kalama, Elspeth Sterling, and Mary Kawena Pukui, Makawao 1-29-63" Honolulu Bishop Museums Archives, 1963

Armstrong, Richard. "Armstrong, Rev. Richard Papers (1834–1837)." Maui Historical Society Letters AR59, Bailey House Museum Archives.

Waialeale, D.K. "Book of Omens e pili ana nā hale." Manuscript A17, Maui Historical Society, Bailey House Museum Archives, 1834

"Hana ʻekeʻeke i ka makani/Hiolo lua i ka pali o Leinaha" Mele of the manuscript collection of Helen Roberts MS SC Roberts 2.2, Bishop Museum Archives

Acknowledgements

The process of gathering needles of information from haystacks of archival documents and trying to make sense of them has been daunting, thrilling, and often tedious. My loving husband Harry suffered much "alone time" to see *The Love Remains* to completion, and without his support and encouragement, there would be no novel. Below, in alphabetical order, not in order of contribution, are dear friends, family, and talented professionals who gifted me with their expertise, genealogy, historical information, encouragement, and companionship on Honokahua hikes. Mahalo piha for your willingness to join the quest to redeem Kale and recreate Honokahua; I thank you.

The Aiwohi Family
Amy Rice
Auntie Donna Kahahane
Auntie Elizabeth Lee
Auntie Kuʻulei Perez
Barbara Cossow
Bonnie Donovan, RN
Caroline Peters Belsom
Catherine Kahahane Asami
Charles Kaʻupu
Christopher D. Smith
Claire Paishon
Clifford Naeʻole
Cynthia A. Smith
Daniel and Valerie Hoʻopai
Dawn Duensing
Dean Pua Kekoʻolani

Dennis John Donovan
Derrick Keʻeaumoku Adams
Dr. Steve Walton
Edwin Chico Gomes
Ellen Malizia
Emmett Cahill
Eunice Garcia
Francis Palani Sinenci
George Kaʻimiola
Gloria Ball
Grale Lorenzo Chong
Harold Teves
Jason Latas, Maui Eco-Adventures
Joel ʻĀwaʻa DeCoite
Julia Neal
Juliette Lum Lung
The Kaneshiro Family

Karen L.Twichell
Kekai Kapu
The Kekona Family
Kennedy Makekau
Kim Carpenter
Kimo Adams
Kimo Walker
Kualono, Ke Kahua Paʻa ʻŌlelo Hawaiʻi
Kumu Aloha Kekoʻolani
Kumu J. Kuʻulei Alcomindras-Palakiko
Kumu Kealohi Rogers
Kumu Kaniela Kuʻulei Palakiko
Kumu Liko Rogers
Laurel Murphy
LDS Family History Library, Lahaina
Leah Caldeira, Bishop Museum Archives
Lee and Ginger Hirshland
Lisle and Lei Baybayon
The Mahuna Family
Liz Marquez
Manny Guzman
Mapuana Akana
Mary and Richard O'Connor
Mary Buersmeyer

Miriam Kaʻaihue
Ola Austin Shaw
Ollie Wizner
Punana Leo o Maui
Pua Mohala Nichols
Randy Bartlett
Reverend John Patrick Riley, C.S.C.
Reverend Robert S. Pelton, C.S.C.
Rick Knowles
Robin Reith
Rory Buff
Roslyn Lightfoot, Bailey House Museum
Rubellite Johnson
Ryan Churchill
Sam Foster
Sarah Svetanoff
Silla Kaina
Susan DeCoite
Sylvia Hunt
Terry Kūʻauhau Wallace
Terry Laszlo-Gopadze, LMFT
Uncle Willy Yama

Isaac 'Aikake Davis Family Tree

*m.*1 Nākai Nālima'alu'alu

1. Sarah Kale Kani'aulono Davis
   m. 1. James Kānehoa — [no issue]
   m. 2. Alexander Adams
      1. Isaac 'Aikake K. Adams
      m. Keli'iopunui Kalanikaukeha [5 children]
   m. 3. Pāha'aikaua
      1. 'Uwaikikīilani
      m. John Joseph Halstead
         1. Elinor Milnor Halstead
         m. Charles K. Wilcox [10 children]
         2. William H. Halstead
         m. Lameka
            1. Charlotte
   m. 4. Kānekuapu'u
      1. Amelia Nākai
      m. George Hū'eu Jr. [8 children]
         1. William K. Davis
      2. Fanny
      3. Mele Kuamo'o
      4. James Young Kānehoa (aka JY Davis)
      [no Issue]
   *m.*5. Kaholokahiki

2. George Hū'eu Davis
   m. Kaha'anapilo
      1. William
      2. George Hū'eu Jr.

3. Elizabeth Peke Davis
   m. 1 George Humehume
      1. girl (hānai)
      2. boy ✝   3. Wahinekipi
      m. John Meek Jr. [6 children]

   m. 2 Antone Sylva

*m.*2 Kalukuna

261

John 'Olohana Young Family Tree

m. 1. Nāmoku'elua

1. Robert
2. James Kānehoa
   m. 1. Kale Davis [no issue]
   m. 2. Ha'ale [no issue]
   m. 3. Hikoni [no issue]

m. 2. Ka'oana'eha

1. Grace Kamaiku'i
   m. Thomas Rooke [no issue]
2. Fanny Pane
   m. George Na'ea 1. Emma (hānai to Grace)
3. Jane Lahilahi
   m. Joshua Ka'eo 1. Alebada (hānai to Kānehoa)
                      2. Peter Nāhaolehua (hānai)

   King Kauikeoauli   1. Albert Kūnuiākea
                         m. Mary Poli

4. John Keoniana 'opio
   m. Julia Alapa'i Kauwa [no issue]

Honokahua

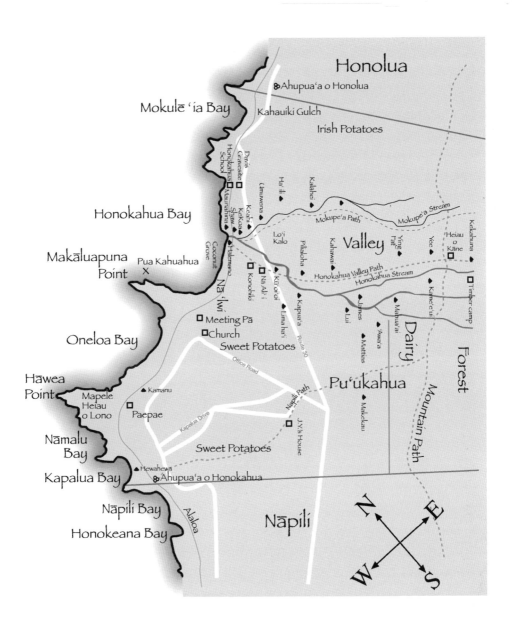

Attention Book Clubs!

Visit www.theloveremains.com to arrange an in-person discussion, live chat, or teleconference with Katherine Kamaʻemaʻe Smith at your next meeting!

Be sure to register for Kamaʻemaʻe's special gifts to book club members.